Venetian Tunnels

Venetian Tunnels

Gale Ets Marie

iUniverse, Inc.
Bloomington

Venetian Tunnels

iUniverse books may be ordered through booksellers or by contacting:

iUniverse
1663 Liberty Drive
Bloomington, IN 47403
www.iuniverse.com
1-800-Authors (1-800-288-4677)

ISBN: 978-1-4697-3870-3 (sc)
ISBN: 978-1-4697-3871-0 (e)

Printed in the United States of America

iUniverse rev. date: 02/01/2012

Chapter 1

"There is someone to see you, a Mr. Von Sligriver.

"This late. Show him in," said Likus.

"It is late I apologize yet Prince I need to ask if we may switch places and I can work on the tunnels for you," said the Engineer.

"Sure but who are you," said Prince Likus.

"My name is Joseph Von Sligriver not Prince just yet but soon when I complete this project," said Oseph.

"You never used your title," said Likus.

"No, and I am hear to allow you to go to the Chateau de Chambord if you want too," said Oseph.

"Yes I do I need to get inside there as soon as possible and you may have this building and the position of construction of the tunnels now right now and I will leave tonight," said Likus..

"Here is your check for your troubles and I was wondering if we could have a late supper right now and you could leave in the early afternoon when it is safer to travel," said Oseph.

"I could yet I do not know you so we will have a security problem, I will sleep in," said Likus.

"I know your brother, Detva yet I have not called your family to let them know I am here because this is your decision, you want the Chateau and I need the work that I enjoy and besides there is my helicopter that is here and you can go home in it and return next weekend for a visit," said Oseph.

"Now I remember your name there is no need of security and when you mentioned construction I did think of you but I was still not sure," said Likus.

"I know all about you and using the same name as your brother," said Oseph.

"I did that because I was the second marriage while they separated and then divorced and remarried and my mother is still part of me and not them," said Likus.

"Yes she did name you after your brother to control your Dad," said Oseph.

"But she did not and not even me," said Likus.

"Good, how is she.?" said Oseph.

"Fine and still living in Paris," said Likus.

"Nice and I hope we can be good friends and maybe you can visit soon I know I said that before and a question." Why would you want to leave this beautiful home all in gold look at it and this living room is incredible.?" Said Oseph.

"Chambord is my life and I want to live there," said Likus.

"Ok, then will give you the salary that my boss gives me," said Oseph.

"I have already received all of it," said Likus.

"It all went into this house.?" said Oseph.

"Yes, but I have expensives taken care of," said Likus.

"Will your Mother live with you.?" said Oseph.

"No, not now seeing I have a dear friend that will visit me too you will visit me maybe every other weekend.?"said Likus.

"Yes, I will and we can go shopping I am not good on my French so you can me," said Oseph.

"Oh, you just speak Italian.?" said Likus.

"That and German where I worked on another site," said Oseph.

"I remember that you received a home and a stipends for your work," said Likus.

"Yes, but I rented it while I am living here," said Oseph.

"Just my luck and now I can leave in the morning here is our dinners and coffee," said Likus.

"When will you visit me.?" said Oseph.

"Next weekend and then you should visit me for the next weekend so you can relax and remove all of that stress every time you are visiting me," said Likus.

"Alright I will and I will see you in two weeks right here or I will come and get you," said Oseph.

"I will be here," said Likus.

"It is afternoon, and the late evening went by so fast and the morning hours too," said Oseph.

"I know here is your cab and we will have to wait seven days," said Likus.

"It will go bye fast you will be very busy there and all the papers are ready for you to sign," said Oseph.

"Seems quite interesting and the rest fo my gear you will have it shipped," said Likus.

"Yes, and the maid will get all of your belongings in your room ready when you returned in two weeks," said Oseph.

"Here Is the cab the water is very calm too," said Likus.

"It is and the journey is very adventurous and exciting, the house you have always wanted is now yours," said Oseph.

"Ours, and we will see each other in seven days. Into the Venetian tunnels or going to any other tunnel, jewelry will be the better identifier," said Likus.

Chapter 2

"Yes, they are now I am going to call you, Hello, we could not start yelling in the channel many would think those two lovers have gone mad. So you agree now this time next weeks we will say good bye but it is for my work I need to keep busy. So you agree and now I need to talk to the staff so have a safe journey bye and I love you and have loved love for a very long time," said Oseph.

"Sir that was the Prince leaving and on the phone is your new boss," said the Butler.

"Thank you, Frames. Hello, yes I did and thank you for calling I will be there in about a half an hour. All right I will wait for you to arrive and then we can see each other tomorrow," said Oseph.

"Sir, here is your coffee and when your guest has arrived I will serve again," said The Butler.

"Thank you Frames and we will have lunch also," said Oseph.

"Very good Sir, will that be all," said the Butler.

"He should be here shortly in fact in a few more minutes he was on his way when I talked to him," said Oseph.

"This is he now Sir," said the Butler.

"Good show him in right now and thank you," said Oseph.

"Good afternoon and once again my government thanks you so much for taking over this project," said Mr. Barry Watersalt.

"May I call you Bob," said Oseph.

"Yes, you may and yourself," said Barry.

"Joe in fine in the house and Joseph among our employees outside," said Joe.

"I can not stay we are getting more new pipe in this afternoon so I let you look over these new plans for the tunnels and we can talk tomorrow. So I need to leave and thank you again," said Barry.

"Thank you and I know we will work together on this successfully. Are the small automobiles started and are able to fit into the tunnels nicely," said Joe.

"Yes, you will see a complete auto tomorrow at the site," said Barry.

"Good a small auto in a tunnel not that much bigger and I would need to crawl in it to the other end," said Joe.

"Yes, one needs to be in the car to get to the other end on the tunnel," said Barry.

"So how high up are the tunnels," said Joe.

"A little bit more than the tunnels itself, another tunnel on top and a boat would not hit it but all four are on the sides on the canals," said Barry.

"Good see you tomorrow and let me know if there are any problems," said Joe.

"Sir, there is a call for you in the library," said the Butler.

"Good and thank you for waiting until I closed both doors. Frames, Hello, what, what stop and talk to me you are where, you are three minutes away, and I hear the boat I will be in the library," said Joe.

"Frames, please do that for me, O.K. said Likus.

"Good morning and what is the matter. ?" Said Oseph.

"Good morning, I suppose you bought this house for yourself, you bought that house for me the chateau for me," said Likus.

"First is good morning and second is my name is Oseph and third is that I said," I was always in love with you," said Oseph.

"Dam these tunnels," said Likus.

"I will I am, it is a dangerous thing, a terrible ordeal many are losing their own homes and I must do something," said Oseph.

"You are too funny and I do not know what to do," said Likus.

"You have that home and this one they are both yours," said Oseph.

"You do know what you are doing," said Likus.

"I love you," said Oseph.

"I love you, I am very confused right now and I need a environment that is making me sane not moving back and forth," said Likus.

"I know and I wanted to tell you last night and hear it is see this photo this submarine will be here tonight if you want to leave I will understand," said Oseph.

"A submarine," said Likus.

"I tolded you, I loved you ever since I saw your photo I was in a classroom with Detva," said Oseph.

"I need a drink," said Likus.

"You can wait for dinner," said Oseph.

"You know that I do not drink either," said Likus.

"Yes, I know everything about you and the fact is that you like me," said Oseph.

"I am beginning to love you more yet it is a fact of traveling that does scare me," said Likus.

"Then we will work it out," said Oseph.

"I do love more and more each minute yet this is totally new," said Likus.

"I have always been on my guard also, I did think this way would work and it did.," said Oseph.

"Shall we get ready for dinner," said Likus.

"We shall and in fact we are ready to live and enjoy a good relationship together," said Oseph.

"Is there, well yes, you are right, yet is there anything else that is going to surprise me," said Likus.

"No, other than a new car outside but you left the Chateau and you did not see the automobiles on the second floor too," said Oseph.

"I did see them and then I signed the papers and left," said Likus.

"Ok, then there are no new automobiles outside or in you know that right," said Oseph.

"Very funny, and thank you for those also," said Likus.

"Your welcome and someday you will enjoy using them," said Oseph.

"You are so good and mean too at the same time," said Likus.

"Dinner is served my Lord," said Frames.

"Thank you we will be right there, By the way would you please sign these papers too," said Oseph.

"Here I stay I guess, please do not tell me you were married," said Likus.

"No I will not just divorced, now that you are staying you may know too there is a little baby three months off. "Oseph.

"I suppose if you want the baby here some times it is alright," said Likus.

"Good because I phone my ex-wife who wants to live with her new husband alone if it is alright with you, she and he want a new start in Russia," said Oseph.

"Or you mean some quiet time alone," said Likus.

"Oh, oh, right and this dining room is so elegant look at all the gold," said Oseph.

"I know remember it was mine," said Likus.

"It is now yours you just signed it and the lawyers will receive the papers in a few hours," said Oseph.

"Dinner sir," said Frames.

"Thank you," said Oseph.

"Yes, thank you this room is very beautiful," said Likus.

"I need to take this message, good the baby will be here in twenty minutes. Then my ex-wife will be leaving just a soon as she and he get my signature on the papers that I have receive the baby boy my little Joseph our little Joseph," said Oseph.

"So you are not going to see her at the door," said Likus.

"No, I made sure this was very legal and she will be paid when she gets the papers with a check too inside. Then they both leave for Russia arrive to her new house that I bought and is ready for her," said Oseph.

"Ready for her so she can not sell it," said Likus.

"Right," said Oseph.

"Very wise of you," said Likus.

"What do we have here.?" said Oseph.

"This just arrived, Sir" said the Butler.

"What is it.?" said Likus.

Chapter 3

"I do not know. It is a letter and two checks one for me and Paul leaves a note to me congratulating me on this construction approval and one for you as well," said Oseph.

"What.? Oh, a commission and a finder's fee and a discontinuous check of employment," said Likus.

"Good that is still not your spending money while you live hear," said Oseph.

"I know ok, there is someone at the door maybe it is the baby," said Likus.

"A nannie to see you sir," said the Butler.

"I need a signature from you and I am also a part-time nanny so here is my card of the agency and if you need part-time help we will send over a nanny for the both of you to approve of," said the Nanny.

"Due you work full-time time.?" said Likus.

"No I actually give the children to the new parents this is also a service of ours, but thank you for asking and I need to leave right now especially while the child is in the hands of a parent. It was lovely meeting you both and good-bye. Good-bye little baby," said the Nanny.

"That was nice and easy and look at you, you look just like your Daddy," said Likus.

"Hear is another thing I received a commision too, from England and it is for this work I am doing In Venice. Now with a title and I be receiving or we will receive a visit from the royals and their approval of my work and it will be an official of the job as it is mentioned in the letter," said Oseph

"They mailed it to your wife because of the house being yours," said Likus.

"That is correct she moved in that day and I moved here," said Oseph.

"So she only gets the house in Russia? Now what is your new Title.?" said Likus.

"First the house is sold and the check is is the library it arrived an hour ago," said Oseph.

"Good that is your spending money and please do not buy a new car we do not need it hear," said Likus.

"Good one and the check is yours for house money or actually save it is case something happens," said Oseph.

"In case they are sued I can own their house for none can sue me especially when they can not find me. Or course in writing it is yours. You are so cute here little Ose, here is your bottle of warm milk," said Likus.

"Thank you Frames, now little baby Ose maybe he would like to have his bottle in the crib and go to sleep," said Oseph.

"That is a good idea and now what is your title," said Likus.

"Lord LiOseph in the home and Prince Li Osephil in public," said Oseph.

"That title is very impressive, Sir. My names are very unusual too, Prince Likus and Count Morrobe because my Mother just remarried," said Likus.

"You should envite them both hear for a few days," said Oseph.

"Soon, we are just getting to enjoy this new home of ours.?" said Likus.

"Look the baby is sleep lets bring him up to the nursery," said Oseph.

"That is a good idea," said Likus.

"I think this elevator will be quiet enough," said Oseph.

"There look a new crib is in our room and we need to let him sleep right now," said Likus.

"I does not seem possible that all of this has happened," said Oseph.

"Are you aware that this baby is going to cry, maybe in one hour or a least in the early morning. He will need a new bottle and to be changed into a clean new diaper," said Likus.

"I guess so I just did not think of that," said Oseph.

"Here are his favorite toys, this one is to be put into the crib with him," said Likus.

"It is a charger's pillow," said Oseph.

"Yes, I used to play that game but in my last estate it looked as if I was going to read the gas meter," said Likus.

"I knew you played that charger's game so here is another one, a new for both us. Each of us too," said Oseph.

"I think I could play this again," said Likus.

"You can not go outside with it unless it is in a travel bag getting into the cab could be difficult," said Oseph.

"Right, here the batteries are working to run it and to charge at the same. This is correct because many like to purchase a new one and start right away. My first question is how many new babies are adapted today in Venice.? " said Likus.

"That is easy one, my baby, our baby little Ose," said Oseph.

"Do not be to sure, the nannie might have been in another cab while this one waited or she was driven to another cab," said Likus.

"That sounds true go on," said Oseph.

"And to the next home waiting for her to annouce the new baby to the parents. That would right after us too," said Likus.

"So lets see who won.? I put in two," said Oseph.

"I put in another I realized that many more because you might not have been the first this weekend," said Likus.

"I am wrong," said Oseph.

"Right put my second answer was over 35 in Venus. Italy was 300 hundred and in Europe was 58 thousands," said Likus.

"You won, Venice, Italy and Europe," said Oseph.

"Thank you, Good that was 50 thousands points each," said Likus.

"Why so much. ?" said Oseph.

"Because we thought of it, it was original and many more players were included. They get their answer a little bit later. What would you like a gift.?" said Likus.

"You keep the money," said Oseph.

"It is not money to be paid out we need to put it into something, how about rings," said Likus.

"By the way would you marry me, right here.?" said Oseph.

"Yes, I would but we need time yet we can still wear some rings," said Likus.

"It is agreed and the jewelers will be here late tonight," said Oseph.

"Now we need to rest today is was another day with those photographers and the royals from England they were quite a joyfull yet a I am so tried this afternoon it went so fast," said Likus.

"That was very nice of them to cater and bring a lot of extra food. The cooks are especially pleased to have lot of food in the house," said Likus.

"I was just going to order today and have it sent over," said Oseph.

"I did suggest that one of the them stay over for a few days," said Likus.

"They needed to return and the usual business for the week starts tomorrow," said Oseph.

"Now we did fun and thank you including me in the pictures," said Likus.

"We are not married yet so I did think it would be friends right now and let the public get use to us," said Oseph.

"I understand if you want the marriage quiet we can do so.?" said Likus.

"Not is allright I need to get the construction underway and then we can get married, it will be very private I hope you do not mind," said Oseph.

"No it can be private and it does not have to be discussed outside of this house," said Likus.

"Thank you, it is just that I need to work," said Oseph.

"It should work out the press just wants to be invited in sometime," said Likus.

"I do know of a small chapel in Venice that will marry us," said Oseph.

"Where.?" said Likus.

"It is on the left-hand side when entering Venice but towards the last canal," said Oseph.

"Good," said Likus.

"If not there, I will give a new chapel in the building next door," said Oseph.

"No, put it in the building on the corner just before you see this house. It will be done in fact I will purchase the house right now. I just love Mondays and you, and hear is little Ose I love you too," said Likus.

"I love you too Likus and we will have a good time tonight but I need to go to the work site for a few hours, ok," said Oseph..

"Do you want me to call you Oseph it sounds more like a name for the business Oseph does sounds like an oil company," said Likus.

"Sure it does sounds better, yet Venice is oil country," said Li Oseph.

"Good one it tells me your right on the ball this morning I am so sleepy I think Ose and I will sleep right hear on the second floor and this way I can control my anxiety waiting for you," said Likus.

Chapter 4

"Lets go to sleep little baby Good bye dear see you soon Li Oseph and I hope you have a successful day," said Likus.

"Yes I will and I love you dear and also this little baby have a good sleep you too. By the way dear I had my will change for the both of you will be alright if something happened to me," said Li Oseph.

"I can not believe this is happening you are so good to us both, now go so I can cry alone," said Likus.

"Alright, ok, I am going see you in a few hours," said Li Oseph.

"Lets go to asleep little Ose oh, you are," said Likus.

"Ooo bebe to ee a do," said Ose.

"Yes, Frames," said Likus.

"Excuse me my Lord, you did sleep for about two hours but Prince Likus your Mother is down stairs," said Frames.

"I will be there shortly and when I am down stairs please stay with the baby if she take him out of the home kill her," said Likus.

"I will inform you and the police," said Frames the Butler.

"Good, said Likus.

"My goodness what a beautiful grand staircase this is and how are you son," said his Mother the Countess Rollefta.

"Thank you, I guess you are hear the see the baby," said Likus.

"Yes, and you will be good to him, I have no intensions of removing the baby legally or kidnapping either, I can only stay the weekend," said his Mother.

"How is father.?" said Likus.

"He is buried, because of a massive heart attack and hear is your inheritance as a check only," said his Mother.

"Thank you, where will you go after this," said Likus.

"I will be living in my new estate in the Northern part of Italy I managed to purchase the Emanuel property," said his Mother.

"Wonderful when Ose is older he can stay with you during the summer if you want him too," said Likus.

"When he is older or the three of you must stay at least for at couple of weeks or a summer time," said the Countess.

"Here I am good afternoon everyone," said Li Oseph.

"Leadrill I want you to meet my Mother, Countess Rollefta," said Likus.

"Hello, I insist that you stay at lease to the weekend or longer," said Li Oseph.

"Thank you just until Monday morning, I am due to sign the papers to officially open up in Northern Italy Emanuel's house," said the Countess.

"So that was you who was on the news but I did not hear your name," said Li Oseph.

"It was, then no one knows that I am hear because I stopped at my new home early today. the three of you must visit this summer or especially in the spring time," said said the Countess.

"Should I call you Mom.?" said Li Oseph.

"Yes, both please do," said their new Mother.

"We can visit in the spring time it will be cooler," said Likus.

"Luncheon is served," said the Butler.

"Thank you, Frames," said Li Oseph.

"It is good to see you son it looks as if you are taking care of yourself," said his Mother.

"Thank you Mother and you are looking very beautiful, as usual," said Likus.

"I am keeping an eye on him he still does not know that I have kidnapped him to stay with me," said Li Oseph.

"You both should go to the Chateau for one weekend next month with all of this beautiful weather we have having," said the Countess.

"We should go Likus or we should visit your Mother.?" said Li Oseph.

"I want you both to be at the chateau and we can see each other next spring," said Mother.

"We will see you Mother next spring and go to the chateau in two weeks," said Likus.

"Good, this lunch in divine and that baby is so handsome," said their Mother.

"Thank you Mother, Li Oseph's ex-wife gave the baby to him so she and her new husband can start a new life and a new career in Russia," said Likus.

"That is the way things are sometimes done, yet it brings happiness to all," said the Countess.

"She is quite in love so she needs a new start," said Li Oseph.

"It is true it can save a marriage while creating another I know all of you will be happy," said the Countess.

"Yes, it will," said Li Oseph.

"Yes, Indeed it will," said Likus.

"This is a lovely Palace," said the Countess.

"Thank you, we can have a tour after lunch," said Li Oseph.

"That will be wonderful," said their Mother.

"Yes, that will be good and I have a piece of jewelry Mother that I think you would like and I am finished with my lunch so I get it right now," said Likus.

"You are so adorable thinking of me," said Mother.

"Yes, and I would like the combination which I did not receive yet," said Li Oseph.

"That is right I will give it to you in writing right now," said Likus.

"That is just like his father he bought me a new car a Rolls is fact and forgot to give me the keys," said the Countess.

"There has been a lot happening these last few weeks," said Li Oseph.

"Here is your gift Mother and here is your combination Ose, I wrote it down," said Likus.

"Oh, that reminds me, I put the car in the Chateau and I few things inside the trunk. If I had moved from the house and left it furnished to sell, there would still be something for you from your father. From both of them in fact wanted you to have something," said the Countess.

"Thank you again, that was a nice auto and I just can not imagine what they left me," said Likus.

"I could give them a ring and have the trunks delivered if you want me too," said his Mother.

"Thank you that would be nice of you," said Likus.

"Good let me give the Chateau a ring and I tolded them to wait for further instructions for the two trunks are ready to be mailed," said his Mother.

"I bet the two trunks or not upright and they do not even have the dividers inside," said Li Oseph.

"You are correct," said the Countess.

"What does that mean.?" said Likus.

"It means the trunks are not the usuall ones for being on a ship for packing your belongings for a cruise," said Li Oseph.

"That is correct again, the trunks do not open on the vertical so without the draw insisted you have large objects to look forward to, quite a good inheritance. That is why with your approval now there is a delivery," said his Mother.

"So we wait a few days," said Likus.

"Yes, but the deliveries here in Venice they call that day and even that hour before it is delivered at the door. You even get the draws back," said his Mother.

"Do you know what it is," said Likus.

"There is all the jewelry they both bought and including some of mine. By the way let me open this now," said his Mother.

"Oh, this is beautiful I will wear it tonight at dinner," said his Mother.

"It looks nice on you," said Likus.

“Thank you it is a lovely gift,” said his Mother.

“Very those are very nice diamonds. It is a beautiful ring,” said Li Oseph.

“Thank you and the both of you are so wonderful to me and this is becoming a very exciting weekend,” said the Countess.

“I am glad you are pleased with your ring,” said Likus.

“Yes, I am did you look at the check.?” said his Mother.

“Yes, I did it was for 5 million dollars,” said Likus.

“I hardly new the man and being in school we were seldom together,” said Likus.

“I know but he saw how pleased I was when you would call from school so I made sure both checks were not in a trust fund, you are very good with money,” said his Mother.

“Thank you for that I think of all othe money I have received I will invest it safely and wisely too,” said Likus.

“The short and long term are good and you always receive your money back in full and there is always a profit too. But that is for you to decide Likus,” said Li Oseph.

“Not wanting to change the subject dear, but this tour was magnificent and the building is so elegant and so much gold too,” said his Mother.

“Thank you, I do like this building, I am going to show your Mother the jewelry in the library safe, wait just a few minutes in the hallway alright,” said Li Oseph.

Chapter 5

"I told you both to wait and here is more excitement," said Li Oseph..

"I thought you did not have the combination," said Likus.

"You just gave me it," said Li Oseph..

"I thought the combination was for a safe upstairs so where is that one," said Li Oseph.

"Look at all this splendid jewelry and the silverware in magnificent, this is why Likus you should not live alone here," said his Mother.

"I know and I tried to get there just as soon as possible too," said Li Oseph.

"Thank you Li Oseph, it is good to know someone cares and will protect my son all the time," said his Mother.

"Thank you Mother I intend to watch over these two for a long time," said Li Oseph.

"Say why not sell your house and buy right across from us it is expensive yet I know we all will be moving after Ose is finished with this project," said Likus.

"I will I can sell the small estate tomorrow and when Li Oseph is finished with this project we can decide on what to do after. There I put in the offer with my real estate agent," said his Mother.

"Then let me leave a message with mine about the building on the opposite side of us," said Li Oseph.

"If I were to live with you, more money from your Father," said his Mother.

"From both," said Likus.

"Yes, or you were to have that when I die. Or as a live-in with you it is now all yours," said his Mother.

"Alright but you need to live next door it is better and there is a crosswalk over the water, I just remembered it because I wanted to purchase it for you anyways. When he died you did not call.?" said Likus.

"I needed to wait for the checks to come in and get all of the belongs together to be mailed. He was cremated and no one was there," said his Mother.

"He wanted that? ," said Likus.

"Yes, he did," said his Mother.

"Now we are all together," said Li Oseph.

"Yes, and look at this husband little baby little Ose and I have some toys for you that are on there way," said Grandmother.

"That is nice of you, Mom," said Likus.

"I found out that there was an infant here so I call a store from here and ordered," said Grandmother.

"What store delivers.?" said Likus.

"Mostly call of them when it is Venice," said Grandmother.

"You will be able to see us both married this weekend," said Likus.

"Yes we are going to put a chapel next door now it will be two doors down," said Li Oseph.

"You know what you should do instead of a chapel get married in this building and that way the traffic will not be so severe," said his Mother.

"That is true," said Likus.

"I know where there can be a chapel and all of the other blocks are stores that will be closed on Sundays anyways," said Li Oseph.

"Excellent that way it is always in the commercial area," said Likus.

"Very good gentlemen you see the business world together perfectly," said the Countess.

"We enjoy talking about the business world," said Likus.

"Mother I myself will be truthful Li Oseph took this business over and I was going to live at the Chateau then we had a wonderful time the first weekend, and I returned finding out he had purchased that building for me," said Likus.

"Then you stayed and here is this lovely little baby he is so and he just makes everything, life so wonderful, perfect and so beautiful for three very handsome gentlemen," said Mother.

"Thank you, Mom do you want to celebrate with an Exile bottle of champagne right now," said Li Oseph.

"Sure but we need to ask for one or the first nanny to be here today," said Mother.

"Right I have my phone and I will call," said Li Oseph.

"This is so exciting, maybe the two of you will be in charge of this business once the tunells are at least half way completed, why I say that is because Paul placed the late Lady Chardinrey in charge when her Edvard died," said the Countess.

"Lord LiOseph, there is a call on the house phone," said Frames.

"Mother and I have an interesting topic and we should discuss it," said Likus.

"Good what is it. Oh by the way we get our first nanny in about one hour," said LiOseph.

"Great," said the Countess.

"We might be the next to run the Eurotrain in Italy, in Venice since the Hermitage is very busy with their own businesses," said Likus.

"I was asked to do that and to give Paul an answer, we are all going to be very rich. I will phone Paul right now to let him know I accept the offer and now we need the house on the other side of us too," said Li Oseph.

"I cannot believe this we are all going to be very wealthy," said Likus.

"I can believe this, I am so glad I put the both of you in my will," said Mother.

"When did you do this.?" said Likus.

"Just a few minutes ago," said Mother.

"There we has given his approval and Mother is approved also if she wants to work, maybe on the phone and PR work too," said Li Oseph.

"That is wonderful but work if I find a husband.?" said the Countess.

"Then that is when you two are across the canal and you need to be alone for sometime," said Likus.

"Ooohoh," said the Baby.

"See even Ose is excited he has a place to vacation when he hears to much of the business and not enough about himself," said Li Oseph.

"Good now we all have a safe place to visit and a new modual across the canals to each building that can be started right now," said Likus.

"Here is the answers a new contract, we now took this business away from the Hermitage and Princess Ulmake has her own business to run," said LiOseph.

"She will not mind that I bought three of her wigs she is doing very well," said the Countess.

"How could three do that.?" said Likus.

"At ten thousand each that is a lot of money, for a weekend work she received the check at the Hermitage anyways. Say I might just get a free wig and so will all of us," said the Countess.

"Ose in a wig," said Likus.

"Sure I saw those at the concert hall in Russian. He can be wearing a Napolean hat of his head for no reason," said Li Oseph.

"Why and who were you with.?" said Likus.

"Here is a photo of all of us with Lady Ulmake," said LiOseph.

"You did not unpack that small case," said Likus.

"No, because it has work files in it but that photo was in there when I moved," said Li Oseph.

"I am sorry I was just wondering," said Likus.

"Look Frames has served us food in the dining room," said the Countess.

"Good lets have dinner," said Likus.

"Right look the maid is taking the baby for us so we can enjoy our dinner," said Li Oseph.

"Sir, here is the Nanny and she is willing to help us with the baby in the kitchen and then she will talk to you later after your dinner," said Frames.

"Nanny it is so good to see you at this high part of the early evening we will talk when the baby has been fed and you may have your dinner with the staff right after Ose is finished with his dinner, then we can all talk," said Li Oseph.

"Thank you, Sir," said the Nanny.

"Now the dinner is ready and it is our first together," said Li Oseph.

"I am wearing my new ring this evening," said the Countess.

"I have jewelry also and so does Li Oseph it is from the safe in the bed room," said Likus.

"I did not know you looked into the safe," said Li Oseph.

"I did and I put all the jewelry into my room and these are some of the nicer rings. Here Mother is a necklace that has the same color stones as your ring," said Likus.

"Lovely, thank you and I we have an excellent feast before us look at all this food," said the Countess.

"The staff are having the same I hope," said Likus.

"Yes, we decided to have the two turkeys, I know it is a few weeks early put the occasion called for a lot of food now that there is two more to feed," said Li Oseph.

"A very wise choice Leaddrill you are right there for things that have to be done," said Likus.

"Yes, it was we can all have sandwiches later on this evening," said their Mother.

Chapter 6

"Thank you both, it was a very good dinner and now we will talk to the Nanny and I hope this interview is successful," said Li Oseph.

"It will be, Nannie I am Likus with Prince Leaddrill he is the owner here and my Mother the Countess Rollefta," said Likus.

"Good evening my name is Nanny Moreeve," said the Nanny.

"Lets sit down and talk for a little while," said Li Oseph.

"Do you have a replacement for the holidays and vacation and your weekdays you will be off," said Likus.

"The agency will send a regular part-time nanny this Thursday and Friday I know her an she has been with the agency for a long time do you wish to interview her sooner. said the Nanny.

"That is not necessary," said Li Oseph.

"I will work weekends, holidays and my vacation is in may for next year that is not the baby Ose birthday, so it might be helpful this way for all of you," said the Nanny.

"Yes, that would be very helpful and in Rome or a Venice vacation hotel will be given to you as a gift for your vacation," said Li Oseph.

"Thank you so much and another country the next year is that how you would plan my vacations it would be appreciated so much," said the Nanny.

"Yes, a two week vacation in a new city," said Li Oseph.

"Yes, and I new wardrobe we want our employees to have to best when they travel," said the Countess.

"Thank you so much I should take care of Ose right now so you may enjoy your evening, and discuss my employment if there is anything if there are any questions please ask and the family history and education is in this file," said the Nanny.

"Do you complete your college degree.?" said Likus.

"Yes, I did in France. A home care in the Protocol Displacement Supervisory and Criteria management counseling," said the Nanny.

"That is the newest programs in her home care degree she is an authority if I were to have a degree in assisting with contracts with Leaddrill as my boss that is all I would do," said Likus.

"It is directly to one function as the degree allows, in this case it is child care. Because that is what I applied for and was approved for," said the Nanny.

"So this degree is for one especiallity," said Li Oseph.

"Yes, Sir, should I leave now to be with Ose," said the Nanny.

"No just go to the kitchen and have some more food and coffee and then to your room and in one hour we will call for you," said Li Oseph.

"Yes we can have one more hour to be with Ose," said Likus.

"We will," said the Countess.

"Alright then I am sure you have a few things to do in your apartment so please enjoy your dinner too, Nanny Moreeve. What is your first name.?" said Li Oseph.

"Anne," said the Nanny.

"Then Ose may call you Naany Anne, alright?" said Li Oseph.

"Yes that would be fine and I see wait for your call Lord Li Oseph. Will you please all excuse now.?" said the Nanny.

"Yes, there an excellent interview and I am delighted about her," said Likus.

"She is very polite and very generous about working weekends, holidays," said the Countess.

"Yes, and the vacation plans are reasonable too," said Li Oseph.

"So maybe I can accompany her to Rome and she can do what she wants in the evenings," said the Countess.

"Nonsense all of us will go and she can be alone in another Hotel and just call I mean there is the sights and rest," said Likus.

"She will wear makeup and have her hair done first before she leaves this house this is her vacation," said the Countess.

"She should have a monitoring device with us rings after she is outside and kidnapped. All of us should have one," said Li Oseph.

"I will ask the staff if they will.?" said Likus.

"Good idea the security is new put having one of the concealed chips might be a good idea," said Li Oseph.

"Yes, put not underneath the skin," said Likus.

"There should be better devices and more relievable then that something in jewelry," said the Countess.

"The jewelry would be ripped off of us so fast and the implant is not a bad idea. Actually if you want to be with us Mother you are going to be implanted," said Likus.

"I do not mind it is for Ose anyways," said the Countess.

"That is right he would have your title," said Likus.

"He will be Count Ose it is a genuine title," said the Countess.

"He will, why thank you," said Li Oseph.

"Actually he is a Prince too my last husband was," said the Countess.

"My goodness if my wife hears this she can not do anything can she," said Li Oseph.

"I will run to the Chateau and she can never find me if I am living in Versailles in one of the wings," said Likus.

"Like Ose can live there with Likus and not be seen and Ose is still in a pre-school until your wife leaves this building. Besides she has a business now and a new home there is to much for them to lose," said the Countess.

"I will call them and tell her know to say there and that she is not leaving to have a title but to apply for one in Russia," said the Countess.

"If she does not do this.?" said Li Oseph.

"Do not worry then she is in a court of law with me and she has to pay back before he is returned," said the Countess.

"Do you have a picture of her.?" said Likus.

"Yes, and one of them both, I case I see him again," said Li Oseph.

"There give me the picture and I will enlarge it and give it to the staff," said Likus.

"There if they keep this picture on their wall it would remain them and our own pictures too. Especially of the baby," said the Countess.

"You are doings so much for me," said Li Oseph.

"You have given me a handsome grandson and Likus is very happy, that is enough," said the Countess.

"Yes, I am the first in a long time," said Likus.

"Then I am pleased and you may call her but do not mention about any more money she gets a check once a month," said Li Oseph.

"Alright I will call in a few days or we can now think it over while she is getting those checks," said the Countess.

"Right I am sure she will not say anything and she know enough to apply for a title anyone else is," said Likus.

"That is not true the statics say there is only a few a small percentage," said the Countess.

"She did say she would leave us alone because of the money," said Li Oseph.

"I remember now I did suggest when the business was succesfull to apply for a title in Russia," said Likus.

"Good lets see on the computer if there was an application.?" said the Countess.

"In the news there would be something, mentioned," said Likus.

"Thye did apply in Russia so it looks as if they have not only received a title tere has been many contracts for the government too," said the Countess.

"Then we will not hear from her at all," said Li Oseph.

"No we will not hear from them and she is expecting her first child that is the way it was written so they are there to stay," said the Countess.

"I am so sorry Li Oseph," said Likus.

"So am I," said the Countess.

"Thank you both I need you both, the three of you," said Li Oseph.

"I am glad we know and I have made a copy of this to show that she has no intensions of calling Ose her son due to the marriage and their new business. That is grounds enough to dismissed her case," said the Countess.

"Here is the copy right now," said Likus.

"There it is and I will put this into the safe that is in this room," said Li Oseph.

"Wait first I will make four copies for upstairs," said Likus.

"Good I think there a safe in my closet and I will take one, ok," said the Countess.

"Sure mother I was just going to give you one," said Likus.

"I think Paul is behind them with governmental contracts," said Li Oseph.

"Give him a call, we are now in charge of the operations of the industries so he has to give us all of the corresponds right," said Likus.

"I will just ask him for all the paper work," said Li Oseph.

"The copy machine is full," said Likus.

"We have more paper he might send everything to cover up their agreement," said Li Oseph.

"So now we just wait in might take a few days," said the Countess.

"There will be the newest papers that were signed electronically and the rest we would have to make a copy while the files itself is in our computers," said Li Oseph.

"This is the only computer system in the house that is connected the net. Said Likus

"Yes, that means the staff use the solitaire and other games only and are connected," said the Countess.

"Ok, looking at our files this is the newest one, it indicates as title it is called, Russia," said Likus.

"Now lets see, sure it is her, both too and a signed agreement," said Li Oseph.

"Wait this last statement to her mentions that you are the new owner to work on the Eurotrain accounts and run the business for awhile," said Likus.

"She agreed with Paul about that too," said the Countess.

"We have them we will win," said Likus.

"I need to stay here after all, so it looks as if we are doing the correct thing with getting a nanny and the part-time help will be here soon," said the Countess.

"Is there anything that we have forgotten," said Likus.

"One thing for her to sue she needs to return all of money first all at once," said the Countess.

"So we need to watch them when contracts are accepted I better mention this to the lawyers so far it is contracts that were not reported and approved by us," said Likus.

"The lawyers will take care of this and give them reminders," said Li Oseph.

"You can ask them to report purchases and sells, right," said the Countess.

"If you did not ask them if they want to be apart of a tax-free Belgium systems," said Likus.

"That will only suggest a helpful alternative to taxes and nothing else," said the Countess.

"That should be it," said Likus.

"Yes it should and I do not have to talk her at all," said the Countess.

"I will call her right now and ask," said Li Oseph.

"No, let the lawyers do it and ask to be polite and to see if she will accept this offer," said the Countess.

"That does sound better, she would not exspect you to call and her husband would just complain," said Likus.

"Right again," said Li Oseph.

"So lets appreciate the baby being with his new governess and have some coffee and relax the day is finished. Everything is fine" said the Countess.

"Here are excellent desserts.'" said Likus.

"We do half a lot to be grateful for," said Li Oseph.

"Yes, we do and that baby is so handsome and such a good boy I am going upstairs to see him, ok," said the Countess.

"We will be here," said Likus.

"Alright just a few minutes," said the Countess.

"Now Likus I think your Mother has become a great help to us both," said Li Oseph.

"I am glad everything is working out," said Likus.

"Did I say today that I love you," said Li Oseph.

"Yes this morning and I love you too," said Likus.

"Now then, I ordered some food for the Nanny and when Ose waits up there is another bottle," said the Grandmother.

"So all is finished for this evening too," said Li Oseph.

"Yes, it did seem a like a working day," said Likus.

"I go in a half-day tomorrow," said Li Oseph.

"This is nice dear," said Likus.

"Yes, it allows me to see Ose for a little while," said Li Oseph.

"Now I better enjoy more coffee," said the Countess.

"Me too," said Likus.

"Here is a call, and a new message," said Li Oseph.

"All is in your favor you make the decisions," said his Wife.

"Everything else," said Likus.

"That is all," said Li Oseph.

"Good and things better stay that way," said Likus.

"Everything has worked out for the better," said the Countess.

"I hope so," said Likus.

"You are both correct," said Li Oseph.

"I am," said the Countess.

"I am too," said Likus.

"Good morning, I did relax and this morning Ose and I did sleep together," said the Countess.

"I heard him this morning so you brought him into your bedroom," said Likus.

"Yes, he stopped crying only when he was in my arms so he was in my room," said the Countess.

"Ok," said Likus.

"I wanted to remove that crib last night and put it into my room," said LiOseph.

"It is up to the both of you I do not mind yet she is a she and you need to wear a bathrobe," said Grandmother.

"Your right Mother, but I sleep in jogging pants or sweats," said Likus.

"So I guess you might be the one who gets Ose at ther door," said Li Oseph.

"I do not mind but I am not inviting her in, early on the morning," said Likus.

"No, just say thank you and take the baby," said his Mother.

"I will do that," said Likus.

"Good," said his Mother.

"Now I need to go to work it is a half a day so I will be home for lunch," said Li Oseph.

"Good bye. Also Likus have a priest marry us in this house, this Sunday," said

"Good I will," said Likus.

"Then I need to get a new outfit and the taylor can be at the house today for a fitting, so do you two want to be in formal wear," said the Countess.

"Sure we will," said Likus.

"Good, I need to go to work right now good bye," said LiOseph.

"LiOseph and Likus I am going to have the staff fitted today as well," said the Countess.

"Now just a little more breakfast," said Likus.

"There another hard roll warm is just fine and coffee," said the Countess.

"I will have yours ok," said Likus.

"Sure," said his Mother.

"Anne while you are hear we all of us are going to have a fitting for new clothes and I will pick out some good uniforms while you are in the house," said the Countess.

"Thank you, both of you so much," said the Nanny.

"I will call you and let you know when the fitting are, each of us will be alone with the designer," said the Countess.

"Even Ose need new clothes," said Likus.

"I know and so does the staff on their days too," said the Countess.

"Here is the designer he is right on time," said Likus.

"Good bring him in here and you will be first so you can take the baby after," said the Countess.

"Now let me get the Nanny and she will wait outside of your sitting room," said Likus.

"Good then you are next first I am ready so Paire, good morning," said the Countess.

"Nanny, please wait right here with the baby," said Likus.

"Good, I am next I will be right back then it is your turn, Anne," said Likus.

"Good you are here my son will be out in a few seconds," said the Countess.

"They are quite fast," said the Nanny.

"Oh, he has the measurments he will just check a few," said the Countess.

"Good now the kitchen help Likus get on the phone and call Frames he will be first," said his Mother.

"I will be on the first floor with Ose he can play with his toys," said the Nanny.

"That would be nice thank you. See you very soon Ose," said the Countess.

"Now the two cooks and we will wait for LiOseph to come home," said Likus.

"So all is completed and we can soon begin to enjoy our new designs," said the Countess.

"Now all is well and the day is here and I am just so glad we are getting married right now this Sunday and can hardly keep still," said Likus.

"What are you doing Likus.?" said Li Oseph.

"I am getting everything ready," said Likus.

"Please do this for me, wake up. Oh no, what is wrong you were sleeping and dreaming," said Li Oseph..

"I was dreaming we were getting married right today, it was Sunday," said Likus.

"Not today, I will desaint you in two days," said Li Oseph.

"What," said Likus.

"Right when we get married, I do not know if we will get an invitation to see the Pope right away," said Li Oseph.

"We could apply to see him it is more respectable," said Likus.

"We will the four of us," said Li Oseph.

"What did you mention the Pope and welcome home Li Oseph and by the way the seamtress needs your measurments so all of them may leave very soon within this hour too," said the Countess.

"Likus explain to your Mother about the invitation," said Li Oseph.

"We are going to apply to see the Pope when we are married," said Likus.

"So the four of us go. I know one of the titles that work in there he is a Prince like you and will get us an invitation. So what was the noise I heard.?" said his Mother.

"I slept for little while and Leaddrill woke me up when I was yelling in my sleep," said Likus.

"There, all is done and they are packing and tomorrow many of us will have our new clothes and designs and accessaries," said Li Oseph.

"Is that what they said to you.?" said the Countess.

"Yes it was," said Li Oseph.

"Good then all will be done and maybe buy tomorrow instead Paire you will have everything ready by tonight," said the Countess.

"I am trying by late tonight is that alright," said the Designer.

"Yes, even if it is two in the morning," said the Countess.

"Alright, I see you soon," said the Designer.

"Good and thank you," said the Countess.

"Now we can enjoy another meal by our fantastic staff," said Likus.

"Yes, we will," said Li Oseph.

"Now we have a wedding and is there anyone you would want to invite.?" said the Countess.

"No, I have no one all are deceased," said Li Oseph.

"There is just you Mother," said Likus.

"I do wish that Prince Edward was here your real father. I finally died of his cancer a few years ago," said his Mother.

"I am so sorry, so you do not go by Princess.?" said Li Oseph.

"No, I had to choose Countess with my second husband while his castle and land we both lived there," said the Countess.

"Your husband Edward he is the father of Edvard who lives in Grenaire the new castle that looks King Ludwig's building he sold another franchise of that building in Finland," said Li Oseph.

"Yes, he and I lived with each other for one year and then Likus was born and he then he went back to Lady Chardinrey," said the Countess.

Chapter 7

"At last the day is over and you two are married," said Countess Rollefta.

"Yes, we are and we decided to stay here because of this house in elegant and new to us both," said Likus.

"Besides Mother we I need I need to be here," said Li Oseph.

"Yes, he is committed to his job for a least until it is done," said Likus.

"Right if anything does go wrong you need to be there immediately. This is not an ordinary job, you could loose all of the money if you did not report," said the Countess.

"I am so glad you understand this is also a Architectural achievement when completed," said Li Oseph.

"Yes, it is is there anything in France that could be done maybe a new dam perhaps," said Likus.

"I do not know but I will try to get you home in that Chateau soon," said Li Oseph.

"Not without you, I think I might stay because of you and Ose," said Likus.

"Thank you, but we will return," said Li Oseph.

"I have admit I do enjoy the salt air when outside but this is a good place for me I might stay I a few more years," said Likus.

"Then this house is yours until you want to move," said Li Oseph.

"Thank you Lord Li Oseph but I want to move nearer to the plaza, or to the shopping and all that excitement," said the Countess.

“Ok, then when I told you that Li Oseph and I moved in we were going to get married. What did you think.?” said Likus.

“You called and let me know that you were in the Chateau,” said his Mother..

“Nonsence I tolded you that he had given me a check that was in the Chateau for payment and that I had returned here to thank him and to stay in Venice,” said Likus.

“I do not understand. ?” said his Mother.

“Wait the India or the Hindu population of India decided to sell their home phone operating system,” said Likus.

“Then you have a lawsuit Likus, they gave anyone a temporary party that sounded alike and the other party became much more avoided that we are right now,” said Li Oseph.

“We only have prove that what my Mother has told us,” said Likus.

“There is a one dollar fee that we can call and have it traced. This is how you do it just answer the questions. Now just listen,” said Li Oseph.

“He gave his name address and the dates of the call approximately,” said Likus

“Now we wait for the answer on the computer and we will know where the call came from,” said Li Oseph.

“We will wait it will only take a few minutes. Right,” said Likus.

“If it was very recent so why not you were there inside the Chateau for one afternoon and back here in the following morning,” said Li Oseph.

“So here is the call, it went to a Northeastern state in the United States,” said Likus.

“Right now it was not to serious, but right I will put in this order in, see answer this apart yes or no. I pressed yes. So now with a dollar they charge me we should have clarification of how damage and a check in the new saving account that was issued brand new and it was now finally used,” said Li Oseph.

“I wonder,” said the Countess.

“I know, I get a little more than you because it was on my phone,” said Li Oseph.

"Here it is you get 25 million and the you two of us only get 20 each," said Likus.

"Right only because the system has taken advantage of and makes sure many people stay at home or do not uses any other phone while visiting," said Li Oseph.

"Making them stay home is what the home is for," said the Countess.

"Spoken like a true European," said Likus.

"Do no be mean Likus. Now we can never blame this on a new tunnel at all such as the ones in Europe especially when no one realizes it is the satelite in space that does it and not the space station," said Li Oseph.

"I am sorry Mother," said Likus.

"That is alright," said his Mother.

"No it is not, what should we do take away his check," said Li Oseph.

"No, but he will learn soon with a little baby in the house," said the Countess.

"I know we should do more with the baby but these things have to be adjusted," said Li Oseph.

"I know it was very harmful that last phone call we had together, Likus," said his Mother.

"Now who is delivering at the door.?" said Likus.

"My wigs, our wigs for all of us. There, place them right there thank you and all of the staff, all of you must wait until I call out your name," said the Countess.

"Here this is for Frames right here, the two cooks and two maids and Nanny," said the Countess.

"Here is Ose and Likus and LiOseph and myself we will try on ours. Now the staff is off to the kitchen and we will have coffee, in a few minutes," said the Countess.

"Will they be wearing theirs to show us.?" said Likus.

"I left that up to them," said his Mother.

"This is something it is my name on it and look," said Li Oseph.

"I will take it if you do not want it," said Likus.

"That is ok, I have to wear it this way," said Li Oseph.

"It looks fine on you," said the Countess.

"Yes, it does it looks very nice. Here are mine see this one," said Likus.

"There I like this one. Here is a note from Princess Ulmake she has indicated that there is one more large shipment because we moved into this building," said the Countess.

"Nice we are going to be a success," said Likus.

"There here is my last one," said Li Oseph.

"Now here is mine," said the Countess.

"All of them are very flattering on us all," said Likus.

"Likus you look good in them here are mine I will wear a George Washington wig if she mails it to me and a wig shaped like Napoleon's hat," said Li Oseph.

"You are not big on the thrills of society," said Likus.

"You are more for sports," said the Countess.

"Besides the other two if she makes you a football helmet as a wig would you wear them," said Likus.

"Sure I will give her a ring and leave a message for you and also let her know they arrived," said Countess.

"Thank you, you both look cute and lovely too," said LiOseph.

"Now we can enjoy our coffee, Frames you look very handsome in your wig," said the Countess.

"Thank you, Countess Rollefta," said the Butler.

"Frames are your to wear it all of the time because it does look very good on you," said Likus.

"Yes, it does," said Li Oseph.

"It truly does look good on you, if you do not wear it please do not give it away or sell it," said Lkus.

"You should," said Li Oseph.

"You deserve another one, Frames," said Likus.

"Thank you, all of you for your concern and I will do what all of you say," said Frames.

"Be polite, Frames, Lady Ulmake wants the both of you happy," said Li Oseph.

"Thank you, Sir," said Frames.

"Say that wig looks good on you Mother," said Likus.

"Thank you dear, now I know what to wear on a bad hair day," said his Mother.

"How about this one.?" said Li Oseph.

"It does not fit," said the Countess.

"Then this one must be mine," said Li Oseph.

"Li, this one must be yours too, it does not fit me at all," said Likus.

"Thank you, now I know which ones are mine because all of us have two," said Li Oseph.

"I never thought of that being mixed up, I needed to tell her about this and let me take a picture of yours and send it to her so she knows what size you wear," said the Countess.

"Should I put them on.?" said Li Oseph.

"No, she needs a description only," said the Countess.

"Maybe I make a good model," said LiOseph.

"You have another job you are staying right here with us," said Likus.

"I will," said Li Oseph.

"Look at Ose, he is so adorable in that wig," said his Grandmother.

"Ose you look so important and grown up too," said Likus.

"Here are your trunks," said the Countess.

"Please put them on the elevator Frames and I will open them up tonight," said Likus.

"Yes, Me Lord," said Frames.

"He did not do that himself.?" said his Mother.

"No, the men did it and will put them into the room," said Likus.

"Good now we can see what is inside later on tonight," said Li Oseph.

"There should be a messenger in a little while with two letter," said his Mother.

"Here Sir, I signed for this," said Frames.

"Right on time they do not fail," said Li Oseph.

"There are two letter. Here is the one from my real father," said Likus.

"There is a note too," said his Mother.

"Here read it Mother," said Likus.

"It is very nice, short and direct too," said the Countess.

"Oh, my goodness Dad must of missed all those years. Look at this check," said Likus.

"He was always rich and he never beat you, because he was never with us, and no matter what the reason for missing a parent the financial says it time and time again. When the children are older they do appreciated what was given to them," said his Mother.

"What was it, this is killing me.?" said Li Oseph.

"The checks are both the same," said his mother.

"Yes, they are and look I can cash them in right now," said Likus.

"50 million both, I can not believe it," said Li Oseph.

"There is more when you are older and if anything happens to your financial situation and you have nothing, a rent or mortgage is always paid," said his Mother.

"This is to good to be true," said Likus.

"Every ten years you get this check until you are with us both in heaven," said his Mother.

"That is for certain as far as the money is concerned but I do not think we will be all be in heaven, I intent to stay here on earth for a long time," said Likus.

"Then use the money wisely watch the Euro train and it tunnels and make sure the prizes do not increase for that was your father's goal, with Gail and Ed gave his son Edvard to help with the tunnels in the states," said his Mother.

"Was that why I was born.?" said Likus.

"Yes, and many other reasons mostly for me I love you and I want you, the both of you to be happy in life," said his Mother.

"Why did you marry dad, and cause a divorce.?" said Likus.

"I did not cause a divorce," said his Mother.

"Maybe I should leave the room," said Li Oseph.

"No, it is allright please stay, I married your father yet the divorce was because Lady Chardinrey had a persistence suitor and he died after they were married," said his Mother.

"It still is not clear to me," said Likus.

"I feel in love with your father and he was looking elsewhere became of his wife being interested with someone else. Then he became interested in me and she needed a divorce and soon. Because her new boyfriend swept her off her feet and was very masculine and had muscles too," said his Mother.

"Now it was all very innocent," said Likus.

"Yes but Ed did what was done with his new wife to before he died, he went to a south Pacific Island and becme a citizen and the marriage is different now.Even becoming a Mormon no one knew and all was legal," said his Mother.

"Yes, when you regisiter as a citizen and laws and rules are different on those Islands like a war, people can not always be married," said Li Oseph.

"Even poverty is a war, and given to many," said his Mother.

"That is correct," said Li Oseph.

"People do remember they just want those building occupied for many reasons such as psychological reasons like depression people are connected with a building that is lived in," said his Mother.

"Now when they drive by Versailles even when there is now a tunnel to use the the building during the holidays you can see the festive lights and people become happier," said Li Oseph.

"I do know we have one religion," said Likus.

"Yes, but the war with poverty there is not to many festive opportunites and the involvement to still based on nourishment many are in a war that is endless," said his Mother.

"Give me an example of this Pacific ocean laws," said Likus.

"If I was in love with another and registered on one of islands, a certain island before my new wedding and I lived next door when I live with you we can still be married," said Li Oseph.

"I understand what love yet after the first, we never need another," said Likus.

"If something happens to me I would want you to remarry, after all Ose will be in a private school," said Li Oseph.

"Yes he will and could we keep him home until he is ten years old," said his Grandmother.

"Of course and we will let him decide where he wants to be educated at that time," said Likus.

"Ok, you both win on that one," said Li Oseph.

"I went upstairs and all of Dad's, both Dad's belongings are in the two rooms nicely placed by the staff," said Likus.

"I would like to see them alone, would that be alright," said the Countess.

"Certainly Mother," said Likus.

"Are you pleased with the objects that were sent to you.?" said Li Oseph.

"Yes, I am," said Likus.

"I looked at all of them and the price tickets are at home with my other things I will have forwarded to you very soon," said his Mother.

"Are you pleased with the selection," said Li Oseph.

"Yes, I was with them both when we decided together," said the Countess.

"I will look right now," said Li Oseph.

"You are going to have the first object at the door," said Likus.

"Thank you," said Li Oseph.

"Mother you may own the vase at the window," said Likus.

"Thank I have always admired that since I bought it for your father," said the Countess.

"Did you enjoy the collection.?" said Likus.

"Yes and thank you for the miniature and very original spy camera," said Li Oseph.

"Your welcome," said Likus.

"I need to let you know Likus all of those items need to start at auction at 50 thousand," said Li Oseph.

"I am sure and by then it will be 100 thousand," said Likus.

"Yes, indeed and I am glad that you delighted with the pieces we had purchased over the years," said his Mother.

"Now when I die you get the house next door and the other, the only one is sold and the belongings will be a sent here and furniture too in a few weeks," said his Mother.

"That is good, I do not need that house so you have made the right decision," said Likus.

"It was one thing about you Mom, I never heard anything from my Dads both of them loved you very much," said Likus.

"Thank you dear, it was very hard to give up your real father, but he needed to return to his wife after her divorce," said the Countess.

"Did know you would be back together.?" said Likus.

"When her husband died I know we would be divorced," said the Countess.

"Lets talk about something more pleasant look at Ose he is in his wig," said Li Oseph.

"We should take it off, there he looks a lot better, he looks like Ose," said Likus.

"Yes, he does he is so cute," said the Countess.

"Yes you are," said Li Oseph.

"Now lets have some coffee and we can talk about what is next," said Likus.

"We need a new Versailles pre-school for Ose in the neighborhood," said his Grandmother.

"Your right," said Likus.

"We do need one," said Li Oseph.

"Then it is all settled there will be one in my new home next door," said the Countess.

"No right next door to your new home is the pre-school and I will buy that house for Ose," said Li Oseph.

"You are a good man one who loves his little boy, little Ose I still can not believe I am here right in Venice," said the Countess.

"Yes, you are," said Likus.

"Likus we need to set up a trust fund and get our wills taken case of," said the Countess.

"Yes we are, by tomorrow ," said Likus.

"Good my lawyer is going to arrive in the afternnoon," said Li Oseph.

"Thank you," said the Countess.

"Thank you," said Likus.

"We must be uo to date with everything right," said Li Oseph.

"I think so," said Likus.

"We are. How is the computer with the businesses as it can be run in here," said the Countess.

"Good I have secretary at the office and she runs it for me," said Li Oseph.

"It it to much for her to handle," said the Countess.

"No, but she is getting more help when it is needed," said Li Oseph.

"That is good, there is to much work to be done," said Likus.

"Now the second cup of coffee and always good food," said the Countess.

"We need an advertisement for sure with the tunnels for the size of the smallest cars in the world, to the Eurotrain business being advertsized in Venice is important," said Likus.

"Yes, a new campaign right here inside the house too," said the Countess.

"The both of you would do this, I love you both," said Li Oseph.

"Of couse we will this is our new business and we need to make a lot of money and now is the time to do this," said the Countess.

"We can make a tele ad in this house," said Likus.

"We sure can," said the Countess.

"I know just what, I can say. "Hello, as a Countess I have been very quiet for a long time and I would like to say the Euro train to the United States is a tremendous energy of good will," said the Countess. "Yes and we feel as if here in Venice which is now the headquarters we need to use that energy to give more discounts to all of us," said Likus. "Yes and for myself and here is baby little Ose and we will do more and give more too and soon the tunnels will be completed, there is us," said Li Oseph.

"I will edit the music myself personally and it should be on the tel soon," said Lu.

"A grand and famous commercial," said Likus.

"We have finally started," said the Countess.

"Yes, we did, that will be all Lu and I will see you tomorrow ok, thanks again," said Li Oseph.

"Thank you and bye I will see you in two days for my wigs," said the Countess.

"Lu, did a fine job on the photos of the staff too," said Likus.

"Yes, he did," said the Countess.

"Now I need to show you something see this cam on the computer it will show my work station and the results of putting the tunnels underweight the water," said Li Oseph.

"Not all the time and everyone.?" said Likus

"No, but many will see the different sites," said Li Oseph.

"This will be good for security some day," said the Countess.

"It will not be for a public to use," said Li Oseph.

"We can not start knowing what everyone does," said the Countess.

"No, It is against the law," said LiOseph.

"It is a law," said the Countess

"Likus, do you call me Li Oseph.?" said Li Oseph.

"Because you are never phil," said Likus.

"You are Prince Li Osephil," said the Countess.

"He is still not Ose, there see the baby looked up a me," said Likus.

"I understand so Likus is being with me," said Li Oseph.

"Just you then Ose then Mom," said Likus.

"Oh, thank you," said the Countess.

"I need all three of you," said Likus.

"I know this is a real family to you, you did not mind going to school far away," said the Countess.

"You have us all," said Li Oseph.

"Yes, you do dear," said his Mother.

"My world became so much better living here I do not know what it would be like living in the Chateau alone.?" said Likus.

"You would have been very busy in a building like that," said Li Oseph.

"I think so and I am very pleased and delighted it turned out this way, I need to talk to the cook for a little while," said the Countess.

"I am pleased too," said Li Oseph.

"I hope so I am so happy and it is because of you," said Likus.

"I am happy too and we have a lot to be thank for, if I told you right now that I am in love with you would you be pleased.?" said Li Oseph.

"Yes, I would be," said Likus.

"I love you," said Li Oseph.

"I love you too, and we both love little Ose too," said Likus.

"Here is the mail," said the Countess.

"Lets see. Is there everything that I am missing," said Likus.

"What is so funny.?" said the Countess.

"He is not missing me," said Li Oseph.

"Oh, you two love birds," said the Countess.

"That is right," said Likus.

"Now behave you two remember Ose can tell by the sound of your voices. So be cheerful and pleasant," said the Countess.

"We do have something new besides the major tunnels that are for the small autos only we have to use the tunnels all of them the tunnels go into our houses also All to each house," said Li Osephill-Rageon.

"There I told her and I new you would not like it," said Likus.

"But I do, you did not hear about the business.?" said Li Oseph.

"Yes, did and at the bottom are the trucks and larger cars as well," said Likus.

"So what do you think of that.?" said Li Oseph.

"I think it is wonderful and exciting what you and the others are doing, but it we ever move to NewYork that building would have to be as large as a chateau in the heart of the city," said Likus.

"I could buy one if all of us go there for a vacation but we have to wait at least until three-quarters of the work is done in Venice first," said the Countess.

"Good under Exile Real Estate we will start looking for properties in the city," said Likus.

"Ok, but it should be a least a little more than three quarters, ok," said Li Oseph.

Chapter 8

"There is great news," said the Countess.

"What is big.?" said Likus.

"The home in New York city it is over 40 rooms and it is a little more than that to purchase," said the Countess.

"52 but what is nice they will wait for us to purchase and the house next door. For 90 more buy both at once and then I can stay for a few more days and come home later after all of the shopping I do for all of us." the Countess.

"Good and by the way are you arriving home with a husband by any chance," said Likus.

"No, I would however like to be marry here in Venice to someone I could love and be loved but he would have to be a little older than me," said the Countess.

"Now that I do not mind at all and it is a deal. Hear that Oseph, we might marry her off," said Likus.

"I did not know a man that is wealthy and older. I do know someone that this 45," said Oseph.

"Thank you, but no thanks," said the Countess.

"Do we really buy these houses or not," said the Countess.

"Yes, I am sorry about teasing but we can not leave here until it is also done," said Likus.

"I do not mind that and we all half to stay so we stay," said the Countess.

"We will wait until the work is completed then we will go to New York for two weeks," said Likus.

"Yes, and then you can shop for all of us and return after two more weeks there for yourself, or better we will stay for four weeks," said Li Oseph.

"Four weeks that is so good to hear," said the Countess.

"Yes and then to the Chateau," said Likus.

"Oh of course yes, the Chateau," said the Countess.

"Yes, the chateau as I had promised you Likus," said Li Oseph.

"It is a deal and then we are back to Venice and make some plans for your new job.," said Likus.

"I hope I have work like this again it is not easy to obtain a job like this it was because of you I was approved because by Paul," said Li Oseph.

"I never did think of that until you mentioned it right now," said Likus.

"So now I can get more employment because of this position," said Li Oseph.

"You will many are recognizing your ability right now," said Likus.

"You see Paul thinks you hired me, he has no idea that I am In love with you," said Li Oseph.

"Oh, I do suspect he thinks we fall in love, I think he and many others think that," said Likus.

"I am sure of it and I know you two are in love now I need to go and talk to the Butler and Chef," said the Countess.

"Yes, all right Mother, Li Oseph you need to build up your confidence in your self we and many appreciate your work, you saw something and someone who needed help," said Likus.

"I know you did. It was you who hired me," said Li Oseph.

"I know but it was you who knew that the work was impossible for me to understand," said Likus.

"I know you did not know anything about engineering," said Li Oseph.

"I did not and I do not care if you did not know anything either. I did not want to travel each day in the morning," said Likus.

"I did not know that is all," said Li Oseph.

"It is easy to understand when was I on an engineering job," said Likus.

"I never thought of that," said Li Oseph.

"Now you know you have completed me here and with Ose, there is no other way," said

"Now your Mother is here she is very helpful to the both of us helping us as one family," said Li Oseph.

"We are one family now and I like that about us," said Likus.

"So do I, but I especially love you," said Li Oseph.

"I love you," said Likus.

"Here we have a little baby with us so lets not make him feel alone," said Likus.

"He will not, here is a new toy for him," said Li Oseph.

"Here Ose here is your new toy," said Likus.

"There I have talked to the Butler and our dinner has a surprise it is warm enough to be on the third floor roof," said the Countess.

"Good that is a good place for a dinner," said Likus.

"Yes, it is," said Li Oseph.

"There is certainly is enough gold on those wall to start a bank," said the Countess.

"Or to give to the poor," said Li Oseph.

"It is gold leaf you would need to remove all of the gold in the house to start a bank," said Likus.

"Are you sure it is not thick sheets of gold.?" said the Countess.

"No, the butler told me the first day I was in here, "If all was melted it would amount to much," said Likus.

"How much did he say.?" said Li Oseph.

"About a few thousands dollars and that is not much collecting it," said Likus.

"It was about 32 hundred dollars I believe the real-estate agent told me when I purchased from Likus," said Li Oseph.

"So that would be a lot of unnecessary work," said the Countess.

"It would," said Likus.

"There would be a few men to cut off the plaster when the debris would be collected and maybe they might burn the gold. Yes, it is a waste of time because these walls are in good condition," said Li Oseph.

"It would still be shame to cover up the walls with a very expensive and good wall paper or paint," said the Countess.

"I do not think of city would allow that when applying for a permit for repairs," said Li Oseph.

"That is good, I forgot about the permit so this house is protected," said the Countess.

"Yes, and we are not allowed to touch anything without the permission of a council," said Likus.

"Right it is just like my last too castles I could not do a thing about anything," said the Countess.

"That is why you were able to sell it at a good price," said Li Oseph.

"Your right, Li Oseph we need to decide that right now what do we leave Ose should we keep all of the houses we have purchased and just rent them out for his new income," said the Countess.

"What do you say you're the engineer.?" said Likus.

"It is very good idea," said LiOseph.

"So now we have two new houses for our wills," said Likus.

"Also the one next and across from us we have not done a thing at all to secure Ose future. My house in New York I am going to give it too Ose so he has his own rents now," said the Countess.

"Thank you Mother," said Li Oseph.

"Yes, thank you Mother so much it means a lot to us," said Likus.

"This calls for more champagne at this dinner," said Li Oseph.

"I think this also calls for a lemon cake that is covered in white chocolate that has been turned to gold for this evenings dinner," said the Countess.

"Why sure and look at the sky it is a good evening too," said Likus.

"It is. We are on the desserts so I do not know if it will rain tonight," said Li Oseph.

"It is later tonight," said the Countess.

"Excuse me Sir the baby would not stop crying and I did not want him to continue may I place him in the crib here and I would like to be able to rest after his screaming," said the Nanny.

"Sure what do you think is wrong," said the Countess.

"You are having a later dinner than usual so he is with you at this time her likes to hear you talk," said the Nanny.

"So ok, little Ose here we are you enjoy your bottle, ok," said Likus.

"Anne, have something to eat while you are away from the baby alright," said Li Oseph.

"Thank you, Lord Li Oseph," said the Nanny.

"We did ignore him but not intentionally," said Likus.

"Now I have to tell you that the security has pick up no unfair treatment to this child," said Li Oseph.

"She knows where the security is she was given a tour of every room," said the Countess.

"I know but still it is best that she was told of the cameras in all of the rooms," said Likus.

"I know and she is good with him," said Li Oseph.

"There is nothing to say, we ignored him, she is correct," said the Countess.

"Right," said Li Oseph.

"We are not looking to blame her for anything we made a mistake and now we are showing our guilt," said Likus.

"More coffee Ladies," said the Countess.

"Very funny Mother," said Likus.

"I know what you are referring too and Mother you are right," said Li Oseph.

"What , what are you two discussing.?" said Likus.

"That is our first cartoon in the newspapers," said Li Oseph.

"Astronomical," said Likus.

"We need more description for subscriptions," said the Countess.

"Yes, it will be with us for a few to come," said Likus.

"Showing hesitations could back up one of the canals," said Li Oseph.

"Proper precautions is a necessity," said the Countess.

"Ready and to be prepared as a virtue an absolute denial of a chateau too," said Li Oseph.

"Then it was not haste makes waste," said Likus.

"Nothing mean unless it is very funny that is what sells the gossip and yet we are still allowed to sue," said the Countess.

"We need to write these things down," said Li Oseph.

"Better than that, remember anything was to be forwarded to this home by Paul, well I have the editor that will handle this for us right now," said the Countess.

"So you are the Countess in the house go for it," said Likus.

"We will us my title in an awful manner if the public thinks you two are braking up," said the Countess.

"Alright, when the public is thinking you broke us up Mother when you will be called Lady Meat," said Likus.

"Ok, now lets let the newspapers handle everything," said Li Oseph.

"Yes we will, I really did not have that in mind," said the Countess.

"Yes, I know. this the only reason why I was in a boarding school," said Likus.

"Now if someone starts talking to loud we just might get the-" said Li Oseph.

"I know and I can not believe this is how I left for school," said Likus.

"Should I take the baby now. ?" said the Nanny.

"Yes, please do, my son is not himself," said the Countess.

"Yes, please do, her Ladyship is having trouble breathing," said Likus.

"Now that is not the truth, I am perfectly fine," said the Countess.

"Yes, please take the baby and later on have another dessert if you want," said Li Oseph.

"Thank you all of you know that the chef leaves a large pan of vanilla custard, in the smaller refrigerator," said the Nanny.

"Good, thank you Anne good night and good night little Ose. We need to call the lawyers tomorrow," said the Countess.

"Why did you forget to leave the boarding school something," said Likus.

"Now Likus calm down," said Li Oseph.

"Yes please do, and I never sent them any money," said the Countess.

"I did find out that too," said Likus.

"Now calm down and lets all go to the second floor or the living room it is to cold here," said the Countess.

"We will all go to the second floor and relax," said Li Oseph.

"Yes, good night dears I love you both," said the Countess.

"Yes, good night, Mother," said Likus.

"Yes, good night Mom," said Li Oseph.

"Now Likus I am going to ask you never to do that again especially in front of the baby," said Li Oseph.

"I know I need to hug you," said Likus.

"Ok there, now calm down," said Li Oseph.

"I am sorry, and in a whisper I am only pretending," said Likus.

"Ok, go and apologize to you Mother," said Li Oseph.

"I will see you in our room in a few minutes," said Likus.

"This is unusual, Bill but my son and I have a fight," said the Countess.

"Mom, can we talk.? " said Likus.

"Yes, alright Bill I will talk to you another time," said the Countess.

"Mom I apologize you have done a lot of u," said Likus.

"I forgive you and to make sure that you forgive me I want you to go into your bedroom and keep Li Oseph company. Do not leave him alone," said the Countess.

"Good night I love you," said Likus.

"Good night and I know you do and I love you too," said his Mother.

"Likus come here and say good night," said Li Oseph.

"Here I am, Li Oseph, I apologized," said Likus.

"Good now get ready for bed," said Li Oseph.

"Can you set the alarm I want to wake up right away.? " said Likus.

"Sure in these buildings you do that," said Li Oseph.

"You are up early lets go to the living room, I smell the coffee," said Grandmother.

"Say what are you two doing up so early," said Likus.

"I could not sleep Ose is up so I told the Nanny to get more sleep," said the Grandmother.

"I have to go to work early and I can come home in the lunch hour and just have a half a day today. So good bye and enjoy the morning," said Li Oseph.

"Bye," said Likus.

"Yes, good bye son," said the Grandmother.

"Son, so if he is your son-in-law what does that make me," said Likus.

"My only child I love," said the Countess.

"So you can not say it.? " said Likus.

"Likus do not tease me in the morning it is very early, please be a very good step son, before you are disowned again," said his Mother.

"So you admit that, that private school was the best thing for us both.?" said Likus.

"No, it was your father who wanted you in Military school in the states," said his Mother.

"He did not want me.?" said Likus.

"No, that is not true he had three children that lived with their mother and he wanted us separated from them," said the Countess.

"Now where are they.?" said Likus.

"She is dead and two of the children died in the same car crash shortly after your father died," said his Mother.

"So where is the other.? " said Likus.

"He is in the school you lived at," said his Mother.

"The Catholic boarding school in France," said Likus.

"Yes, and if you invite him in to stay here it will ruin your marriage," said his Mother.

"What if he returns after vacation and weekends too and goes right off to college," said Likus.

"If he does that, what about the summers this will be the first one coming up," said his Mother.

"Gee then we do not have much time, do we, lets let him stay over a few weekends until the summer start ok," said Likus.

"Now you are a good house wife and a caring Mother, you are proving yourself every day that is what marriage is all about," said his Mother.

"I will call Li Oseph right now and let him know what is going on," said Likus.

"Yes, let him know what has happened and still get his permission," said his Mother.

"He is answering I will go into the other room," said Likus.

"Good, I am sure everything is. What happened you are back so soon you just went to the door and," said his Mother.

"I told him I have a 12 year old brother and he said, Then let him live here." and he needed to return to work and talk to someone else," said Likus.

"That is the professional, one who answers and gets right back to work, did you ever think that unloading those heavy pipes from those barrages can tip over and sue the company or country and bye the way congratulations," said his Mother.

"You mean I can raise him here and of course he goes off to college too," said Likus.

"Yes, you may and you both need to raise him and adopt him also I will give him the necessary homes and get rents too," said his Mother.

"We could in fact you are his Mother right now," said Likus.

"When she dies he agreed with me to stay at the school and I told him when you see me at this address it might be a little while but I let him know when he can be here for the summer time, I hope you can forgive, me," said the Countess.

"Yes, I do lets him so he can visit this weekend," said Likus.

"I think he can go home only this thanksgiving vacation which is in a few days, about 5 days. I cut it close and I told last night I was getting him home here and I need to let him know right now," said the Countess."

"You are a good woman I see it all now, all the times I was never there with you and it all means for us right now we live and are happy and comfortable too," said Likus.

"Thank you but remember I needed you as a good student and now we have to do the same for another," said his Mother.

"This is good please call him right now," said Likus.

"I sent him a text message right now that I had written and let him know this is the way it had to be and my plane will pick him up this Friday," said his mother.

"I left it just like a business memo so the kids could see the plane when it leaves this excitement is the way he gets home to Venice and we are all happy," said his Mother.

"Now there is just one thing I have to ask you, did you send me Li Oseph at my door step and please do not let him know I ask you this question," said Likus.

"No, I did think that you would have a foreman and just watch the payroll and extra cash which I am sure Li Oseph has a foreman," said his Mother.

"Thank you so please do not repeat this to Li Oseph," said Likus

"No I will not, I could never think of another person entering this house, I could understand your brother using my jet because it is a part of my life," said his Mother.

"Now what is his name.?" said Likus.

"I am so glad you mentioned that this is the best part of all of this he was named after you. His title is Prince Likus Deerames," said his Mother.

"When were you going to tell me this, I am sorry you told me now when he needs us the most," said Likus.

"He is rich on her side and has enough money to buy all of Venice so when he is older he might be a lawyer and help out financially with the Atlantic," said his Mother.

"The Atlantic project is done yet it can be wider in the middle for more underwater hotels and housing too," said Likus.

"Sure, and we would not mind it at all," said the Countess.

"Now we will not tell him yet when he suggests to help out financially he puts us right back into making more money than ever, I am sure that he would be pleased about that," said Likus.

"Yes he would and we will wait for him ask, is that alright with you Likus," said the Countess.

“Yes it is and now we will meet my little brother very soon,” said Likus.

“We will the dean mentioned he could arrive here today in about three hours,” said the Countess.

“So the jet is there now.? ” said Likus.

“No, it just left the airport in France and will arrive at the school soon,” said the Countess.

“So he will be here in a few hours,” said Likus.

“We will let him arrive here alone to enjoy being an adult,” said the Countess.

“You are home Li Oseph good my brother our new son will be here in a few hours,” said Likus.

“Good, what is his name.? ” said Li Oseph.

“Princess Likus Deerames,” said Likus.

“Likus another one in the house now all we need is two of me,” said Li Oseph.

“Two of you would do wonders for me but I can not wait for him to arrive,” said Likus.

“It will be soon he is on the canal as we speak,” said his Grandmother.

“Here is the cab now I can not wait for him to be in this house,” said Likus.

“We will have him introduced to us by the Butler, remember your own teaching at that school,” said his Mother.

“Prince Likus Deerames,” said the Butler.

“Likus come here I am ours and I did tell to wait and here you are my boy give me a hug. Here are your new parents if you approve of the adoption Likus and Li Oseph,” said his Countess.

“Likus, I am so please and delighted that you can live with us, may I have a hug too,” said Likus.

“Yes, so here is my new son and a hug from me,” said Li Oseph.

“Thank you all, it is very nice to see Countess Mother and my new parents too,” said Likus.

“I think you should be called Likee in the house,” said Likus.

"Thank you, Sir," said Likee.

"There we can start the paper work today for adoptions today," said Li Oseph.

"Very good and here is your brother, little Ose," said Likus.

"Where would you like to go to school there are many fine schools right here is Venice," said Li Oseph.

"Hello little Ose, my Dean told me there is a boarding school in Venice the most, or the best in the country," said Likee.

"Then you will be there in one week right after this Holiday," said Li Oseph.

"It is settled you may live here in Venice and return on weekends unless there are other activities that might make you stay," said Likus.

"So the Dean was prepared to let you go that was nice of him to give you some names of schools in Venice," said Li Oseph.

"My guess is the Dean only gave him the boarding name is that correct Likee," said his Countess.

"Yes, that is correct ---," said Likee.

"Grandmother, I decided not to confuse little Ose," said his Grandmother.

"Thank you now I can be with my little new brother," said Likee.

"He needs you he is lost during his waking hours and just listening to us talk and of course he is sitting with me or my my lap," said Grandmother.

"Or mine and he will listen I think he is wondering what could happen if he talks," said Likus.

"I do put him into the crib being his new father, I guess he will understand my role is not an easy one," said Li Oseph.

"Enough of that talk he can sit right now with you," said Grandmother.

"Ok, here we go little Ose I am your very busy father and here is Likee your new brother," said Li Oseph.

"There it is good to see them both sitting down, here nanny we can have a photo together," said Likus.

"Nanny was very good she insisted on the entry of Likee to on film and it is now on the computer with the pictures of us that she just took. Here is the computer Likee see we filmed your arrival and here are the other photos of all of us sitting and then one with the Baby, you and Likus," said Grandmother.

"These photos are good the nanny does exceptional good work in photography, she should be hired while little Ose is asleep," said Likee.

"That is a good idea I hope you have more of them," said Li Oseph.

"Thank you, Lord Li Oseph and Lord Likee."

"Maybe you should come home instead of staying at the school there are the local residents that do not sleep over. Good here are the other cameras to work with Anne," said Likus.

"Thank you to Lord Likus for this new position too," said the Nanny.

"Your welcome and I say that for all of us, Likee are you going to come home each day.?" said Likus.

"I think many other do return home from that school the Dean told so that is why I left as early as I could from France," said Likee.

"Good then it is settled," said Likus.

"Could I try that camera.? " said Likee.

"Sure, me Lord may I please go on a break while I now have a new assistant taking pictures," said the Nanny.

"Sure take about 45, the baby is asleep," said Likus

"Here Likee take my picture I might want to enlarge it soon," said Grandmother.

"Likee, look at this my son is asleep that what I mean I will be know as a human and very large teddy bear to him in another year," said Li Oseph.

"Yes, and you do speak so one out of two is not bad," said Likus.

"You need more work in front of him when he is older you two can go fishing on the back porch, every one else does in the back of their second floor porch so why not you two," said Grandmother.

"You can take that hobby with you at the Chateau," said Likus.

"I will join in for fishing too," said Likee.

"It is a deal and we can do this today when it is warmer, or tomorrow, we had a lot of fishing to do this year," said Li Oseph.

"Are the fish edible.?" said the Grandmother.

"Most and occasionally you might find a large tuna who uses this waters to find from danger," said Li Oseph.

"The first day I was here a person found a large tuna and the police put it back into the sea," said Likus.

"Do you think there are sharks.?" said the Grandmother.

"No, there is not any?" said Li Oseph.

Chapter 9

"It is a wonderful day and Likee will be home from school and then we can celebrate our first Christmas together," said the Grandmother.

"Here are the decisions that were made and we are going to be the first family to run the business bringing in a large Euro train stock of it own as Venice Euro and we have 52 persent and now the stocks will start," said Li Oseph.

"Congratulation may I have one quarter of it and I will give Likee a quarter too. But we will pay back," said the Grandmother.

"Good I will take the rest and now we own the controlling shares and we will control the business as an authority," said Likus.

"Thank you, all of you I am so proud of all of us and here is my little Ose, our little baby and look who came in but the prodigy son the first born Likus who is a million because of Grandmother bought your first stock in the Eurotrain Venice," said Li Oseph.

"Thank you Grandmother I will purchase them from you in about when do I get control of my money.?" said Likee.

"I found out today that you may receive a check each month and the spending will be approved by us and then the lawyers second," said Grandmother.

"A large purchase such as the stocks will be paid to Grandmother right away because it is a sound transaction," said Li Oseph.

"Now you are a business partner," said Likus.

"Are you pleased.?" said Grandmother.

"Yes, I am and thank you Grandmother," said Likee.

"Good now go upstairs and get ready for dinner, ok," said Likus.

"Yes, I will," said Likee.

"I know we decided to ask him first but we did not have time too," said Grandmother.

"I know you did the right thing and now because of that we are in controll that is good in front of the public very good, Mother," said Likus.

"Thank you dear I am glad to be of a help to us all," said Grandmother.

"Thank you so much as Likus said, "Because of you we are in charge," said Li Oseph.

"We are united at last with this business," said Likus.

"You have a great future in front of you Likee but you should become a lawyer a business corporate lawyer that will help us out," said Likus.

"You will be pleased with me I will not let you down," said Likee.

"We know that, you have already been a help showing us you believe in our stocks," said Li Oseph.

"You have to thank you Grandmother about that one, she purchased my stocks," said Likee.

"Yes, you did there have been so many times you have helped out, Mom," said Li Oseph.

"I know you have Mom and I have not helped at all complaining," said Likus.

"Oh, be quiet Likus I have only been here for two weeks," said his Mother.

"I did think you would just get a complaint in and I have done very little to deserve you," said Likus.

"Oh be quiet and here is a hug from me I love you, you are my son," said his Mother.

"I have done a lot for us, Likus said Li Oseph.

"You both know I was joking to Mom and this is what I get, two against one," said Likus.

"I do not keep sides and this is the last of the teasing," said his Mother.

"I forgot I was not suppose to tease anymore I am sorry," said Likus.

"You better stop Likus the baby is going to pick this habit up from you," said his Mother.

"You did stop me, thanks I asked you both too," said Likus.

"We will again," said his Mother.

"Thank you both, I do not want the baby to get this habit of mine," said Likus.

"The little guy will survive," said Li Oseph.

"Yes he would, he is my little brother," said Likee.

"We can have some snacks in the living room just to hold us over until dinner," said the Grandmother.

"See the Nanny will stay here and let little Ose sleep, I will send in some food for you Anne," said Likus.

"Thank you, Sir," said the Nanny.

"He needs some more sleep he was crying two morning in a row," said Li Oseph.

"He never cried when he moved in," said his Grandmother.

"I could be his early teeth. Everything else was a positive," said the Nanny.

"Here is your snacks, Anne," said Likus.

"Now lets go to the living room and we will return shortly," said Grandmother.

"Is this 6:oclock evening dinner to late for you Likee or would you like to have your meals earlier.? " said Li Oseph.

"Yes, I know I sent you upstairs to get ready for dinner and it is many different hours to eat around so would you like a certain time," said the Countess.

"No, six is fine I can study and do my homework and after too there is a lot each day," said Likee.

"There it is settled, he has extra time for his studies in the afternoon and early evening too," said Likus, his Mom.

"You should get to bed early I went to your room last night and you were still reading that was near nine o'clock," said Li Oseph, his Father.

"I am fine, this schedule is a good way to keep busy too. So we have a good way of life here now and the dorm is I hope never apart of me again" said Likee.

"Why you did not hate the dorm, you told me on the phone in France it was not that bad," said Grandmother.

"I know but when I was at this school for one day all of the students go home while living in Venice. The Dean told me that," said Likee.

"It is more convenient at home I am sure, and you do have good homework hours a very good schedule," said his Father.

"I quiet agree," said his Grandmother.

"Yes, it is and I hope you do stay and not return to any other school," said his Mother.

"When you two move in here was it so quiet even during the day it is quiet for studying," said Likee.

"I moved in first and then your father, then Grandmother and we are the only ones on this side making any noise," said Likus.

"On the corners and around it are the shops front doors while they occupy these block," said Li Oseph.

"So around the corner is actually all of the shops there is only just a few," said Likee.

"Right and most are interior decorators and their own furniture antique stores too," said Grandmother.

"Then at the other end around the corner is the shopping stores, groceries and clothing where both stores take up the first floors too on both sides," said his Father.

"At the other end on the left is a new Versailles pre-school and a new fashion house using its own Versailles runway for Venice," said Grandmother.

"Do the models live upstairs.?" said Likee.

"No, but the condos on both sides all of the second and third floors are for the models to get ready ," said Grandmother.

"Who owns all of these," said Likee.

"We do as a franchise but someone else runs them for us," said Grandmother.

"This is getting more and more exciting for me," said Likee.

"Please do not go there yourself we never do and we have received a great deal of money on these properties the yield is astronomical and a great living too," said Likus.

"I will, yet some day we all must go there and give our praise and get a few photos too," said Likee.

"He did it again, he arranged our new photo session for a business," said Li Oseph.

"I arranged it and yet father you called the shots and it looks as is we have became our own models for our own ads that means we take the money for all the work," said Likee

"He is thinking just like a corporate executive," said his Father.

"Your there with the money too," said his Mother.

"I will book him, too," said Grandmother.

"I made a good impression on the boss the first day too," said Likee.

"Yes, you have," said Likus.

"Yes you did, it does not seem as if we have included everything, will be a lot more months before we have a total grasp on everything," said Li Oseph.

"With Likee, we will get there," said Grandmother.

"I do have a plan for today it is so lovely and tonight we should be at the top of the building on the porch for it will be probably the last warm day to stay outside," said Li Oseph.

"Good Li Oseph, you can barbeque once again, steak, chicken and corn again," said Grandmother.

"Sounds good already for dinner and just think it is a weekend no business, no school and no cooking for the weekend," said Likus.

"That is right no cooking," said Grandmother.

"I will help Dad tonight and be a good cook when I am older," said Likee.

"I think we can all nickname you Likes," said his Dad.

"Good idea, yes good idea," said both his Moms.

"I do approve I was your Mom now a Grandmother to you, but this nickname is more grown up and will be better," said Grandmother.

"We all agree then," said his Father.

"So there is a busy day after all," said Likes.

"But I will let you know Likus with your real name do you have any homework to do this weekend," said Likus.

"Just for Sunday late afternoon but my trunks are upstairs and I am going to put everything away this evening," said Likes.

"Look who died the Grandmother of Edvard in Bavaria, she died in Belgium in her own estate. She lived outside of the capitol in a very small castle," said Grandmother.

"I remember her we should send flowers to Ed, Paul and the families in Belgium," said Likus.

"Her name was Constance and she had a few titles mainly in Belgium one the those marriages that were silent and yet she helped a nation during a struggle and a war. Then she went back to her beloved after the war, she was kept out of the history books for the schools," said the Countess.

"Does it say anything there about any marriage at all," said Likus.

"Her second marriage mentioned the king's youngest brother would be on the throne when the died and she as the Queen she made sure he was," said the Countess.

"So she was the person to give him the throne when the King died. Then she marriage him the youngest brother," said Likus.

"That is right, she was the youngest of all of them and marriage the king's closest friend in the states," said the Countess.

"She saved a nation and no one knew it, that is what they could do in those days," said Li Oseph.

"It is right here in printed she was given credit when she died as their Queen and what a ceremony there was," said the Countess.

"We were so busy with our own family we forgot to turn on the news," said Likus.

"I confess I saw it and decided not to let anyone know due to the fact of her son married me and I left their family with you, Likus," said the Countess.

"That was your right and privilege, Mother," said Likus.

"I know but she was your Grandmother too, and I am sorry that you never saw her," said the Countess.

"The kids would mention her to me and yet I never did talk about her to anyone," said Likus.

"Thank you for that and today we all have the Eurotrain and tunnels and now a chance of receiving more new wealth that we need," said the Countess.

"I does seem as if we just left her castle and woke up here today," said Likus.

"I know and I am glad the road for you to here was pleasant one," said his Mother.

"It was the boarding school was not that difficult," said Likus.

"She was Queen then a Princess and then a Duchess when she died. Her husband was part of the government and would sell stocks of all their companies they owned. As part of the family he earned his title too," said the Countess.

"So you are a Princess also," said Li Oseph.

"Here is the Express mail. Who is it for Frames.?" said Li Oseph.

"Princess Likus," said the Butler.

"What is it.? " said his Mother.

"It is a check from Grandmother her will was opened and here is a gift from her," said Likus.

"That was nice you did not have to go there," said his Mother.

"See what it is," said Likus.

"Very good and this is what you get from me, from your Father he gave me the same thing when he died and I am going to give it to you," said his Mother.

"See Li Oseph," said Likus.

"Oh my, 6, I can be believe it," said Li Oseph.

"Likus do you want to see a check for more than a tril," said Likus.

"Sure," said Likes.

"Thank you, Mother I am so sorry for being upset with you but you did go the events at the school," said Likus.

"Of course and I remember all of your calls and most of the boys only wanted one assembly program because many of some of the students did not have parents," said the Countess.

"We did think of them and it was a long ride and we all made it," said Likus.

"I did not want to go back to that school ok, Dad and Mom and Grandmother," said Likus.

"You will stay right here and Likus I am so sorry about your Grandmother dying," said Li Oseph.

"Thank you the both of you I do not know what I would do without you two and my Mother has been truly wonderful to me since she has lived with us. I thank you too Mother," said Likus.

"Your welcome dear," said his Mother.

"I am going to save this and we should save of our largest checks and these will be coming in soon with the business," said Likus.

"That is what I heard," said the Grandmother.

"Just as soon as the stocks reach full ownership for only the owner we invest," said Likus.

"Meaning all were owned by the owner of the business, I heard of them doing that too," said Li Oseph.

"They invested until all the stocks went highter in prize again and again each trillion was given to each of them too," said Likus.

"To good to be true but the kids were talking about that too," said Likes.

"So we just give the highest check to the each of us right," said the Grandmother.

"Yes, but that could be over done about four to ten times and then it stops," said Li Oseph.

"It is only us Grandmother, Myself, Likes, Li Oseph and little Ose," said Likus.

"Just the five of us first but I do remember when the family has been awarded it does not stop until all of the members of every family is given their share," said the Grandmother.

"When we are finished getting our share we give it to the families of Paul in Versailles and then Edvard in Bavaria," said Li Oseph.

"Yes, we were three months late when Princess Ulmake was giving everyone their share as she was in charge in Moscow," said the Grandmother.

"Princess Ulmake was in charge of this project for quite a few years," said Likus.

"I know she was and she earned it just like we are helping of this business for now Li Oseph is in charge," said the Grandmother.

"I know it was all yours likus but each one of us did their share I do no think you could run it and be their every day to keep your checks coming in," said his Mother.

"No, I could not and I think I would be very angry if I had to go their every day," said Likus.

"I know we owe you a percentage Likus but in fact it would be a lot more to owe Li Oseph," said the Countess.

"I know but give me a reason why that is so," said Likus.

"He is there everyday and works with the men and has a foreman," said the Countess.

"He is a foreman too my foreman," said Likus.

"So we just forget about the percentages and that is that," said the Countess.

"If there is only three stocks left then we each get one each," said Li Oseph.

"That is right and it there is 100 left Likus all gets one third," said Likus.

"How about 90 90 90 and Likes gets 10," said Likus.

"How about 20 20 20 20 and 20," said Likes.

"How about that Likee you have saved the corporate a lot of overtime," said the Grandmother.

"Just Grandmother will call you Likee so you remember your place here so is that agreeable with you Likes, and by the way good corporate work, son," said Li Oseph.

"Just what is my percentage," said Likus.

"I would be third on the receiving end of the money but we are going to invest in more stocks if one does not do it right away so we have things to do," said the Grandmother.

"You do have controll all of the time you Likus are in charge you are the President of the Corporation, I could not apply for all of this, I would have to be the engineer in charge and that is all I owe you regards of who is in line first," said the Li Ospeh.

"Yes, you are in charge you owe it all, so Likee what would be the amounts," said The countess.

"I think it could be voted on, and yet Likus is in charge so he can demand all being the owner," said Likes.

"This is the truth but what about the amounts what would it be.? " said Li Oseph.

"Is spite of being in charge for such a short time I know he could ask for it all," said Likes.

"So our percentage is very small because Likus will be protected because he started the business technically he stayed when every left," said Li Oseph.

"So would be likely if we got ten percentage after being in court yet we are responsible and own a business now due to Likus," said the Countess.

"No, it works on the time scale also and we not get anything it is to soon there is not enough time to be President and other appointed titles," said Li Oseph.

"As soon as the titles are given we could be replaced by Paul he is next," said the countess.

"However the titles can be given among ourselves yet the business I believe might give us a check each to buy. said Li Oseph.

"So I own 50 percent right now," said Likus.

"No you right own 99 percent. The judge will give you the total of 100," said

"How did you get 99," said Likus.

"I was not thinking, the judge will give you 100 percent," said Li Oseph.

"So we are to split up the largest checks," said Likus.

"No, this the time we are allowed to run up the total of a trillion dollars for each of us then we have give each one of the others a check just one each and then the rest is yours," said Li Oseph.

"So we are next and we need to purchase the stocks right now as they are sold," said the Countess.

"Right and the largest of our stock holders we can ask them if we can purchase," said Li Oseph.

"So they are getting something they could never have so they will sell," said the Countess.

"They have to sell to the owner first. We have to watch for the smaller people who sell to the public," said Li Oseph.

"So the large investers invest in us," said Likes.

"That is correct Likee and you and I are the largest investers so far and we need to make sure one of us gets the purchase our next stock on the market," said his Grandmother.

"So we are the first to be in the company by popular demand," said Likee.

"It does not have to work that way this, time we were lucky we had money.!" said his Grandmother.

"It will always work that way for the five of us," said LiOseph.

"Yes, It will," said Likus.

"Now come we have a lot of food to get on the grill, to the elevator right now and we will begin to feed the staff first," said Li Oseph.

"You can put all of the food on this grill so we do not have to wait," said the Countess.

"Right and I understand after the meal in about an hour the chef is going to bring up a large pot of stew and several types of homemade breads that have been toasted by him," said Likus.

"Yes, and with apple cider and two warm drinks also," said the Grandmother.

"I did this meal so they did not have the cook," said Li Oseph.

"I mentioned that and the chef indicated to me it was a very good time to introduce a new meal with different type of baked breads. said the Countess.

"Did you indicate that he have been here for about a month and all of his meals are new and exciting," said Likus.

"I certainly did because all of his dinners are fantastic," said the Countess.

"Good so now we have a new dinner to look forward too," said Li Oseph.

"Stew is easy to make, but the chef wanted to use that spare time to polish one of the three silver tea sets of this house," said the Countess.

"He just wanted to know if it is was in good order and then we will decide if we should use it again," said Likus.

"Should we leave it on display and it someone wants to buy it they may," said Li Oseph.

"No, we will use it and leave it on display," said the Countess.

"What if it belonged to another building.?" said Likus.

"Then of course the owners may purchase only, no wait not so fast, these are antiques that will enhance the selling of this house and all of the others houses with many antiques, what if we were broke," said the Grandmother.

"Good point and I think when we do leave we should rent," said Li Oseph.

"Right after all it is Likee's fortune that he makes on the rents too," said Likus.

"I need to help my brother or has everyone forgotten he needs his own fortune too," said Likee.

"Likes is right we need to set up a fund for both of them," said Li Oseph.

"We do not have to worry about my tuition I applied for a scholarship with the Dean and I might have an answer this weekend," said Likee.

"It is for you," said Likus.

"Oh, I forgot I was so taken by everyone when I first entered the house. Your tuition is reimbursed like mine the school gave many tuition free and a trust fund was set up when we are twenty one," said Likee.

"I am over twenty one and I did not receive any money yet," said Likus.

"This dean is new and he just started looking at the past graduates and many new ones who are now on the list so he mentioned you will be first to receive your check from me, it is upstairs I will get it now," said Likee.

"In all the commotion and not putting his own these away it was neglected but that school must have been given a very large amount of money recently," said his Grandmother.

"I think that is very unselfish of them was this the intent of the donor," said Li Oseph.

"I think so it is beyond the year 2000 and it is a very good deductible," said the Grandmother.

"Here is the check," said Likee.

"It is made out to you Mother," said Likus.

"It is the computer.!" said Li Oseph.

"Here I can endorse it to you but let me put it into my account and here is a new check for the right amount that way I can put it into a money maker for three weeks," said his Mother.

"Thank you Mother I guess the school think I am 21 years old," said Likus.

"No, I read about this is a certain type of tuition reimbursements especially if the student is deceased," said Li Oseph.

"But this is the entire school and years in the past," said Likus.

"Right and as tuition is used by our employee it is best to get increases as soon as possible," said Li Oseph.

"There are credit cards that are for tuition and the students right after graduation there is the final imbursement," said Likus.

"Exile bank has that card. too," said the Countess.

"That is Paul's bank right," said Li Oseph.

"It is our bank right now," said the Countess.

"Versailles has it own stock exchange and now we need a new policy with their insurances too along with Lloyd's too," said Li Oseph.

"Good now with these increase in insurances we can use the lawyers to sue for the privacy laws," said Likus.

"I put it on the phone, a message to do just what you wanted a new policy in both places," said the Countess.

"Now with the last of the insurance problem that was in the news about of us we can include all of this as a precautionary insurance for the last it is considered a sabotage ok. Do we all agree.?" said Likus.

"Yes, this is time we hit them hard because we have worked and it can not stop our work and their wrong is our successes," said Countess.

"Yes, I agree because this is the makings of a proper war with using the press," said Li Oseph.

"I agree too and Likee," said Countess.

"Yes, I agree because they did not let me have one perfect thought to this new freedom by wars of the press vs. people who do good work. Now tomorrow I want to play with my electric boat in the back yard alone my little brother does not have to see me in the water in the boat he is two young. Also someone needs to be with me and for the submarine ride also," said Likes.

"I did think we were going to save the submarine as a get away because it fits all of us," said Li Oseph.

"I thought we were going to be keeping the staff we do not have to use the submarine I just want to visit," said Likes.

"It was decided, I would let them return home. They had a long visit maybe they would like to return now and when they do we must use the facility in the submarine to stay in for kidnapping and place the guards at the front and back doors," said Li Oseph.

"I know you would not tell any of your friends Likee but there is the question about a sleep over too," said ther Grandmother.

"I do not need those things at all," said Likee.

Chapter 10

"Look at the computer, the others are selling their own stocks to you they are giving up their shares of Eurotrain and the other companies because of the Venice tunnels because you are in charge, Likus," said his Grandmother.

"Grandmother, I see other agencies such the Versailles runway, the preschools, sleep and loitering and look the Atlantic tunnels stocks all have been purchased with the money for this project," said Likee.

"These are all the clients that have worked with Ed and Paul these last years," said Likus.

"We are on their roll this is how Paul in Versailles allowed Princess Ulmake living in the Hermitage to get her second and third fortunes," said Li Oseph.

"She received more than that even before she gave a trillion to all of us," said Likus.

"You used the words," To all of us." what did you mean Likus did you received a trillion plus from Lady Chardinrey too," said his Mother.

"I do have it coming to me but she said," Wait until at least five years." and I have two more," said Likus.

"So we can in invest again just before Paul takes all of this away," said Li Oseph.

"We both will I was going to inform you when first and last payment was due," said Mother.

"We are the both of us are getting a payment at the same time so we must use them while we are placing the tunnels in Venice," said Likus.

"I do not mind you both keeping the money but thank you for including the tunnel project," said Li Oseph.

"We do not mind we want the work," said Grandmother.

"Of course this type of work is fun for us," said Likus.

"Right," said Grandmother.

"Likus was this your first job.?" said Li Oseph.

"Yes, it was and that is why I was so glad we were together the first night," said Likus.

"Good, I am a help to all of you," said Li Oseph.

"What a thing to say we are here because of you, because of both of you I am here and I want to stay even more with a two grand children," said the Grandmother.

"Good then we will have another cook out this weekend to celebrate," said Li Oseph.

"Why not the both of us Father prepare the foods tonight and we can use the dining room," said Likee.

"Wonderful idea and we can have another stew also and I want to have sausage with chicken and pork ribs in tomato sauce it is my favorite and we can have it tomorrow if we want," said Likus.

"The chef the trilled you are cooking again but tomorrow night he is giving us one of his favorites. Likee what about you do you want one of your favorite dinners too," said Grandmother.

"There is and we are having barbeque tonight is one and the chicken is sauce is the other," said Likee.

"Of cource there is a good steak too which is tonight," said Grandmother.

"We can have the steak dinner and one of everything too," said Likus.

"Sure it will not go to waste the staff and us will have everything finished by the end of the evening," said Li Oseph.

"Then it is settled and now I will get ready and wear one of my new wigs that was delivered today," said Grandmother.

"We can go upstairs right now there is a bathroom to use and we can wash our hands there," said Likus.

"Grandmother mentioned she wanted to take a tub bath first and so will I," said Likes.

"The while the food is cooking I will take a shower when they return," said Likus.

"This is going to be fantastic evening with the food and I think it is to chilly here right," said Li Oseph.

"It is too chilly for Mother so we can use the dining room," said Likus.

"Say what do you think one drink right now.?" said Li Oseph.

"No, maybe later if I am going to help you right now I need to be sober," said Likus.

"Good idea," said Li Oseph.

"Say what is this you are in your robe.?" said Likus.

"I had a good shower but I want to have a swim and then I will take another warm shower if the water is to cold," said Likes.

"Ok, here I am, what is Likee doing in the pool it is to cold.?" said Grandmother.

"Yes, get out right now and dry off and put the robe on right now you must be very cold," said Likus.

"I will do better than that," said Likee.

"What is going on now.?" said Likus.

"He is just going to put something on that is warm," said Grandmother.

"He is going to be the last one seated for dinner," said Likus.

"If that is true then he took something off of the dump waiter," said Grandmother.

"He does have something he has a cart from the elevator and from the kitchen too," said Li Oseph.

"What did the chef give you.?" said Grandmother.

"Water melon, and popsicles sticks," said Likee.

"Oh, I guess we are put in our places, do you think so.?" said Li Oseph.

"No, this is as tipical dessert for a cook out," said Grandmother.

"It sure looks good and the watermelon is already cut," said Likus.

"By the way if we are going to raise your son together we need a better form of leadership, this pool is not to used without one of us here, and I want this door locked when we leave and Likes please do not use this pool ask first and someone will go upstairs with you, ok," said Likus.

"Yes, this is serious Likes you know we want you to be ok," said Li Oseph.

"Likee please I do not want anything to happen to you that is awful," said Grandmother.

"Ok, we love you," said Likus.

"I know I should have ask you both if I could swim for a little while, it would not happen again," said Likee.

"Thank you dear you made me very happy," said Grandmother.

"Here have some more everyone it has been a fun day," said Likus.

"Yes, but it seems as if we have only had fun with a few dinners," said Likee.

"That is because we are alone where we live and we do not see anyone from up here," said Grandmother.

"It is very lonely on this side of the city and very private," said Li Oseph.

"It is very far away from the excitement of the city yet we do get the privacy we need for our work," said Likus.

"It is alright here it is lovely to listen to the birds and not really hear anything or anyone from the city," said Grandmother.

"Someone has broken into our home in New york," said Li Oseph.

"The phones are ringing," said Likus.

"It is Edvard in Bavaria, yes I will tell them and there are no charges at all," said Li Oseph.

"Apparently the 12 year old boy from Newport, Rhode Island his nephew went into the house because his father punished him to severely," said Li Oseph.

"I have her number let me talk to them in Newport and I will comfort them. Hello, this is Countess Rolefta Yes, but there is no charges at all," said the Countess.

"What is yes, for.?" said Likus.

"That is fine I do not mind it at all. Good night and take care all of you," said the Countess.

"What is yes, for.?" said Likus.

"I am, going to have another brother," said Likee.

"Boy are you both very smart," said the Countess.

"We both went to the same boarding school, and you invited him here," said Likus.

"If he acts out he goes to his Uncle's Ed's house, to his castle immediately," said the Countess.

"I will ask both of them in a few days if both boys would want to go to school here or in France. Thank you Mother you are very kind but the next time we need to talk first," said Likus.

"So will Ed be calling for him soon," said the Grandmother.

"You may handle this call too Mother. Here is the phone it is Ed right now," said Likus.

"Hello Ed, Countess Rolefta., Yes, but not Countess, I will take the boy if he does not improve I will let him know he is going with you. This is the way I need to handle the situation. He will be with my 12 year old, your brother Likus is here from France to stay with us. Ok, then thank you, I will have him call you when he arrives. " said the Countess.

"So it is ok.?" said Likus.

"It is now he wanted him there," said the Countess.

"I do not mind but is his name, Likus by any chance," said Li Oseph.

"He is titled, Earl apparently he is completely away from them, this last year he lived in the other Estate and manage it," said the Countess.

"I guess Lady Chardinrey, named the world ," said Likus.

"Yes, but your step brother did not mind when you were there instead of him because of the education for you both received was completed fully," said the Countess.

"Was he with you at some point in time," said Likus.

"Just one time for a three month he visited then he went be with Ed for two weeks and then finally settled after the divorce in France, doing what you do now," said the Countess.

"Do not look at me when he left Italy and you showed up I know who I wanted." So we have three Likus here and Ose we should call him Likus too. We call him Earl, but then Count Likus is his formal name," said Li Oseph.

"This is getting better, thank you, Oseph," said Likus.

"I know what is problem is he needs his title and to work for the company, he has proven that this year," said the Countess.

"If he wants to run the house next door and watch it let him, I do not mind it at all," said Likee.

"What a good boy you are, Likee to think of your brother needing his very early independence," said his Grandmother.

"I will ask him if he wanted to stay there at night and of course he will be paid," said Li Oseph.

"No, this will be done much later, we have to let him know he is needed by us first," said Likus.

"Your right is in the need for a lot of love and understanding," said his Grandmother.

"So he will be here with in the next few hours," said Likus.

"Was there a message.?" said Li Oseph.

"It was Ed, he is sure willing to give him a chance in life," said Likus.

"He should watch both houses that is how he got in, he watched one house for a year and then he know how to get in it," said Likee.

"You are correct and should be given a job to watch the property, we will let him start his job when he is ready too," said the Grandmother.

"We need an insurance project for him instead of him harming himself," said Likus.

"Me too," said Likes.

"Yes, probably the both of you together instead of harm, how about their own business together and each one having another for themselves," said the Grandmother.

"This summer we can both be in the Chateau to watch it together, or I could go there as a guest as a B and B that will give him some training for sure," said Likee.

"You help him when he needs it ok," said Grandmother.

"They will need a staff and someone will get groceries too," said Li Oseph.

"Please do not cook without someone watching alright, that way you can still learn," said Likus.

"Learn they will be learning quite a lot too," said Likus.

"So little Likee is going to become a man and have his first job and a business too," said Grandmother.

"Maybe they might just both be in different school a boarding school after all because or is it for their own name sake first," said Li Oseph.

"That is true when children are given their names it is because they are the only ones with it to it called in the house. This is the story the insurance the boys are in the chateau and away from home a new boarding school each," said Li Oseph.

"I do enjoy what I hear go on," said Grandmother.

"Yes," said Likee.

"This is mad, insane and legal go on," said Likus.

"Thinking it was to confusing in the house, and it takes time to do this no one would think of it as impossible or that it could not happen to us," said Li Oseph.

"Right then the fortune starts again," said Grandmother.

"Why not for Newport they themselves the family was in charge and now in the news and several times the insurances are for them too," said Likus.

"Likee you do not mind being as an insurance deal with us it is a fact you to need to be in a boarding school the two of you and it will be a good vacation at the Chateau," said his Grandmother.

"We do want both you home but I think you are going to grow up when it is less confined," said Li Oseph.

"He might use the boarding school and first if there is trouble ask about him staying next door it could save it all and right after we stay at the Chateau," said Likee.

"Eight hours have passed where is Likus, he is late.? " said Likee.

"I know we did get some sleep and there is a taxi at the front door," said the Grandmother.

"Count Likus," said the Butler.

"I am your new Grandmother hre are your parents and you brother Likee and your little brother Ose," said the Grandmother.

"I am sorry I am late I called last night to let all of you know that I would leave Grandmother's house early in the morning to arrive here," said the Count Likus.

"Your brother called and wants you to live with him yet my Mother and myself and all of us want you to live right here," said Likus.

"You are not Count Likus you are a Prince, Prince Likus," said the Count.

"I know. Your late Grandmother was my father Prince Edward" said Likus.

"I can use Prince but I hope you do not mind if I use Count because of the Countess here and is a part of the Euro train now and all of you are a good and important inspiration," said the Count Likus.

"Excellent and I am Likee and I was wondering if the both of us could stay at the Chateau in France this summer and watch and manage the building," said Likee.

"Sure and when we, the both of us are finished there with this project in Venice we could be off to the Chateau until something else is ready for us both," said His Brother.

"Wait a minute I know I could use you both but I do think that land is your better investment, especially at the castle," said Li Oseph.

"Ok. then Brother here we are lets see my room, ok," said Likable.

"Likee return after about one hour and Likable you are going to have the phone ring upstairs and you will talk to your Uncle Edward and apologize to him that you can not live there, alright," said Grandmother.

"Sure Grandma and the nickname is Liker as in me," said Liker.

"Alright Liker and as in me as Grandmother, the one who got you here, you can return with any slightly any new type of verbal deviations or physical too. Being to rough on each other wresting or anything from you two then you are separated, finished, do you both understand," said the Countess.

"Yes, I will him talk to him and I am so sorry for the slip up," said Liker.

"Yes, Grandmother," said Likee.

"This might be the most difficult house to live in for communication but it is going to be the most politess and very comfortable too," said Grandmother.

"I do agree and this will work," said Likus.

"Yes it is, I think the summers in that building and some work will do them some good," said Li Oseph.

"Things will work out I am sure of it," said Likus.

"I hope so, both of them can enjoy life without major problems," said Grandmother.

"It will take work and trust," said Li Oseph.

"A lot of love for them and it will work," said Grandmother.

"That is it," said Likus.

"I am sure Ed would not mine it," said Li Oseph.

"He has no choice I was appointed by the court," said Grandmother.

"Only You.?" said Li Oseph.

"Yes, because I can leave with him and go into Venice city and he knows he will loose a great deal, too," said Grandmother.

"Ok, it is the court, so it is fine," said Likus.

"It is final, Likus is here with us so we will give them the summer home," said Li Oseph.

"Yes, and maybe they will make a business out of what they have," said Grandmother.

"This could work for all of us and we have service year round," said Likus.

"But if I visit I will not take a very large room or suite this is their lively hood," said Grandmother.

"I know if we are there for a while we do not need a suite," said Likus.

"No, but two rooms will do it," said Li Oseph.

"I think our visits will not be to long," said Likus.

"What, my dear I do not know you thought that way, but after this we will live there alright," said Li Oseph.

"Sure it is a deal and they still can run the b and b, right Mother," said Likus.

"Of course I do not need that much room and I do not mind answering the phone to book people," said their Grandmother.

"Thank you, Mother," said Likus.

"Say, you did buy that building maybe for months ago why not let the Versailles runway use it now before we are even living there," said the Countess.

"You are right again could you call the company in Paris and let them know they have three years to work there," said Li Oseph.

"Good and to them there for these three years I will let them know the fee is negotiable and would not be money maybe its own stock," said the Countess.

"Thank you, this is all to perfect," said Li Oseph.

"What it is going to get better not anything else right now or at any time," said the Countess.

"No, I mean as I did not have to do anything and it was done for me, just as if I was the President of the company," said Li Oseph.

"I saw that you giving my Mother a signal and for that you are the President of the company until this job is done," said Likus.

"Thank you I love you so much, Likus," said Li Oseph.

"I need to check on the boys and let them now we are going to have lunch now," said the Countess.

"Good Thanks," said Likus.

"You made me President of the company do you know what that means I can start my own company by doing the architectural blue prints and designs too and we can be living right in the Chateau," said Li Oseph.

"You do not have to be on call and the trips to the sites do not have to be so on the job, especially with the foreman that you can trust," said Likus.

"Also you can be prepared to have a few more infants there with their own nannies for the future it is not a bad environment for a child," said Li Oseph.

"We do have a clientele to watch over as well as our own business," said Likus.

"It will work out and we need to watch the boys anyways so why not get paid too," said Li Oseph.

"Great idea, huge amounts of money, too," said Likus.

"Here we are," said Likee.

"What a nice pool," said Liker.

"Dad we need a cook out tonight, alright," said Likee.

"Yes, we do," said Likus.

"As Likitoria we do need a cook out," said Grandmother.

"I agree too, as Ose is LikeOse and I am in agreement with all of you as LikerOseph," said Li Oseph.

"LikerOseph it sounds like, Pharaoh LikerOseph," said Likus.

"You should us it and become the Pharoh of Egypt instead of everyone being the King of France it was over a hundred volumes already and Egypt has only 55," said the Grandmother.

"Yes, it is important and it is a good name to use," said Likus.

"What was this started for by Paul.?" said Li Oseph.

"Not to have any assignations or kidnapping of our rulers," said the Countess.

"The students are complaining already about the extra amount of studying there is," said Likus

"It is not the majors of the programs, it is the extra books now in the classrooms remember it means," Thou shalt not kill.?" said the Countess.

"Right and now we have an extra book for each year in my high school too," said Likee.

"This will do it," said Li Oseph.

"I am sure of it," said the Countess.

"We need to remember some thing else and I have a good idea this family is going to the be a big part of the public eye and do the right thing is our goal," said Likus.

"We have, it take a long time to be a part of the public and now I think this is it," said the Countess.

"Good we are in charge and now officially public," said Likus.

"Good and we will do our best at the chateau," said Likee.

"I know you two will be very useful and you might want to think of a career," said Grandmother.

"We both think the law school is good," said Liker.

"Terrific we can use our own lawyers," said Grandmother.

"I will be needing you both in England, France Venus and here in France," said Li Oseph.

"That is perfect," said Liker.

"That all costs money Dad," said Likee.

"Oh, my goodness now Likee before you get to rude," said Grandmother.

"That was funny," said Likus.

"I am glad we can laugh and enjoy this business because right now is the money from the insurances so lets think of what the press is going to do," said Li Oseph.

"Maybe what is next is the fact that there is one more here, and the press will say he was always ours," said Likus.

"Or much more we can all deal with it, but the children do not have to read these things in print," said the Grandmother.

"We collected enough money for Lady Urlee and her family also in Newport, Ed and Paul all were paid. Now it is Moscow with Princess Ulmake then it becomes all ours for along time," said Li Oseph.

"All have been paid, that is right, I am so glad now we have done our share for the ones who help create and get where we are today. Said Grandmother.

"Yes, and we ourselves will be looked at with great admiration too, especially our Li Oseph who completed this project.?" said Likus.

"Boys if you wan to learn here is when we talk about the business. So please add if you want too," said Grandmother.

"All of us will be remembered for what we have accomplished in Venice," said Li Oseph.

"Hear that boys the both of you can work at the Chateau as a B and B with your wives and children . Still making money as a lawyer and delivering special documents to Paul and the others to sign is not a bad idea," said Grandmother.

"We will get it done we were here first and Ose can help, he is our assistant," said Liker.

"That is good but I need him around me when I am older," said Grandmother.

"You will be with us at the chateau," said Likee.

"Yes, you will," said Liker.

"Thank you boys, remember when Grandmother mentioned important things we can do. Now you are very helpful, yes you are but what about this idea.

"I know what you are going to say go on," said Grandmother.

"Grandmother goes to Paris after owning a Parisian building and very expensive too and gets surgery done on her face this week too," said Likus.

"Your right, I will go now, I have a house rather a fortress for myself for a great money I decided that ashould be done and Paul and the others have not thought of," said Grandmother.

"Please tell please, please," said Likee.

"Yes, please," said Liker.

"An older person moves in yet a group of contractors and carpenters as themselves. The older gentleman gets them to work on all of his apartments," said Grandmother.

"Yes, said all of his apartments," said Liker.

"True, if they build a new kitchen he would buy it and the wives were happy with the money yet they would have to start all over again," said Grandmother.

"What next," said Likus.

"He would buy them out giving them land with a house, and several new cars as well somewhere else. This was decided so they would not sue him for mental stress and damages," said Grandmother.

"Are you going to Paris and by the way we are all helping with that movie," said Li Oseph.

"I know the doctors and the building I will buy tomorrow and I will leave for the hospital, so I will return with a private nurse so please all stay here ok," said Grandmother.

"Mother, please I do not mind getting the movie done or you going alone to Paris. I do mind it if you get a nurse please make sure that he or she is older than you a female too," said Likus.

"Why dear.?" said Grandmother.

"That he or she will push on when you are well, family I do not mind it a bit Liker is wonderful he will stay even if I have to hind him from Ed," said Likus.

"Stop that when and where I pick a nurse all will be a right," said Grandmother.

"I can not have a total stranger here again as staff, family is just fine," said Likus.

"He or she will move on, to right next door that I own that chateau we need a nurse here for this family this is Venice it takes a while just to get even a taxi," said Grandmother.

"Ok, your right both what sex are you going to convince to stay here for three years," said Likus.

"Maybe someone who is a good nurse," said Grandmother.

"I need to sit down for a minute she is going to bring in a family with three children," said L:ikus.

"Likus sit down and relax, I hate to be cold at a time like this and not comfort you but I have to say this right now. "Likus go with her and interview," said Li Oseph.

"Why thank you that was not cold and it was very sweet and lovely of you to say. I know Mother agrees because the surgery will be postpone her to get some shopping done while in Paris while she can still sleep in the hospital," said Likus.

"No Z's or sleep to use or a hotel as a traveler, now you can own a building of your own and get a surgery you want too," said his Mother.

"That is perfect you do not need it, but you can become a lot more handsome than anyone could expect," said Li Oseph.

"Shopping for one day, surgery and then we are home with a nurse who will watch this house," said Likus.

"Please do not be offended what I just told you Likus when you are home you can hate me," said Li Oseph.

"I will I know I will, I will be wrapped up for a while," said Likus.

"You will be a wrap star out of all of us," said Grandmother.

"It is true, you will be in the news," said Likee.

"They will make fun of you Mom," said Liker.

"Then we do make more money that is the best way we need to have this happen," said Likus.

"It will you are scheduled right after me tomorrow so we need to leave right now if we want to shop," said his Mother.

"Ok, we do not need to have bring anything with us and we can have dinner in Paris late this evening," said Likus.

"So we have the phones and the nurse will be calling you," said Grandmother.

"Hope this goes well," said Likus.

"Everything will be fine," said Li Oseph.

"Good by, all of you and you best behavior for your father," said Likus

"I will get the chef to start the food," said the Butler.

"Good and we will have dinner of the roof," said their Father.

"Good by," said Likee.

"Good by," said Liker.

"Good by, I love you," said their Father.

"By, Love you," said Grandmother.

"By, I love all of you see you in a few days," said Likus.

"Now we do have a dinner to have children so lets get this done and we can wait for a phone too," said their Father.

"Lord Li Oseph," said the Butler.

"Oh yes, Frames, children lets have dinner," said Li Oseph.

"This is getting very exciting around here it reminds of my home so tonight I will call my Mother, just like last few nights I called and I will tel her about this ok," said Liker.

"Sure it is allright the others put in the the news I will call the editor we have to let him know," said Li Oseph.

"There is a message for you right here from Grandmother," said Liker.

"Ok, it is good what I was going to do had been done by your Grandmother she called the editor," said Li Oseph.

"I will take Ose now to feed him in the other dining room near his bedroom on this floor," said the Nanny.

"That is a good idea there is going to be a lot of loud talking tonight," said Li Oseph.

"This is so wonderful of Grandmother and Mom to do this," said Likee.

"When they return all of us can go for the same surgery and could look handsome," said Li Oseph.

"Could I, I need to get rid of these baby checks and baby fat in my face," said Liker.

"I think your bones in your face have grown as it will be when you are older. We will let the doctor know right now.? There it is in the phone so we might hear from him in just a few minutes too," said Li Oseph.

"I will not mind it if I have to wait a few years," said Liker.

"There is the answer if it is for being handsome only he will see you in about 4 years the both you," said their Father.

"I do not mind if I wait that long," said Likee.

"I do not mind it either," said Liker.

"Good the both you and the doctor have made a wise choice," said Li Oseph.

"Will you be going alone," said Likee.

"No, I will take Frames and his wife, the other two cooks will have everything under control," said Li Oseph.

"That is thoughtful of you," said Likee.

"Yes, it is," said Liker.

"Thank you both and here is dessert," said Li Oseph.

"The dinner is very good," said Liker.

"Yes, and so is this dessert," said Liker.

"Good and thank you and we can have some more in the living room later," said Li Oseph.

"So is there anything on the tel tonight or is anyone interested in looking at the computer and for messages too," said Li Oseph.

"I will look at the computer I will take this one over here," said Likee.

"I will wait and watch the tel first," said Liker.

"It seems as if they are in Paris and are shopping with orders that things are being delivered to us in a few days," said Li Oseph.

"Anything about a few new toys such as a new phone for the both of us," said Likee.

"Demand more that is the new thinking of our generation," said Liker.

"You are getting some new gifts she did not say what," said Li Oseph.

"Liker you get more being polite that is what your Grandmother would have said right now," said Li Oseph.

"I am sorry but I just said it in front of us men," said Liker.

Chapter 11

"Here they are and with the new nurse too," said Likee.

"Wait here and let them come in and settled down first they could be in a lot of pain do not touch them," said Li Oseph.

"Good morning Mom and Grandmother," said Likee.

"She waved and so did Grandmother and they have their faces wrapped up," said Likee.

"You should use the elevator and relax upstairs we will be up to see you one at a time," said Li Oseph.

"I apolgize boys I should have had you go to the third floor first. It is my fault please forgive me," said Li Oseph.

"Will they wrappings be on them all of the time.?" said Liker.

"Yes, for two months," said Li Oseph.

"Then we had to see them," said Likee.

"I know," said Liker.

"I am so sorry boys please forgive me," said Li Oseph.

"It is not your fault we had to know," said Likee.

"Right," said Liker.

"We will go upstairs in a little while but first you need to be upstairs," said Likee.

"Yes, with both of them," said Liker.

"I will and then you may come up one at a time, ok," said their Dad.

"Now you may go see them first Likee," said Liker.

"Good and who is next," said Likee

"It is Ose, next it is his turn," said Liker.

"Right, dad you are back so soon," said Likee.

"Yes and I am going to the hospital and I will be back in a few days," said Liker.

"You both may go upstairs and one of you must wait outside the door. Good bye and I love you both," said Li Oseph.

"I love you," said Likee.

"Love you, too," said Liker.

"Come on lets go upstairs now," said Likee.

"Wait, I hear the elevator," said Liker.

"Hello, boys and I am here so your Dad left and I hope Frames really wants this surgery too," said Likus.

"He does he was very excited about the decision," said Liker.

"Do you want anything, Mother.?" said Likee.

"I will let the nurse know everything and thank you," said Likus.

"This is very usual all of us having surgery," said Liker.

"I know it was for the visiting nurses who all with be here in a few days," said Likus.

"Then all of them will stay," said Liker.

"I do not know it all depends upon how well we heal," said Likus.

"Is it painful.?" said Likee.

"No, I am allright," said Likus.

"We have to go to bed now or in a little while do you want to go upstairs and rest," said Liker.

"Yes we should, I can hear your Grandmother calling us," said Likus.

"I can," said Liker.

"Yes, we should," said Likee.

"I will see the both of you in my bedroom or wait at the elevator," said Likus.

"We could get in see," said Liker.

"Very good then here we go," said Likus.

"I will say," Hi," to Grandmother again," said Likee.

"Yes, we both will," said Liker.

"Yes, and please do say," Hello," to Grandmother again," said Likus.

"Hello, boys," said Grandmother.

"Nurse I will see Grandmother, if you are tired I will take them back," said Likus.

"There, in my room finally, it takes a lot out of you me with my bandages on my entire face," said Likus.

"It is for your entire new face and tomorrow we will show all of your face from the head, forehead to the cheek bones only," said ther Nurse.

"Good do you know how many nurses we will have left if my Mother has her own, when we are better," said Likus.

"If all of you are on medications then the nurse will be in to administers of the scripts and she will check all of the people in the building of their own vital signs if you want them too," said the Nurse.

"At least two to stay if it is possible.?" said Likus.

"No, their will be a medication stay inside a box to lock up when she leaves," said the Nurse.

"Alright for anyone who has medications.? " said Likus.

"Yes, anyone," said the Nurse.

"What if I got a private duty nurse without your help, several in fact.?" said Likus.

"Then we have the right to hire anyone anywhere and take away their license no one is a private duty nurse," said the Nurse.

"I do not know, I apologize," said Likus.

"Thank you it is your right to know and I am glad to help, I will repeat anything from over talks," said the Nurse.

"Thank you," said Likus.

"Good night," said Likee.

"Good night," said Liker.

"Good night boys, I will see you tomorrow," said Likus.

"Good night, I am leaving too," said the Nurse.

"You know where your room is," said Likus.

"I need to go home and pick up a few clothes," said the Nurse.

"We plan to give you and the others anything from your own designer, would you like that it is our treat to the staff from us," said Likus.

"Alright thank you I will stay tonight and I will let you tell the others tomorrow so good night I will be in the room in between the both of you, so good night," said the Nurse.

"Good night and thank you," said Likus.

"Good night," said the Nurse.

"Nurse my face hurts," said the Grandmother.

"You were sleeping on it, but I could not turn you, you did not want me too," said the Nurse.

"What is this.?" said Grandmother.

"Two pills for the pain and I will bring you the portable chair it is time to get up if our want to do that," said the Nurse.

"I would like to have breakfast now I can smell the coffee from here," said Grandmother.

"The tray must be out side the door," said the Nurse.

"What a sleep," said Grandmother.

"Here I am Grandmother good morning, I am going to have breakfast with you ok," said Likee.

"It is the only server cart for dinner time for the second floor, so there is enough food," said Grandmother.

"Good," said Liker.

"You are up too so we need to be quiet so the baby does not wake up," said Grandmother.

"We have another Nanny while Anne is watching Ose," said Grandmother.

"We will be good," said Liker.

"I know but we will all have had surgery at the end of the month so it is necessary for the both of you to obey besides it is a man and young man and will play ball with you both outside," said Grandmother.

"The garden is not large enough," said Liker.

"Yes, it is beyond the wall is still ours," said Likee.

"Good we can play a game of base ball this morning," said Liker.

"Right after school this afternoon," said Grandmother.

"Good, we will do that," said Likee.

"Sure and now I need to get ready for school," said Liker.

"Yes, have a good day, Ed sent these to you they are two books he wrote and Paul too," said Likee.

"Here is the reader it reads your books aloud the same time as a movie," said Likee.

"Also there is the movie itself at the bottom of the draw," said the Nurse.

"Yes, I will see you when I leave Grandmother," said Likee.

"We both will." Grandmother.

"Alright go get ready right now," said Grandmother.

"I thought they would never leave and get ready for school, they are so worried about you," said the Nurse.

"They are good children," said Grandmother.

"They will look after you when they are grown up," said the Nurse.

"I hope they are married with children," said Grandmother.

"Let them live a good childhood and college and they will bring someone home," said the Nurse.

"You are awake," said Likus.

"I sure am and I had a very good breakfast," said Grandmother.

"Here is little Ose he had a good sleep too," said Likus.

"Did he sleep with you," said Grandmother.

"Yes he was, he was in his new crib in my room to give the nurse a break," said Likus.

"You have your face wrapped from your forehead to your cheeks and are showing," said Grandmother.

"I am leaving or we are leaving so you can get ready," said Likus.

"Thank you, I will see you down stairs for coffee," said Grandmother.

"See you soon," said Likus.

"I will want my bath right now," said Grandmother.

"Boys good bye." and Grandmother said Good bye too, she does not want the two of you late again," said Likus.

"We are not, this is the first school cab, so good bye," said Likee.

"Bye," said Liker.

"Good bye and be good and do a lot of work today," said Likus.

"There Mom we are alone and I do not want Ose to see me this way or you," said Likus.

"No, you are right and I think that elevator needs a little maintenance," said Grandmother.

"I will put it in the phone. I see your forehead and cheek bones are visible," said Likus.

"Thank you and I do want some more coffee," said Grandmother.

"I do too," said Likus.

"I wonder if we are on the news about these surgeries or not," said Grandmother.

"Lets see.? Both nurses are here," said Likus.

"We were just wondering if the both of you would like a head and neck message," said the Nurse.

"Yes, please," said Likus.

"Yes, I would indeed," said Grandmother.

"Good here it goes and I hope, we hope this relaxes the both of you," said the Nurse.

"It is this is so good," said Likus.

"Heaven that's what it is," said Grandmother.

"Good we will continue this tonight we have twenty more minutes and we hope this agrees with you both," said the Nurse.

"I could fall asleep," said Grandmother.

"Here is the news," said Likus.

"Good, please turn it up," said Grandmother.

"The very first news item, we received surgery, the children neglected and ruling the staff and Prince Li Oseph has run off," said Likus.

"We can sue, what did they say about the butler," said Grandmother.

"The butler is accompanying him to turn down his bed for him," said Likus.

"His wife is not going to be to happy," said Grandmother.

"What do you hear that she is laughing," said Likus.

"I can here her laughing," said Grandmother.

"See if she is alright nurse, and if she want s to talk I can meet her in the library," said Likus.

"I will," said the Nurse.

"What is next,?" said Likus.

"You know that I have become beautiful and so are you with also a sex change," said Grandmother.

"I hope so, so we can sure for a lot of money," said Likus.

"I know these stories are not going to get any better," said Grandmother.

"We will not let the children see this and we will have movies tonight," said Likus.

"There, I cancelled the news on their tel," said the Nurse.

"Thank you," said Grandmother.

"I hope they return tonight," said Likus.

"That would be nice and we will certainly get a few more nurses too," said Grandmother.

"Yes, we will and thank you Mother for letting me bring home some nurses that I had picked," said Likus.

"Your welcome, now do not accuse me of having a stay brought home to marry," said the Countess.

"Sorry about that I just did not want the house filled with people," said Likus.

"I know ones that do not have a reason for being here," said his Mother.

"We all do every single one of us that has something to do in this house," said Likus.

"All that is needed now is the cooks to go to the hospital for surgery if they want too," said the Countess.

"What do we do about the nurses.?" said Likus.

"We gave them clothes that are designed before they all leave," said the Countess.

"All prepared here I hope," said Likus.

"Yes, our own clothes, our designers and all will be ready before they leave," said the Countess.

"Here are the boys, time did go by when we are waited on," said Likus.

"Yes, but I did mostly keep quiet and did rest all day long," said the Countess.

"That is good," said Likus.

"Here are the boys, how was school," said Grandmother.

"Good, we are having a Christmas party this Friday," said Liker.

"Each classroom is having a party and we need to bring a food item," said Likee.

"Are the both of you in the same classes," said Grandmother.

"Just outside sports," said Liker.

"Each sports has two homerooms in it. I need a large bag of chips for Friday," said Likee.

"I need a large bag of chips too," said Liker.

"You boys are so helpful and polite when we are going though this," said Likus.

"They are good boys and now tell me about your day," said Grandmother.

"Just the same I was wondering if I could have something to eat right now," said Likee.

"Please do I did not thing of that, we can talk later," said Grandmother.

"I am hungry too," said Liker.

"Yes, please and you may go up to your room if you want," said Likus.

"So I did not get anything out of them do you suppose they know about the news," said Grandmother.

"I am so glad you waited until the door was closed, I do not think they know anything," said Likus.

"I whispered to you," said Grandmother.

"Yes, I know forgive me," said Likus.

"We need to tell tonight," said the Countess.

"Remind because I do not want to do it right now with two people out of the house that makes this house function," said Likus.

"A very clever point of view and accurate," said the Countess.

"Yes you are correct.," said Likus.

"We can tell them when they come down stairs or just ask them right now or when they are finished with their snack," said Grandmother.

"I will give the kitchen a call," said Likus.

"We have to know about this ourselves," said Grandmother.

"They are going to be here in a few minutes," said Likus.

"You ask them and tell them what we saw on the tel," said Grandmother.

"Look Grandmother here are some cookies," said Likee.

"Thank you dear the both of you," said Grandmother.

"Likee and Liker did anyone mention to you about the news we were on the tel and we now have to sue. Yes, the press did say what was not true," said Likus.

"Not all of the press reports were lies," said Grandmother.

"No, nothing," said Likee

"Nothing," said Liker.

"Alright, and if you are bothered by anyone at school let the Headmaster know," said Likus.

"Sure we will, Grandmother," said Likee.

"Grandmother we both will," said Liker.

"Thank you boys, I guess you may go upstairs right now until dinner," said Grandmother.

"Why not, for a little while study and get whatever homework done," said Likus.

"Right," said Likee.

"Ok," said Liker.

"I do not think they would spare our feelings and fib do you.?" said Grandmother.

"If I wanted to protect you I would fib," said Likus.

"Maybe not I think they would tell us," said Grandmother.

"If I was asked that question and saw it on the tel I would fib to protect you," said Likus.

"Lets have some coffee," said Grandmother.

"I will and here is yours," said Likus.

"Thank you and I am feeling much better there was no more pain,?" said Grandmother.

"The doctor will be in tomorrow and to examine us," said Likus.

"Then he will tell us how long does this wrappings have to stay on," said Grandmother.

"Here are some cookies they are for you," said Likus.

"I know someone does love me they both do, but this around my head does not give a positive even inspite that we are both going to look better than before," said Grandmother.

"I know it to confining," said Likus.

"Too confining, it seems to be permanent to me," said Grandmother.

"No, it will be off soon," said Likus.

"This dinner smelled divine and I did think we would have a good dinner too," said Grandmother.

"With these painkillers either I am napping more or the world is passing me by very fast," said Likus.

"It is a painful world but these pills are letting us nap to forget what is going on," said Grandmother.

"It is true a person that is uncomfortable and ill and in pain the world is slower to move with them," said Likus.

"For the Asthmatic while suffering in the world it seems to go by slower," said Grandmother.

"Right and for the asthmatic and the anorexic when they are better the world seems to go by faster," said Likus.

"It does seem unfair," said Grandmother.

"This is why we are younger and will contiue with the tunnels in Venice and the Atlantic tunnels as well there are now over one hundrend and twenty tunnel cities," said Likus.

"It that our next advertisment," said Grandmother.

"I think so it is our next goal to own underneath the ocean too, according to Paul," said Likus.

"Gale I hope I never see the day he is in the Lounve as Duke Paul an exile Prince and he will be the only owner of these trains and tunnels systems always as he is right now," said Grandmother.

"There is someone at the door the nurse is getting it right now," said Likus.

"It can not be Frames and Li Oseph you are both home, quick Frames go see your wife she is first," said Grandmother.

"Li Oseph you are home and there is no bandages and you look so very handsome," said Likus.

"How did this happen.?" said Likus.

"I asked for all the shots to reduce the swelling and pain and here I am. The doctor is going to be here tomorrow so he will give you the shots, he told me," said Li Oseph.

"Shots, why not the same day like you," said Grandmother.

"Would you have gone to do more shopping.?" said Li Oseph.

"Yes," said Grandmother.

"That is why," said Li Oseph.

"What is entering the door look at all of these packages and gifts," said Grandmother.

"We both had a few hours before the surgery so we went shopping," said Li Oseph.

"Boys come down stairs right now and do not run," said Likus.

"Thank you so much for shopping," said Grandmother.

"I even bought out almost all of the collection in Ulmakes wig for the both you too. What we do not need we can put into our own shop in Venice as I bought a franchise too," said Li Oseph.

"Is that the only franchise for Venice," said Grandmother.

"No, but we can talk more about them all later here are the boys. My sons how are you and here are some gifts for the both of you.?" said Li Oseph.

"Dad your ok, what about the wrappings," said Liker.

"You're here that is so good, Frames is back, and what about your wrappings," said Likee.

"Tomorrow all should be better for the both of us, now go see Frames and there are gifts for the both of you and for all of us," said their Mother.

"Li Oseph, you look more handsome," said the Countess.

"You two will be better tomorrow there is an ointment to use so let him be the first to use it and apply it when it is needed," said Li Oseph.

"I had it removed and the nurse washed my face and I had a tub bath," said Grandmother.

"That is good so far it was for when you start to go outside then it is used," said Li Oseph.

"The only time we were outside is when we arrive home," said Likus.

"I am having a lot the things delivered from five stores so we can look forward to this in the next few days," said Li Oseph.

"Li Oseph, please sit down and let me look at you," said Grandmother.

"You do not regret going shopping do you," said Li Oseph.

"Now sit here with me and Mother can get a better look at you from here," said Likus.

"You should sit down there," said Grandmother.

"Alright now, are both of you please at these lists.?" said Li Oseph.

"Oh, this looks very good," said Likus.

"Indeed.!" said Grandmother.

"Here we are," said Likee.

"Some food arrive it will be out shortly," said Liker.

"You bought food too.?" said Likus.

"We had time to shop than you too," said Li Oseph.

"He must have taken the two of you at least by five and six o'clock," said Grandmother.

"I was four-thirty and Frames was at six," said Li Oseph.

"That was how it was done," said Likus.

"These toys and puzzles are alright," said Likee.

"Good dear enjoy them," said Likus.

"Great," said Li Oseph.

"Let me see," said Grandmother.

"Now I am delight because the purchases are so the boys will not feel neglected," said LI Oseph.

"It is really good to see you again," said Likus.

"You did think I would return," said Li Oseph.

"I do not know what to believe I just realized right now that you had all that money and could have left me," said Likus.

"I just, you just reminded me I forgot to run away," said Li Oseph.

"It is not funny," said Likus.

"I know you did just reminded me about running away with my share of the cash but I can handle the situation and I am not upset at what is going on. Also, I love you Likus and that is the truth," said Li Oseph.

"I love you too," said Likus.

"Children there is a small dinner for us the three of us and with desserts too so lets have our food now and we can open up some more gifts later," said Grandmother.

"Food," said Likee.

"Right," said Likee.

"We are alone and here I am with a medical wrappings over my head that is good for one more day," said Likus.

"Here I am better for you and I making you happy," said Li Oseph.

"Yes, you are," said Likus.

"Did I come home saying I found someone," said Li Oseph.

"No, you are for me and that is the way it will remain," said Likus.

"Good then lets go and have dinner and be apart of a family," said Li Oseph.

"We will, Sir," said Likus.

"Your plates ready and we can enjoy a good dinner at last we can rejoice," said Grandmother.

"Here Grandmother have a few more hot dinner rolls for your gravy," said Likee.

"Thank you I did start to sound like a person who was about to give a speech or a few quotes," said Grandmother.

"Very funny Grandmother," said Liker.

"Yes, it was," said Likus.

"But I did think that was my job," said Grandmother.

"Mother you can start tomorrow," said Likus.

"Good wisdom never hurt and neither does good words," said Li Oseph.

"Yes thank you, Li Oseph," said Grandmother.

"Yes Li Oseph thank you for being on Mother's side I can not seem to do this, that is why the children come home from school," said Likus.

"They will stay with us but it did get you to this point after being at a boarding school," said Li Oseph.

"I know but there were serious times of being alone," said Likus.

"You are here with me now and all of us," said Li Oseph.

"I know it has to be the pain killer I am taking," said Likus.

"It will be a few more days ," said Li Oseph.

"Just think we would be seen by all of you if we did not go shopping. Oh, but say this food is wonderful and very delightful too," said the Countess.

"Awesome," said Likee.

"Truly," said Liker.

"Truly awesome," said Likus.

"Awesome," said Grandmother.

"Very truly awesome, indeed," said Li Oseph.

"We are all in agreement, so that is the policy of how words effect agreements in groups I never knew that before until now," said Grandmother.

"So we will have dessert and then what.?" said Likus.

"A few new games to see and then we are off to sleep," said their Dad.

"Right Li Oseph and then we have a busy day tomorrow for those other deliveries might arrive," said their Mom.

"Yes, and as their Grandmother I do insist on one thing," said Grandmother.

"What is that.?" said Li Oseph.

"The nurse will help me to the elevator and the boys will take one game each and you Li Oseph will put them to bed when they are sleep on their bedroom floor," said their Grandmother.

"Good lets go good night," said Likee.

"Yes, good night," said Liker.

"Good night, Dears," said the Countess.

"Good night," said Li Oseph.

"Good night, Mother. I am not tired due to this medication," said Likus.

"I know it hit me that way too and this excitement is good too but your Mother had some wine and is very tired," said Li Oseph.

"They are all upstairs I want you to know there is no reason why I would leave you," said Li Oseph.

"I know that," said Likus.

"I am having so much fun with this business and the family is ideal. Truly I do love I told you the first time I saw you on the tel is the time I would try to have you for myself," said Li Oseph.

"I know and I am very grateful to you and all that you have done for me and the children and my Mother but it is just these pills are doing a terrible wrong right now. I do love you," said Likus.

"I love you, it has been a dream and a fantasy come true," said Li Oseph.

"For me too," said Likus.

"Did you see the children faces when they saw all of the games," said Li Oseph.

"Yes, they were thrilled and that was a nice thing to do," said Likus.

"Thanks and there is still more gifts to be delivered," said Li Oseph.

"Now lets go upstairs and we can watch some tel," said Likus.

"Alright I am so tired," said Li Oseph.

"I am not so I am going to have coffee and use the computer right off of our bedroom," said Likus.

"Alright I will understand and in the afternoon you must get some sleep," said Li Oseph.

"Good night I am going to call up the lawyers and start the proceedings right now for what the press has done," said Likus.

"Good you do that dear and good night," said Li Oseph.

"Good night," said Likus.

"Now Hello, I do have a lawsuit for you," said Likus.

"Now then when can we get this done. Wait I wan to put you on the speaker phone," said Likus.

"OK, here I am we meet at your house tomorrow night and you sign the papers ok," said the Attorney.

"Sure be here for dinner also," said Likus.

"Good bye see you tomorrow evening about 5 o'clock," said the Attorney.

"Yes, and good bye," said Likus.

"Are you coming to bed.?" said Li Oseph.

"Not yet, now to start my first book," said Likus.

"Check if we are receiving now the new money from that account," said Li Oseph.

"I will start it over again for us only it is now for us it is our third time for it to work," said Likus.

"Good now we continue to have the trillions for us only," said Li Oseph.

"There that is good now my book I am on page 25 right now," said Likus.

"Lets go to bed," said Li Oseph.

"Ok, just a few more pages," said Likus.

"Be quick about it or I am going to put you to bed.," said Li Oseph.

"Then that is the way it has to be but I am not tired," said Likus.

"Ok, dear now I am very angry so I will keep you busy if you can not get any sleep. Turn off the computer because I am going to pick you up and you are coming with me," said Li Oseph.

"What happened did you get an operation done there too," said Likus.

"Yes, and today is the best day and evenings for the rest of your life too," said Li Oseph.

"I hope they do say it is King size in the news," said Likus.

Chapter 12

"Hope you did enjoy all of the gifts last night, Mother," said Likus.

"I did and when does the doctor get here.?" said the Countess.

"That is why I am in this room to tell you he is in the dining room and I am going to be first, ok," said Likus.

"Sure, I do not mind, should you see if he is ready and have a cup of coffee with him ok," said the Countess.

"I will Mother, hello doctor I yelled across the hall so I would not scare you," said Likus.

"You did not and we can being right after your coffee," said the Doctor.

"Do you want another.?" said Likus.

"I have a full cup so help yourself," said the Doctor.

"Mom, if you want to be here said the nurse to bring you. These little phones are so helpful," said Likus.

"Will she be here.?" said the Doctor.

"No, I was wondering if you are going to see Li Oseph today," said Likus.

"Yes, why.?" said the Doctor.

"Is there any way of him getting muscles and not having any side effects," said Likus.

"There is a monthly shot now and with his work he could use it," said the Doctor.

"Please convince him I need him to look very strong and with enormous muscles too," said Likus.

"I will and I do have the one month shot with me," said the Doctor.

"Thank you, Doctor," said Likus.

"I will get Li Oseph and please tell him, ok," said Li Oseph.

"We do things very that are very important yet I try to relax. Please forgive my son this visit it is part of their career too," said the Countess.

"That is alright, now your surgery is a success as well as your son so I was wondering it there is any discomfort," said the Doctor.

"No, I am fine and I look and feel good too," said the Countess.

"Good," said the Doctor.

"Here I am doctor," said Li Oseph.

"I will go into the dining room right now," said the Countess.

"Thank you and could you have Likus return," said the Doctor.

"I will let him know right now," said the Countess.

"Li Oseph, you need to remove all of your clothes. We need to wait until Likus is here," said the Doctor.

"Here he is, stop running," said Li Oseph.

"These shots are based on the size the smallest is small pecks and to the largest then to the biggest of them all, the M.P," said the Doctor.

"What about the others parts of me," said Li Oseph.

"It is based on manhood and the other parts of you become large depending upon the shot," said the Doctor.

"Side effects.?" said Li Oseph.

"There are none it is based on you becoming a large man and there is a need to have you a photo of you alone and then with the family," said the Doctor.

"Stating the success of this project is a concern and the staff were not taking me seriously," said Li Oseph.

"I do have tell you that your success all the employees will respect you more because of money that went with the job this will make them listen and look," said the Doctor.

"I will sit here Doctor," said Li Oseph.

"Yes, and Likus and I will watch over here sitting in front of you," said the Doctor.

"Alright I need my shot right now," said Li Oseph.

"Ok, I decided it is best for you to remain seated on the couch. Now Likus watch and the extra weight on him will help in the right places," said the Doctor.

"What about Mr. Talk.?" said Likus.

"Yes, position yourself so it is over your leg. Now here is your shot a surface shot in the middle upper part of your chest," said the Doctor.

"Will it be now.?" said Likus

"It is now so watch and if any of us are ill we will be seated," said the Doctor.

"Oh, my you look like a heaven or someone to watch over me and no one can get into the house. Please stand up," said Likus.

"Ok," said Li Oseph.

"My goodness you are enormous Oseph and it moved into a round shape and fall and hit the floor," said Likus.

"I know I watching it turn go into a round ball like shape and fall to the floor, it was fun and exciting," said Oseph.

"I need to examine and then you to can go about your business," said the Doctor.

"Sure," said Likus.

"I need you to be the first to pick it up so I can examine it that way you were the first," said the Doctor.

"Say I should arouse you now to be the first," said Likus.

"Now I need all this in my hand," said the Doctor.

"Here," said Likus.

"Now that is a fine bit pleasurable and desirable and a handsome man too you have there Likus," said the Doctor.

"Ohhhh," said Likus.

"It is a good thing the door is locked," said the Doctor.

"Ooo," said Likus.

"I need to know if you can produce and go to the bathroom today those three things are essential to stay on this medication," said the Doctor.

"He got one," said Likus.

"Now here take this. I need to stay for the other two parts and then I can leave and I need to see them," said the Doctor.

"I did think," said Likus.

"I need to know that he has gone to the bathroom I need to see him go. I need to see him because I can not trust anyone this is my licence," said the Doctor.

"You want him to go," said Likus.

"You need to see him make urine," said the Doctor.

"So you both will see me, I have to go right now," said Oseph.

"Here is the bathroom. Go in front of us," said Likus.

"Ok, I will," said Oseph.

"There is not obstructions at all. Normally you would be in the hospital for this procedure," said the Doctor.

"Two out of three," said Likus.

"Yes, it was clever of me to help," said the Doctor.

"I know it was," said Likus.

"Yes doctor, you have very warm hands," said Oseph.

"That was clever of me it was the lonely way I could leave here today seeing all three," said the Doctor.

"I might need to sit down and go," said Oseph.

"Good, this is the last out of the two that I needed to know of," said the Doctor.

"Doctor it was not the first one you have such smooth hands and," said Oseph.

"Look now sit down and Likus be pleasant with him and then I will go into the Den and ask the Butler to get you some clothes," said the Doctor.

"I could get him some thing from upstairs," said Likus.

"Yes, get me those jogging pants and a sweat shirt too," said Oseph..

"Now I need to ask you some questions," said the Doctor.

"Are you still sexually aroused," said the Doctor.

"Yes, but I am in control," said Oseph.

"Good than tell me is anything hurting with this drug.?" said the Doctor.

"Here are your jogging pants and a sweat shirt," said Likus.

"No, nothing hurts exspect since we all stopped," said Oseph.

"Oseph, do not start this you are not hurt," said Likus.

"No, you are not hurting and I suggest the both of you stay here and talk and I will see myself out. Please call me and I will give you a monthly shot if you wish to continue," said the Doctor.

"Does this stay the way it is and in a few months all of this will disappear.?" said Oseph.

"It will take six months to get rid of it all, yet you need a shot each month to keep its firmness and length of all parts so good day to you both and I will call about your next shot," said the Doctor.

"Good bye doctor and thank you for helping me," said Likus.

"Yes, good bye and thank you," said Oseph.

"Good bye," said the Doctor.

"Now it is going to get use to," said Oseph.

"He closed and locked the door so lets see how used to it you are.? Here stand," said Likus.

"No, I have a better idea, sit down right here," said Oseph.

"O and say nothing," said Likus.

"That was just fine. Do not stop," said Oseph.

"Here," said Likus.

"Good there is a movie," said Oseph.

"I all seems to be over," said Likus.

"Yes, it is and thank you I need to put on my jogging gear," said Oseph.

"You need to put that thing away right now," said Likus.

"I will and you and I are going upstairs," said Oseph.

"Ok, then lets take the elevator. I am now calling the for photos to be done tomorrow ok," said Likus.

"Now here is our room," said Oseph.

"I will send up a tray for lunch," said Likus.

"Good I need something to eat," said Oseph.

"I need some sleep for about two hours," said Likus.

"I do too so give your Mother a call and thank her are resting," said Oseph.

"It is nice to relax on the bed. I just heard the cart it is now in front of the door," said Likus.

"I will look for it," said Oseph.

"Good and let me know when we are ready," said Likus.

"I look alright," said Oseph.

"Looking at your new muscles you are a different person," said Likus.

"It that good," said Oseph.

"Yes, I mean a different person as a handsome person," said Likus.

"Thank you," said Oseph.

"You can not think of you as seeing those muscles, someone would never think it was you," said Likus.

"This is ok," said Oseph.

"It is a good thing for me that we do not have sidewalks in Venice," said Likus.

"I was just going to say that sidewalks," said Oseph.

"You do not want me to be in public ?," said Oseph.

"On the tel, in the news sure but personally I want you right here with me," said Likus.

"I know you do," said Oseph.

"Do I ever say lets go to a movie in the city or do something else.?" said Likus.

"No," said Oseph.

"I want you for myself," said Likus.

"Certainly you do and I need and want you too," said Oseph.

"We should go and see the children they all must be wondering what I look like," said Oseph.

"That is true but do they know.?" said Likus.

"I do not know give a call to your Mother and have her tell them we are going to be in the living room shortly," said Oseph.

"Hello, Mom ok, then you know we will be in the dining room shortly," said Likus.

"Shall we go my love.?" said Oseph.

"Yes, we shall but they are all on the second floor," said Likus.

"Why.?" said Oseph.

"Mother wanted to lie down and we all are having pizzas upstairs and maybe we might roast marsh mellows on the third floor.?" said Likus.

"But it is to cold right now," said Oseph.

"Good reason I think we can persuade them to watch you flex your muscles," said Likus.

"They will have to ask.?" said Oseph.

"I forgot that I will wait until they mention it first," said Likus.

"Yes, they should," said Oseph.

"Here we are they are in my Mother's suite," said Likus.

"Oh, boy here they are oh my," said Likee.

"Oh, this is.?" said Liker.

"My goodness," said the Countess.

"Hello boys," said Oseph.

"Dad," said Likee.

"Dad, are you going to get any bigger.?" said Liker.

"No, this is where I stay," said their Father.

"If the doctor used it I would marry him in a minute.?" said the Countess.

"I hope you do but the both of you need to live with us or at least until in we are in the Chateau and Oseph has worked in France," said Likus.

"Good orders, President," said the Countess.

"We just did the photos just the two of us is what the papers wanted," said Likus.

"I was wondering who was downstairs.?" said the Countess.

"Now lets have some dinner the pies have arrived," said Li Oseph.

"Very good," said Likus.

"Yes, I need some food too," said the Countess.

"Could we see some flexing of your muscles.?" said Liker.

"Please, just a few times," said Likee.

"Alright here is a biceps and now with the shirt off and this is all," said Li Oseph.

"I want to have that when I am 14 years old," said Liker.

"I will have it right now if I could," said Likee.

"Then one or both will have it done at the ages of 15 years, ok," said their Father.

"Ok, then it is me," said Likee.

"You have a few more years to go, look at that food we need to have a good time tonight and play with all of your new toys, there are adult toys too some are very good puzzles and a new reading book each," said their Father.

"Mother, I do hope Likee does not remember that at 15," said Likus.

"I know, I do not think he will be interested," said the Countess.

"I did not tell you how beautiful you are," said Likus.

"You are beautiful," said Li Oseph.

"Thank you both and I am very serious if the doctor uses that drug I will marry him tomorrow," said the Countess.

"What about his practice.?" said Likus.

"I have lived in Europe long enough to treat him like a diva and he can live with me for 4 months out of the year," said the Countess.

"You really did have an education here in Europe," said Likus.

"You sure did," said Li Oseph.

"Right and Oseph maybe when we are living in the Chateau I should give you 4 months so you can work someplace where you want too," said Likus.

"Maybe it all depends on how important it is publicly," said Oseph.

"Maybe the Atlantic tunnels and start a new project next to the other tunnels but not attached, use it as back tunnel and then for the police use all the time," said Likus.

"I could apply for it now and get the necessary paper work going and grants too," said Oseph.

"Good so when you come home you and use the tunnels the journey will be a safe one," said Likus.

"More food boys.?" said Grandmother.

"Mother did you hear.?" said Likus.

"Yes, I am glad you have finally have plans that could work," said the Countess.

"I know it is perfect and so is he," said Likus.

"Thank you dear," said Oseph.

"How is your wrting when I saw the light on from the court yard I knew you were writing a book," said his Mother.

"Are we in the book," said Likee

"Yes, are we," said Liker.

"Both of you are creating a design of how the both of you will go on drugs, thinking you will both be three feet taller," said Likus.

"It does not.?" said Likee.

"Then forget it," said Liker.

"Now we do not need to be in a book," said Likee.

"Yes, we do I think that is a great story to tell," said Liker.

"Then I will use it," said Likus.

"Good then you can tell about the doctor and myself getting married," said the Countess.

"Just as soon as it happens," said Likus.

"I think he is good for you so lets have him to dinner because he was so nice to you," said Li Oseph.

"I will ask him and he will be here tomorrow night," said Likus.

"Good then you should ask to invite his wife," said Oseph.

"I will and if he says there is no one that would be good for Mom," said Likus.

"I hope so," said Oseph.

"Need I tell the both of you I am right here is the palace," said Grandmother.

"We need you to have someone and it is him," said Likus.

"I can not argue yet I feel as if I do not have a say in this at all," said Grandmother.

"You do not have a say so if you did he would not be here tomorrow night," said Likus.

"Ok, then I surrender I will do as you say," said the Countess.

"Boys do not repeat this to anyone outside of this house alright," said Likus.

"No, please do not," said Li Oseph.

"No, please do not and your rewards will be in the summer time at the Chateau," said Grandmother.

"Now they will remember," said Li Oseph.

"Indeed they will," said Likus.

"He accepted, a definite yes and he is he arriving alone at 5," said Likus.

"So there is a marriage soon I hope.?" said Li Oseph.

"I hope so too," said Likus.

"We will see.?" said the Countess.

"Things will go as planned. Yes, and I know you are looking forward to a marriage and it looks promising," said Likus.

"We will not appear to be this eager," said Oseph.

"We need to give him a chance to relax and enjoy us here first," said the Grandmother.

"I know it will fast and painless and the you two will be on a honeymoon in two weeks," said Likus.

"I hope so I do want to vacation and enjoy someones company for the rest of my life," said the Countess.

"You will be happy the two of you," said Likus.

"I hope so I want it all and so far I have been very lucky and fortunate," said the Countess.

"We will make sure things are done, he would not accept if he was not sure," said Li Oseph.

"It all makes sence to me and I know you will enjoy his company," said Likus.

"I called the doctor and ask him if he would like a dinner with you alone due to that it was still early enough to have something to eat and would he mind it if he slept over to see my scalp in the morning," said Li Oseph.

"So he will be here in a little while, what was wrong with your scalp.?" said Likus.

"I had a red area on my forehead and it was all over my arms and chest," said Oseph.

"Oseph, I have to let the doctor know these things maybe he should move in for a little while.?" said Likus.

"That is good I never did think that far into the picture," said Oseph.

"If it is the plasma that I think it is, it is staying on," said the Countess.

"Good because he is here right now so go downstairs and have dinner with him right now," said Likus.

"I will use the elevator," said the Countess.

"See you both tomorrow if you are still here," said Likus.

"So what happen," said Oseph.

"I let her know I will see her and him tomorrow or it should be three weeks after the elopement, but I did not think of it," said Likus.

"Let them work it out and remember you did say the correct," said Oseph.

"I know, always the correct thing to say," said Likus.

"Here we are alone the boys are asleep and is there anything you want before I go to sleep," said Oseph.

"Just let me stay here with you for a little while and I will be up most of the night because of these pills.? said Likus.

"We can talk," said Oseph.

"I did as much as I could," said Likus.

"I know I was some help right," said Oseph.

"Yes, if it was not for you she would not be downstairs with him. You called him not me," said Likus.

"I know I had to think of something," said Li Oseph.

"You did and it worked," said Likus.

"Do you think they will go next door.?" said Oseph.

"My guess is they will ask for a lot of prepared food even in spite of the fact there is food over there," said Likus.

"Good maybe in three days will ask for us to go over and they will be married.?" said Li Oseph.

"I hope so, she deserved to have someone," said Likus.

"Yes, she does I can not believe little Likee was waiting for her to call him at the school," said Li Oseph.

"He was and I am glad she did not wait to long," said Likus..

"He is in good hands and so is Liker," said Li Oseph.

"Yes he is, they both are, all three are," said Likus.

"What if your Mother gets married he is a Doctor, it is very impressive but he does not have a title," said Li Oseph.

"He has his family, they do live here a few blocks down," said Likus.

"Why not ask the staff on the phone," said Oseph.

"I will," Hello, it is Likus, I was wondering do you know about the Doctor's family ok, and good night and thank you, Frames," said Likus.

"What did he say.?" said Oseph.

"They are going to stay next door, the maid is there and they brought with them a lot of food. The parents are five blocks down and they both use their titles," said Likus.

"What is he.?" said Oseph.

"He is a Count himself, Count Orelift," said Likus.

"Ok, good night know you want to write," said Oseph.

"Ok, I will write in my book and I will not call them at all," said Likus.

"Good now start to type," said Oseph.

"Here is goes, first the stock and cd's too and to see if we should transfer," said Likus.

"Good," said Oseph.

"Another trillion it is mine and then Mom and then you," said Likus.

"Hello, yes Mother, good, you are big adults now and both of you know what you want. Good and you will be back to sleep next door," said Likus.

"What.?" said Oseph.

"They are eloping now and returning tonight to Venice to stay in the city," said Likus.

"Your Mother wanted happiness," said Oseph.

"She did get it. I think she was lonely too.?" said Likus.

"Now she is happy," said Oseph.

"What about the witnesses.?" said Likus.

"I think they have them at the city clerk's office," said Oseph.

"The phone is ringing, yes we will, see you in a few She mentioned that the preacher is on duty and is willing to be there is a few minutes, and we are to be witnesses," said Likus.

"Then lets go I will take a shower, you just did and I will meet you down stairs," said Oseph.

"Here you are and in a hurry I like that shirt," said Likus.

"Ok, we are in the cab, and now here is the first step," said Oseph.

"Hello, Mother and Count," said Likus.

"Hello, you too I want the both of you to be witnesses," said the Countess.

"Sure we will and good evening to you both," said Oseph.

"Shall we begin," said the Preacher.

"Yes please do," said the Countess.

"I hear noise out side," said Likus.

"And now you may kiss the bride," said the Preacher.

"There is is quite quarded out there is or is it not.?" said the Countess.

"If you to leave now we can talk on your behalf," said Likus.

"Alright we have a cab in the back," said the Count.

"I will go outside and you follow me and stay at the door," said Likus.

"Did your Mother remarry," said a Reporter.

"Yes, she did," said Likus.

"Excuse yourself Likus and come in here," said Oseph.

"Thank you for interrupting me I did expected a lot of questions," said Likus.

"So she did it and now she is happy. Yes and we both are for her do you have a certain amounts of pages to write, you should do so," said Oseph.

"I will start right now and finish up," said Likus.

"Good, good night," said Oseph.

"I guess my Mother is going to live next door for a little while," said Likus.

"Maybe.? " said Oseph.

"There I am finished for this evening. Lets see if mother or if we were on the tel," said Likus.

"Maybe.?" said Oseph.

"Now we need something bad in the news it always happens some newspapers says something wrong," said Likus.

"The phone, let it ring and I will listen," said Likus.

"There just someone who wants info," said Oseph.

"I know what is the first thing, Mother had to get married," said Likus.

"No, that, that it is best too," said Oseph.

"I guess so," said Likus.

"Turn it on," said Oseph.

"Lets see if anything is on the tel.?" said Likus.

"So we missed if there was anything at all," said Oseph.

"I think so," said Likus.

"What else did I say.?" said Oseph.

"You mentioned, turn it on," said Likus.

"So here it is," said Oseph.

"Oh, good here you are and oh boy I hope no one can hear this," said Likus.

"Oh boy, I do love you," said Oseph.

"I know, and you are the best thing that has come alone in a long time," said Likus.

"I love you," said Oseph.

"I do love this bedroom that all of this is happening to me," said Likus.

"I love you, I need you," said Oseph.

"Oh this is incredible, you are not wearing any shirts this summer," said Likus.

"I will just wear a swim suit at the pool. Here I am and I will turn on the lights right now," said Oseph.

"Oh boy I can not believe this.?" said Likus.

"You will again right now," said Oseph.

"This is fun and good oh my goodness. I love this as you squeeze me and let out my air," said Likus

"So it is your turn and squeeze me right here. Good now a good tug, harder and let them both bounce. This is good and I enjoy it and I need more," said Oseph.

"Alright I will," said Likus.

"This is wonderful," said Oseph.

"Ok, I need a rest," said Likus.

"So do I," said Oseph.

"I know someone else owns this joke, I think it is Edvard of Bavaria, but Oseph I do have to say it," said Likus.

"Say what.?" said Oseph.

"First, why do you pronounce my name O-se-f," said Oseph.

"It is because of Ose who has his nickname and it could work that way for Lloyd's when he is older," said Likus.

"What did you want to say.?" said Oseph.

"As Prince Li Oseph you are a Prince but that is certainly King size," said Likus.

"Good wasn't it just a few hours ago we were talking," said Oseph.

"Yes, and I tried to take advantage of you in your sleep with all of your muscles and this is why I am writing so early too," said Likus.

"Why what do you mean.?" said Oseph.

"I touched you and you through me off the bed," said Likus.

"I will have that small bed from the den brought uptairs if things are to difficult or I become dangerous make sure I am across the street, ok," said Oseph.

"You could be allergic to the medicine, what about male nurses.?" said Likus.

"No, they just what to have me, so call the police department and ask if they can watch me until the medicine is out of my system, and pay them overtime too," said Oseph.

"I will, I think you should introduce yourself and give them equipment as you can go on assignments with them and get some guards to watch the project," said Likus.

"Very nice tell me more," said Oseph.

"Maybe you can help them keep law and order. At least you will help them out as a charity too," said Likus.

"So I could look for a few guards to help with the business," said Oseph.

"Yes and still the police charity," said Likus.

"Good I will do this today and," said Oseph.

"This is Sunday so go and give them a check or go to a store," said Likus.

"I will just give a check so I can talk," said Oseph.

"Ok, then you have something to do and now I am going to write.

No, I hear the boys I need to get to their room and tell him that their Grandmother," said Likus.

"I will go too," said Oseph.

"Yes please do, boys I have something to tell you we both do. Your Grandmother and the doctor were married last night," said Likus.

"Our Doctor.?" said Liker.

"Yes, and now he is your Grandfather known as Count Orelift too," said Likus.

"Grandmother got married," said Likee.

"She is very happy and will live here or next door," said Oseph.

"We can visit right.?" said Likee.

"Yes, the both of you and sleep over," said Likus.

"Ok," said Liker.

"Then you must respect her wishes and they will be away for a few days or weeks I do not know," said Likus.

"I will miss her," said Likee

"You both will all of us will," said Likus.

"Maybe your Mother is trying to tell you for a while it might be by invitation only," said Oseph.

"Yes it is, but we must call first," said Likus.

"Ok," said Liker.

"We will," said Likee.

"Then that is that, and we will be happy for Grandmother," said Oseph.

"So why not go to your rooms and get ready for breakfast and have some food in the second floor dining room so we can talk later," said Likus.

"Yes, we will," said Oseph.

Chapter 13

"There two weeks went by, when are they going to arrive.?" said Liker.

"You were asleep last night when they called," said Likus.

"When will they arrive. Please tell me?" said Likee.

"Today at 9:00 a.m. because they are going to be next door," said their Mother.

"I here them they went into their house," said Oseph.

"Do you want to go to see Grandmother and her new husband," said Likus.

"Oh, yes Mom and we will behave ourselves," said Likee.

"For the future I want you to call me Likus and let yourselves become more matured after all the two of you could run the b and b at the chateau. Dad you can call Dad," said Likus.

"Ok, should we leave now.?" said Liker.

"Yes, I think enough time went by for Grandmother she wanted a few minutes," said Likus.

"We will be there the whole day and evening.? " said Likee.

"You both are returning to sleep in this house," said their Father.

"Now I am closing the front so good bye. Oseph, there is going to be a great difference if they do not move in," said Likus.

"I now I will let them know right now moving in as soon as possible. Letting the Count to set up his practice there," said Oseph.

"Mention to her to ask to return at the end of the week so he can work in that house," said Likus.

"He might set up a practice here.?" said Oseph.

"There is an office in Venice so why was the surgery done in France.? said Likus.

"Remember the surgery when purchasing a building in France," said Oseph.

"I did not think of that," said Likus.

"Remember because you might get some ones hopes to high," said Oseph.

"I will remember. There what you are you doing or looking for.? We are in the bedroom no more than two minutes and look, did you find it," said Likus.

"Find.?" said Oseph.

"A very large back," said Likus.

"Come," said Oseph.

"What.?" said Likus.

"Look, watch out of you big ass, what, you put me on the on your large back and then I landed right into your big bum. Oh, that was heaven again I hope the children stay for three weeks," said Likus.

"Here," said Oseph.

"What ? I do not want to call them," said Likus.

"What is the phone ringing, pick it up, it is probably for you. Here use the desk phone. ? " said Oseph.

"Hello, Hello, Hello," said Likus.

"Let me talk," said Oseph.

"Here, What, what the hell.?" said Likus.

"Lets go bolling," said Oseph.

"When," said Likus.

"Right now," said Oseph.

"What, what.?" said Likus.

"You are the only pin," said Oseph.

"Lets talk, right now on the phone," said Likus.

"Hello, it is so good hearing from your again. Now the people can hear the truth why the tunnels got done because Ed did it and worked too," said Likus.

"I know I have to leave, I only have a half a day today," said Oseph.

"Right, so get dressed and I am more disappointed than you here," said Likus.

"No, I am, are all of us having dinner here or there," said Oseph.

"Here our dining room is a success now that we have our new blue goblets and pale white plates with your coat of arms in the center that is very small too," said Likus.

"Why so small.?" said Oseph.

"It is to hide the lions that are actually two males have oral sex with each other," said Likus.

"Really," said Oseph.

"No, it is the center yet prepared foods such as lobster and the vegetables cut and narrow could enhance the center. Even steak cut up and narrow can do it too," said Likus.

"Very good and I am sure the long steamed carrots will get the work out," said Oseph.

"That reminds me, I can wear my ring tonight that is a white diamond that has been around the world in auction plus I received a gold mesh shall with a hood that looks like Ownsites, Princess Ownsites that used the same in Newport so do not tell Liker," said Likus.

"Give him the cash or better a check and you say he bought it for you as a gift, we need gifts from all of us.!" said Oseph.

"I got gifts from us of us so there is not need," said Likus.

"You gave her, her pattern," said Oseph.

"The store new her building so she can exchange it and the same credit goes towards her decision," said Likus.

"This was the store decision," said Oseph.

"Yes, and including ours now I will kick you out to go to work," said Likus.

"Ok," said Oseph.

"I should be trying to keep you here yet you need to make an appearance that is what is required," said Likus.

"Bye, President Likus," said Oseph.

"Good bye,Vice President Oseph," said Likus.

"Good bye," said Oseph.

"Now for the menu and to tell the staff. Frames is the dinner going to be ready on time and serving steak," said Likus.

"Yes, the dining is all set and the London broil steaks prepared out side will consists of two steaks each all cut into long strips and served in a cream steak droppings, along with the mash potatoes served in the hard skins also," said Frames.

"The mash hot potatoes will have the seasons package of what.?" said Likus.

"It will still be the steak droppings, butter and a lite cream cheese in side," said Frames.

"Good the table is perfect elegant and again you did out do yourself," said Likus.

"Thank you my Lord Likus," said Frames.

"We are combining this dinner with a young America couple who are living next door to our right," said Likus.

"So is that the reason for the home steak dinner for them too," said Frames.

"No," said Likus.

"Are we sure."" said Frames.

"Yes, I told mother they are invited and we are going to have an home made ordinary meal from the states," said Likus.

"Very good, Sir," said Frames.

"She may have a lobster dinner tomorrow night here and we will have everything from the grill on the third floor I do not want to smell that lobster in the house," said Likus.

"Then she will exspect you to invite them again for the cook out," said Frames.

"I will let them know right now, hello, you too, I was wondering if tomorrow evening you two can be here for a cook out. Good no that area is sealed off we will be in doors. Not at all see you at 5 tonight, and thanks, yes I have it. Ok, bye," said Likus.

"She was surprised you included their gift," said Frames.

"Yes, I included everyone we all have given her a new crystal glass bowls to cups to goblets," said Likus.

"I will let her know the gift and my collection of the Venice company made a very good price for everything," said Likus.

"For dinner tomorrow bedises the cook out could you serve two each of the dough and the ham and eggs mixture rolled up with a white cream cheese sauce, I still want this appearing as if it was a dinner," said Likus.

"The dough is usually a sandwich you can hold in your hand and eat," said Frames.

"Make it three each and serve two with and one without," said Likus.

"Very good Sir we have extra cooks now that everyone is out of the hospital," said Frames.

"What about the cooks when is your wife going into the hospital.?" said Likus.

"The three left last night and are returning tonight with all of their shots that are to be given here when they get into the house," said Frames.

"Good the land deeds went as planned so now the houses are yours expect the one you picked, you may pick one next to them that you want," said Likus.

"Thank you, Sir I will," said Frames.

"Now the children will be back soon with their Grandparents so I will talk to you later and thank you again for all of your help," said Likus.

"I will take care of the desserts too," said Frames.

"Now who is at the door.?" said Likus.

"Surprise we had lunch and we brought over our dinner to add to yours," said Likee.

"Ok, hello Mother I am so glad you decided to be over here earlier because I have to tell you something," said Likus.

"Look see my new ring," said the Countess.

"Yes, and congratulations to the both of you and it looks elegant and so lovely, oh, goodness," said Likus.

"Hello, son please call me dad," said the Count Orelift.

"Ore let Likus decide," said his Mother.

"Dad is fine with me," said Likus.

"He is going to have his practice right here for all of Venice," said his Mother.

"Then it is settled that is so good, thank you Dad," said Likus.

"Your welcome and thank you for arranging all of this to happen," said his Dad.

"Likus does a lot of good," said his Mother.

"Yes, he does he helped me," said Liker.

"Me too," said Grandmother.

"Me too," said Oseph.

"Me three," said Likee.

"What is that noise.?" said Likus.

"A alarm," said Oseph.

"Follow me the dogs are safe," said Frames.

"There wait just one second more. Now I can open this door and step into the elevator that is from the basement," said Frames.

"We can all sit down in a square," said Likus.

"Now I closed the door behind and now you will descend and walk to the end and open the door and close it immediately," said Frames.

"The police were called, and where are you going.?" said Grandmother.

"I am letting your elevator closed keep your hands in and then I go upstairs to deterrent their position and yours," said Frames.

"The elevator is out of sight we can not see his feet," said Oseph.

"There keep on moving.look the door is opening," said Likus.

"This hallway is long," said Grandmother.

"The door closed behind look another door and the garage door, now the door we left is the cedar block as not looking like a door at all," said Grandfather.

"Look another door there are the maids," said Likus.

"Please enter immediately and now I can closed all the doors," said the Maid.

"Look it is a bank vault door. Did you know this Likus.?" said Oseph.

"Now what is that sound, it is happening this corner wall. That is to big for a laundry shoot," said Likus.

"The door is opening I think it is Frames, I hope so," said the Maid.

"Thank you for being so prompt and willing to cooperate," said Frames.

"Frames, are we safe now.?" said Likus.

"We will be, right now I need everyone to stand over here," said Frames.

"What is going to happen.?" said Likus.

"Before I can give you the tour I need to get rid of this elevator, remember the chimney and now it is electric this elevator is going below and the steel and cement will follow from the third floor," said Frames.

"The chimney stopped," said Likus.

"See the light," said Frames.

"Yes," said Likus.

"Remember the large brick wall and walking to the dining room into the kitchen it is going to leave us.?" said Frames.

"Now let me show you why there is a brick wall," said Frames.

"Look this is exciting, wheres Ose," said Likus.

"Here he is," said the Maid.

"Good baby, Ose here we go," said Likus.

"Now let me put the combination into the door, and now the tour," said Frames.

"Look at this lovely living room and a kitchen when we first enter," said Likus.

"Wonderful there is a bathroom and a long hallway," said Grandmother.

"There is a television set lets find out what happened or we should just listen," said Likee.

"Now down the hallway is a library and it own bathroom and bar," said Frames.

"Where are the bedrooms," said Likee.

"Right down here parents first guest room for the Countess and Count," said Frames.

"So the living room is in the middle the kitchen and dining room on the sides. We both have sitting rooms Mother," said Likus.

"Nice," said Oseph.

"Now a hallway across and it has a bathroom it is the first just on one side," said Frames.

"Closet space," said Oseph.

"Here is a room and to on the right hand side are two bedrooms and this door at the end on the right also is a living room for children and adults who wish to observe," said Frames.

"Now we have uniforms to wear in case we are here to long," said Frames.

"How long will it be.?" said Oseph.

"The wall and chimney will take about a few hours to get it back into place," said Frames.

"Why it is not electric.?" said Oseph.

"No, it is manuel and the police have the parts and the combination for the safe as the third part is in their own safe, provided by the company," said Frames.

"So the station has two parts," said Likus.

"Right and we have to wait a while," said Frames.

"So lets all go and see if there is a snack or even an a dinner at all," said Likus.

"I took the liberty is fix the food and I did bring it down stairs just before the alarm went off," said Frames.

"So you knew.?" said Oseph.

"Yes, they told me there would be a problem that the police would turn on the alarm, and the food was ready," said Frames.

"Right we are not really inconvenience today or in any harm because of Frames, he is the local hero," said Oseph.

"Yes, but it will not be in the news," said Likus.

"Thank you, Prince Likus.

"I do remember Frames telling me the first day and it was his instructions only and to see the system when it was necessary," said Likus.

"So lets all have dinner and the staff can be at the table next to the kitchen and with the children would you like that," said Likus.

"Good by the way where are the nannies and the nurses.?" said Grandmother.

"There are upstairs and I could not tell them to go outside this was the decision I had to make," said Frames.

"You did a good job," said Likus.

"I did have time enough to give them a dinner at the other house and to let them see the Villa and enjoy a few hours per order of Oseph and Likus," said Frames.

"Oh, you are a good man," said Likus.

"Yes, you are and quite aware of what to do," said Oseph.

"Is there coffee next door that was the only thing I could not do," said Frames.

"Frames please have dinner with us," said Oseph.

"The maids and I prefer to have dinner with the children, there are other ways to show gratitude," said Frames.

"Yes, there is and we will talk later on tonight ok, right Oseph," said Likus.

"Right the three of us, will talk," said Oseph.

"When we talk about this he should keep that house and at least let them vacation this year," said Likus.

"Good it is done he has the deed already," said Oseph.

"If he wants to buy someplace else they can sell it back to Grenaire. You can tell him that," said Likus.

"Frames you may keep the house and sell it to Grenaire and invest or purchase a home here in Venice," said Oseph.

"Thank you, the both of you I will sell to Grenaire and then purchase stocks in the tunnels in the Atlantic project and wait until either one of you wish to purchase," said Frames.

"Thank you Frames you are worth the invest you and your wife who should be back soon possibly tonight," said Oseph.

"Yes, they will return late at night," said Frames.

"So we have a partner who is willing to wait for us the purchase," said Likus.

"I could buy the house from him why not get it does with Grenaire so it does appear to be a normal transaction," said Grandfather.

"Oh, you are such a good husband," said the Countess.

"Thank you dear now we can resume our honeymoon," said Count Orelift.

"Thank you dear lets go to our living room with the children so there will be a quietness after all we have been through," said the Countess.

"Oseph, the boys and may be with us right in our suite," said Likus.

"What is that noise.?" said Grandmother.

"The walls are manually being placed back, it will take two or three hours. They might release the bank door during that time," said Frames.

"Frames the staff may be with you in the kitchen and we will be in the apartments," said Likus.

"Soon we will be upstairs again," said Oseph.

"I miss the house already," said Likus.

"This living room looks quite nice and in Baroque too. Lets see the other room," said Oseph.

"We will. This bedroom is lovely, I wish there was another one," said Likus.

"We will survive and remember we can not stay here," said Oseph.

"I know we fortunate this is here," said Likus.

"Yes we are," said Likus.

"Lets relax and there is actually candy, something we can use," said Oseph.

"So this is how an emergency works here," said Likus.

"It does serve a purpose," said Oseph.

"We still do not know if this is real," said Likus.

"I understand this when we leave we will be safe," said Oseph.

"Excuse me here are some snacks and coffee," said the Maid.

"Thank you," said Likus.

"I hear the noise is still there," said Oseph.

"It is I hope we do not have to listen to this during our sleep," said Likus.

"It should be one hour left," said Oseph.

"Here Oseph have some coffee, tea and cookies," said Likus.

"Alright I give up and surrender we will be here until tonight so lets go to bed right now," said Oseph.

"No, we need to use a little restrain," said Likus.

"I now we can not let anyone know we are annoyed being here," said Oseph.

"No we must act as if it is everyday there is something," said Likus.

"We can but be inquisitive this is their job," said Oseph.

"We are there will be a lot to think of and ask when we are upstairs," said Likus.

"So we might even be sleeping on the first floor," said Oseph.

"No, I think we will all be upstairs" said Likus.

"Besides there is Frame's wife to return also," said Likus.

"She will," said Oseph.

"Knowing something did not happen is the final answer," said Likus.

"So we do know this is still exciting," said Oseph.

"That is because we do not know if anyone is murdered. upstairs we can not expect," said Likus.

"We can however try to each the police," said Oseph.

"I think Frames mentioned the police will reach us here each," said Likus.

"They will," said Oseph.

"We should go look at the boys.?" said Likus.

"Right now," said Likus.

"This hallway is beautiful," said Oseph.

"It is lovely. Lets go see the children," said Likus.

"So children how are you both," said Oseph.

"Do you need any food.?" said Likus.

"No thanks," said Liker.

"No," said Liker.

"Now we need to return and be with the baby Grandmother is watching him," said

"Bye," said Liker.

"Bye," said Likee.

"Here is the baby and Ose is just fine," said Likus.

"Here is my baby," said Oseph.

"Yes he is," said Likus.

"We need to be with you more often," said Oseph.

"He is a good baby," said Likus.

"Yes, you are," said Oseph.

"Frames I want you to hear this. We have an excellent opportunity to transfer the house and money today and it will somehow be connected to this emergency," said Likus.

"But Frames might go to prison and be there for a while," said Oseph.

"Wait this is how they found out. When the staff received there housing," said Likus.

"If anything happened we still do not know," said Oseph.

"It is the only theory right now that someone a group wanted their own property and tried to invade us," said Likus.

"Maybe it is but we can not let anything happen to Frames," said Oseph.

"No, we can not do this transfer and I do not want him in a prison," said Likus.

"We will just have to wait," said Oseph.

"There is nothing of a transaction in the computer so this is the only thing that has happened," said Likus.

"I do not think anything will happen because of the surgeries were done there that itself is evidence," said Oseph.

"Good we have to use this as the focal point of this intrusion so the press and the world will know there was surgeries given to the staff," said Likus.

"So far so good," said Oseph.

"The nursing and nannies when they leave are given a new wardrobe," said Likus.

"There I hear the walls have stopped and the bank door should open soon," said Oseph.

"Thank you Sir, the both of you clearing up and please use this it tends to be important so it should not be ignored," said Frames.

"Hello, we are the police," said the Sargent.

"Was there anyone in the house, are the nannies alright," said Likus.

"Yes, they are alright but we needed this time to fine out if there was anyone else in the palace," said the Police man.

"It is a palace but the castle can not be seem that well since the palace was here first and disappear again and reappear for the last time in, I do not know the date I was wondering, why were they here.?" said Likus.

"The reason is to be included in on the surgery a few at a time and to get the properties and your money also," said the Detective.

"There is not to much money here right now, my main concern is Frames and his wife will return in about an hour and I do not think she has thought of being a witness to something earlier or to be a suspect in a crime," said Likus.

"His wife is due home right with surgery so that fact and himself who just got out of the surgery too is enough to solve the case," said the Detective.

"The case is closed.?" said Oseph.

"Yes it is and the people who went to jail to be booked were the only ones involved," said the Detective.

"No one else," said Likus.

"We will always be investigating that part of the case especially when they are to be going to a trial," said the Detective.

"Well thank you so much," said Likus.

"Your welcome here is my card and all of you may go upstairs," said the Detective.

"Thank you again, Detective do you want to stay and have some coffee and sandwiches," said Likus.

"No but thank you for the food earlier," said the Detector.

"If there is anyone here the dogs would be barking," said Likus.

"That would not make a difference," said Detective.

"Oh, now I wonder if you should check all buildings on both sides and across the street," said Likus.

"Is the alarms on.?" said the Detective.

"Yes, they are I can see the one across from us," said Likus.

"Detective, I think all is in good hands and the search is done for now could you leave a few quards in each building," said Oseph.

"Sure I will send over a few of my people tonight I will call right now, excuse me please," said the Detective.

"Oseph, I hope they arrive soon.?" said Likus.

"They well. We better have Frames get some food and coffee," said Oseph.

"Right for the three buildings," said Likus.

"No, the four buildings," said Oseph.

"Right, you are right four," said Likus.

"Prince Likus, my security people will be here this evening as soon as possible and I will stay right here until they appear," said the Detective.

"Thank you so much would you like to wait in the living room.?" said Likus.

"Yes, I will thank you," said the Detective."

"It seem as if the police are here," said Likus.

"Good I will right back and I need to assign them their building," said the Dectective.

"Alright the door is unlocked," said Likus.

"If we are to ask them for the security maybe they can appoint someone from their team," said Oseph.

"Here he is, I was wondering if there are any of your officers would like to work some overtime until we can furnish our own staff," said Likus.

"All of these gentlemen will work overtime yet they are here to watch the place not do any work of any kind," said the Detective.

"Fine we need three weeks planned if you could do that.?" said Likus.

"Sure I will ask right now," said the Detective.

"Thank you and what is your first name and may I call you by your first name," said Likus.

"It is Mike yet it will not do you any good for I am going to work in Rome in two days and these three separate pages are the new schedule I put their names on them," said Mike.

"Enjoy your new job it will be a good opportunity to be in Rome," said Likus.

"I can not even wait it is going to be very exciting," said Mike.

"I am sure of it we were just there," said Likus.

"Now here is your schedule and I left the copies with their messages," said Mike.

"Good I will talk to these guards tonight, only the ones that are in this house," said Likus.

"That will be perfect and I need to return to talk to my boss about leaving. Now I do need to leave and thank you both for helping this evening and cooperating too," said Mike.

"Thank you for all your help," said Likus.

"Good bye and thanks," said Oseph.

"Now this is wonderful we have security at last," said Likus.

"Lets have a snack and coffee," said Oseph.

"What is all the commotion all that noise is at the door," said Likus.

"It is Frame's wife, they are home," said Grandmother.

"Frames take your wife upstairs and the rest of the staff can continue and tomorrow you can start a normal shift an hour late too, unless all of you want the day off," said Likus.

"Now we can go to our suites and call it a night so you can still talk to the staff tomorrow," said Oseph.

"Ok, come on everyone lets go to our rooms," said Likus.

"There we can eat in our rooms, I ask them to place our dinners there," said Oseph.

"There Ose is in his bed and the guards are downstairs so we do not need to worry," said Likus.

"No we do not have to worry , I believe that Mike is going to stay here in Venice and he is going to call tomorrow while I am at work all day," said Oseph.

"What would it be for," said Likus.

"He is going to have a schedule made up and drop it off and then on the tour of this building he is going to kiss you," said Oseph.

"He is not," said Likus.

"Oh yes he is and I will not be jealous if you want him and others just let me know," said Oseph.

"Why do I need yours.?" said Likus.

"Not many at once just one," said Oseph.

"Why.?" said Likus.

"Because I now have to much for you and it is going to get bigger and just to make sure I keep you," said Oseph.

"So you are going to be greater than what you are right now.?" said Likus.

"Yes and I am going to keep you by my side," said Oseph.

"Ok," said Likus.

"But there is just one thing, one side effect that I noticed when I stated the shots," said Oseph.

"What is that," said Likus.

"I never did like going out side and now that these shots are given to me the problem is greater," said Oseph.

"So now what.?" said Likus.

"I like the shots and the doctor is going to be here is a few minutes," said Oseph.

"So you are going to be larger.?" said Likus.

"Yes, and here he is," said Oseph.

"Good evening doctor," said Likus.

"Good evening when Oseph wants to be larger the shots start all over again," said the Doctor.

"What am I saying my Mother just married you, you live here now," said Likus.

"This could be pleasant for you by watching so sit down and he is going to stand," said his new Father.

"Dear I should have given you more time to think but I need you to help me when he is finished," said Oseph.

"Then Oseph please strip. Here he is," said the Count.

"Oh, boy what is, is so good oh, my," said Likus.

"Now I need you to be a nurse for me, Likus," said the Doctor.

"He wanted to be an M..P. three times as greater than he was," said Likus.

"Sure now place in my hand his larger sacks, I need to examine him," said the Doctor.

"He will stay right there for now," said Oseph.

"Now he is ready so stay just like that and now I will get this done too," said the Count.

"A blood test.?" said Oseph.

"Sure right now. One prick first," said the Count.

"Oh, I can not blame Likus look at me in the mirror," said Oseph.

"As if wakes up give it to him," said the Count.

Chapter 14.

"Oh, Likus are you awake.?" said Oseph.

"He is not. There how about that.?" said the Count.

"Oh, I do believe anytime your in the neighborhood doctor," said Oseph.

"It is hard to believe that your balls are extremely larger than what I expected," said the Doctor.

"Say what are you doing there is another one and where did it go.?" said Oseph.

"It took at lot not to east it Oseph. But if you want a scandle let me give it to someone in the city of Venice that needs a child," said the Count.

"Who knows we could make another fortune.?" said Oseph.

"So I will try one more time," said the Count.

"No, I think you should wake up Likus," said Oseph.

"Oh, boy what did I do. Oh, Oseph you are better than before," said Likus.

"Say why not do something like this," said Likus.

"Leave it alone now," said Oseph.

"No, I need to give you a," said Likus.

"I am having," said the Count.

"Ok," said Likus.

"Alright," said Oseph.

"There," said Likus.

"I am locking the door," said Oseph.

"You can stay, the more the better," said Oseph.

"Say it is nothing like taking right over," said Likus.

"Do you want a problem in the newspapers," said the Count.

"Sure why.?" said Likus.

"Say Doctor you are really getting this done, here it is," said Oseph.

"Here no major lawsuit in a cup," said the Count.

"I guess they will try this too.?" said Likus.

"You can call me your worst father. Expect us to gather at the bedside all together because but last night I sold his first," said the Count.

"What, why.?" said Likus.

"If he is going to put in these tunnels their has to be many a press release," said the Doctor.

"Ok, then," said Likus.

"I called your Mother and she knows there is a examination going on," said the Count.

"Good lets get started now Oseph, please get on the bed," said Likus.

"Ok, just for today," said Oseph.

"There the stress has it and if you are weak lie down, the shot just upset his stomach," said the Doctor.

"Why are you so serious.?" said Likus.

"I am going to give him his third and final shot. Work on him now you need to desaint him as soon as possible. Here let it drip in this cup," said the Doctor.

"Go on get on top and work him over," said his Father.

"You are a good step Dad and Mom knows about this.?" said Likus.

"As a precaution she will not enter and will make sure no one else does," said his Stepfather.

"Good," said Likus.

"Ok, but I warm you we need to sell and lot of them at a great price," said the Count.

"Why are you tying him,?" said Likus.

"Two reasons to promote a very good or another release and if he wants to be here for a while then I can get him an attorney when he needs one," said the Doctor.

"It is a lot of sex and then he is a good surrogate or we tie him for awhile and then he is desainted," said Likus.

"Sure it should take about six months," said his Stepfather.

"I know but I think it will be faster," said Likus.

"I think so too and when he sees the ties on his hands you need to stop his yelling or voice with kisses," said his Father.

"Now as a nurse and he is the largest he can be give me again his parts for another examine," said the Doctor.

"He is moving," said Likus.

"Now he is waking up give him so kisses and talk to him," said the Doctor.

"Good keep it going and talk," said the Doctor.

"Likus please and by the way I am tied are you sure I was going to run outside naked," said Oseph.

"Outside running but not naked," said Likus.

"What do you have in mind, Likus.?" said Oseph.

"I need you to be home so we can desaint you and this is the second one we poured into a small container," said Likus.

"What.?" You do not need to tie me I am convinced. Give me the phone please," said Oseph.

"Ok, I trust you," said Likus.

"Hello yes this is Oseph give me the boss please. Hi, you are in charge of for a few months and a good increase too, ok, bye," said Oseph.

"Oh, good Oseph I am so glad now I do not have to worry," said Likus.

"Now I do not want any more talk unless it is not on this meter," said Oseph.

"Then let me continue and we can go to heaven together," said Likus.

"We will and I am labeling and the dates are on the bottles," said the Count.

"Good, what do you get for each one.?" said Likus.

"Likus this is for him, it was his idea and he will need it for the lawyers' fees," said Oseph.

"Ok, it is his, lets get it done again," said Likus.

"No, a few more minutes," said Oseph.

"Alright that it is good "Likus.

"Any time you are ready," said the Doctor.

"Ok, now what I want from you Likus, are some good kisses," said Likus.

"Oh, ok, there is fine too, alright," said Oseph.

"Here," said Likus.

"Ok, I will hold him," said the Count.

"It is better than before," said Oseph.

"You approve," said the Count.

"Ok, but there seems to be something wrong or different," said Oseph.

"Tel me what.?" said the Doctor.

"Oh, Ok. I do not see you," said Oseph.

"I am relaxing and so is this," said the Doctor.

"Now I guess all of you are pleased," said Oseph.

"Not until the container is full," said the Doctor.

"What did you say, Likus.?" said Oseph.

"Tell me," said the Doctor.

"Now and more," said Likus.

"He wants you to get working," said the Doctor.

"There done," said Likus.

"Now we can rest a while," said Oseph.

"Sure just let me know when it needs it again," said Likus.

"Sure I think you would know that.?" said Oseph.

"Thank you hon, Dad why not give it a try," said the Count.

"If it is for a cause, now let me work right now," said the Count.

"Oh, what a good deal," said Oseph.

"Looking absolutely handsome," said Likus.

"Yes, you do," said the Doctor.

"Now I need the both of you to be mean," said Oseph.

"To the finish I will jerk you off," said Likus.

"I will work the nuts along with my hands," said the Count.

"Yes this is good, a little more, now, ok there it is," said Oseph.

"Great now you can not even be King of one the Italy's regions," said Likus.

"Or at least King of the country," said the Count.

"Now we need a exercise and this too is what I am going to do, I am staying here and talking to you," said Likus.

"That is not talk. That is singing," said Oseph.

"Just cooperate it is my order. We need some food. So Oseph here is a sandwich," said the Court.

"So Likus. Have some food," said Oseph.

"Here Father I am not tired," said Likus.

"Hay wait one minute," said Oseph.

"If you wet the bed I will just remove the bottom sheet that remains. Yell and I will stuff your mouth," said Likus.

"No, I will not but what about a bathroom. I will take care of that," said the Count.

"There two legs and two arms what is next.? Here Dad take his weapon," said Likus.

"I will," said the Doctor.

"If he calls the police then they will be paid to go alone with it," said Likus.

"I will not call. Oh boy, what a morning," said Oseph.

"This what I am about to say is still professional. Did you ever feel embraced or something on your dick or totally around it like this.?" said the Doctor.

"Yes, when I was left alone by you two I did notice maybe a running of pee but nothing there," said Oseph.

"Then you were in a life picked and is going on in a dimension in the room you are in," said the Doctor.

"Like visual reality," said Oseph.

"Militaries style," said the Doctor.

"So I have been held.?" said Oseph.

"Why sure and I do believe you stopped wetting the bed as a child," said the Doctor.

"No, I leaked anywhere I could find," said Oseph.

"Just like this one," said Likus.

"Just like that one," said Oseph.

"Well I have to tell you that is why you leaked to a good and young teen," said the Doctor.

"I guess so," said Oseph.

"You guess so, you will be doing it quite often with us," said the Doctor.

"That is no good," said Oseph.

"Please do not cry," said the Doctor.

"Here Likus give him a bath lick him good and here is a face cloth clean him first," said the Doctor.

"Did you have this planned doctor," said Oseph.

"Do you want to be a saint," said the Doctor.

"No," said Oseph.

"What did you say something," said the Doctor.

"No," said Oseph.

"That no, tells me you did not think of it at all," said the Doctor.

"He did because he does say sentences," said Likus.

"Oh, that talk did feel good," said Oseph.

"I know and where I talked makes me desainted," said Likus.

"I wish I could," said Oseph.

"I just realized something that this is not desainted," said Likus.

"It is because I did not give my permission," said Oseph.

"We tied you up and you enjoyed it," said Likuis.

"I did and now that I want more it is just fun and I will have more do you understand because now I am in charge," said Oseph.

"Good finally it is a great moment, you enjoy it and I enjoy you Oseph," said Likus.

"I love you," said Oseph.

"I love you," said Likus.

"There we love each other and I think we need more food," said the Count.

"Good idea. There I have given a memo to the staff," said Likus.

"Let me put it on the house phone," said Likus.

"Oseph, I need to tell you that you need to rest for two days after these shots," said the Count.

"Alright then what.?" said Oseph.

"We go downstairs and you see the children and if you need to be on the second floor we will leave," said the Doctor.

"Now it is clear of what to do," said Oseph.

"Likus are you going to stay the entire weekend too." Oseph.

"Yes, of course," said Likus.

"Then it is settled," said the Count.

"We only have just a few days left," said Likus.

"Then it is done and we now have a plan," said Oseph.

"So lets go sit on the bed, Oseph," said Likus.

"We need to touch you," said the Count.

"Now we need to start putting our hands on your back," said Likus

"There moving on your back and then some reasons why we will not stop.?" said the Count.

"The reason is, this is our job," said Likus.

"Our job," said Likus.

"Here is the food," said the Count.

"Smells good. The building has never been the same," said the Doctor.

"We have done our share of good and love too," said Likus.

"This does seem alright," said the Doctor.

"It is alright," said Oseph.

"Lets celebrate too," said Likus.

"I just realized about the family," said the Doctor.

"What.?" said Likus.

"Always very busy," said the Doctor.

"We are all to be blame.?" said Likus.

"No, not to be blamed it is up to us to get Oseph off the desainted list and the other," said the Doctor.

"We do have a situation," said Likus.

"Does this mean I stay here or get ready because since I have been this medication I have wanted to be naked and with a few good ones at a time," said Oseph.

"No, it is for Liker his little brother died and she wants him to stay here. Plus he is a going to have a new baby sister," said Likus.

"Alright he will and we can tell him, I do not think he wants to go.?" said Oseph.

"There is a group of doctors in Newport and now in France and they allowed the boy to die," said Likus.

"We will find out if they are in France now and using their titles.?" said Oseph.

"I will write it in now, it is on the work day timer he will receive it at 9 am," said Likus.

"Good we will run them out of Paris, France that day," said Oseph.

"Dad, do you have nothing to say.?" said Likus.

"No I do not. We can not really get into trouble for this because I mentioned to you I wanted to see his penis to examine and you gave it to me," said his Father.

"So here it is, after I put it on your head," said Likus.

"Looking this long we need another cartoon in the papers we this I will be crowned perfectly among the world," said the Count.

"Hay that was a good," said Likus.

"The cartoon right, what about this.? Now it is very good and I am very convinced," said Oseph.

"Good then Likus has done this worked.?" said his Father.

"There all done for the bottle," said Likus.

"Specimen container," said his Father.

"Dad I think you need this more than me.?" said Likus.

"I do sound as if I needed more sleep.?" said his Father.

"Then go to Denmark," said Likus.

"Very funny, Oseph you need some nude pictures," said his Father.

"Take both of us," said Likus.

"Guys I can not see you but from where you are the both of you are making me come again," said Oseph.

"There I saved it," said the Doctor.

"Another press release is that this is not a cleansing," said Oseph.

"Ok, so I was a little messy," said Likus.

"No, I need that but was not done in a camp," said Oseph.

"That one I got, living in Venice," said Likus.

"Good," said his Father.

"But we did have two cook outs on the second flo," said Likus.

"Flo is good," said Oseph.

"Flo is good, would you prefer a back rub," said Likus.

"Yes," said Oseph.

"Ok, then, when I am finished," said Likus.

"No, we have to get back to the children," said Oseph.

"Here is a t-shirt it is the only thing and you might even rip it," said Likus.

"There it is torn," said Oseph.

"You know there is a first shot and once a month that shot will keep you at this third level which is the last," said the Doctor.

"This is fine, here just sit down and put these covers over you and I will order some new suits now," said Likus.

"Now they can visit," said Oseph.

"You have a cold," said Likus.

"Here they are my two boys," said Oseph.

"Hi Dad, I hope you are feeling better," said Likee.

"Yes, I hope so," said Liker.

"Could we go to the pool.?" said Likee.

"No, it is to cold out," said Oseph.

"Ok, hope you are better," said Likee.

"It is lunch time so I will or we will talk later," said Liker.

"Ok, I will see the both of you later," said Oseph.

"Here is our lunch," said Likus.

"Is someone going to be a house to measure me.?" said Oseph.

"Yes, he is going to be here in a few minutes," said Likus.

"Good," said Oseph.

"Lunch," said

"Now I have to get some work done later," said Oseph.

"Looks good," said the Doctor.

"I think everything is perfect on this plate," said Likus.

"It is," said Oseph.

"Indeed," said the Doctor.

"Here is the news and here we are the media indicates it was their fault he died," said Likus.

"They are no good and low even the dead was the reason why he is here," said Oseph.

"We will sue, I will let the lawyers know," said Likus.

"Good," said his Father.

"Now we have completed some thing that we did not expect," said Oseph.

"Now there is war," said his Father.

"We can not get this away from the courts we will not settle outside," said Likus.

"It is awful how they interpret events," said the Count.

"It is only the press," said Oseph.

"Lets try to own," said his Father.

"Then it is our business that is why we can sue," said Oseph.

"True. There I called," said Likus.

"Again good idea," said

"Here is sometime for the stress and relief for you Likus," said Oseph.

"Oh My God, you are a God look at the flanks on the shoulders and neck too. It looks as if you are wearing a large collar over coat " said Likus.

"Now you must stay in and again I need to examine them Likus, this part of the meds if you do not want these on your neck and shoulders I can remove them with a drug," said the Count.

"There I filled the cup while you were writing in a log so look at this it is for you Dad," said Likus.

"I will in fact this is the last part of the meds and if you do not mind I would want you to have a few women that I know of. They can be here and at the back door in about a few minutes," said the Doctor.

"I do not mind the size or the extra women," said Oseph.

"Good then I will get them over here right now," said the Doctor.

"So let me have one more try at this new source of entertainment and lets talk right now," said Likus.

"Here they are they are with their wives and the husbands will take control and get this done. Here they are," said the Count.

"We are both cops and I would think you need to go to the police station in the back to get as many as you need," said the Policeman.

"Now here and do not talk to him now and stop wasting my time and his," said the another Cop.

"All having their clothes off and look at the cops stimulating him, he is enjoying this very much," said the Doctor.

"Good so he goes with them and gets what he can," said Likus.

"Here, look at that he is finished with the first," said the Count.

"Here goes the last and final," said Likus.

"Their man that was easy I do not think I need or we need to return," said the Cop.

"There is next year, is that, ok," said the second Cop.

"There might be more and I have friends that are in need of him," said a Wife.

"Yes, we will be outside in the other building waiting for the both of you," said the other Housewife.

"Sure can we get it now that they are out of the room," said the Cop.

"Sure I am ready," said Oseph.

"You sure are what a great surprise this has been," said the second Cop.

"Ummm," said the Cop.

"That reminds me Likus get on the other side and Oseph let me know when to take it," said the Cop.

"Oh, right on schedule," said Likus.

"Here is my, thank you," said the second Cop.

"Say man any time just to help out let me know," said the Cop.

"Ok, stay and let him take these homes and the wives and have her call in," said Oseph.

"Sure have a seat on the bed and Likus on the other side rub the chest and shoulders and look at all of that charisma and say look at all of that, that, why I bet you can talk a full three minutes," said the Policeman.

"Oseph likes it if you talk to him while on his ball," said Likus.

"That is my speciality and here is this other to get him good and angry here how did you like that kiss and now for his therapy while I sing the Lord's prayer," said the Cop.

"Say what is your name.?" said Likus.

"What he is praying Likus come here, there do you want another.?" said Oseph.

"Why sure a kiss is alright. Now another," said Likus.

"Here I am, I am ready," said Oseph.

"Turn on your side so I can get it in the cup. There it all went in and Likus this is what to do right after, there a new cup," said the Cop.

"There is something now I am sure the police man does know this is the control for the medicine any small mole is another way to start the process all over again and the next drugs to do that are to mum the smallest muscles and press it and then the muscles will appear," said the Doctor.

"There must be another way," said Likus.

"Yes, we do have a new way about it taking the medications and only hit the spot where it should be," said the Doctor.

"So we will continue with this one and the good policemen will bring in the necessary ladies," said the Doctor.

"Say lets get him all set and fine now for it is my turn but I need him to be tied," said the Cop.

"That is good say Likes be giving kisses so I can take away his breathe at this end too," said the Cop.

"He will not have an Asthmatic attack," said the Doctor.

"I have stopped those," said Oseph.

"He might.?" said the Cop.

"No, he does not have them.?" said the Doctor.

"What is going on.?" said Likus.

"I think he was one of the first victums.?" said the Doctor.

"You were.?" said Likus.

"We will talk later," said Oseph.

"Now he is here and a cup," said the Cop.

"That was good so you are going to keep we in," said Oseph.

"Say I do recognize you, you did have a hell of a time where you lived. Now I am going to bring in a few girls and let them settle in with a baby," said the Cop.

"Here I do not have to forgive you but I am here for a correct move in my life and the Pope can rest so I am going to do all I can to populate," said Oseph.

"I am sure we can get along and there is a good deal of come to be eaten and abused is not a question say you can save a great deal of money on rubbers and I intend while I am here to make sure you are a ver large and enormous individual for fun," said the cop.

"Good," said Likus.

"Right we will be waiting," said the Doctor.

"Yes, this looks as if you will be here for a long time. Say I do need a shower and then I will get back, Likus share one," said the Cop.

"Sure," said Likus.

"There he went in I am surprised he did," said the Doctor.

"Good now you can get busy just like when I was nine years old. I did recognize you," said Oseph.

"We do not need to tell Likus," said the Doctor.

"No, just get to work," said Oseph.

"Right now," said the Doctor.

"There it is, yes, for the count is accurate and I will be needing a lot more done, do you understand," said Oseph.

"Sure your demands without a though for a consideration of others is the most in your mind right now, but your self control with the police is a discipline you need," said the Doctor.

"I was all right with the guests.?" said Oseph.

"Right they were yours to do what you wanted and the women were, the both of them stacked they were enormous and never got out of the house that is what you wanted," said the Count.

"What I do want to know is I hope that cop has no diseases.? Say I will just go in there and find out" said Oseph.

"Plesase do not start anything I will go first there my clothes are off anyways," said the Doctor.

"Say officer you, you are clean, no diseases.?" said Oseph.

"Say I am going to enjoy working with this guy and I will bring back three tonight all clean. It is amazing she is all yours and nothing happened. Doc can we talk outside.?" said the Cop.

"Sure here we are and they can be left alone," said the Doctor.

"Right, I got seven words out of him and one was mine I am going to love to work here with him but I will not tease the big guy anymore," said the Cop.

"Good do not tease and you can stay What is your name.?" said the Count.

Just Uno and my partner is Dos and we make an appoint each time we are here so I will have three tomorrow night and you know where the police station is right, two doors away. Please do not call if we are there then he gets them," said the Cop.

"Ok good bye. I will walk you to the door," said the Doctor.

"That was wonderful he just took a bath and I saw him, that is all I think he wanted you to come in and you did twice," said Likus.

"It was good, yet there was only six words," said Oseph.

"I ask him if he was ok and healthy but he could not stay and he said," That I have you anyways, maybe some other time." Darling you have not said to much since I have known you," said Likus.

"You are right," said Oseph.

"I know so when tonight is happening you do not have the say a word not one word and let him do the talking and working," said Likus.

"He does not want me to talk," said Oseph.

"No and the girls do not, they all want to leave and are home all day long and they want their pickle ice cream," said Likus.

"So it is like being at the store for them," said Oseph.

"No, and not when they all see this and look at your shoulders you are enormous and I love it every bit of it and I like holding your shoulders and putting my arms round you," said Likus.

"That I like. Here we have a few hours lets see if I can go downstairs and use some control," said Oseph.

"There they are," said Liker.

"Here we are," said Oseph.

"No sooner down the stairs and we are praised," said Likus.

"We are," said the Count.

"I do hope Likus you know what you are doing about a desaint of Oseph as a future father of many and what about the other men in this house and what do I do," said his Mother.

"We will take out insurance for all of us especially for those who think it is easy to rob me," said Likus.

"Thank you, I forgot about that, London and its insurances are the best in the world," said this Mother.

"So I think we need an office in Belgium, one in Paris and in London. We can rent space with the others, where they are," said Likus.

"Good I will call your step brother in Belgium," said his Mother.

"Detva is fine," said Likus.

"Likus or Detva it is better to have Detva, he did not mind leaving Chambord and Likus did not want to run Venice so I do not think he would want this job right now. Especially after running the business with Detva and helping their Mother after my Ed died," said the Countess.

"Alright I will ask Detva he might be still at Chambord living there until we arrive at some point in our near future so I will call him right now and leave a message," said Likus.

"I hope we get a good place for the work the last one was not so good," said his Mother.

"There, it is done," said Likus.

"Wondering or not if I think my new husband was gay, at my age you marry for love of that person and not his faults," said the Countess.

"No, I did think only about the desainting of Oseph and this route was the better instead of interfering with the business, especially it, the tunnels is his business so nothing should go wrong," said Likus.

"I know so we must expect a scandle about my husband so if he loves to have Oseph I do not think you will loose him," said his Mother.

"I know I will not and I am so sorry about a scandle we need to investigate all of the policemen and women who are here and look for anything in the press," said Likus.

"We will look for anything mentioned and sue right away after all this is very private and the people should remember they can sue too," said the Countess.

"Good so I think it will be given to the press by the policemen who are on duty and do not like the fact their overtime is not from us," said Likus.

"Lets go have some coffee with the others and I will let the Count know what the plans are," said the Countess.

"Good idea," said Likus.

"Also with the media and make sure he does not encourage any kind of press release," said the Countess.

"Good so we have a plan at last and I have an answer," said Likus.

"The answer is, we have locations in all three countries and Detva was just about to set them up, so most of the orders will be filled out and we will get the copies too," said Likus.

"All is alright with the family.? " said his Mother.

"Yes, they are all in good health. We are going to have offices in Paris, Rome, London, and in Belgium with theirs," said Likus.

"Rome too," said his Mother.

"Yes, I just remembered," said Likus.

"That does sound perfect, just what we need," said Oseph.

Chapter 15

"So we are still in charge according to Paul so why not start the ball rolling and see what the press has created and lied about," said Likus.

"I just looked at the computer yet my good husband is looking at the computer right now," said his Mother.

"Dear, I have something right here as we speak," said the Count.

"This is not nice and I want to know if it was on the news too.? Look at this Likus," said the Countess.

"Look, Oseph, maybe you should go to work for a few days. No just stay at home and give a call right now," said Likus.

"I will, give me a phone ok," said Oseph.

"Here use mine," said Likus

"I hope all is fine at work.?" said the Countess.

"Ok, then you can here this right now, I need to go next door and few of the guys are going to meet me with their wives right now. They are all getting off from work and are going to be here right now," said Oseph.

"We need to move right now do not open the door, let Frames do it and do not let the children hear," said the Count.

"We will be back soon," said Likus.

"Alright be careful and if you have the number of those policemen I think you should call them now, it will be good for their overtime," said the Countess.

"I have their number and I will call right now," said Likus.

"I hope they say, "Yes," said the Countess.

"Here we are ready to leave this floor Mother and the police agreed too," said Likus.

"Good lets go right now," said the Count.

"Good luck Dad, I would like to join in when I am older," said Likus.

"Me too," said Likee.

"Boys go into the other room, please," said their Grandmother.

"Now I am going to close the door, and I will ask just what you are talking about," said their Grandmother.

"It was on television, I do not mind because I do not want the Pope with us," said Likee.

"No, I do not either he will make a saint out of all of us if we do not watch out for what is going on," said Liker.

"What.?" said their Grandmother.

"The kids said," Their own Father and Mother are having affairs, so they will not be picked," said Likee.

"We need to do something for ourselves too.?" said Likee.

"We are insured and to be a lawyer and embezzle, we do not mind only keep the money in the home," said their Grandmother.

"I did want to be picked like Dad," said Liker.

"There is other ways too," said Grandmother.

"At lease can you with Paul get us you and Grand Dad and Oseph and Likus be King Likus and King Oseph and you and Granddad be King and Queen and many more Kings and Queens of Venice and start getting the second book done besides the first book of many Kings of France," said Liker.

"Good I will have a statement that King Oseph and King Likus will rule a different providence and then myself as Queen and my husband as King and then you two are King Likus and King Likus at two other different providences, How is that.?" said Grandmother.

"That is wonderful can we at least give some titles at our school.?" said Likus.

"Anyone can apply they need to fill out an application I will put it on the computer right now see. Name address and their own title they need," said Grandmother.

"That is perfect and thank you," said Liker.

"Here is the answer from your Grandfather." Hoping that the boys will like their new territory that is theirs to watch," said Grandmother.

"Oh, thank you Grandmother, I will like owning the square some day," said Likee.

"I hope the square is not one of us, like me. We are using the first ten square blocks that are with us now," said Grandmother.

"I know just keep it in mind," said Likee.

"You will, you will pursue that when you are older," said Grandmother.

"Here is statement from Grandfather it is the first twenty five blocks we are in and there are seven of us," said Grandmother.

"Good and now we are, Kings Liker," said Likee.

"There is so happening here I never think of home," said Liker.

"That is the idea and now you are apart of us and no one can take you away," said Grandmother.

"You need now is to look outside every time you go out because now you are a money maker and you are valuable to all," said Likee.

"Yes, Likee is right you must watch out all of the time. This will keep you interested and it is the final autos chosen to use in the tunnels see," said Grandmother.

"The design are new and the autos are very strong looking and could be very practical in an accident," said Liker.

"They always stay in the tunnels that is why it looks like a few wheels on the side of it. It keeps the driver in one line as one tunnel both sides on working for them," said Grandmother.

"Grandmother here is Frames," said Likee.

"Thank you, Frames, here Likee and Liker these are new phones and are program to go off at the police station and will ring our phone if you leave it somewhere so it can call when you set it down and it does not notice you moving," said Grandmother.

"Thank you, Grandmother," said Likee.

"Yes, thank you," said Liker.

"Your welcome the both of you," said Grandmother.

"Lets have some refreshments and food," said Grandmother.

"Sure that is good," said Likee.

"Yes it is," said Liker.

"We need to have more fun," said Likee.

"If the both of you can wait all of us will be having our first vacation in Chambord," said Grandmother.

"Good, finally in France," said Likee.

"Yes but I do not know if your Father, Oseph is going to be with us all of the time.?" said their Grandmother.

"He might be there on weekends at first.?" said Likee.

"At the beginning he might be there for a few months," said Grandmother.

"Probably he might visit Venice for a few weekends.?" said Liker.

"Do not get your hopes up the government might ask him to go to Venice and stay there due to his project and work. Also so they, the French are not to be blamed if the work is behind," said Grandmother.

"We would not have to leave, he does right," said Liker.

"Right, he would have to leave by himself," said Grandmother.

"What about Likus.?" said Likee.

"They would both leave and Likus would return in a few days," said Grandmother.

"I know," said Likee.

"The three of us will stay here right," said Grandmother.

"Are you sure.?" said Liker.

"No, Likus just might stay here and enjoy his home," said Grandmother.

"That is true," said Likee.

"Very true," said Liker.

"The both of you have to remember if Likus stays here then Oseph can work without us around," said Grandmother.

"We are in the way, he needs to work so if we are at the Chateau we will be helping," said Likee.

"Right you are, Likee," said Liker.

"Both of you are right we need to have this project to go smoothly so far it is," said Grandmother.

"I am for a good summer at the Chateau," said Likee.

"Me too," said Liker.

"We all need a rest," said Grandmother.

"All there is, is work," said Liker.

"I know," said Likee.

"That is what gave us our money it was all connected to the tunnels other than that Likus and myself were on a budget. The chateau was purchased were the money that was given with connections to the Venice tunnels," said their Grandmother.

"So we had the Chateau anyways due to the tunnels and Oseph was there anyways to help with the engineering," said Liker.

"He, Oseph really knows what he is doing with these tunnels," said Likee.

"He does and he is responsible for the largest checks to come in because I do not think we would have that money if the tunnels were neglected," said their Grandmother.

"Here they are and Grandfather we were just talking about Dad and how he is responsible for all of our success and yes we love Dad," said Likee.

"Yes, I do too," said Liker.

"Thank you, boys," said Oseph.

"Yes, I love him too and we would not be here all together, I was all ready to call my Mom and have her sell her house and live with me," said Likus.

"You watched all of this happen," said Liker.

"It took only three weeks to have success and a great deal of more money than we could ever dream of," said the Countess.

"Yes, and now for me to have a Countess by my side," said the Count.

"We are all apart of this fortune it could not be any more better and even your little brother is a millionarie," said Likus.

"He is asleep," said Grandmother.

"He is the only wise one all of us are always doing something and not resting," said Liker.

"We need to relax more, Liker is right we need to get into the Chateau this summer and have a good time," said Grandmother.

"We can leave right after school is let out," said Oseph.

"We will," said Likus.

"We are going," said Likee.

"You do not believe me.?" said Liker.

"We do now," said Grandmother.

"I do now," said Likee.

"Not so loud the baby will wake up," said Grandmother.

"I am going to bring him downstairs and to stay right in the next room," said Likus.

"We do have to be quiet now that Ose is in the next room," said Liker.

"I must start right," said Likee.

"Me too," said Liker.

"He is asleep in the dining room," said Likus.

"Now that the baby is still sleeping why not get our plates of food and stay here in the living room for dinner," said the Grandmother.

"Great idea," said Oseph.

"I will get the boys plates ready and Mother listen if Ose if he is awake then please will bring him into this room," said Likus.

"No, you watch for the baby and I will get their plates, come on boys here is the food," said their Grandmother.

"On the computer, I am looking at Duke Paul who lives in the Palace of Versailles he placed the troopers back into the Versailles and the Hermitage after living there for one year," said Liker.

"I know that is so amazing, and very good Liker, you may read more after you have your dinner," said their Grandmother.

"I knew that, but we can not do that there," said Likee.

"We can ask him if he did any thing about the troopers in the Chateau," said Liker.

"I will put it in my phone," said Oseph.

"That would be nice to see this summer," said their Grandfather.

"There is an answer, he suggests that due to the building having its own money at one time to place the guards who want a different environment and use the Pope's quards," said Oseph.

"He is going to work on this before we are all there this summer right," said their Grandfather.

"I am sure he will.?" said Oseph.

"This is exciting I can hardly wait to see them," said Grandmother.

"I know I want to be a quard this summer too," said Likee.

"I will but I want to be a lawyer," said Liker.

"Me too and a guard just one time is ok but not for a lifetime, we both are needed else where," said Likee.

"That is just fine one summer for me and that is that," said Liker.

"The both of you might have a uniform to use but you will do this as a quard just once a week and not in front of the tourists or the building," said Oseph.

"Your Father is right we can not start this, it can be considered interfering with their job," said Likus.

"We need to use another strategy we will ask to do this once and then mentioned we do not want to interfere," said Liker.

"Very good and sensible," said their Grandmother.

"Yes, it is," said Likus.

"Good choice," said Oseph.

"So do both of you want to be a lawyers.?" said Likus.

"Yes," said Likee.

"Yes," said Liker.

"Good we need someone to represent us and watch over our and your own fortunes," said Likus.

"Remember children you both or just one of you will not be in charge and have contol over the money," said their Grandmother.

"That is right even about your own money we need it to buy stocks but you will have enough to live on to make your wife comfortable and not hate you or all of us," said Likus.

"This is very true and my own money from the company buys stocks," said their Grandmother.

"Now here is a meeting in progress and from now on Grandfather is included in on a one seventh of his share as of now," said Likus.

"Thank you Likus and Oseph and especially you my wife and Likee and Likus too," said their Grandfather.

"Your welcome," said Likus.

"Your welcome," said Oseph.

"Your welcome," said Likee.

"Your welcome," said Liker.

"This is wonderful now there is a full equality and Likus will still be our President of the company," said the Countess.

"Here is news the lawyers have settled out of court with a much bigger amount," said Likus.

"How could that be, a bigger amount," said his Mother.

"The larger the some now a days hinding the unnecessary information to the press gets a larger amount," said Likus.

"This works most of the time," said his Mother.

"Now it does," said Likus.

"What a good idea," said his Father.

"Here is another good idea at the Chateau we need to have a small cars," said Likee.

"What about the cars and a small trucks too," said Liker.

"There should be something to drive on the property," said Oseph.

"We can order if there is nothing there," said Likus.

"I hope so and I do want to go camping too," said Liker.

"We will there are empty of camping ground near by," said Oseph.

"That is right there is a woods near by," said Likee.

"Do you want to go riding bikes we need two," said Liker.

"I need to ride our bikes I do not know how," said Likee.

"Then we will all buy one for ourselves," said Oseph.

"We can use a bike built for two dear," said the Count.

"That does sound great could we do this Oseph, please," said Likus.

"Sure but you and I will still buy our own," said Oseph.

"Ok," said Likus.

"We do not have a web site about this family.?" said Liker.

"I will get right on it the secretary is still here I will go and talk to her right now," said their Grandmother.

"Give her a call and stay here," said Likus.

"Alright I will stay at the other end of the room," said Grandmother.

"Mother and you Liker are really keeping up with helping the family and letting us know about improvements very good I am proud of you," said Likus.

"Thank you does this mean it is part of my contributions and I can get an award too," said Liker.

"I am glad you ask so the electric cars are being shipped soon and should be here in one day," said Likus.

"Good I am so glad Likee did you know that if you give good advice about the business there could be an award too," said Likee.

"Why not think of other things.?" said Liker.

"What about a grand prize as a boat to take us to school, or even right now with a driver," said Likee.

"We were both wondering if we can have a boat with a driver to take us to school.? " said Liker.

"It is a good idea wait until your Grandmother is off the phone and let her call," said Oseph.

"I agree it is a good idea for security purposes and the both of you are to return home right after your school is dismissed," said Likus.

"I guess there is another phone call for me too make," said Grandmother.

"Yes, we need a new boat to bring the boys to school," said Likus.

"I just had a call the other day from a boat owner who was selling his small and large yacht and I was going to mention that to you," said Grandmother.

"We will take them both but first get a picture of it," said Oseph.

"Something better than that, on the porch from the third floor we can see the yacht it is a nice boat he is waiting for your answer," said Grandmother.

"I will go look do you want to go with me boys," said Oseph.

"Sure Dad," said Likee.

"Thanks Dad we need something like this," said Liker.

"This will keep us busy for this weekend I am sure of it," said Likus.

"It will be of some use when we have it brought to the Chateau," said Grandmother.

"I think I will go see this yacht too. said Grandfather.

"Good, give your opinion and I am sure you will agree with me, we need this," said Likus.

"I will be on your side," said his Stepfather.

"Good," said Likus.

"Yes you will and be reassuring," said the Grandmother.

"I will, I will," said Grandfather.

"I know it is for you too," said Likus.

"Right," said Grandfather.

"I want to have a good time on that yacht too," said the Grandmother.

"We will hear from him soon.?" said Grandfather.

"Yes, very soon," said Grandmother.

"That is good, where is Oseph.?" said Grandfather.

"He went upstairs," said Grandmother.

"I will go see him," said Grandfather.

"Where is Grandfather going," said Likus.

"Upstairs you should go with them for a little while at least," said Grandmother.

"I will the nannies will help with the children. I will return soon" said Likus.

"It is important. "said Likus.

"Yes, it is, I went to this room a few minutes ago and he was right there," said Grandfather.

"He is busy," said Likus.

"I can not believe he is going to have a very stacked girl with him and she is all alone," said Likus.

"Doc what about the nuts.?" said Oseph.

"Likus give me a hand take the one on the right," said his Father.

"He is surely agreeing with my movements," said Likus.

"Keep it going," said his Stepfather.

"Is there anyone else that you know of that will be here today.?" said Likus.

"There are two girls that will be here in a few minutes but I am not going to stay," said the Girl.

"Ok, so we have another appointment that is good to know," said Likus.

"Thanks for the baby," said the Girl.

"Anytime see you next year," said Oseph.

"Here are the other two," said Likus.

"Good. Who recommended you," said the Count.

"The girl you just saw," said the first Girl.

"Yes," said the second Girl.

"There is plenty for anyone," said Oseph.

"We do not need take home," said the second Girl.

"No," said first Girl.

"Now for this next girl, and we are then finished I guess," said Oseph.

"This is nice but why are you doing it for free, or just why.?" said the second Girl."

"To desaint him," said the Count.

"Then you need to purchase a building next to your work place and let the press do the rest," said the second Girl.

"Right and if there is anything else please, do have me now if anyone is hungry," said Oseph.

"That does sound good maybe just a little to say thanks," said the second Girl.

"Good, and I know it does get better, but we need to leave now," said the first Girl.

"Ok, maybe next year," said Oseph.

"Could be," said both Girls.

"There that seems to be the only ones," said the Likus.

"That was very fast and you still got great enjoyment," said the Count.

"Likus how about a great time of it for a little while," said Oseph.

"I hope this means me too.?" said the Count.

"Sure this is what the desainting is anyways," said Oseph.

"Ok, there is a call," said the Count.

"Mom," said Likus.

"Yes, I will see you later and their will be private dinners for you both in the dining room in about an hour and a half," said the Count.

"Thank you and please let them know ok," said Likus.

"I will send a message anyways right now, Good bye," said the Count.

"Thank you, Dad. Here we are at last alone and I need to help myself," said Likus.

"Then lets go have a shower together," said Oseph.

"Here is the tel, lets see what the news is and here, let me wash your back," said Likus.

"Oh, this is not good, you are," Ofist is not the Gem who is now getting his hand full finally," said Likus.

"Praying on single women, is not the case here, or is it," said Oseph.

"The media is getting smarter and not very nice," said Likus.

"Here is more news," He is not a saint after all," said Oseph.

"Is it just one channel.? That is so good and I will do your back one more time," said Likus.

"Now all of them are saying De Sainthood," said Oseph.

"Here is the source, and is he going to say we were in the shower together.?" said Likus.

"He did not say anything about you," said Oseph.

"Here it is see the other did say you two were in the shower. I am so sorry I put you in this position can this kiss make up for it," said Oseph.

"Sure but we better get out since we are finished and you need to make things better or it was not me who called you a new name," said Likus.

"You mean Ofheall," said Oseph.

"I hope they do not but it could get worse for all of us," said Likus.

"They will make sure we are not together," said Oseph.

"This can not happen we are both good subject for this because no one else wants this type of publicity," said Likus.

"You are right we need them to say everything," said Oseph.

"We just let them say and do what they want until it is beyond the truth or very hurtful for the entire family," said Likus.

"Ok, we will do that. Are we finished here, lets go see the family and let a few know what is going on," said Oseph.

"Yes I had fun did you,?" said Likus.

"Of course remember I love you and always have," said Oseph.

"Thank you and I love you I could not get this far with the business and you have helped me. You have done it all for me and no one else has," said Likus.

"Thank you, now here we are and we are with the entire family," said Oseph.

"Yes we are all together," said Likus.

"Would you like a drink.?" said Oseph.

"No, I think I will just to have some coffee," said Likus.

"I do think the next time someone is here you should give them am appointment," said Likus.

"I do not think it could work that way," said Oseph.

"Right, especially when someone just might find someone and is interested and they need to be careful too and so do you," said Likus.

"I know now here is your Mother and she wants to talk to us so we can discuss this tonight, ok," said Oseph.

"Sure, hello Mother," said Likus.

"Good evening boys," said the Countess.

"Hello, Mother," said Oseph.

"Hello, Oseph I need to apoligize to you both but I think there is quite a large fortune, if you two want to see the tel right now we can talk later," said the Countess.

"No, we can see the tel right from here and this is something the boys will need to know eventually," said Oseph.

"Here it is," said the Countess.

"Today sunshine and tomorrow a new Dad, it appears from the heavens as the talk is that Oseph is somewhat of a new father for the community and is giving out babies from his heart or rather his hardness since Likus does not have the final say on the or who reigns in any building," said the reporter.

"How do you sue.?" said the Countess.

"We use Lloyd's that is why we pay them," said Oseph.

"Then we wait until we are brutally hurt by words on the tel, and it is going to be soon too," said the Countess.

"What is wrong," said Liker.

"Yes, what?" said Likee.

"Your Father is being desainted by me before he is ever considered to being a saint," said the Count.

"He is going to help with the construction that is in progress for the Atlantic new tunnels, brand new and it is going to be enough to have two large cites in the middle of the Atlantic ocean," said the Countess.

"Your father is a very good man yet we need to make him look like a bad person or someone who is good yet not to friendly to many," said Likus.

"So he is doing a man thing," said Liker.

"Yes, he is," said Likee.

"I need to two men to be my very good little boys who I love and to be on my side,Ok," said Oseph.

"We need you too," said Liker.

"We need and Love you Dad," said Likee.

"Yes we do love, I love you and we would have a home tudor and to be right with you and help with the business, ok," said Liker.

"You are leaving school and you will help with the business and look kids here we are right now and baby is upstairs and see here we are the two of us," said Likus.

"Great and we will have a tudor," said Likee.

"This is great," said Liker.

"If I were the teacher I would you write, type on the computer why you think that a tudor is great," said Likus.

"Oh," said Likee.

"Also if you say that a tudor is great and compared to a new car is bigger then I think we still have a lot of work to do," said Likus.

"I know he or she is fantastic, wonderful, amazing and very accomplished," said Likus.

"Right now we will start every day excellent manners and if there is a problem one or both of you may end up in a high school again," said Oseph.

"I will teach you until we get a tudor so your behavior will be your defense and it can work your way," said Likus.

"I will help you too alright Likus," said his Mother.

"Just think someone asked where you went to school then I could say my tudor taught me. If they wanted to know her name we can say a,"Countess and Prince in Venice," said Likee.

"That does seem to be in our favor yet we need to work on the names we need a new tudors who can give us everything," said Liker.

"Just got finished with telling you both about to do now be sure if you two want to continue this you both can stay in your rooms," said Oseph.

"I apologize," said Liker.

"I apologize too," said Likee.

"Alright so lets watch the tel and have a good evening," said Grandmother.

"Sure it is a time to be happy we can stay here and invest in our future with our own company," said Likee.

"We can after all we do not need a future anywhere else," said Liker.

"You are correct and we can make a lot of money and be on our own some day," said Liker.

"Yes the both of you can work for the company and make good money and still live in your own castle," said their Grandmother.

"That does sound good and perfect," said Liker.

"It does," said Likee.

"I am glad the both of you approve," said Oseph.

"They do and I think we are on to a good start," said Likus.

"We have decided that the two of you will grow up fast and this summer the you both will be at the chateau for a vacation then when you are being taught by the new teacher you will be on the payroll with the business if you want to," said Oseph.

"Will we be on location if we want too.?" said Likee.

"A few times it is not mandatory," said Oseph.

"Then we are in the office.?" said Liker.

"Until you both get tired and want to see the field or if something is about to happen that is important," said Likus.

"You both will see us too," said their Grandmother.

"Yes, we all can work it out," said their Grandfather.

"We need to work next door and let the office people be there too," said Likus.

"The building next door on our right-hand side facing the front door is the better work place there is more space available and I also think our purchase went was accepted. I will give them a call right now," said the Grandmother.

"Good, thank you," said Likus.

"We need you two, there is a good possibility that the both of you will work out," said Likus.

"Sure they will how about full-time after the summer, we will put you in a suit and tie and you both can take my place during the day and grow right into my job," said Oseph.

"This would give your father time to look at the films and cameras of the men who are working under water. He does this on the computer already and both of you can do this too," said Likus.

"We look at the camera for troubled spots and we will let you know. I like that very much," said Likee.

Chapter 16

"There are empty cameras under the water," said Liker.

"Sure but there are other responsibilities," said Oseph.

"Making sure everyone has his hours in," said Likus.

"I have the decisions on all the building where was too much water at the city buildings so they moved and a rep will be here tonight for you too sign," said their Grandmother.

"Thank you Mother, then it is a deal boys.?" said Likus.

"Yes," said Likee.

"Fine with me," said Liker.

"Now the two of you will not miss things that happen in school," said Likus.

"Going public, we both discussed before and besides football or baseball is truely on the sport of Venice," said Likee.

"We did not miss any practice because there is none," said Liker.

"Ok, it is a deal and you may witness your own building tonight being approved," said Oseph.

"That will be interesting," said Likus.

"Coffee or smoking Not until you are older," said their Grandmother.

"No drinking until you are both of age," said Grandfather.

"I do not think I will be drinking to many of ouir friends have no parents because of alcohol," said Likee.

"Just last week a parent died from drinking," said Likee.

"That is right and there was no one to take them home, the two boys in the dorm that we both could have had," said Liker.

"Are the others cared for that still have a parent," said Oseph.

"Yes, they have one parent left," said Liker.

"Then I will call the school and make sure they are living there even for the summer too, until they graduate," said Likus.

"They could be with us this summer mention that to the Dean," said Oseph.

"Hello Dean, the boys that just lost there parents can we pay for their tution and for the summer they may be with us if they want. Ok then, thank you," said Likus.

"What happened.?" said Oseph.

"If make it official as guardians the school will bill us and they may just visit this evening or stay the weekend," said Likus.

"Good we like them," said Likee.

"Yes, they are both funny guys," said Liker.

"We need to make it very warm and inviting for them to stay permanently," said Likus.

"We will it is fine with us," said Liker.

"Fine with me too," said Likee.

"It is permanent they stay over and never return unless they wish to stay at the school," said their Grandmother.

"As soon as the Dean heard we were going to have a tudor permanently after the summer. There is now a teacher on his way and will live here," said Likus.

"We have school until the summer right," said Likee.

"Yes the four of you do," said Likus.

"There then we need to keep quiet when I am at the other house just say I am in my bedroom resting," said Oseph.

"Yes we need to keep that quiet the teacher should not be involved only the Count should know," said their Grandmother.

"Right again, Mother," said Likus.

"Discretion is key, if anyone ask no one knows anything," said their Grandmother.

"Right," said Likee.

"I will obey," said Liker.

"I just have one question," said Liker.

"Yes, and what is that.?" said Oseph.

"When can I have a very stacked woman," said Liker.

"I could use one my self," said Likee.

"You both like women that are emorous," said Oseph.

"I could handle them both when you are with someone and I can see if either one of them really want her, one each," said their Grandfather.

"Then I will watch and see if they have her again," said Oseph.

"For this they can not go back to their school," said Likus.

"No these young boys need a lot of enjoyment of life living here with us and this should be first before any introduction of having women," said their Grandmother.

"Right," said Oseph.

"We will follow this plan," said Likus.

"It should be or I will be the next Italy's state bird the canary and I might even have to work for less money that could even be a plan I am glad they are working three shifts," said Oseph.

"The Holly lands have finshed the tunnels and we are certainly adding more to the Atlantic than the original plans so why not start the second groups of tunnels in Africa," said Likus.

"Good idea," said the Count.

"Do we stay in the Chateau.?" said the Countess.

"Yes and I do," said Oseph.

"I do not mean to be selfish but does Paris to Moscow need a new group of tunnels too,?" said Likus.

"I will be selfish and say by the time I finish with Venice those tunnels could use the help so I will do both," said Oseph.

"Thank you so we can visit you in Moscow and then in Africa," said Likus.

"Yes, and the tunnels in Africa this time as before will be near each other yet from Morocco to straight down to the shore," said Oseph.

"Good I will go there," said Liker.

"On the top of Africa to the bottom," said Oseph.

"That is for me," said Likee.

"Then the equal proportion as the other side and then there are new resorts and residencies only," said Oseph.

"Good," said Likus.

"That sounds like all of us," said Grandmother.

"Indeed now lets have some refreshments we all worked hard at this meeting," said Grandfather.

"It is not over I need to know if we are to invite your own dates over who do not mind companionships," said Liker.

"We should have given you permission to apply for a new title such as: Prince Roguetel, it will be done now because the other Houses have done it during their own administration while on the tel," said Oseph.

"We all will keep the same names except Likus is the Prince yet still Prince Likus and what your father is saying if the girls have their own way at home then we will let you know if she is good for the house," said Likus.

"When do we get new names," said Grandmother.

"In one month the boys and Oseph will put the first or Letter capitol I after their own names and Mother and I will put Ets Marie," said Likus.

"After I place the roman numerals I then will add Ets Marie due to the House is the Palace of Versailles as the founder of this world wide project," said Oseph.

"Yes, and Grandfather and the grandchildren should wait the children at twentyone and grandfather when you are seventy and not before," said Likus.

"Now everyone will know that I have worked the hardest," said the Count.

"Oh, Granddad now stop that," said Liker.

"Maybe by then I hope it will be four boys or five in this house," said Likus.

"Good idea," said Likee.

"I need to have a baby," said the Countess.

"You better not," said Likus.

"Now that the boys are watching tel when the others arrive our two children still might still go to the classroom," said their Grandmother.

"They know already about a tudor being hired," said Likus.

"We are in agreement that they should go to school are we all in favor of this.?" said their Grandmother.

"Alright," said their Grandfather.

"Sure," said Likus.

"Sure thing," said Oseph.

"Of course it is a sure thing you still get all of the women," said Likus.

"Now do not start or we need to get upstairs," said Oseph.

"Now.?" said Likus.

"No, I can wait," said Oseph.

"Oh, you two are back and now we can start having some food or later in the evening and as soon as the boys arrive," said Likus.

"There is the door," said their Grandmother.

"Boys I am Likus these two are your Grandparents, Oseph your father and of course you both know Liker and Likee," said Likus.

"Yes good evening my name is Prince Raytoll and Prince Grolate," said Prince Raytoll.

"Lets all sit down for some to eat in the dining room. Please be seated, did your Dean tell you about your new teacher you may have a tudor here if you want too," said Likus.

"I will speak for my brother who is very sensitive and he does miss our parents, but we need to be with people that love us and I think being home having an opportunity to see our new parents immediately is important right now," said Raytoll.

"We do understand so here we are," said their Grandmother.

"Good, then you are all taught at home," said Likus.

"Thank you from all of us," said Likee.

"We are all going to enjoy this summer at the Chateau too," said Likus.

"I can not wait," said Liker.

"The Chateau, the Dean told us this before we left," said Grolate.

"Then we have a future in front of us," said Oseph.

"We do have a good opportunity to work and all of us to make a great deal of money," said their Grandfather.

"We will we already of and boys the both of you are apart of the business so please give your opinion and input and we will discuss everything," said their Grandmother.

"If you have any ideas right them down and we have a talking session about the business each evening," said their Grandmother.

"Yes, we do and we are pleased to let you both become a partner in this business," said Likus.

"Thank you all of you for the offer and I will make sure my brother all of my brothers will be honored to serve you," said Raytoll.

"Thank you, that is the attitude we need here," said Likus.

"Right we will ge things done," said likus.

"Also I do not mind it, it I can participate in a group of the ones that were written up in the news. I do enjoy a good time of it and if the I have to watch I do not mind it at all," said Raytoll.

"I want too," said Likee.

"Me too," said Liker.

"I could give it a try," said Grolate.

"Then they have voted so your Grandmother and I will be in the living room while all of you are next door," said Likus.

"If you wish to have food it will all be on the third floor porch," said their Grandmother.

"That is excellent if you boys bring anyone over then you do loose out some way I am not sure of any of the penalties," said Likus.

"I am sure glad we got the real estate agency appointment over with and he will not be back, he will mail anything for us to see," said their Grandmother.

"Yes, I think this has gone far enough, not that I do not want you with me but remember it is a long time before you get to the university," said Grandfather.

"That is why we are here with a tudor and a business, if I want at wife I will make sure I get one even if it takes money to keep her at home," said Liker.

"You know what you want that is very good," said Grandfather.

"Yes, and I like privacy so I do need to stay here with a tudor that is why I left home in Newport," said Liker.

"He is right I do like privacy or more than that like getting the sun and cool air from the third porch and going to school is a lot of energy that I do not have," said Likee.

"I need the sex before I go after a girl my age," said Raytoll.

"I could use some and soon," said Grolate."

"I do not think I need to hear anymore, Likus I do want you to continue with this conversation with the boys right now. Remember please Likus I do need them desainted," said their Grandmother.

"Yes, Mom I will make sure we have an agreement tonight to go ahead and for them to start very soon," said Likus.

"Ahead it is, and they can start tonight when the boys will have anything they want and for them to remember they do not see their conquest, if nothing happens then you get it again," said Oseph.

"So Grandmother is for this.?" said Raytoll.

"Yes, it was my idea because Oseph is very popular for his good deed," said their Grandfather.

"Yes, and tonight I will have three and you three will have one each and Grandfather will make sure they all leave," said Oseph.

"Thanks and by the way can we have her for over night.?" said Prince Grolate.

"It is a goal and a business," said Likus.

"I know," said the Prince.

"Now we need to go to sleep and I help you will be pleased tomorrow, say good night," said Likus.

"Good night," said Likee and Liker.

"Night," said Raytoll and Grolate.

"Night," said Grandmother and GrandDad.

"Night," said Oseph.

"We need to talk, they need at least a new tudor but not the having a good time and a possible marriage that might end," said Grandmother.

"I agree and as soon as the other ladies see me they will be more than pleased to wait, or in my case they will participate and that is when the boys are going to be discouraged," said Oseph.

"I hope so, you know what you are doing," said Grandmother.

"I do not I know what your husband is telling me to do," said Oseph.

"But my husband is older and wiser," said Grandmother.

"I still do not know if I am approved for this next deal in the Atlantic," said Oseph.

"You will get it you might need a lot of references or the skill of your own work to proof enough," said Grandmother.

"I hope so," said Oseph.

"There the four of them are asleep," said Likus.

"We were discussing the sex part of life with the boys yet they could use a tudor," said Grandmother.

"Tudor of course but I do hope they will not in any way interrupt Oseph," said Likus.

"I am sure these girls will let them down gracefully," said Grandfather.

"I hope so," said Grandmother.

"I know they will, they will want Oseph," said Likus.

"Of course," said Grandfather.

"Then it is settled I will be naked and when those boys go downstairs the two of you will watch them so they will not be upset," said Oseph.

"Do you think being naked will work," said Grandmother.

"Yes we all get naked in one room and enter the other," said Oseph.

"It will work and most likely the boys will be to upset to do anything," said Likus.

"Tomorrow it is," said Grandfather.

"The phone, wait I have a plan, ok in a few minutes. We need to go upstairs the six girls are arriving in a few minutes," said Oseph.

"Now," said Likus.

"When I call you I want you both to try and get the boys up and ask them if they want to have a girl," said Oseph.

"Ok," said Likus

"We are here in the other house I will be with the girls soon so and in ten minutes try to wait the boys up just our two," said Oseph.

"If they show up as you requested.?" said Likus.

"Just do not wait up the others, or if they are awake then ask them. Thank you Grandmother," said Oseph.

"Now if I am correct they will both refused and say they are to tired," said Likus.

"Right and I am leaving and I will be back soon please wait for Grandmother," said Oseph.

"I will, so I will hear from you later so we might be in the living room," said Likus.

"I do not want to go but I need the sex since this medication has given me a boost," said Oseph.

"For you to be hung about a foot and a half and more when you walk around in the bedroom I can see why the meds give you another, foot," said Likus.

"I know and I enjoy it so I am leaving and we will be back soon," said Oseph.

"I ask them and they are both asleep," said Grandmother.

"Good I will return," said Grandfather.

"Good thanks I am glad they did not wake up," said Oseph.

"Me too. We will wait in this living room," said Likus.

"Ok, see you both in a little while," said Grandfather.

"Yes, we will," said Oseph.

"They are gone lets have some coffee," said Grandmother.

"Oseph, mentioned that the did not want to leave me, "But it was the medications," said Likus.

"That was nice of him that he had feelings," said Grandmother.

"Are you upset about this," said Likus.

"No, he is the one doing all the work he needs to desaint myself for being that good," said Grandmother.

"What about me.?" said Likus.

"You are not in that position you are not helping the world he is and for you too so do not ever say anything negative about this," said Grandmother.

"No, I have not," said Likus.

"Good, we also will gain a lot of money which is his," said Grandmother.

"I would call Grandfather to make sure the men or women do not attack him but they want the money for the child," said Likus.

"Everyone gets something. So call your father to make sure he is not attacked and to find out if they are keeping the baby and to make an offer.?" said Grandmother.

"I will, I will give him a message and to make sure he gives us an answer on the phone," said Likus.

"Good, I hope he gets an answer soon because we can adopt just like the others," said Grandmother.

"Mother what others," said Likus.

"Paul and his wife and Ed and his family because he did adopt those children after she had a few of her own," said the Countess.

"That is right and we should be doing the same so now we are," said Likus.

"We are, and we are going to get every one of those children," said the Countess.

"I will have Oseph offer all of these women money," said Likus.

"Give them a check after the birth, they want to be paid," said the Countess.

"I will," said Likus.

"I left a message to all of the other women if we can be considered first to purchase their child. " said Likus.

"Good they will call us first," said Grandmother.

"I hope so," said Likus.

"They will," said Grandmother.

"I think they will at one hundred and fifty thousand," said Likus.

"Yes that is a good fee and if they want more there is an agreement with you and the bank," said the Countess.

"All that is fair enough," said Likus.

"Yes, more than fair and I hope we do not get into any severe problems," said the Countess.

"There will not be," said Likus.

"If anything happens to our own fortune, or to you and Oseph, he will need to leave France and you will see him only when he can see you," said the Countess.

"Then the papers will be calling him Ophiss again," said Likus.

"I think we better tell this plan to Oseph so he can be given some money and he needs to apply for the Atlantic position immediately, maybe he has an answer from them," said the Countess.

"There was a letter he never told us there was an answer," said Likus.

"He needs that address at the Atlantic ocean office and use their residential program," said the Countess.

"He needs an address and use it tomorrow night so we are not sued," said Likus.

"He leaves tonight or tomorrow especially if there are more children that are going to enter this house, he needs more money," said the Countess.

"There are two new offers accepted the first two women agreed to give them to us because we are wealthy, and will settle for the 1 and a half," said Likus.

"That sounds like one and a half mill," said the Countess.

"I know it is one hundred and fifty thousand I will not forget," said Likus.

"Here they are," said the Countess.

"Oh, honey we have thought of very horrible financial problem tell us first what the decision is about with the Atlantic. Here is the letter.?" said Likus.

"Yes I hope it is the answer," said the Countess.

"I can start tomorrow," said Oseph.

"Good we were just saying how you need an Atlantic address so you will not be involved with a lawsuit," said Likus.

"Yes and if the crew can go to many places as residents I think you ought to start first in Paris," said the Countess.

"Right so tomorrow go to work and stay there and go to a small country estate that no one would want it needs a lot of work, then go to a hotel and get a condo with them," said Likus.

"Right with these two residents no one will sue and for a while lets hope you can stay there on the job and not worry about a cold night at the farm but this is what has to be done," said the Countess.

"So I get an old small house a bed room and kitchen and fix it up," said Oseph.

"It is that or get it attached by some lawyer," said Likus.

"I need a place where I can meet you Likus," said Oseph.

"I will have a place and a rented automobile now first I want you write out the checks and the lawyer will be here tonight with the forms for them to sign," said Likus.

"You are not really on the run and yet it might be very exciting for you and the employees. They will watch what is going to happen next," said the Countess.

"I will tell no one that I had made a mistake only because it was fun and desainting too. Ok, now here are the checks," said Oseph.

"Good they will be given to them as soon as they sign," said Likus.

"I did make a suggestion to them so life will not be unbearable they still maybe a part of the rearing such as breast feeding. We need to pack my overnight case for this weekend," said Oseph.

"Yes, all right we can go upstairs right now," said Likus.

"Yes, to our own rooms," said Grandfather.

"I know I am so tired, and by the way my good husband when are you leaving home," said Grandmother.

"Why I did not do anything, it was Oseph," said Grandfather.

"Something was contributed by you.?" said Grandmother.

"Nothing," said Grandfather.

"Aiding, and accessory to that fact is helping," said Grandmother.

"He is an adult it it was a minor then sure we will all go to jail," said Grandfather.

"Then these boys can not until they are of legal age," said Grandmother.

"Or if they give their consent and so does state it in front of witnesses," said Grandfather.

"No, I think it is still aiding and abetting.?" said Grandmother.

"Then if Liker wants it, he needs to have his Father there," said Grandfather.

"Okj, thank you and please let me know when he is to return with us," said Grandmother.

"Good night you too," said Oseph.

"Yes, Good night," said Grandfather.

"Look, I can not mean for you to go Oseph but you need to get that money for yourself and to get a home in Paris," said Grandmother.

"He will he gave himself a purpose in life," said Grandfather.

"Good night you two," said Grandmother.

"Yes, good nght," said Liker.

"Yes, good night and see you both tomorrow," said Grandfather.

"There is your underwear all washed and your white and colored shirts too," said Likus.

"Good socks and slacks and just one suit," said Oseph.

"I do not want you to go but I know you will be safe," said Likus.

"Thank you, I do know that I have shamed you and over stayed my welcome," said Oseph.

"You have not shamed me and you are going to return this weekend and then you will be using a nice yacht," said Likus.

"The yacht will not work," said Oseph.

"Then we might have a case.?" said Likus.

"Yes, then and only then we can buy back the babies, as I am visiting and working too," said Oseph.

"I think we have a good price.?" said Likus.

"I hope they do not want more.?" said Oseph.

"It was mentioned that we would make a deal with the bank and them," said Likus.

"It will be ok and we will not have worry about anything," said Oseph.

"Good then you go to sleep and I will work on my book and Ose is asleep I just looked at him," said Likus.

"I did too and his nanny is very good with him," said Oseph.

"I need more security at the door while you are away," said Likus.

"Yes, you do," said Oseph.

"I only did one page and I do not want the baby to wake up," said Likus.

"Ok, good night and I love you," said Oseph.

"I love you to and thank you for getting a new resident," said Likus.

"Good night," said Oseph.

"Night, I do not think I will sleep at all," said Likus.

"Please,?" said Oseph.

"I am going to miss you," said Likus.

"I will miss you," said Oseph.

"Now did you want to get up early.?" said Likus.

"I set the alarm for 6:00 a.m.," said Oseph.

"Good," said Likus.

"It is great," said Oseph.

"Stop, now you are sleep," said Likus.

"Yes, you awake," said Oseph.

"Here there is someone I want you to see," said Oseph.

"Who?" said Likus.

"Let me turn on the light," said Oseph.

"See meet Mr. Stipend," said Oseph.

"Now that is a fact and a good reason to stay up. What did you get bigger balls.?" said Likus.

"That is true and they will be larger," said Oseph.

"How large.?" said Likus.

"Large as a, open your mouth, wider, all the way. That is how large," said Oseph.

"I can not get both in my mouth right now," said Likus.

"This is going to be a jolt but I am going to look like an oxen which is what I need. But I will not be castrated," said Oseph.

"I will make sure of that so please appoint a foreman for the site and if there are any men who will ask you about being a father again for them do not refuse," said Likus.

"I guess you want me to stay at home with you.?" said Oseph.

"Yes, I do and with a foreman at every possible site you can," said Likus.

"I hope so, because I am going to be amorous," said Oseph.

"This is fun," said Likus.

"You are not hearing me I am going to be larger than this," said Oseph.

"Then go to work and come home after asking if you can see most of it by cameras. Also I will make sure that you get another small house near the chateau," said Likus.

"Wait what time is it.? No never mind, a can ask the boss on the phone right now," said Oseph.

"Good get him on the phone right now.?" said Likus.

"Hello, this is Oseph, what I, yes it is good then it will be by cameras, if that happens again, it has, then put all twelve onto submarines. Let them hold the twelve pipes up until all is completed and connected," said Oseph.

"What was mentioned by him at the beginning.?" said Likus.

"He did think that I was going to quit before I could say anything he gave me the job and to use the cameras only they just want someone in charge there never was anyone," said Oseph.

"You called a the right time," said Likus.

"There can not be anyone or to many people working at that dept," said Oseph.

"Is there anything else. Is there anything else ?" said Likus.

"He said as he put the money into my bank account like every check that will be there each month, he placed a trillion-five into my account so I would not refuse," said Oseph.

"There now invest and we all will get a trillion a few times you are in charge of the boys accounts and please purchase next door the first thing you must do," said Oseph.

"Yes, while you are the second acting guardian and be take control of their money at any time," said Oseph.

"Good, I have you home again and look the empty house across the street right next to the ours is now yours," said Likus.

"Thank you, I can go there instead of being at the Atlantic station," said Oseph.

"I have a good plan I will go with you and we will go into that house late at night and stay there for one week," said Likus.

"That is wonderful yet I do not know if we are going to be able to stay there for one week something is always happening," said Oseph.

"If we do not call them up and let them call us," said Likus.

"Ok, but I hope nothing goes wrong," said Oseph.

"Good morning," said Grandmother.

"Good morning to you too. Mother, I know you see Oseph is staying here, he has purchased the small house near the Chateau" said Likus.

"Yes, I have received a trillion-five and we are all apart of that investment," said Oseph.

"Why, how.?" said Grandfather.

"I call up the boss and he gave me the money to stay and I can work at home watching the cameras," said Oseph.

"This is wonderful," said Grandmother.

"Yes, but we are going out and stay across the street for one week is that alright. We are staying in the next house I just purchased for Oseph," said Likus.

"Good, the both of you need a vacation," said Grandmother.

"We will leave in the afternoon and be in that house after two a.m," said Likus.

"When we first bought the house next door I was very pleased when they opened that one too for us to see and the electric is still on," said Grandmother.

"It worked out very well," said Oseph.

"Yes, it did and I am delighted so I hope you have a good time and I will try to keep the children in the living room or the bedrooms," said their Grandmother.

"We will and I will try to look for them without being seen," said Likus.

"Do not give yourselves away," said their Grandfather.

"We will not," said Likus.

"I know I will not," said Oseph.

"I will not because I want to be alone with you for a week, and besides I nearly made you leave our house and I want you with me," said Likus.

"I need you too and I am so glad called my boss because now I am in charge and I am allowed to stay here with you and all of you," said Oseph.

"We are delighted too," said Grandmother.

"Yes, now we are a family again and by the way how are our two new boys who arrived yesterday," said Grandfather.

"They must be still asleep," said Likus.

Chapter 17

"Here is Liker and Likee," said their Grandfather.

"Here is Ray and Grolate," said their Grandmother.

"All of you boys please have some breakfast," said Likus.

"Did you both say you were going to Paris.?" said Likee.

"Yes, but your father is allowed to view the project from the computer," said Likus.

"Good you stay with us," said Likee.

"I will," said Oseph.

"Ok," said Liker.

"Nice going, Dad," said Ray

"Good deal, Dad," said Grolate.

"Thanks guys," said Oseph.

"Yes, thank you boys," said Likus.

"Boys lets get started on your breakfast," said Grandmother.

"Yes, please do but your father and I still have to go to Paris today sarting at one o'clock," said Likus.

"Have a good time in Paris," said Likee.

"You should," said Liker.

"Yes, and when are you both home.?" said Ray.

"In seven days, so we will see all of you this Sunday," said Likus.

"Good, I am trying to think of what you can bring home for us," said Likee.

"Why not a gift card from a store," said Likus.

"The better we are the more money is on it," said Ray.

"There will be an equal amount for all of you," said Likus.

"Could we have our own card.?" said Liker.

"Yes, all of you will get a card including Ose and Grandmother and Grandfather," said Oseph.

"Of course the both of you need your own card," said Likus.

"Very good boys now lets start on our breakfast," said Grandmother.

"The door Sir, I will get it," said the Butler.

"I wonder who that is.?" said Likus.

"Sir, here is the children's tudor," said the Butler.

"Thank you, Frames I am Likus who is their Mother, and here is Oseph their Father," said Likus.

"How do you do, my name is Abid Zona," said the Teacher.

"Please lets talk in the living room. Oseph, Mom, and Dad please sit down with us," said Likus.

"I apoligize for being here to early but I thought I could introduce myself to them and entertain them as students for the day with fun activities. Sort of letting all of you have a day off," said the Teacher.

"Thank you, my Mother will appreciate that service today. We are both going to Paris so she and her husband could use the help," said Likus.

"I understand you have another house possibly one that is not furnished so I can be there until the both of you return," said the Teacher.

"You may stay here buit if you want to be alone the house across from us is unfurnished. I will give you the key to the cottage on the side of this house you need to go by boat because the house does not connect to this main one. " said Likus.

"That would be even better than across the canal I realize that children need to be away from the teachers," said the Teacher.

"Good then that is settled," saidLikus.

"There is one thing if today did not work out as well as it just did, I have my five trucks and suitcases at the steps and I was wondering if I could have them moved into the cottage," said the Teacher.

"You did not plan on staying at the school.?" said the Teacher.

"I was going to stay at my mother's house in Rome if things went badly here which everything it fine. When your Head Master tells you to move to another teaching position you never hesitate," said the Teacher.

"We are going to the Chateau this summer, you are welcome, to be your guest.," said Likus.

"Thank you, I could give French, Italian and Russian language instructions I just point to the object and just try to follow and no home work it is summer time," said the Teacher.

"Thank you very much, you are hired I need them to be taught pleasantly the way you have described the summer," said Oseph.

"Yes you are, I am quite impressed," said Likus.

"Yes, indeed. Let me have the Butler move the luggage," said Grandmother.

"Yes, please I do not want this teacher too leave. Lets go Dear so they may discuss the salaries," said the Grandfather.

"Salaries," said Likus.

"Yes this summer it is like time and a half," said Grandfather.

"You are on the ball again Dad," said Likus.

"It is a deal then we have a contact here," said Oseph.

"Oseph I need to tell you something about your case and the fact is the DNA for correct parenthood needs you making love with a women for hours," said Grandfather.

"I know it secrets moisture and blend into the woman and then it can control the healthiest DNA to her from you, I read it in the work place," said Oseph.

"So you did not have to mind the ordeals and the problems with the case," said Grandfather.

"No we need to talk anyways. Here is Likus," said Oseph.

"Did you know the tunnels are having a roof on them to allow water tight vehicles to run in them," said Oseph.

"That is good did I miss you.? said Likus.

"I missed you too, say this teacher does not need to talk about my children ok," said Oseph.

"Another thing is the lawyers mentioned to tell you about the case all have agreed to settle," said Likus.

"That is good now with the tunnels and its first cover with this Lloyd's first payments I can place a large hotel to the top of the clouds," said Oseph.

"You do know this is to be purchased by, by Paul he is the owner.?" said Likus.

"Of course if he buys at the full amount he might receive a check from the insurance," said Oseph.

"Ask first," said Likus.

"Ok, I will, did you know the entire cover will be on by this week and all finished in three days and will be the largest cover for the base of a building in the world plus it is 30 miles wide and long," said Oseph.

"Six months have gone by already.?" said Grandfather.

"So how long is the building.?" said Likus.

"It has to be 28 miles by 28 and filled mostly with cement so after it will be a regular size hotel yet extremely building because of the salt water," said Oseph.

"Then it will be finished, and opened by the Mayor just in case Paul is not to attend," said Likus.

"He will not go so the Mayor can have another successful campaign," said Grandfather.

"So we are back and the boys and I want to share some news," said Grandmother.

"Good what is the good news," said Likus.

"They both want to use their titles in the newspaper so it will be for with the Euro train charities and especially to the runaways children," said Grandmother.

"That is a fine idea," said Grandfather.

"Yes, said Oseph.

"That is excellent I am very proud of the both of you," said Likus.

"Yes, Likus should be very pleased that they are both named after you," said Oseph.

"What then we can adopt a girl and name her after you," said Likus.

"What is her name.?" said Oseph.

"I will call her Osepha," said Likus.

"Then we can get that baby we never talked about, the agency must have an infant," said Oseph.

"So Osepha, not with a silent A vowel sound. I love that name," said Grandmother.

"It is settled then," said Likus.

"A baby sister," said Likus.

"A new brother and now a sister," said Liker.

"A little Princess," said Grandfather.

"This makes it complete but we do need to have about ten infants to adopt and live next door after all we can afford it," said Oseph.

"We do need this again and soon there will about a hundred children in both houses," said Likus.

"I can still stay there, the both us and watch them with the nannies too," said Grandmother.

"Yes, we can," said Grandfather.

"Do you think they are aware of the bolt that was in the harbor of Venice, it is the size of a two car garage and just as tall. To anchor the building on to it, the cemented foundation so they might enjoy seeing it," said Oseph.

"It is now on the grassy lawn that it is going to level the to enhance more of the natural tall grass that was just removed for the bolt and to be in place and than move to other," said Grandfather.

"I like the idea they went to put in a richer soil now that the plants can be used for a substitute for another plastic," said Grandmother.

"Yes, we can and the report came in today and it we are successful once again. It does not take to much of the plants just an extra salt water to maike it happen," said Likus.

"Good then we will take the children to see a good use of a factory machine part that does another function," said Grandmother.

"Now I guess we hare ready in a few minutes.?" said Grandmother.

"Goods kids you are ready even when you heard water trip," said Likus.

"Yes, good bye we will wait for Grandmother," said Liker.

"Sure and we have the money this time," said Likus.

"Good and when you get home I will reimburse you both," said their Father.

"Bye and please have our baby sister here when we return," said Liker.

"Oh, there is a lot to talk about," said their Mother.

"Then it is all set we should see her when we return," said Likus.

"We will see about that later, now go have a good time and have a dinner the four of you," said Oseph.

"I have plenty of money," said Grandfather.

"What then I will buy a few gifts for us all," said Grandmother.

"Then there are two people who I will be reimbursed," said Oseph.

"Then I will pay Mother. So have a good time" said Likus.

"Thank you dear, Good bye," said Grandmother.

"Now that they are gone, I will call the agency," said Likus.

"Ok, and I will get the chef and let him know about our dinner for the two of us on the third floor," said Oseph.

"Good, hello Mrs., yes it is me I wonder if you have a baby, an infant there a few days old. In about one hour that will be fine and thank you and good bye," said Likus.

"Here is your drink, we will eat in one hour, what did you mean about calling an agency.?" Said Oseph.

"I called the adoption agency and we are going to have a little three day old baby girl brought to this house in about an hour or more," said Likus.

"With a new actual idea being a sentence or an I going to have another full-time employee or who is the victum or the great prisoner which will be the caption for the press," said Oseph.

"No, hardship you sent them both away and even my Mother forgot to stay home and I think she knows I called the agency, right now I think see is talking to her husband about this present to you from me," said Likus.

"Thank you, I hope you know what you are doing.?" Said Oseph.

"I do and we have a doctor in the house and he will be paid to look at even the other children next door. Even for a second or third time around it is still one time with the others that have four hundred infants to raise," said Likus.

"Right I do not mind but not that many in these houses the buildings are too small," said Oseph.

"I know that, this is also a good time to bring her in while the others are at the schools for a few days," said Likus.

"It was nice of the school to have the meetings there to observe new teachers that the school like," said Oseph.

"It was necessarily if we were going to teach them at home," said Likus.

"Venice needs a new school system, several small buildings for just one grade," said Oseph.

"This is true for many cities now here is your daughter do not let the others get jealous," said Likus.

"No, I will treat them equality," said Oseph.

"Just remember she is a little girl and she needs her father's lap to sit on and watch you read the news," said Likus.

"That I can do and the boys are not young they do not need affection unless they are injured," said Oseph.

"Verbal and encouragement is always good," said Likus.

"I will remember," said Oseph.

"Look she comes with a dry bottom," said Likus.

"She does and she looks so beautiful in her pink dress," said Oseph.

"She is beautiful," said Likus.

"Now are the others going to be here is a few days," said Oseph.

"Yes, and the staff we ready sent for we know already," said Likus.

"They will all arrive when.?" said Oseph.

"They be in the building across from our front door, and to our left. Then they will take care of them as a quarantine procedure," said Likus.

"Good idea," said Oseph.

"It is and we will all be there tonight or tomorrow," said Likus.

"Good and now they are back so I quess Mother told them there was someone here waiting," said Likus.

"Hello, we are back but we did do some shopping and had lunch," said Grandmother.

"What happened.?" said Likus.

"Yes, what happened.?" said Oseph.

"We were not able to see it they had to move it again," said Liker.

"We did not get near it in case it fell into the water," said Likus.

"We did get a few gifts and had a good lunch," said Grandfather.

"That is good, now look across the water to the new white building," said Likus.

"It looks as if there are many babies being carried into the Palace," said Liker.

"Did you ask the agency for these babies there must be over forty babies.?" said Grandmother.

"I did," said Likus.

"What about Dad's little girl who is my sister," said Liker.

"Yes, and what about my sister," said Likus.

"She is right here see through the French doors, she is resting right now," said Oseph.

"She is my beautiful and lovely Osepha," said Oseph.

"She is," said Grandmother.

"Yes, she is and we put the crib right next to the door so we can see her all of the time," said Likus.

"There is a hot dinner for all of us. Lets all sit down and talk about our gifts," said Likus.

"Here is my gift I have a new watch and so does Likus," said Liker.

"Good for you, you both bought practical gifts," said Oseph.

"Good for you, I knew you both would do the right thing," said Likus.

"I have a gift from all of us to the both of you, it is a baby girl christening bowl and cup made out of silver," said Grandmother.

"It is from an antique store," said Grandfather.

"This is so elegant and refined," said Oseph.

"Yes, thank you and it is our gift to you both, if you want to reimburse the boys we do not mind right boys," said Grandmother.

"We will, you two have done so much, you boys deserve a gift," said Likus.

"Thank you," said Liker.

"Yes, thank you," said Likus.

"Yes, and the gifts do not stop here, the both of you have been very helpful," said Oseph.

"Now we have about forty or more children within two buildings so we need to give them names" Said Likus.

"Great and we want to have a picture of all of us next door," said Grandmother.

"We will, all of us," said Oseph.

"Good idea Mother and a photo from us and the staff too," said Likus.

"We will now here we are and we will see the babies right now and here is a nanny," said Grandfather.

"Good evening, I am sure you would like to see your children here they are," said The Nanny.

"Oh, they are so cute," said Grandmother.

"Yes, they are," said Likus.

"I sure do have a lot of brothers and sisters," said Likus.

"Here is Ray and Grolate," said Oseph.

"Hello, boys you are just in time to meet your new brothers and sisters," said Likus.

"Which one is mine. ?" said Ray.

"None, they are all in blue or pink," said Grolate.

"Yes, just for this evening," said Likus.

"I talked to the head nurse we are to leave now and I have a list of the children their names and medications too.'" said Grandfather.

"Good you are their doctor," said Likus.

"Right and seeing that I am on duty tonight the hospital is sending over an intern to watch them and the shifts and three intern along with resident nurses too," said Grandfather.

"That is so good to know, you are in charge there so thank you so much you are a good father to me," said Likus.

"I try to be and also a good Grandfather too," said Grandfather.

"Yes, you are dear and a very good husband," said his Wife.

"You are very concerned and caring," said Oseph.

"Now that we are home lets get something to eat and drink is anyone hungry there is turkey sandwiches soon," said Grolate.

"Good, food I am sure hungry but the dinner was very good this evening," said Ray.

"Yes, it was a steak and we are home because the teachers had to leave this evening after their meetings," said Grolate.

"Was Abid there.?" said Grandfather.

"No, but the head master was and he gave Oseph a letter," said Ray.

"Yes, it will be in the mail," said Grolate.

"How was school.?" said Liker.

"I am glad I am being tutored in our own home," said Ray.

"It will be more fun," said Grolate.

"Good then you are with us," said Likus.

"Sure and it is going to be fun and interesting," said Ray.

"I am glad all of you are pleased ," said Likus.

"Yes, we were worried that you might not want the idea of home education," said Oseph.

"They are delighted," said Grandmother.

"They are, and Ray and Grolate here are your gifts," said Grandfather.

"Why are we getting gifts now it is not Christmans or my birthday," said Ray.

"No, it is not but please do not stop it is another great idea," said Grolate.

"Because you are both family, we love you both," said Grandmother.

"Here is a final gift for the four of you," said Likus.

"Now just go upstairs and enjoy and we will be up in a little whole," said Oseph.

"There that was smoothly done we needed to give them another gift because of all the babies they saw tonight," said Likus.

"They are not jealous, they were quite amazed, surprised and were very pleased," said Grandfather.

"I was quite shocked now I have eleven baby girls to be with," said Oseph.

"I you unhappy with that because I could get more," said Likus.

"No, that is fine but I will let you know when we can get more," said Oseph.

"Easier by the dozen but we do not have that problem with Belgium and Lloyd's so we are ok, just let me know when everything is ok," said Likus.

"You mean now that I am the children's doctor I can have Belgium and Lloyd's for myself," said Grandfather, or Likus Father.

"Yes, you can and both ways is fine yet Belgium is a gift from Paul who needs us to run the business," said Likus.

"That does seem very expensive," said Likus Dad.

"That is why Lloyd's is now on our side and with the media we get full payment. The fee is now a part of the company and it is paid once a year," said Likus.

"So when does the company become someone else's," said Doctor.

"Lets say we are finished again with these tunnels in the Atlantic and Venice we can start on the Concorde or tunnels in Africa and South America," said Likus.

"We are in charge Dear," said the Countess.

"Then if someone wants their own project," said the Doctor.

"There has never been anyone other than us," said Likus.

"That is perfect I was thinking of this the other," said the Doctor.

"When Oseph and I are finished we can give the entire project to you two and remember Paul gets 70 percent so we are to work fast with the media," said Likus.

"Vaguely I remember something about this topic a while ago so what do you think we should do," said the Count.

"It was vague the last and discussed over the Christmas dinner and left there. I think we should go ahead and do our share," said the Countess.

"To keep this with us would be excellent," said the Count.

"Just being a part of it is exciting and to get as much money for our future is important especially when the work is over," said the Countess.

"We now have an agreement so tonight we will let the lawyers and this is the only merger is amoung ourselves," said Likus.

"You are a good Prince and Likus and I love so much," said his Mother.

"Thank you and I appreciate everything that you have done for me up to now," said Likus.

"Do not worry, you will receive all of my money but I would like to know where it goes, I hope it is in our stock for investment purposes. said his Mother.

"My money also, we will live on half of mine if that is ok," said the Count.

"Sure and half of that should be stock investments and I will look at the rest when you both start working together," said Likus.

"Ok," said the Countess.

"Sure, ok," said the Count.

"For the sake of knowing that Paul would want a report from all of us. We all need to look at each others reports," said Likus.

"Good," said the Countess.

"Fine," said the Count.

"Good, it is a deal and this time we will advertise, many many times to let the world know we did not do that the last time we talked," said likus.

"The children went upstairs so why not have some Champaign.?" said Grandfather.

"Good ending a good deal with something wrong it is a good idea, do we all agreed," said Oseph.

"It is a good idea with a usual wrong ending so that is fine," said the Countess.

"Likus now that you had mentioned not pursuing what has just accrued I think we were ahead to much with other ideas and the insurances of Lloyd's was ignored," said his Mother.

"Your right and we did nothing about it is the computer calendar," said Likus.

"Here it is now in the calendar," said the Count.

"Now it is, I told you that if you Oseph did not follow up in our insurances and in the present calendar I was going to do this," said Likus.

"Oh no, you did not, let me see," said the Countess.

"Say Oseph you do have quite a large club," said the Count.

"What, what it this.?" said Oseph.

"You are now the first to be in a new calendar for Venice tunnels to raise money for its charity," said Likus.

"Ok, then here is yours," said Oseph.

"Oh, Likus you are very handsome," said his Dad.

"That aught to sell copies it is a good thing you two work at home," said the Countess.

"Yes, you both can and it looks as if you are going too, I just placed it in the Venice computer news of messages and ideas so it indicates that we need just ten more Venetians," said the Count.

"You did not, then lets go Dear and so these to models can be alone," said the Countess.

"Good night, here take the bottle we have another," said Likus.

"Look what you did Likus there are seventeen other photos," said Oseph.

"Oh, my these are very large men and officiers so I we do have to make this a charity calendar so they are not fired," said Likus.

"Good, lets cover them up and do not make a duplicate," said Oseph.

"There now they are ready and here Is the cover see a tgunnels right behind you awith a caption, "Lets go for it," said Likus.

"I am on the cover," said Ospeh.

"Sure you and about eleven others one would like to hit as a big guy," said Likus.

"Me," said Oseph.

"Yes why not," said Likus.

"Why," said Oseph.

"Because you are all brawn and that type many like to tease until it is to late and you give back," said Likus.

"Is this how I give back.?" said Oseph.

"Sure that is great but you are to heavy right now," said Likus.

"I did not want to hurt you so lets have some more champaign and give a copy to the ones who gave a photo with a contract and they will be paid while investing," said Oseph.

"Good I just did you on the cover and as January," said Likus.

"So you did cover me up that was nice," said Oseph.

"Of course before I know it you would be walking outside if we did have sidewalks," said Likus.

"We do out in the back," said Oseph..

"I did make a copy for myself but all is now eased," said Likus.

"Then that is now in the library you better get it," said Oseph.

"I no, it is not in there that is why I ran back and forth," said Likus.

"I wonder where it could be.?" said Likus.

"Some where," said Oseph.

"Yes, what is it," said Likus.

"There are some photos that only I have from the kitchen," said the Butler.

"Thank you, could you look upstairs in the library I do not think any one is there. Call out first and give your name," said Likus.

"Sir I have all of the copies," said the Butler.

"Very good you are quite a help," said the Countess.

"Yes, thank you," said Likus.

"Thank you, Sir," said the Butler.

"Yes, thank you for your help it was very good of you," said Oseph.

"Now lets all get another drink," said Likus.

"No, we managed to stay too long and we are going upstairs maybe we will see your tomorrow morning," said the Countess.

"Alright we were interrupted for the last time lets just stay up and watch the tel," said Oseph.

"We can do this tomorrow, I said," That they are all getting paid," said Likus.

"They will and now we can watch some tel," said Oseph.

"Ok, get something on a good station, ok," said Likus.

"What about a film, here is Paul in Versailles, and look at these two films with Edvard they did two reproductions of other movies with King Ludwig's building," said Oseph.

"Ok, how about this one.?" said Likus.

"Good I enjoy when she starts to sing," said Oseph.

"I do too and it is amazing that the entire movie was place into the castle so perfectly," said Likus.

"We could get a few history movies in Venice done," said Oseph.

"I know and we have to discuss our own movie," said Likus.

"Sure it will be done soon just when the tunnels are all completed in Venice," said Oseph.

"By the way, did you hear what Paul did at Versailles.?" said Likus.

"No, what.?" said Oseph.

"Mother told me earlier today and I did not have any time to tell you," said Likus.

"What?" said Oseph.

"You know the cement sleep, the square cement room with a bed, a shower and a toilet," said Likus.

"Yes, the franchise that is on I-95 Connecticut to Maine to California and also Paris to Moscow what about it," said Oseph.

"He has ten of them in the court yard in Versailles and his clients go to therapy and drug rehab," said Likus.

"Did he use it," said Oseph.

"Yes, he was the first inside to have his medciation for Diabetes regulated," said Likus.

"For four weeks he was in the main square largest building in the middle and is going to be released in three days," said Likus.

"You should send him a card and tell him to visit us when he home," said Oseph.

"Should I invite him.?" said Likus.

"Yes, he might just show up," said Oseph.

"Then I will," said Likus.

"Now am I sure about this, that the coliseum is in the backward covering the canal, with two large buildings behind that for parking and above all of that is a restaurant," said Oseph.

"Yes, but before anyone could get to the coliseum the court yard was there and now the ten buildings are there with the largest in the middle," said Likus.

"We could do the same thing here when they level the glades," said Likus.

"We could buy that right now," said Oseph.

"We could and in the morning we will," said Likus.

"That is right you just mentioned it, so invite him and with the family too," said Oseph.

"Ok, thanks I will," said Likus.

"These individual cement room are the latest in Connecticut, you buy five for five million and the sixth is another one for free. There is one in each city for an owner to use and then after his meeting he sleeps and then goes home," said Oseph.

"We could use that sleep here in the back yard, the state would pay for many of them in many places," said Likus.

"We could fill them in many unused coliseum," said Oseph.

"Ed knows that this franchise belongs to him we are just borrowing it," said Likus.

"Good then lets put it in many different places and vacant places do make money," said Oseph.

"Yes, it does but where did I hear that this was used some place just like it had happened before," said Likus.

"This has been done in many places permanently but not portal that it can move to another town," said Oseph.

"We might have tried it before but now the Ed has used it for himself others will do so," said Oseph.

"I remember something, I think we gave him this idea," said Likus.

"Well please show good behavior and not be unkind it is still a sign of underachievement and not one who is in control, where the orders have been given by another who is unknown," said Oseph.

"I thought is was due to the lack of snow now a days.?" said Likus.

"It is but this is part of the lack of snow controlling allergies maybe bad or maybe good," said Oseph.

"So for the psychosis one might loose verbal control and yet a bad winter does separate the souls too," said Likus.

"Good analyzing and yet we have controlled all of this by using sleep and loitering for psychiatry, while people wait for there appointments," said Oseph.

"Coming to bed we can talk in the bedroom," said Likus.

Chapter 18

"Now I know you did sleep and every well in fact you made me stay up for a while listening to you making sounds," said Likus.

"I was just going to tell you that you do snore," said Oseph.

"I know Mother mentioned it one day when the door was open and she closed it and I slept until noon," said Likus.

"I sleep once in a while in the late morning hours," said Oseph.

"It is just one complete oval circle not quite a circle yet horizontally and attached we do become one as two, yet our sleep is better when it is not planned," said Likus.

"Ok, but my circle being oval shape tends to be flattened not a perfect shape like a piece of rice and my words do not express what I feel and when in writing it is never correct," said Oseph.

"We do have people who can write for us yet I think some where the two pieces of rice are flat yet wet," said Likus.

"Wet, but not ruined, just needing a few more hours to wake up inside and outside is the many who are looking at us and expecting us to do the right thing," said Oseph.

"Years ago in these castles that sort of thing was not mentioned and the republic has its own situational course and yet the guards still do get the work out," said Likus.

"Like Princess Ownsite has had everything under control and Edvard too," said Oseph.

"She is happy and loves him and is appreciated for where she is," said Likus.

"She is happy.?" said Oseph.

"She is and she let me know that all is rehearsed and filmed in advance," said Likus.

"Yes, I know but the keyword I used is work," said Oseph.

"I know my Mother does suggest anything to me at all," said Likus.

"No, and she would only if it meant for the safety of all of us," said Oseph.

"You are right," said Likus.

"This is your house I can not tell you what to do," said Oseph.

"Fate is what I met you for," said Likus.

"Also the love that is created is stronger and it has been tested by good and bad and yet we both know that a poor life from here will eventually grow to love and the hardship is always there," said Oseph.

"I know and jokingly it can get better with only my twin because I can not survive a poor life and still be pleasant," said Likus.

"Then we should hire someone and let them be us," said Oseph.

"As a look-alike we need to think of this when we leave or we stay here the life outside can not demand," said Likus.

"We use Chateau for the summer and then we return," said Oseph.

"That is it you have the answer we need," said Likus.

"Thank you," said Oseph.

"You want humor, I have it, did you know that in the dictionary look-alike is after longwinded and long term," said Likus.

"Long shot is too, I took it and I am very pleased," said Oseph.

"I am glad you did, I love you," said Likus.

"I love you too," said Oseph.

"We can say we can use look-alikes for advertising and if they go out in our place to pick up the children and letting the nannies know and then we can be alone," said Oseph.

"I would but I do not want anything to happen to us being accused of neglecting the children and when the look-alikes are here it will happen," said Likus.

"We do have the opportunity to have a good amount of privacy we have not been called to have photos and when the Mayor saw the tunnels he and I gave a photo and it was with a few other workers as he had a tour of the tunnels," said Oseph.

"We can take advantage and do the correct thing and we do have a doctor here too," said Likus.

"What you are," said Liker.

"You are, you are wasting your money," said Likus.

"What a coinsedence, and you think we should not have our own twins," said Oseph.

"What is wrong, Liker," said Oseph.

"Yes, what," said Likus.

"He called me a name the "N" word and a few others too," said Liker.

"Likus you should know better and if anyone hears this we can not charge the press for listening and remember we are all in a position to be paid for what we do and arguing is bad press," said Oseph.

"Yes, make up with your brother right now," said Likus the Mom.

"Liker, I am sorry," said Likus.

"Thank you and I am too," said Likus the child.

"Now stop what ever it is and none of you are going to purchase anything without my permission," said Oseph.

"Liker wanted a sky mobile and I do not think it is wise it is to dangerous here," said Likus his brother.

"They are outlawed and it is to dangerous," said Oseph.

"How do I know I lived Newport," said Liker.

"Ok, it is over," said Likus his Mom.

"Now the both of you get ready for lunch," said Oseph.

"They have not argued in a long time," said Likus.

"No, and I hope there is nothing to worry about," said Oseph.

"Ask Liker if he wants to go home and my son can go to military school tomorrow," said Likus.

"No, we want to stay here," said Liker.

"No, military school please," said Likus.

"Then I have to tell you boys something, you are both quests in this school and you both can leave by the military school soldiers if you get out of line one more time," said Oseph.

"You mean we should be in a school far away and sleep over," said Liker.

"That is the tradition of Europe and the responsibility of the parents who live in a large house like this one," said Oseph.

"You mean that we do not belong here," said Liker.

"No you do not belong here," said Oseph.

"I would be there in Newport or here when I am older," said Liker.

"In any house when you are older and want to do this business," said Oseph.

"Right this is the only business and position to make a lot of money running Versailles or in another building too," said Likus their Mom.

"When you are ill you can not let your wife run the business, you can let a brother or a business partner who has no control, or just run it at your bed side," said Oseph.

"Most of the time you might have to starve and then go downstairs when you are able and see who is there and then fire them for being in a group that is continuing to let you be ill," said Likus their Mother.

"Just like an anorexic who is ill and even dieing and the parent alone this to happen," said Oseph.

"That is what some staff do and parents," said Likus.

"We will behave we want our education at home and on the computer too," said Liker.

"Ok, then all will be remembered about today that the both of you are quests," said Oseph.

"We can watch over little brothers and sisters," said Liker.

"Also make sure the staff does what they are suppose to do," said Likus the brother.

"Do not spy children and honey we can give them one day on the cameras to know what the work of world is," said Oseph.

"I want to start today alright," said Liker.

"Good that is what I want to hear," said Likus.

"Ok, then," said Oseph.

"Excuse me Sir, a Mrs.Childliverer is here," said the Butler.

"I will take care of everything, Likus she is my Aunt," said Oseph.

"Auntie what are you doing here.?" said Oseph.

"I am here to live here and here is my check and all of my money too," said Auntie.

"You did not call first," said Oseph.

"No, I called to talk to the Countess and she told me just what to do. Here," said Auntie.

"That is right I told her to give you everything and to place her security in your hands. Likus you too," said the Countess.

"Good I will help out where ever I am needed," said Auntie.

"My last daughter to stay at home is with me she is right here. Come on in," said Auntie.

"Hello, and thank you Oseph you are very kind and I do appreciate being here with your family," said Pala.

"Likus, Liker, Likus, Grandfather and Grandmother I want you to meet my Aunt and her daughter Palage," said Oseph.

"Hello, lets go into the living room," said Likus.

"Now where did you live.?" said Liker.

"We both lived in Paris or just outside in a very house house a small Chateau. Palage name is pronounced Pa-la-ge - - - the e is long e," said Auntie.

"But Palage is good enough," said Palage.

"Long A and long e we can remember that are you finished with college Palage," said likus.

"I have just finished a Masters in Psychology and now I intend to return to Paris for a P.H.D," said Palage.

"You must see Venice first and at lease give it one year," said Oseph.

"That is a good idea and maybe you might want to go to the University of Venice," said Likus.

"By the way Grandmother my Countess and a very good Mother-in-law I want to thank you for getting Auntie and Palage here with us," said Oseph.

"Yes, that is good and children please go and have your lunch now ok. We can all have our lunch later now when they are finished," said Likus.

"That is perfect and this evening we will all have dinner together," said Oseph.

"I am quite sure after this trip getting here to your home that I will stay for one year and see the sites," said Palage.

"You do speak French so why not see Venice and go to your classes here and learn Italian too," said Auntie.

"It is going to be just that way and I am thrilled just to think of it," said Palage.

"Good it is going to be very exciting for the both of you this year and for us too and well come to our home," said Likus.

"Yes, well come," said Oseph.

"Lets have some coffee we deserve a treat," said the Countess.

"You mentioned other children and where are they," said the Count.

"George is in London with his family and two children he is a lawyer. And my other daughter Elle is in Egypt on a dig yet the expedition has not given much results in the last two years," said Auntie.

"That is the only expedition right now in Egpyt," said the Doctor.

"It has been advertised any times if I recall and Elle was not mentioned at all," said Oseph.

"That is what happens when you start at the bottom. sometimes I feel so sorry for her, I wish I was there to help her but I have the feeling that I might find something first," said Palage.

"That could happen and the two of you might never be friends again," said Oseph.

"I did think the same think but she reassures me that she is working any day," said Auntie.

"That is good and she must enjoy it," said Oseph.

"I would not mind being there myself. said Grandfather.

"You can not leave Count you have children and a practice to watch," said the Countess."

"I heard that you to adapted many babies," said Palage.

"Yes, you have and I think that the two of us should wait a least a month as a quarantine good practice," said Auntie.

"I agreed one month from today and they are right across from us," said Grandfather.

"Yes, the Count has watching them and we all forgive him yet we follow his instructions," said the Countess.

"We will," said Auntie.

"Of course and they need to be protected," said Palage.

"It is a deal and I hope all of us can be a help too," said Grandfather.

"It is a grand idea and very lovely too," said Palage.

"Helping these babies when they are all alone," said Auntie.

"Who decided to adopt, was it you Likus," said Palage.

"It was actually was our boss Paul who lives in Versailles," said Oseph.

"I remember reading and it has been on the news, the tel quite a few times this year," said Palage.

"He should be visiting soon so the both of you can meet his royal highness," said the Countess.

"That would be wonderful he is the reason why we can be here, it is all because of Prince Paul, actually now it is Prince or King Louie Paul the 18th," said Auntie.

"He is and yet the Prseident will be there until the countries are linked with the euro train tunnels," said Oseph.

"This switch of tunnels and with the Concorde has made a difference in our lives," said Palage.

"It has and yet we can not have both powers at once," said the Countess.

"The population does not realize the military was build up then and now the royals are taking care of the people at last with these great inventions for transportation," said Palage.

"Long live the King, for he is helping the President to do good things of mankind," said Auntie.

"Long live the King," said the Countess.

"Now the Autobus has been a good success and we think it needs expanding too," said Likus.

"I know Hon but I was wondering maybe Liker would like to run the next big project of those ships," said Oseph.

"Also the worlds largest submarine to do and to be soon on the tel and then Likus can run those birds that still go towards the skies," said the Countess.

"Good we have a plan for them and I will go and tell them both," said Likus.

"Yes, you should Liker does not need an audience we he is in front," said the Countess.

"I know this life is still knew to him," said the Count.

"I do not know how Newport was but it was very different compared to Venice," said Oseph.

"It had to have been arguing from the start so the building did not have a chance. I will be right back," said Likus.

"This is so good they have a career and one at a time they will be in charge," said the Grandfather.

"Does that mean we are in charge of this project again.? " said the Grandmother.

"Yes, we do," said the Grandfather.

"So there is always to be enough money to live on," said the Grandmother.

"Yes we will. Especially right now because I just gave this message to Paul and it came back in contract form until that date is here with the next will be contracts are quite deep," said Oseph.

"So these are agreements," said Grandfather.

"Then the paper work is quite intense," said Grandfather.

"I remember when the first contracts came in I had to wait for their paper to arrive," said Likus.

"All is well and both boys agreed," said Likus.

"Fantastic," said Grandmother.

"And also huge!" said Grandfather.

"I hope we are all right in this decision we do need those two accounts in this family," said Likus.

"the will not let us down.'said Grandfathere.

"Do you know what Liker said to me before I left the room." He said," We will be lawyers by then too," said Likus.

"He is a sharp one and right on the ball," said Grandfather.

"What did Likus say or do.?" said Grandmother.

"He came over to me and gave me a hug and a kiss and so did Liker," said Likus.

"He did not say anything.?" said Oseph.

"No, I think he found the answer to bordering school," said Likus.

"Yes they did, it was a tremendous pressure off of their own schoulders," said Grandfather.

"Now they both feel like important and responsible adults with a true meaning of belonging," said Oseph.

"By the way Auntie and Palage would you both want to run the business some day we really earn over money by the press and what is said wrongly in their press releases," said Oseph.

"Let me answer our personal phone for the family and I will learn day by day," said Auntie.

"How about you Palage you see how the afternoon goes with ideas and suggestions," said Oseph.

"I know my love for Psychology, and that P.H.D. can be later, I think to do any good for this family I would need to become a lawyer," said Palage.

"Good we need a law firm and running by someone you do not need a degree to run that firm during its first few years," said Oseph.

"Then Palage can take over the firm we started in Venice so there will be strength and more of that during the years," said Likus.

"Tremendous and humongous too," said Grandfather.

"Do not let the boys hear some of these words that can be considered sang," said Likus.

"That advice is also very great and considered at this time. Yes we need them in this room for a new business decision of theirs should be heard," said Palage.

"Ok, that was good and funny," said Auntie.

"I think the younger generation would just stare at us being so clever," said Palage.

"Or how about take a picture it will last longer.?" said Grandfather.

"Not my haste makes waste either," said Grandmother.

"Oh, and not my, "Lets go the dinner table and we can devour our hurt in champaign," said Likus.

"We need them to be lawyers immediately," said Palage.

"That is very true even if they are not in the office all of the day, they will be very useful during a take over," said Likus.

"Are they both upstairs.?" said Palage.

"Yes, I can see them, Liker is getting some food," said Likus.

"That computer is quite good and especially for security," said Grandmother.

"I watch them all the time," said Grandfather.

"They are good boys," said Oseph.

"Liker waits on Likus and watches quite him a lot," said Grandfather.

"Likus needs someone to tell him what to do," said Likus.

"I agree they are good boys. This is an excellent dinner, Likus," said Oseph.

"Thank you, I know most of us enjoy a hot meal and an oven roast the way this chef prepares it is indescribable," said Likus.

"This dinner is devine," said Palage.

"Yes it is heaven, you are correct about the oven roast he does do exspectional work, Likus" said Auntie.

"Thank you, all of you. I am pleased that all of you are enjoying his cuisine," said Likus

"Here are the boys. Do you want some more food," said Oseph.

"I know what they want, they both want to do into the kitchen and tell the Butler that he can fix the both of you some sandwiches and have them in the your playroom."

"Sure right now.?" said Liker.

"Yes, please and also tell the chef we are ready for some more coffee and dessert. Ok, and thank you boys," said Likus.

"Sure it is quite pleas able," said Likus.

"There we did not get a true response from them, missing them a few minutes ago would have been the clincher," said Likus.

"I think it was good and proper at this moment," said Palage.

"You are right I never thought of that," said Likus.

"I notice Liker is not Likus," said Palage.

"Actually they were named after my first son is giving this fine food and a good hospitality he does give me and took me in too," said the Countess.

"Liker is a cousin and Likus is my little brother who Mother took back after his parents both died," said Likus.

"I am so sorry, I did not want to bring up any reminders of a past thas would hurt even in the slightest.," said Palage.

"It is not painful my cousin did not mind taking him in while Likus was at a boarding school," said the Countess.

"My Mother's last husband was a Duke and he was not in the mood to raise two children," said Likus.

"Now I sold my two houses and gave Likus the money to invest. Just the same advice I gave to the two of you and it will work out," said the Countess.

"I know how Palage and I can get the media seeing that it is the way to create the revenue last is the greatest and most promising," said Auntie.

"How.?" said Oseph.

"This part of the evening I love it is how we invent for the press to do the worst," said Likus.

"I could go into the law office and start taking charge and when I am there to be interview I can mention that I am the only one in this house that does not have a title," said Palage.

"This will do it," said Likus.

"Maybe, we first need to get this done correctly," said Grandfather.

"No, when they ask my name I will say my Mother is the one with the title. Then someone might say oh, "You are single," said Palage.

"I should work," said Likus.

"Yes, maybe he will say," Work all work before pleasure," said Auntie.

"I hope so, then let the media do the rest," said Palage.

"It will work," said Likus.

"They do that the insurances are our biggest investments which is our money and not the company," said Oseph.

"Oh, do not get us wrong we have a good fortune now we just know that some we do hope it will be in the hands of Likus and Liker," said Likus.

"That does sound like a very good name for a law film," said Palage.

"This is the way each of us as a group will make the money right," said Auntie.

"Yes, and the insurances are always paid first and then we do have the stock of Venice, the stock exchange that is where we have the right to take it over," said Likus.

"We did start a bit of the stocks and we are going to ask the investers to give them to us very soon," said Grandfather.

"When the tunnels are completed which is soon and all is working, then we have the right to purchase from others," said Oseph.

"Yes, so your share will be in stock and we are putting your money in as we speak because it is a knew source and now it has confused the others," said the Countess.

"We wanted to be here to invest and I think I should be in the news at the law film this week," said Palage.

"That is good and we need to have things in our control," said Oseph.

"Yes, can start tomorrow if you want to and apply to the University too," said Likus.

"I will I can not wait, I need to be there in the morning and I hope the press will pick it up," said Palage.

"I could call and have a picture done.?" said Likus.

"That would be very nice of you," said Palage.

"Then tomorrow you will be in Venice city and it will be until you are fulltime at the University," said Likus.

"It is a deal," said Palage.

"Yes, it is," said Grandmother.

"Just one thing I do hope every soon the pavarazzi will not use the word single and I can find a nice man to be apart of his life and if he has a title too it would be a good thing," said Palage.

"All will work out you are very young and 22 years old is not the end of the world," said Auntie.

"I know but I would like to get married," said Palage.

"If you concentrate on the work as a lawyer and yet involve with the firm you might meet someone.?" said Likus.

"Yes, then when you are dating mention about the University full time and give the both of you space after an engagement," said Likus

"Good idea," said Palage.

"So then this relationship will work out, remember most house wives are at home and studying is good also," said Likus.

"Right and if you and your husband have your own firm there is a retainer and a new investment for us as another firm," said Oseph.

"Yes do not mind us, this is the way we handle our meetings at home and just with us," said Likus.

"We established, the Countess and I, a business and a family," said the Count.

"Right, they gave us a good point of view on many things," said Likus.

"We do and have all of the time in fact it is just like this evening that we are talking and we decided that Palage will be working in the law office and then at the University," said Oseph.

"We create and then make it happen and usually most of the things are for the better for us and the business," said Likus.

"Lately it has been education for the boys and I am on the computer with just one course along with the Count," said the Countess.

"I am hoping that I pleased you this evening.?" said Palage.

"Yes you have," said Likus.

"I hope you are having a good time and enjoying the University," said Palage.

"I am I have a psychology course and the Count is taking the first course in law and then he will be helping me with it," said the Countess.

"That is very wise indeed I emphasized to enjoy and have fun because of that is not with you then it is not in your best interest," said Palage.

"If you do not like the ocean, then use an airplane," said the Count.

"I always think of being away from Europe and how difficult it was to be in the frontier, the out west or in a desert too," said the Countess.

"I do think of that and how difficult it must have been to leave Europe and ones home only to get away from the government, and maybe not just the King," said Auntie.

"There is the quaker who because of religion were made sure there was land for them is one place. Even to mention their own life style was a hardship too," said Palage.

"We are all very lucky indeed to have building such as this one," said Likus.

"Yes the gold, in the hallways and in this room and the others is incredible," said Palage.

"I do have to admit it was wonderful just to think of living here," said Auntie.

"I was completely selfish and wanted to be here and convinced Mother that we were welcomed and to see right away the properties were sold and to make sure the check was in Likus view and that would secure us both of wanting something very badly," said Palage.

Then it is that attitude that will help us all stay here and fight for our home," said Likus.

"Then a toast to us and our happiness together and that nothing will harm anyone of us," said the Count.

"Nothing will harm us and we do have a Doctor in the house, we are quite fortunate," said the Countess.

"Yes, we are," said Likus.

"Yes, Doctor we probably are not realizing that you are our very own weapon towards good health and mental health too," said Palage.

"Thank you all of you we have to realize anything that is harmful is not the best idea or person to be with," said the Doctor.

"We do have to keep us together with new ideas and giving good guidance about the business is essential," said the Countess.

"That is the beginning of survival," said Oseph.

"We have a good deal here we need to make it work all the time," said the Count.

"Hello, here we are, we just wanted to say hello," said Liker.

"Yes, we missed all of you," said Likus.

"We missed you boys," said Palage.

"What are you watching, a film.?" said Oseph.

"Yes, we are watching Grenaire," said Liker.

"That is a good movie," said Likus.

"Yes, it is we saw it last year," said Palage.

"Come on Likus lets go remember the movie," said Liker.

"Yes boys, control your behavior the children might wake up," said Likus.

"All right we will," said Liker.

"Yes," said Likus.

"They are good boys yet I wonder right now if they are on the computer," said Oseph.

"I wish we could find out but your skills with computers is limited," said Likus.

"I could tell you if they are on the computer," said Palage.

"I will handle anything that has to be done," said Oseph.

"There here we are and see the computer upstairs it has not been on and it never was," said Palage.

"That is good to know I never cancelled out those parts of the computer that gives children the wrong shows to watch," said Likus.

"I can get that done right now," said Palage.

"Thank you," said Oseph.

"Yes, but just that one," said Grandfather.

"Yes, you are something that makes my blood go warmer," said the Countess.

"Thank you dear and I love you too," said the Count.

"We do have something happen every night that is different and unusual with those boys," said Grandfather.

"The two of them are a hand full," said the Countess.

"We enjoyed them this evening they are a lot of fun to observe and they are boys," said Auntie.

"Why not Palage and I go upstairs and she can code the computer for us dear. We will be right back," said the Countess.

“There is our room too,” said Likus.

“Why not show me our house upstairs and Palage can code all of them,” said Auntie.

“Then why not have a drink Count some more champagne,” said Oseph.

“Good night and we love you ,” said Auntie.

“We love you too and we are glad that you are both here,” said Oseph.

“Good night, I love you dear,” said Auntie.

“Yes, good night and we love you too,” said Oseph.

“Yes, good night,” said the Count.

“Come on Auntie my man is never to intimate, he is a Doctor,” said the Countess.

“Oh, my goodness I hope I do not need an exam,” said Auntie.

“It would not be a bad idea for all of the x-ray equipment be here to help us,” said Likus.

“Then I need to move.!” said Auntie.

“No, there is not any exams here, he is my husband,” said the Countess.

“Sorry Mother,” said Likus.

“It is alright. It was humorous,” said Auntie.

“Then we can,” said Likus.

“Likus, it was not your computer,” said Oseph.

“Very funny,” said Likus.

Chapter 19

"I guess everyone had a good night sleep and we are going to have a good weekend," said Likus.

"Likus, we have a good day every day. At least I do with you," said Oseph.

"Thank you that is why I enjoy each day because of you," said Likus.

"Then we are good for each other and we have the world together right now," said Oseph.

"Yes, we do and it is better each day and we do love each other," said Likus.

"Yes, we do and we are loved by many we do have a large audience," said Oseph.

"I know and the fan club mail is always arriving it is a good thing we place the letters next door," said Likus.

"I know people still send us money regardless," said Likus.

"It is recorded and a letter is sent to them," said Oseph.

"Auntie was not upset with you and about the exam, which will not be done but she did in fact wants an x-ray," said Oseph.

"I am very sorry but it did place everyone in a position to think these tests that are done here is very good and important," said Likus.

"I know you you did not want to hurt her but she is very use to her own family of and we have to listen to what we say," said Oseph.

"Now that we have done all that is a necessary I have something that even you did not think of," said Likus.

"I know it is something that is good and grand and will help all of us, because I know you and I love you too," said Oseph.

"I love you too and tonight we are going to have a formal dinner in honor of your Auntie and Palage," said Likus.

"That is so grand and regal and the next time you are teasting your Mother I will interrupt you the same way as the last," said Oseph.

"Alright but please do tell me in case I am forgetting," said Likus.

"I will," said Oseph.

"There see how the table is arranged for us and these blue goblets are so beautiful in this gold room," said Likus.

"I will be in a tux," said Oseph.

"Very good and after you do not even have to dance for us," said Likus.

"None of you can afford me. After where do we go from the dining room.?" said Oseph.

"I think we should go to the large ball room and have chairs a small tables placed for having coffee and some couches with refreshments set up in a few places," said Likus.

"We can do that and also finally be in the largest living room on this floor," said Oseph.

"That is much better and it gives the staff a chance to clean up while we are in the ballroom the staff can get sandwiches ready in the living room," said Likus.

"Then we have seen all of the main rooms that are in gold," said Oseph.

"It all seems so wonderful and we will have some gifts too," said Likus.

"Yes and when they are ready to go upstairs you and I will be in the smallest intimate living room on this floor alone for a few hours," said Oseph.

"Good and the exspense for all of this," said Likus.

"I know it will be exspensive," said Oseph.

"So we are in the small living room just for coffee and then we are upstairs too," said Likus.

"I do not know how long we will be there.?" said Oseph.

"It will be grand the whole night and we will enjoy ourselves, this is our first group we will entertain," said Likus.

"I know why we have not had any formal groups in is because the election people we give to Paul remember," said Oseph.

"I do and they with very grateful even the Mayor of Venice showed up at the door with so many gift of appreciation and the baskets of food and did stay just for lunch that day," said Likus.

"That was very nice of him," said Likus.

"Right that is because he said, "The warm food will be ready in a few hours and he will arrive at noon," said Oseph.

"I know we have our lunch in the small dining room too," said Likus.

"Those two rooms are very nice a living room and dining room just for three or four people," said Oseph.

"It is n ice for a couple who rent out the small apartment on the fourth floor who want to have a lovely reception area for themselves too," said Likus.

"That is all very grand and it is for ourselves now and we do not need a renter," said Oseph.

"No, but we can do what the others did such as Edvard and Princess Ownsite, they rented out to a millionaire," said Likus.

" Your right maybe we can get Auntie and Palage married before the year is up," said Oseph.

"I know two people who can rent on that floor," said Likus.

"Why not my innovator who had given us a lot of money we can ask him who is Prince Soblift," said Oseph.

"Good about that young man who wanted to rent.?" said Likus.

"He is a student who wanted a four year lease and he was a Count, Count Hamesmith but did not use his title because of the studies and the popularity he mentioned could be after graduation is a must," said Oseph

"Good we can call each of our friends right now," said Likus.

"Likus they are not your friends right now," said Oseph.

"I mean you are mine and that is that," said Likus.

"That is right I would not want to get a second for myself at any time in the near future," said Oseph.

"What are you talking about.?" said Likus.

"If I can not win you back by having a fight to the finish, then I must challenge him to a duel," said Oseph.

"No violence, we would have to leave this home and Europe," said Likus.

"No, I would have to leave and then I would not have nothing," said Oseph.

"Do what everyone else has done over the centuries," said Likus.

"What is that murder," said Oseph.

"No, you pay him off," said Likus.

"Then I am thinking of the States, even housewives now have attempted to murder their husbands in public too," said Oseph.

"I know but I think they just wanted to hurt him. Also they did not have a place like this called Venice to resume their romance in privacy," said Likus.

"No they do not and do not invest," said Oseph.

"That is not good, now the court makes sure they invest in a counselor," said Oseph.

"If they do not want to speak to another then let the judge know that they have purchased a home in Europe.!" said Likus.

"So now I can not even have a duel," said Oseph.

"No, and you will be placed in prison is that what you want," said Likus.

"No, I love you and I just wanted to let you know how realous I am," said Oseph.

"I know you are jealous, you did pursue me, that is a big indicator that you are in love with me and I am madly in love with you and your dominance is real and I love you more for it," said Likus.

"Thank you and you are mine please remember that," said Oseph.

"With these renters there is just one objective to get them married," said Likus.

"We have a similar path and objective now to get these ladies married and it leads to another objective for us to have a new goal for this company to have ownership a little while longer," said Oseph.

"That is correct, that is why our talks work," said Likus.

"Yes, the talks do and yet we seem to stay in control," said Oseph.

"We will for a long time there is a sudden attraction Venice gives to the public and the media just can not get enough of Venice. Did you notice that, that we are Venice all want to know what is going on right here.?" said Likus.

"I know and we will stay for a long time and it is you who they have always wanted to see," said Oseph.

"Thank you and I hate to stop this but we are in the smaller living room and maybe someone would want to use this room to talk privately," said Likus.

"Lets go now and see who is in the living room," Well good morning everyone," said Oseph.

"Good morning do not get up and I will wait on all of you so just tell me what you want, more food.?" said Likus.

"Yes, please some more eggs," said Liker.

"There, just let me fill all of your plates. Ok, now the ham," said Likus.

"Here are the sauages," said Oseph.

"Next the toast," said Likus.

"Coffee," said Oseph.

"Juice," said Likus.

"Does any one want anything else," said Oseph.

"Does anyone want me to order anything else.?" said Likus.

"No, then ok," said Oseph.

"Everything seems to be alright," said Likus.

"I guess everyone has had breakfast in their own apartment," said Likus.

"Yes, they did," said Oseph.

"Now here is the news," said Likus.

"Baby girl is now in the force of another," said Oseph.

"Abandoned child is now a teenager," said Likus.

"Look they are both from this neighborhood and see them both I never saw them did you," said Likus.

"No, I never have and she is a very big woman," said Oseph.

"I just want to know who their doctors were.?" said Likus.

"How did they get better with the flu.?" said Oseph.

"What about the shots.?" said Likus.

"What about wanting more food some snacks.?" said Oseph.

"What about toys when she was younger.?" said Likus.

"It is a good thing no one can hear us from over here," said Oseph.

"I think the pros were.?" said Likus.

"Why.?" said Oseph.

"She would have been dead by now without the medicine.?" said Likus.

"Probably," said Oseph.

"I am going to get more coffee do not want a cup.?" said Likus.

"Yes, please and be sure we are not the only ones having that coffee," said Oseph.

"Dad, do you see the girl she lived near by," said Liker.

"Yes, that is quite a shame and she is much better now," said Oseph.

"Ok, dear go and sit with your brother and finish your food," said Likus.

"I will," said Liker.

"Excellent food," said Auntie.

"Thanks, more coffee," said Liker.

"I am ok, so how are the two of you.?" said Auntie.

"Good," said Oseph.

"I cannot complain," said Likus.

"You are alright, Auntie.?" said Likus.

"Sure I am enjoying it here very much," said Auntie.

"Good because we need you the both of you and we want you both to be happy," said Likus.

"Auntie will have a wonderful time here and we have arranged it for the two of you to have a castle in France one each in case something happens to all of us," said Oseph.

"Yes, we do and here are the photos and just where your daughter is and us too," said Likus.

"Why I am so shocked and surprised," said Auntie.

"That is good, look Palage here are your houses just in case something happens to all of us," said Likus.

"Thank you both and I could stay there for a few weeks as a vacation. Plus I could go into the University for a weekend course," said Palage.

"Good and others my follow and they are not to bother you," said Likus.

"No one will and I can drive to and from with all of you," said Palage.

"Then the real vacation trip was the Euro itself," said Likus.

"Perfect I love a train ride," said Palage.

"You know you are right," said Likus.

"That is the one reason why I go," said Palage.

"Stop that you too," said Auntie.

"It is true," said Palage.

"Stop that you both sound like babies," said Auntie.

"It is a big part of it wait and see," said Likus.

"Just remember this Palage we were going to our new home," said Auntie.

"Auntie this, then there is something we need to give to the both of you," said Oseph.

"Here are you are this is for you and here Auntie," said Oseph.

"Why it is a necklace, earrings and a new ring and bracelet," said Palage.

"Thank you my jewelry looks a bit different for my age group," said Auntie.

"Yes, thank you so much," said Palage.

"Also there are some formal gowns for you to choose please take all that you want each time there is a runway we purchase for our guests. Yes, and you will not see me in one of them even during Halloween," said Likus.

"I never do think you had the gots to do that. I remember you being in the news since you were two years old," said Palage

"No, Likus really enjoys the privacy of our existence, so do I," said Oseph.

"Maybe Mother or I can fill in when you do not want to be in the news," said Palage.

"Maybe answering to the press at the door," said Likus.

"That is good," said Palage.

"Or maybe a press room next door across from us," said Likus.

"It will be necessary and just when we do not want to quote," said Oseph.

"Good we will see what happens in the mean while how do you like, do you enjoy your jewelry and those gowns are beautiful," said Likus.

"We choose as many as we can they are all so beautiful," said Palage.

"Good there is more later on. Also I did save one gown and it is in this closet. It is all in black diamonds and I need to call the designer and maybe I need to mail it to him. See it is a rare gown, one of a kind made by Pourfuss," said Likus.

"Mother it is so elegant I remember this gown and the day it was shown, Likus there was never anything mentioned about this gown in the news after it was on the runway," said Palage.

"Good then I hope to see you soon," said Likus.

"What happened.?" said Palage.

"He will arrive tonight to take the gown, he did think I had it and I would eventually call," said Likus.

"My Dear, I hope he does not think you would keep it and you did," said his Mother.

"No, he said there are six more gowns that are in homes where they were photoed," said Likus.

"No, he had another one at a home where there was a show and he leaves them and returns only when the owner wants to return them," said Palage.

"He mentioned it was like a new car you see it drive and eventually he gets a call," said Likus.

"Just think I heard of him doing this and this time I get to see his best gown," said

Palage.

"We need to dine with him in his honor," said Likus.

"I will mention to him if I could try it on before he leaves tonight," said Palage.

"He should stay a few days," said Likus.

"Maybe there might be a show here in one of the buildings," said Oseph.

"If if gives you a yes then let the Countess help you put in on and do not sit down and ask him when the dinner is finished," said Likus.

"There has to be a mistake I called about one hour ago and here he is," said Likus.

"How are you thank you for the call and invitation," said Pourfuss.

"How did you get here so fast, Pourfuss," said Likus.

"I live in Milan for this last year I do not believe it here is my favorite client the Countess how are you maybe you can be apart of the audience I could give a show here this weekend," said Pourfuss.

"That will be fun thank you," said Likus.

"Here is a new model, I hope she can be in the show wearing this gown," said Pourfuss.

"Good then let me go to my room and I will make the necessary calls and I will see all of you at dinner I just need to rest after that unplanned trip here," said Pourfuss.

"Why sure the butler will bring you to your suite," said Likus.

"Likus you just booked this house and Palage maybe a new model," said Oseph.

"I need some water please," said Auntie.

"Here sit down here and rest for a while on the soft couch. Dad see if Auntie is alright," said Likus.

"She is she needs to rest it is a bit to warm in this room," said the Doctor.

"I know my intro was to short, but he needed to make some calls," said Likus.

"That is not it I never slept last night I was to thrilled at being here," said Auntie.

"I did not sleep either and now maybe a model is what is upsetting Mother," said Palage.

"No, but I do know you need to be on your own," said Auntie.

"We do not kow what is going to happen, lets just relax and enjoy our new guest," said the Countess.

"We will," said Likus.

"There she is alright, maybe your daughter could keep you company in your bedroom and we will see you tonight," said the Doctor.

"I should rest for a while," said Auntie.

"We will see you at dinner or if you get some sleep that would be very good too," said the Doctor.

"It is hard for anyone to adjust," said the Countess.

"We gave Auntie the beautiful gold room so I am sure she is trilled with it," said Oseph.

"She is just to tired it is an ordeal to move," said Likus.

"She is just tired and she wants me to read to her so maybe when I am upstairs she will be asleep," said Palage.

"Of course she is very tired but reading will make her relax," said Likus.

"I have ordered the ambulance to prepare the equipment in the room next to the kitchen just in case we need it today or during the week," said the Doctor.

"That is helpful Dear, I wonder if you should order the same equipment for the hospital and use and keep what is here," said the Countess.

"I should do that and have them bill me," said the Doctor.

"Will they miss the equipment.?" said Oseph.

"No, if they want to use it they will but they are getting new equipment soon," said the Doctor.

"New equipment is very good," said the Countess.

"The new equipment should be replaced within the half hour," said the Doctor.

"I am so please being your wife," said the Countess.

"Thank you very much," said Oseph.

"Yes, Father that was very nice," said Likus.

"Mother wants me to thank you for the hospital equipment that was brought to our home, and we can all benefit from it," said Palage.

"I am very pleased to do something, I am sure she will be alright," said the Doctor.

"Doctor please be seated and," said Likus.

"Thanks son that is just what I do need. My wife here sit with me and all of you have a seat we need to talk about when she is better," said the Doctor.

"She will need some rest," said his wife.

"Right and her bedroom is alright, she does not need to be moved. I think she needs to fit in and yet is not expected to work," said the Doctor.

"I agree," said Likus.

"Right, there is to much responsibility for the average person to be involved in this type of company," said Oseph.

"No, that is not it and I know what you mean she is the one she needs to watch and learn and yet does not have to be involved," said the Doctor.

"Like a certain job or aspect, we should get others to help," said the Countess.

"That is it, we do not have to include anyone who does not need to help," said the Doctor.

"We have not exspect everyone to work for us when we have family," said Likus.

"We do have many people in the right place," said Oseph.

"Yes, we do," said the Doctor.

"We will just ask Auntie if we can conduct shop and is it all right," said Likus.

"Well it is good we have this lovely house for all of us to stay in and this is the nicest to use for her health," said Palage.

"Auntie is asleep right now.?" said Oseph.

"Yes she is and I do know what you mean about the work she was very concerned about that before we left," said Palage.

"Then there is talks but do not appoint things to do," said Likus.

"No, we will not," said the Countess.

"It is good to get this out of the way but I think she is under of certain type of behavior that no one can understand while living in the states. Yet she is very happy to be here too," said the Doctor.

"That is right just look outside and we see water, I think she no long needs to worry about who is outside or at the door," said the Countess.

"Yes, there is security and yet I am very very relaxed living here, there is no one at the door and many have to call first," said Palage.

"That is it there is a lot more freedom here in Venice," said the Doctor.

"Your are right," said Oseph.

"Freedom and look at this room it is filled with gold and so is my bedroom suite and Mother's too," said Palage.

"Your right is the our environment," said Likus.

"It is and we have to go ahead and give the public something to enjoy," said Oseph.

"We have a show to do and it this weekend too," said Likus.

"Good this is the most expensive and the best show in a while since Cynthia in India which was given the best reviews," said Oseph.

"We now have a good chance of receiving a large amount of money and not all as the insurances either," said Likus.

"So we will give a perfect performance and I am so pleased that I am in the show too," said Palage.

"Good and I know you will look beautiful," said the Countess.

"You will be in the audience with my Mother," said Palage.

"I do not know, I do know that no one orders Pourfuss," said the Countess.

"In two days and it will be a great day too," said Oseph.

"It sure will. Here everyone your places and it was a fun dinner too. Palage, did your Mother have all of the food.?" said Likus.

"Yes she did and she wanted to sleep a little while longer," said Palage.

"Now there was food, naps and now the group effort or lets see what is on the news instead," said Likus.

"There is something that I need to talk about and it is about the lawyer position," said Palage.

"Sure what is going on," said Oseph.

"I am in the show tomorrow but what if Pourfuss ask if I am going to be a model fulltime with him," said Palage.

"If he does not then I will," said Likus.

"I will save you the trouble, Palage will you please work with me fulltime.?" said Pourfuss.

"Yes I will, I will I have been wanting to work as a model for a very long time," said Palage.

"I am going to tell Mother," said Palage.

"She is on cloud nine and I want you to take a lot of still and private runways and splice them in with the others say, "It is to help you out." and I will pay you when it is over or even start right now," said Likus.

"Thank you for your generosity but she will do alright," said Pourfuss.

"Mother is very pleased but she is going to stay there all night," said Palage.

"Good so now back a few things that you will want and the rest will be mailed later," said Pourfuss.

"I will and where will I stay.?" said Palage.

"I have an apartment for you someone just moved out you are right down the street from me, and not lease," said Pourfuss.

"No lease.?" said Palage.

"No lease, I own the building," said Pourfuss.

"That is ok," said Palage.

"Coffee, sandwiches and snacks lets go," said Likus.

"There all looks very fine," said Oseph.

"Fantastic," said Palage.

"Likus everything is fine and fantastic and do you know that all of this is because of you, so we have to toast you who is the one who made this evening possible," said Pourfuss.

"Yes you did Dear and Likus this is an a very special occasion because of you, so it does demands another toast to show you how grateful we are," said Oseph.

"We are Dear we love you, all of us and all of this is because of you," said the Countess.

"It is true I am right now the best model of the century and it is because of you," said Palage.

"This is true, it is a fact, we are all so grateful to be here and meet the one who is the best in the world," said Pourfuss.

"I am here," said Liker.

"I am too," said Likus.

"Me too you are my son," said the Doctor his Dad.

"Ray and my new other brother Grolate could not be here they are upstairs and they are grateful to be here too," said Liker.

"All because of you we love you we all do," said his Mother.

"The baby does even a he sleeps, Little Ose," said Oseph.

"Now you have me and and you got me at Ose," said Likus.

"I know I love you, we all do," said Oseph.

"We are all going into the large ballroom where we were and we will be waiting or just stay here we do not mind," said Grandfather.

"See here are the maids with more food and refreshments and the other food you see is brought into the ballroom as we speak so we will talk to the both of you later," said Grandmother.

"Thank you, all of you," said Likus.

"Yes, thanks," said Oseph.

"Here have some coffee and look at all of these pastries," said Oseph.

"They are great and some or are all of them homemade.?" said Likus.

"Who cares, some one of these days you can tell them but not now," said Oseph.

"You are right as always," said Likus.

"You are not, you look fine but you are all tense up here let me calm you down I will rub your neck," said Oseph.

"That feels so good but what about you, you need something to eat," said Likus.

"Will you stop, I am a big guy now and I can help myself we just had snacks a little while ago," said Oseph.

"Here is the phone, yes please do," said Likus.

"What.?" said Oseph.

"Hello, my baby," said Likus.

"Hello, baby," said Oseph.

"He was awake so I did think we could just say hello, so little Ose here we go say, "Good bye," said Palage.

"He was just change and had his bottle," said Likus.

"All done I will put him to bed and check and see if he wet first, "good night, say good night," said Palage.

"Here you go here is some Exile Champaign and a strawberry no one ate them do you see that today," said Likus.

"Likus I do know that we had them for breakfast and for quite a few days now," said Oseph.

"We did," said Likus.

"Are you finished with everything," said Oseph.

"Yes I have dad enough," said Likus.

"I have to when you went to the door I phone the Butler and all of us should have food in our food right now," said Oseph.

"Then lets go, please," said Likus.

"There the ball room doors are closed, so lets go," said Oseph.

"Here we are right in our own bedroom and there look, there is more food," said Likus.

"I know and I hear the elevator and all of them are going to there own rooms," said Oseph.

"Yes, this has been a very busy day," said Likus.

"Also draining yet very happy and very inventive for all of us," said Oseph.

"It was and it was good to see Little Ose we have been going upstairs to see him that this was the first time we have seen him on the first floor," said Oseph.

"I did show him to Auntie, I did right, I did," said Likus.

"I showed him to her and you were so busy I did not think of it," said Oseph.

"I can not correct this no matter how hard I try, I did not do anything about this," said Likus.

"I will tel you this right now we all agreed that my Aunt and cousin should not see him untill all of their things were wash again and ironed and put away," said Ospeh.

"Yes," said Likus

"I am not finished and also quite a few baths will be taken before they both see him," said Oseph.

"Ok," said Likus.

"Just like the word quarantine that same day you were not sure how to spell it," said Oseph..

"I know that much but it has been a long time," said Likus.

"It has been a long time and a very good amount of time has passed by and now tomorrow is a good opportunity for Auntie to see him her nephew," said Oseph.

"To long of a good amount of time," said Likus.

"To long of a time it is perfect for many diseases or germs to go by, so now being him in to her," said Oseph.

"I will," said Likus.

"Call Palage at her door first," said Oseph.

"I will," said Likus.

"Palage is your Mother awake.?" said Likus.

"Here I am," said Auntie.

"Here Is Little Ose," said Likus.

"I see him, now I want all of you to go to bed right now and do not worry, it was ten years ago I saw Oseph, it was when you were on the tel in Denmark," said Auntie.

"There Little Ose I will see you tomorrow, I love you and you now need to go to sleep," said Auntie.

"See Auntie understands so you were worry for nothing," said Oseph.

"Likus was concerned and it is alright no one is at fault we need our sleep so lets go to bed all of us and I will see you Ose in the morning," said Auntie.

"Yes Ose and we both will be at the breakfast table at nine in the morning Auntie," said Oseph.

"Let Ose sleep if he is not awake do not wake him," said Auntie.
"Oh, we will not good night Auntie," said Likus.
"Night," said Oseph.
"Good night," said Auntie.
"Good night, Mother," said Palage.
"Good night and congratulations again my dear," said Auntie.
"Good night and thank you," said Palage.

Chapter 20

"There good morning that was not as hard it was a very good sleep I had and all of you are ok," said Auntie.

"Yes, fine," said Grandfather.

"Good," said Grandfather.

"I am fine and I had a excellent sleep, Auntie," said Oseph.

"Good and Likus is still resting I hope with Ose," said Auntie.

"They are both asleep, and I hope for a few more hours for them both," said Oseph.

"Likus was so concerned last night with me I do love so much," said Auntie.

"He was always a very good child," said his Mother.

"Since I have been with him he has always been well mannered and fun to be with, he should be up soon," said Oseph.

"Here he is," said his Mother.

"Good morning, everyone," said Likus.

"Mother I need to interrupt everyone right now I think we should bring the children to the Chateau early we all will leave together at the end of the week," said Likus.

"I think it is about time the boys went outside and we all can sit outside too and the chateau is the place for that," said his Mother.

"We need fresh air and the only way to do that is to be in Ferance," said Grandfather.

"They need to run around we like to talk in one or two places," said Auntie.

"Right and the only way for them to run around and enjoy the fresh air is to leave on Friday," said Likus.

"Yes that way we pack a lot the food that has been cooked," said Grandmother.

"That is time enough to get the house and the other buildings secured," said Grandfather.

"It will be fun indeed. What about the show that is Saturday.?" said Auntie.

"That is another thing I wanted to talk to all of you about," said Likus.

"What is your idea.?" said Grandmother.

"We can invite Pourfuss and the models and crew to the Chateau for another show," said Likus.

"That would be very good for their careers," said Grandfather.

"It will help out with Palage's career also," said Likus.

"You are so wonderful what a good cousin you are," said Auntie.

"Thank you, Auntie. It would help her out quite a lot," said Likus.

"Yes, it would and the others too," said Oseph.

"So all leave on Sunday morning and some the crew can go ahead and be there with some of the staff after the show on Saturday," said Likus.

"Does Pourfuss know.? " said Auntie.

"I left a message at his door. Also a message on his phone too" said Likus.

"He will be here soon," said Palage.

"This is a fantastic idea of yours having another show at the Chateau," said Grandmother.

"Here is Pourfuss now the last to get up again. I wish I could sleep like you even on the weekends," said Grandfather.

"I am usually on the night shift myself, it is what happens when you have good people that work with you," said Pourfuss.

"That is quite true from what I have seen here and witnessed on the phones," said the doctor.

"You are in for a treat at the chateau I have an extra four hundred female models and two hundred males to do that show," said Pourfuss.

"Private schools.?" said Liker.

"I told you, lets go into the living room" said Likus.

"Boys be good and stay in that room there is a lot to do today," said Oseph.

"Where or what time Sunday at noon we all start out," said Likus.

"Sounds and anyone who wants to go Saturday can be with the staff. There teacher is here and he wants to take them Saturday too," said Oseph.

"Could you tell the boys and have them know and to call him before they see their teacher upstairs," said Likus.

"I think I would like to go Saturday and make sure the house is all right and maybe Oseph and you Likus sure be the last two and the baby to leave Sunday," said the Countess.

"Good," said Likus.

"I would like to go Saturday, I think I have sea legs as if I were on a boat," said Auntie.

"Thank you Auntie, That is what I did think when I moved in," said Likus.

"Maybe we should have the foundation look at," said Oseph.

"We will be away in case something needs to be repaired," said Likus.

"I will call right now I know who can look at it today and under the water too," said Oseph.

"What about the insurances.?" said Likus.

"Auntie is not sleeping on the Island itself so we can give her the boys' rooms. With the insurances, we are all covered until the work is done with the tunnels," said Oseph.

"Good then in all of these rooms, all of the buildings will be painted or wall papered. Most of the gold will be cleaned and then polished it needs it again," said Likus.

"These are the origin staff so I think they would want to stay," said Oseph.

"The Butler informed me they would only leave if the building was completed repaired and not even that would scare them off," said Likus.

"Maybe now it is a good time and the chef is ours so he will go with us," said Oseph.

"I have given him the message, then he can tell the staff and we will know if they are all leaving," said the Countess.

"It would be safer for them to be with us and leave a security guards," said Auntie.

"Your right Auntie," said Likus.

"I will still let the Butler know by phone, they do need to decide for themselves," said the Countess.

"That is correct Likus there is not a war going on and I can not up route them this is their home," said Oseph.

"Lets have some more coffee and some pastries there is going to be the security guards here," said Auntie.

"Right, I think their, here is an answer," said Likus.

"The butler let me know they are all going and one nurse needss to go to the dentist to have a tooth pulled and she is going today," said Oseph.

"So the guards will stay here," said Likus.

"Good, and now just me I would have to stay for three weeks in a row and only working on Monday and Tuesday," said Oseph.

"Alright then we will tell the children when that happens or you tell them," said Likus.

"I will soon and maybe in four weeks time and lets if I am missed at all," said Oseph.

"You could get away with it. But are the other children alright across the street ok," said the Countess.

"I will watch them and we can place them on the island after the inspection under the water too," said Oseph.

"I will call and let all of you hear and the nurse will decide watch ones go first with the nannies," said Likus.

"This is all worked out, right now as he calls that nurse in charge she is waiting for his call," said the Countess.

"Yes, allright and thank you I was just thinking of this," said Likus.

"What does she have planned," said the Countess.

"What do we all have the flu, Oseph did we not purchase a ship in the harbor.?" said Likus.

"Yes we do," said Oseph.

"Now I know why we need the miles, after we are the Euro, the tunnels and it is more relaxing," said Likus.

"We do and it is not the flu, just rare and unusual excitement ," said the Doctor.

"We can keep the ship at the chateau to use it for the staff. If they would like a large cabin for themselves then many of us will have a vacation," said Likus.

"That is a difficult decision for us, we are very spoiled," said Auntie.

"I do agree, so we will use it when the staff returns to Venice, then they will have an excellent vacation too," said the Countess.

"So, we are near the end of the first show and now the second one will begin when we are about to be enter the Chateau," said Likus.

"Ask your Mother about the staff," said Oseph.

"Mother are your plans for the staff are they liking the ship because they all do not have to be in that building. Good, then see you soon in a few minutes," said Likus.

"Why do you say, ok, then bye.?" said Oseph.

"Because we are not going to see her right away when we enter this building right now," said Likus.

"She is tending to something else, maybe the dinner.?" said Oseph.

"I do not know but here we are and what a wonderful surprise the boys are in front and the nanies have all of other children," said Likus.

"That went well, you do say they would be very quiet seeing the toys and food on top with doughnuts on the top it did keep them from making extra noise," said Oseph.

"It sure did and now that they are all seated in the dining room milk and also one doughnut is a good surprise and will not fill them," said Likus.

"What is going.? I hear nothing at all and you brought in extra hot food so that will be our dinner and the staff may have their choices too," said the Countess.

"We did spend a lot of money on food the food alone is about a thousand and the same for the desserts. That is not even the doughnuts that was separate," said Likus.

"We have a lot of doughnuts for snacks tonight and maybe at breakfast but I do not think so," said the Countess.

"I hope the silence is constructive they are all eating.?" said Likus.

"I will hug you later but do recognize the older boys and girls the two of you," said the Countess.

"Look at all some doughnuts are you going to finish your dinner, I am just being silly," said Likus.

"Here is a little baby lets bring in all the babies to the nursery and get them settled in," said Oseph.

"It is a cool afternoon so they could go in," said Likus.

"There is a lot of food and children they were just having a walk before they settle in," said Grandfather.

"That is this house, all is rested then the pleasure of elegance, especially when it was build for the enjoyment of just one person," said Likus.

"The quests and the staff are well taken care of," said Oseph.

"Right and the staff will alternate their stay with at the Chateau and then the ship," said the Countess.

"Some are on vacation so they do stay longer or how is that done.?" said the Grandfather.

"We are all staying until the work is done and it could take a few months or a year," said Likus.

"Oseph and everyone my brother Detva who lived here and sold the Chateau is about to arrive with his wife Marie," said Likus.

"Nice, my stepson will be here," said the Countess.

"He did miss the only show, all of them have left about twenty minutes ago," said the Grandfather.

"Did the crew leave and the show went on in the early afternoon so is it not going on again.?" said Likus.

"No, but Pourfuss did say he will be back before we leave," said Auntie.

"Now that he took Palage they all might return for a few times, if we have to stay a long time," said his Mother.

"Good Detva's wife is a designer and she has her own company, maybe she wants to use this building too," said Auntie.

"That would be good and letting Pourfuss use it often he might have four shows here before we leave," said his Grandfather.

"Then missing this one might not be so bad but here we are and I am finally in the building that I always wanted," said Likus.

"Yes, I took it before anyone could claim this building as theirs," said his Mother.

"We do owe you something for that," said Likus.

"A finder's fee I would imagine," said Oseph.

"That is good then we can start by giving Mother some stock," said Likus.

"I got right in the phone," said Oseph.

"Thank you for the fee. Likus. Before I forget the owners' have another place and did let me know where," said his Mother

"Ok, I will need that address," said Likus.

"Ok, what I wanted to say is all of us were quite helpful and Auntie was in the car and made sure the children were resting while she read to them," said his Mother.

"Thank you all of helped and were so good I need to give all of you something," said Likus.

"So I think all of us deserve cash or stock option," said his Mother.

"It will be cash, then they can return it as payment for the stock," said Likus.

"Very good of you," said Grandfather.

"Thank you Dad and all of you, this is what our meeting are about we tell, we decide and all are get paid. It has to be that way to divide the money and to secure all of us," said Likus.

"So now I am going to take Auntie and we are going to talk and have coffee and the both of us are not going to be disturbed until I call Oseph to let him know," said Likus.

"The staff has the food ready for you both in the room next door," said Oseph.

"Thank you we will only be a few minutes this was mentioned only when a few of us were in the room Auntie and the children were not there," said Likus.

"I would like some coffee," said Auntie.

"Here you are now, is this about Palage she could use a career with a lot of money then be a lawyer," said Likus.

"Yes, it is I want her with me and I do not want her to know that," said Auntie.

"I know," said Likus.

"I could and ask Palage on the phone in this room after we stop talking," said Auntie.

"That would be good and you need to tell her anyways and I hope I did not hurt you about the quarantine but I know it did not help your situation and I apologize," said Likus.

"That is justifiable and it is not about you," said Auntie.

"Here is an order from the top right now I will get on the phone to the head nurse, yes please to head nurse, hello, I want to let you know we are having a quarantine for those children and myself and my quests and family are not allowed to be there," said Likus.

"You know how to give orders," said Auntie.

"Yes, I am sorry that came about by having our evening meetings. But I did set the both of us up and the others right. Wait until my Mother hears this then she will know the same thing happens when we go home," said Likus.

"That is a cruel idea," said Auntie.

"I love you and if anything does not sound perfect it is because life is not perfect, until we have all under control and so far the largest and biggest babies among us who have now taken controll are those two homes we all live in together," said Likus.

"You have mentioned and explained everything now so let me talk to Palage," said Auntie.

"All right I will get her," said Likus.

"No, we will go in together," said Auntie.

"We will and how about this we will have another cup of coffee in the other room and the staff will give us this food later," said Likus.

"That is a waste of food," said Auntie.

"I know and when the staff cleans up no one will know the difference," said Likus.

"Ok, then just one cookie," said Auntie.

"Good and I will take the tray," said Likus.

"Likus you are so good to us all do you regret at all not being alone here," said Auntie.

"No, that alone time has been controlled by using my sleep time for privacy. With whatever is the brandy at night settles in and I think there should be more of everything. Then I know what is working," said Likus.

"It does take over," said Auntie.

"Right and that is why I am glad allof us are in bed. When you told us to go to bed the other night that was very good," said Likus.

"I think I can handle what goes on it is now what I realize like the quarantine is also a restriction for the others not just children and these are rules of etiquette," said Auntie.

"That is what you have mastered and we need you with us if you are silent then we know you are observing our social behavior. There will be a new title for you," said Likus.

"Thank you Likus a new one would be good," said Auntie..

"More coffee. Oseph, I sent a new rule there is a standard quarantine for the babies even when we go home," said Likus.

"It is so good you that it is reinforced now," said the Countess.

"Good choice," said Oseph.

"Yes new house and new germs and especially a new country," said the Doctor.

"Yes, here is more cookies to go with your coffee," said Likus.

"Thank you," said Auntie.

"It has just been on the computer right now a franchise was not taken over 85 of them in one state so we have them again," said Likus.

"Which one.? " said Oseph.

"The block that you put on the bottom of your record player and just as it is then it has 5 plugs and four plug in to the walls and it gives you perfect picture and color on your old set or what ever," said Likus.

"That is the one that gives color to the black and white," said Grandfather.

"No one brought them out.?" said Oseph.

"No, so I need to get the others interested," said Likus.

"Maybe the mid west couple they just received a title from Austria that is different from the ones they have been using for France," said Oseph.

"Lord Teerunderland and Lady Nollgoallift, I will ask them," said Likus.

"It seems to Princess Nollgoallift mentioned at one time she and her husbhand would never refuse Louie Paul the 18th as the future King of France and Emperor of Austria," said Oseph.

"No she would not refuse, give her a call, that is what she just said on a interview," said Auntie.

"The interview was not about the encyclical which was the topic before that and the consequences of forcement and immediate retraining due to alcoholic behavior and its treatment to the public, It has started the twin and corrections secretly," said the Countess.

"Yes, but they are titled and the class distinction is many reasons this time," said her husband.

"They are talking about the recycled come one lets go," said Ray.

"The difference is this time it is not imprisonment at all. Hello boys Ray it is about time for your bath," said Oseph.

"Good then we can snack and then go to bed," said Ray.

"I heard they are talking about something very important," said Grolate.

"Sure," said Oseph.

"That is not a franchise but we could buy it and make a better law," said Likus.

"I will give the lawyers a call and leave a message," said Oseph.

"We will use this next money that came in," said Grandfather.

"First invest as usual and then we pursue this. " said Likus.

"We will," said Oseph.

"Then we have accomplished again something worth while," said Likus.

"Why not start a police meeting and seminar for many who want to stay over and enjoy these buildings," said Oseph.

"We are in Venice, at the square a ball can be given in costume also," said Likus.

"Then we managed to get some good work this evening," said Oseph.

"We need to get charity events done it is important for the community," said Auntie.

"This really is not the land for fund raisers," said Likus.

"No, Venice did have its problems and still does except for new hospitals do we need another," said Auntie.

"No, there is not a problem right now but how about a few more and to take your time putting them in," said Likus.

"As a twenty year spand and get the land ready," said Oseph.

"Yes," said Likus.

"I know just where they should be placed," said Oseph.

"You know by its locations," said Likus.

"Yes, I do and twenty years to prepare is a good amount of time," said Oseph.

"So we take it to the committee," said Likus.

"If we did would there be a tremendous write off.?" said Auntie.

"I could ask the committee to examine the possibility towards the supplies now that I have seen the territories of Venice.?" said Oseph.

"That is why you are a Prince," said Auntie.

"Thank you and you are very gracious as a new Duchess," said Oseph.

"That is excellent now we are all with titles even the boys are given Prince as a title," said Likus.

"A Duchess, Duchess Ildegiver I do love Venice," said the Duchess.

"Auntie you are a great lady now," said Liker.

"Thank you, Liker," said Auntie.

"A Duchess, I Love you," said Likus.

"See Auntie you now have all of the boys with you," said Oseph.

"I hope so I enjoy being spoiled," said Auntie.

"Ray and Grolate did not care about their titles at all," said Oseph.

"They did think their new names would be taken away if they were bad," said Likus.

"My boys will never be bad, they will always behave themselves," said Auntie.

"Of course they will and they are always good boys," said Likus.

"They are all very good and have excellent manners," said Oseph.

"Boys have some refreshments now because there is a lot to see at this Chateau," said Likus.

"There is the jewelry building we can see that tomorrow ," said the Countess.

"We will," said Likus.

"Good I wonder just how much that room is worth," said Oseph.

"So we finally see the building for what it known for," said the Count.

"Things did not cost that much in those days," said Oseph.

"True and we all do enjoy this life," said the Countess.

"It does have its good points," said Oseph.

"Yes, this place does give us a good time," said the Count.

"Many of these buildings are quite unique for what could serve an individual or a family too," said Oseph.

"The staff is wonderful that we have and that does make a difference," said Likus.

"Excuse me, I have to talk to one of the nannies," said Oseph.

"I hope she is not leaving," said Likus.

"The nanny agreed to help herself when she needed the money but it goes to her children and not her," said Oseph.

"She is sharing the C.D. with this house. I know I am right," said Likus.

"That nannie is very wealthy and is going to give us the stock," said Oseph.

"She goes home for a vacation," said Likus.

"She loves this job and gave up another one while she lives here." ? said Oseph.

"She is a Roman Catholic nun," said Likus.

"I am shocked," said the Count.

"What dedication," said Auntie.

"She is very dedication," said Palage.

"What to do.? " said Oseph.

"Duchess and Countess I need you to talk with her and let her know you two are on her side and give her personal things that she would need and a check this one because she is us now," said Likus.

"We will go right now and visit her and we will be on the right side of this building," said the Countess.

"Be back soon, I want to know what is going to happen," said Oseph.

"You could not let here go with a fat stomach Oseph," said the Doctor.

"No, but I will give it to her," said Oseph.

"I need to call the Countess," said the Count.

"Do not worry Father, I called the convent and she is going back to her home," said Likus.

"Now she is to stay away from all of us we can not encourage anything at all," said Auntie.

"You are right and there is a few guards at the door," said the Countess.

"I know this is wrong to isolate her but if she is strong in her religion then she can get the advice from her convent as Mother Superior had mentioned on the phone," said Likus.

"I have to treat her this way she can not interrupt our lies now that I am Louie Paul the 18.th said Likus or Louie Paul.

"You are given a position by Paul himself at the Palace of Versailles," said Oseph.

"Yes, here it is in writing," said Louie Paul.

"He was quite impressed with you my little brother," said Detva.

"Detva you are here," said Likus.

"I want you to meet by fiancee, Marie," said Detva.

"Hello, I am so please that you two are engaged and that you are both here, I want you to meet my Mother, Auntie, Grandfather my for boys and Oseph my one and only," said Likus.

"Pleased to meet all of you," said Marie.

"I know everyone that this intro is not the best but we do have a lot to hear about," said Likus.

"Yes, my son is now Louie Paul of France. Hello, Detva my other son who is so busy he can not even call. For that he works very hard so I am very proud of him and I love him dearly.," said the Countess.

"Thank you I love you too and congratulations brother," said Detva.

"Congratulations," said Marie.

"We should all kneel," said Detva.

"Yes we should, I love Louie Paul," said Oseph.

"Yes, here my son this is still a throne room, let me open up the stage," said the Countess.

"I will help you, Countess," said Marie.

"It only takes one, just make sure the children are out of the way of the wall," said the Countess.

"There Likus who is now who is His Royal Highness Louie Paul the 18th now the newly son and appointed by the King of France and as the uncrowned Prince and Prince regent and with God he will reign some day as King of France, the Prince of Navarre," said Marie.

"There he looks fine Mother in his crown and the press has arrived so lets have the photos now and give them a refreshments of coffee and pastries only," said Detva.

"Right on time for this what is wrong Detva," said the Countess.

"Now it does look obvious yet I have not seen my little brother in years also you Mother," said Detva.

"I know that is everything all right with you are you ok," said his Mother the Countess.

"My second reason and I was not sent here by the King, I had an idea that as soon as Likus was in France he would be appointed King if Paul was not here in France for any unexpected visit somewhere else," said Detva.

"Countess I will tell you and you must be silent Detva is too proud to say he is here in case he takes the place of Likus and Oseph and we both live in Venice," said Marie.

"To do what work.? " said the Countess.

"The Venice project and not the tunnels in the Atlantic and only the work that involves Venice," said Marie.

"Likus might be called to Versailles this evening," said Detva.

"I know now why I loved so much and thank God your Mother could raise you all of those years" said the Countess.

"You need to make sure we go to Venice and Oseph and Louie Paul go to Versailles and right now while you stay here at the Chateau again," said Detva.

"That is right he needs to go there now just Likus and Oseph and at this present there needs to be only six children to go to the Palace of Versailles," said the Countess.

"The press is finished and he heard one of them say you need to go to the Palace and Oseph heard it too," said Detva.

"Here my Louie Paul a phone call it is Gale from Versailles," said his Mother the Countess.

"Yes we could right now and the train has been here on the grounds for the last few minutes, alright we will go to Versailles, thank you and good bye," said Louie Paul.

"We need to start right now and I just told just Detva he can watch Venice for us," said Oseph.

"Alright, he indicated we will be staying for a while," said Likus.

"Yes my lord let your Mother run this house again and Detva and Marie will go to Venice now," said Oseph.

"I hope I see you in Versailles Likus and Oseph please give a call to Palage I am sure the modeling it would be good for a few new shows," said Auntie.

"Yes, good bye," said Louie Paul.

"Good let him I do not need the commission but Versailles could still be in need a few shows and another designer who is in need of a runway," said Auntie.

"We need to go Marie just mentioned that our wedding will be in Venice in the Palace tomorrow," said Detva.

"Good Bye you two you can do whatever you want to your new home we moved out everything when we heard the house needed repairs," said the Countess.

"Now we have the news to look at," said Auntie.

"Duchess we do not have to, and all this food the staff will be very pleased to know they are here to say. That always happens when I move inland," said the Countess.

"The security guard I am sure he will appoint many before he is here to serve us," said the Duchess.

"I have a feeling that he is going to stay at that computer alone, I only saw him three times," said the Countess.

"When was that.?" said the Duchess.

"When I arrived, when you arrived and when we left," said the Countess.

"Will we see Detva again.? " said the Duchess.

"Yes, he will be here and all of us will leave for Versailles because Detva will receives his title. Then we will all leave the next day and return here. He will return with us and stay one day and he and his wife will go back to Venice," said the Countess.

"That is very promising and his wife will be floating on air, if a may say that.?" said the Duchess.

"Go for it Liker is not here," said the Countess.

"What about Liker and Likus and the others.?"said the Duchess.

"I have a surprise one the children is growing up very fast and she will stay with us with one little baby boy," said the Countess.

"That is wonderful and all the rest will be in the Palace of Versailles," said the Duchess

"That is perfect too, now I remember the security guard, oh no he will be back at all," said the Duchess.

"That is right and he did remark that he will miss you too," said the Countess.

"He did, no he did not," said the Duchess.

"No, but the Palace was of Trump Lloyd and optical illusion so maybe he was having us both," said the Countess.

"Oh, now you are acting just like the kids," said the Duchess.

"No, I am enjoying my freedom once again," said the Countess.

"Watch reminds me I have to ask you this, do you want to live at Versailles and be with your daughter Palage," said the Countess.

"No I will stay here if I was she would never work," said the Duchess.

By the way you do have a commission, I took from them before they left or would like to have a security guard as your own it will be his yearly salary, unless you to marry and you own this home we are going to give you surgery in Paris you will be eighteen again.?" said the Countess.

"No a beautiful 55 year old and married that sounds good," said the Duchess.

"With your first title what was it," said the Countess.

"Baroness," said the Auntie.

"Now you are trhe Baroness Von Likeor," said the Countess.

"Why the Baroness," said the Duchess.

"It goes perfectly with Von Likeor and all of us will know who you are," said the Countess.

"Alright," said the Baroness.

"We need a new especially the two children need to grow up in Austria it is too soon fore them to be raised in France," said the Countess.

"Fine with me and they will be models too," said the Baroness.

"We leave for Austria in the morning with the staff and children. The rest of the infants Gale wanted them in France. Said the Countess.

Chapter 21

"Hello, Likus or Paul how did Oseph take it being a French citizen. Good, now I took Auntie's money out and mine the investments made it that way anyways," said his Mother.

"Tell him about my new face," said the Baroness.

"The Baroness has a new face and the Chateau and this castle will be yours when we are not here anymore," said the Countess.

"Enjoy the Palace of Versailles dear we will not be calling unless it is urgent good bye," said the Countess.

"Good bye Mother and tell Auntie that we love her," said Louie Paul.

"That was your Mother and the Baroness," said Oseph.

"That is show business or in this case and like all of yours it is the sake or fate of the building. Just as Detva told me a year ago he was staying in Venice and did just as I am watching the tunnels in the Atlantic by computer scope," said Oseph.

"Just as I am watching our for my little Louie Paul who is gale's or Paul's child who someday will be on the throne of France," said Likus.

"You and I enjoy our position and the pay is incredible. Not bad for someone who was just working in the mud piles of Venice," said Oseph.

"Do not put yourself down when you do it in front of the children they are all laughting that is good and fun," said Likus.

"Now are you turning pro because of this building. ? " said Oseph.

"What you are the comic, I am not," said Likus

"Is it because you lost your Mother, Detva and my Aunt too because of many laws and a new building," said Oseph.

"By the way the Chateau and the building in Austria and also the money was taken out and your Aunt has her money too," said Likus.

"I did think it was deceased but it was not much and I birthday is next week so I did think I was getting a new ship a cruise ship," said Oseph.

"Cruise ship sure you can get your ship because they took their earnings too," said Likus.

"I do not need a ship and it was their money," said Oseph.

"Ok, then we can not sue and for what," said Likus.

"Look if your Mother thought of a good idea to gain some cash she did invest with us and Detva saw it too and so did I and I told you the first day you to hired me," said Oseph.

"Your right I do miss them and I do realize it was me who Gale and the others took out of Venice because I could not report to work, what type of work.?" said Likus, who is now acting as King of France.

"Gale is giving us a financial break so we are going to take after that and he is returning as King and then whomever is President at least we know there are the new tunnels in Venice and the Atlantic," said Oseph.

"You are correct," said Likus.

"The Atlantic tunnels will still go on so I will always have work and we can stay here all of our life time," said Oseph.

"We will," said Likus.

"Good now I am pleased with you," said Oseph.

"Say it is Detva, how are you, let me put it on speaker," said Likus.

"Good and I know the both you or all of you are fine," said Detva.

"Yes, the media does speak for us and yet the speaker phone lets me think that I am back in Venice. said Likus.

"Then go and call the staff and have some coffee with me, they are all knew so you will not know anyone is Oseph there," said Detva.

"Sure here I am," said Oseph.

"Receiving your friends I do not mind and you have excellent taste in large busted woman I do have to say it was exciting and a few of them," said Detva.

"It could get expensive just give them a business deal and take your own children back and then you decide and help them adopt that is what to do," said Oseph.

"It is ok, plus being quite good friends right now with the girls and my wife did not say anything so it looks as if I desainted myself already," said Detva.

"You know what to do Detva it is now acceptable yet we just wanted to take control of their fiances," said Likus.

"I know and now there is controll and of course very enjoyable too," said Detva.

"Be careful," said Likus.

"Is there anyone else who can hear me.?" said Detva.

"No we are alone just the two of us," said Likus.

"That is just the way it should be with you two," said Detva.

"Enjoying ourselves and it is just the life we want in this Palace," said Oseph.

"Good I need to go and it is fun talking to you yet we are in need of a business security reach with Gale and myself and you can both watch if you want to," said Detva.

"I am here yet they are not they are in another room. I did have reach with the tunnels in the Atlantic and all is fine," said Paul.

"First thank you Sir and here is the newest of the placed tunnels this is the last section and we will be finished soon" said Detva.

"Hello, Paul," said Marie.

"Hello Marie and hello Dep and it is good to see you are you enjoying Venice.?" said Paul.

"Yes, I am and I need to go to take care of the baby so we may talk some other time alright," said Paul.

"Say hello to the little one Edvard for me it is quite nice to see your wife and Dep they are doing fine I can see. Now I am sure you have another place for see to see and I hope these tunnels are fine and they are just being placed," said Paul.

"Yes they are and it is being lower right now," said Detva.

"The level is good and it went very well I do have to say all of that gold is beautiful and it is very distracting too," said Paul.

"We like it here," said Detva.

"Good when it ends and there is not more money to earn you both will be paid the same to watch the tunnels for a least ten years," said Paul.

"Thank you Sir I really do appreciate it," said Detva.

"Now I need to leave and you let your wife know," said Paul.

"Marie I need to let you know that we will be paid up to ten years when the tunnels are in and working by this winter so do you like the fact that we do not have to move soon," said Detva.

"I do not mind being here but with the water as a streeet when we move we will have a country castle that needs to be repaired and then we can still be isolated," said Marie.

"I know we are isolated no matter where in Venice we live," said Detva.

"Good are you finished with Emos or am I on and in with the total French government and they all can see me now," said Marie.

"No we are not on as of this time yet I need to tell you that Oseph gave them a business and received all of his own children back so I am going to so the same and I am going to make sure these couples have their own adoptive children," said Detva.

"Good I am pleased and delighted to have them live with us and so well the hired nannies and help too," said Marie.

"I guess I was, I know I was wrong and I apologize too," said Detva.

"If it happens again I suggest that at the work site make it a living arrangement there for your employees because you will live there even if you go out for a bottle of milk," said Marie.

"You are saying divorce.?" said Detva.

"No, I am saying a very expensive divorce because I need this house to raise all of them that you never thought of," said Marie.

"What if she or they could not have children.?" said Detva.

"Here is the phone and talk to Oseph and when you have the answers and all of their names of every one of those girls that gave birth for the others, then we will talk again," said Detva.

"We will not alk at all.?" said Detva.

"Here," said Marie.

"I will talk to Oseph right now," said Detva.

"Say Oseph I need a list of names of all of girls and the babies too. Wait I need to a paper to write on, what you have it all ready and you will fax it. Thanks, but it does not bye," said Detva.

"No, it is not funny, ever," said Marie.

"Thank you for talking to me," said Detva.

"Thank you getting on this phone again and buying three building for your employees, and now I can have a photo done with all my children you and I with all of them. said Marie.

"I will do it now I know of a few buildings that they can use immediately," said Detva.

"Good," said Marie.

"Now it is done and they were all notified and they all can move in now," said Detva.

"Good," said Marie.

"I hope I can stay here with you I love you and I am very sorry for what I have done," said Detva.

"You do not have to leave but I would like to be alone for a few minutes more here take Dep for a little while longer," said Marie.

"Here is a letter for today it just arrived, Sir," said the Butler.

"Thank you, PierceScore, it is yours Marie it is from the Palace of Versailles. It was sent by Paul and addressed to you.," said Detva.

"There is a notice of title for me from him as a French citizen too. Our two children also," said Marie.

"I know I need my own as a Belgium born citizen while I am on these projects," said Detva.

"Is that true.?" said Marie.

"Yes, if you want to tell the government here we are going moving to France it is, yet my business does call for a Belgium citizenship," said Detva.

"It does.?" said Marie.

"Yes, it does," said Detva.

"It is important to have an address in Belgium and certainly from the original family who started these tunnels," said Detva.

"You do have castle to live in," said Marie.

"I do and it is mine when I return if it is not rented," said Detva.

"Do you move them to a better home and I better deal," said Marie.

"Only if I like them and they are good tenants," said Detva.

"Most of the time they are given a better deal if you want to move back in," said Marie.

"Yes, I do hope you want to stay here with me," said Detva.

"I will but when we move from here we still purchase the large building with a lot of land for privacy," said Marie.

"We will and I am sure I can get the position away from Oseph because he does understand that Belgium needs to be in charge just before he is finishes," said Detva.

"Then in ten years it is finished and we move and I do not want to die from any disease you have from another, do you understand.?" said Marie.

"Yes I do and I do not have any kind of germ in me right now," said Detva.

"Ok, now just let me sleep here only a little nap for about and hour or so," said Marie.

"I can not let you do that unless it is about three hours from now," said Detva.

"Ok, then watch them in here and I will talk and rest at the same time," said Marie.

"Ok, but you are not sleeping at all," said Detva.

"Ok," said Marie.

"Ok, doctor she is out can you do anything," said Detva.

"There I have induced vomiting and now it is clear of drugs. Let me do a pregnancy test," said the Doctor.

"You can use sex on here like kissing and talking and feeling her, but I do not think you need to enter to wake up from what is a severe case of stress and denial of a woman that is having your third child," said the Doctor.

"Ok, baby and you are having my baby so wake up and talk to me we have a lot to say. A lot to say. Right here, ok, here she is, she knows me she smiled when she heard of right here. She knows what hear is,. she is smiling again" said Detva.

"Is her eyes open.?" said the Doctor.

"The doctor wants to know if both eyes are open. She smiled again," said Detva.

"Here you are drink this," said the Doctor.

"What is it.?" said Marie.

"It is inside the water and it will make both of your breasts grow," said Detva.

"I am awake you do not have to say anything else," said Marie.

"Good then I know you do not take anything it was just a hard conscious with the baby trying to make you talk it out," said the Doctor.

"That was the baby on the phone all morning long to talk to the Doctor," said Detva.

"You are so silly," said Marie.

"I know I am in love with you, you are my life. You complete me as the term goes," said Detva.

"The other term is, you had me at, inside the water, if you want I will get very large boobs for you," said Marie.

"I will get a very large house a Chateau in France today it you want to move to the main land," said Detva.

"We will do our ten years with pay and the house and land will be finished by then. Because I complete you" said Marie.

"I need to write out scripts and see you before I leave," said the Doctor.

"Ok, I know you complete me even at new boobs now so I had you at with me at a new chateau being finished," said Detva.

"You could say new boobs a new Chateau and a new baby so come too and completed this much better than before, give it a try," said Marie.

"You had me at boobs, completed me twice, now may I love you a third time," said Detva.

"Much better and now for all of us get on that phone here it is and give a call right here about that new home of ours," said Marie.

"There see it is in a message for the butler," said Detva.

"Good see the building and now with this I say it is good and out of all of the vineyards in France I am very glad you to picked mine," said Marie.

"With that total finish of that Chateau do you really want a vineyard too," said Detva.

"That is something for you to think about before you look for something somewhere that could get you into a lot of big financial problems," said Marie.

"We could watch this house from France another ten years to complete the first bottle of, "you had me at." C-h-a-m-p-a-i-g-n," said Detva.

"You did spell champagne incorrectly but in side you were thinking of me and it became a campaign I could be a military order for you, that is still thinking as a man," said Marie.

"You are my goal to pursue at all risk, to obtain my objective is to control and love," said Detva.

"Instead of for better or for worse I will leave it as do you think we could do this when the walls in our chateau are not all gold and the ceilings too," said Marie.

"There are better things to do at night time," said Detva.

"Ok," said Marie.

"The Chateau is now ours and I have even better gifts for you Exile Jewelers is going to be at the house today and you may pick what you want for here and in our homes too," said Detva.

"Thank you, I love my husband you are good to me and the children," said Marie.

"I love you too and you may buy something for the children too," said Detva.

"We do need some silver items too," said Marie.

"Good buy it all," said Detva.

"Some gold chargers and light blue goblets would go perfectly with the gold walls in the dinning too. Then gold silverware," said Marie.

"I was just going to mention you do need a fur coat maybe several old ones," said Detva.

"Right and it is cold here and in the country Chateau also," said Marie.

"We could use for the chateau all of the items for this house too," said Detva.

"We do I think that slipped by me when you said it again then I knew you wanted to spend a lot of money so we well," said Marie.

"Did I ever thank you for thinking of taking over this place and no one told you too," said Marie.

"No there would be an opening when they went to France so I visited," said Detva.

"Yes, thank you" said Marie.

"Making sure that you were with me before we started out to France," said Detva.

"Yes, I know and I would this weekend to renew my vows again like an anniversary just before dinner the two of us maybe even tonight, could you get a priest what, I think we renew as many times as we want," said Marie.

"Sure I will have the butler call," said Detva.

"Thank you," said Marie.

"Do you still want a divorce.?" said Detva.

"No, I do not remember I think I was demanding before I ever did any thing about it. I am very sorry I love you but I do not want you to do the wrong thing I need you here not in prison," said Marie.

"I am right here and when you want to be alone there is a nurse right here to watch you," said Detva.

"Are you going to look at the tunnels by computer for now on.?" said Marie.

"I will," said Detva.

"Good because I need you here with me and I can not even pick up my child I get so weak," said Marie.

"I well stay here with you but I need to tell the doctor about you being weak," said Detva.

"He is still here he did say he would be here tonight right," said Marie.

“Yes he is going to stay for dinner and then maybe he might stay over.?” said Detva.

“Good I need him here and you, you I can hold on too,” said Marie.

“Do you want anything a nice cold a soda, juice or some ice cream.?” said Detva.

“No, I do not need anything but you,” said Marie.

“I know everything is still not alright,” said Detva.

“I have you here that is enough,” said Marie.

“Thank you and I well stay and watch the computer right here with you,” said Detva,.

“That is good I need you and I can not be alone I get afraid or nervous and I do not want to be alone,” said Marie.

“The doctor will see us at dinner time, he wanted to see if the pills got you ill so do not take any more at all and try to rest before dinner,” said Detva.

“I should I do feel very tired,” said Marie.

“I just asked about getting some sleep and he wants us to talk and for you to just to rest for a little while,” said Detva.

“Ok, so what about names if a girl then Epavay and if a boy SoeDetvar,” said Marie.

“Good names we can have one of both why not,” said Detva.

“You are to silly and yet that is not a bad idea we should have asked the Doctor for a multi-birth,” said Marie.

“Maybe six or eight of them at once,” said Detva.

“Why not we can afford it,” said Marie.

“Next time first we will talk to the doctor and then decide,” said Detva.

“Sounds fine with me,” said Marie.

“We will talk in about seven months from now,” said Detva.

“Good, and we will be happier,” said Marie.

“Here is the news Likus is on the throne for a few hours to open up the tunnels to Austria and to the Hermitage from Paris as the Atlantic is finished,” said Detva.

“Now Oseph would want Venice again.?” said Marie.

"No, here is it is the new publicity is for the countries to use the tunnels to Austria to the Hermitage so the public needs to know just where they can travel," said Detva.

"Publicity just for the two new locations," said Marie.

"Yes while both dedications are separate it allows the citizens to celebrate," said Detva.

"Then what about the Atlantic," said Marie.

"He will still work for them even if it is for a smaller pay and to get more stock," said Detva.

"That is the way things again with all of those businesses. My own magazine is now with them," said Marie.

"It is good now you properly insured for the business and the clients who use yours," said Detva.

"It is good I was very ill for the days few days and my business is run without me now so I am glad I am in the control of the client worlds," said Marie.

"That s right they ask you on the phone and then a formal letter to invite you to ""their business as the clients of the modeling and world" invited you to their business," said Detva.

"Yes, it is abbreviated as "thatcotmaw "and pronounced "Batmawco," said Marie.

"Now you know they do look after your business and you," said Marie.

"Sir you have a phone call," said the Butler.

"Thank you PierceScore we would like more refreshments and ask the Doctor if he would visit us now," said Marie.

"The Doctor is asleep and wanted you to do the same or just rest a while and the Doctor is named at home Lord Frozanegood," said the Butler.

"Thank you," said Marie.

"There, what does the Doctor have a title he does not use did I just hear that," said Detva.

"Yes, who was on the phone.?" said Marie.

"Likus wanted to let me know he is Prince Likus again and that his and my Mother and Auntie were at each ceremony to represent all of us for the King," said Detva.

"I was not in the mode to go," said Marie.

"They were the only ones invited and only because they left to live in Austria my Mother always knows what to do see has many years of experience of entertaining and Auntie with her new face and name of Baroness Von Likeor is just beside herself being apart of this," said Detva.

"Gale now is Louie Paul the King of France he did not waste anytime returning even with the Euro Train to be at the Hermitage and he was home after three hours of entertaining," said Marie.

"That is his new life being able to run Austria, France and Russia and leave and have the President in government after major openings of his businesses," said Detva.

"I did think you would be the owner of this business," said Marie.

"I am only when it is sued," said Detva.

"That is correct it is a Federal governmental project. There are only insurances and only while buying the tickets and that includes the price," said Marie.

"Should me change our names when we moved into France.?" said Detva.

"We have too we want that privacy," said Marie.

"This is getting better every minute as we speak," said Detva.

"I need to rest was the other advice of the phone but I do not feel tired and this is relaxing," said Marie.

"Yes, and therapeutic," said Detva.

"It is very relaxing and coping with your selves too," said Marie.

"I need to tel you something in my Mother's grave at her burial and in her tomb where we go she is in a gold mesh to her waist and a black diamond headdress," said Detva.

"That is so lovely," said Marie.

"Yes, it is and was a Military funeral. She wore that with me when we retrieved my brother Likus from the underground beneath the Palace of Versailles," said Detva.

"When we live in France we will not mention it and let someone else do that," said Marie.

"Why.?" said Detva.

"Because that was her gift when she died," said Marie.

"There will a duplicate made up for you and you will wear it in the gold living room and you will be on the front cover of your own magazine," said Detva.

"I will not," said Marie.

"Yes you will for an advertisment of your own business, life and home," said Detva.

"Ok, you win and you are right so then we have a picture of the two of us and then with the children," said Marie.

"It is a deal and I want to get paid and so are the children you need to take," said Detva.

"Even for the jewelry.?" said Marie.

"Yes, then you can own by an outstanding loan," said Detva.

"Then I only call it in when there is a law suit," said Marie.

"Right and it works for you, they give you a small check each month," said Detva.

"Is this what Louie Paul has done for him in Versailles.?" said Marie.

"For small accounts and lots of checks small checks for spending during the week," said Detva.

"So I can ask for the total profit too and give them stock.?" said Marie.

"You can ask for the total now because you were on the cover but for the stocks you need to own the Versailles patent," said Detva.

"I did not know that and now I do," said Marie.

"The Palace and its grounds too because you are taking not earning," said Detva.

"If I do great things with this magazine I could give it to the Versailles company," said Marie.

"Yes, with the final ownership, yes you can," said Detva.

"I still own so I could make a fortune and still be in charge of the production too," said Marie.

"You can be in charge of all of the business for a certain amount of years and have a lot of creative people working for you," said Detva.

"You did work and was in charge of Versialles at the same Chateau and you lived doing creative work too," said Marie.

"Yes, for Venice there is a creative work shop in the square using a very large building to work in," said Detva.

"What is done there.?" said Marie.

"We still are drawing the cars to be use in the tunnels and the interior as well," said Detva.

"Do you see the front hallway and doors and ceiling too it is in gold yet a very beautiful red gold," said Marie

"How about using that red gold and making the cars a rolls and in fact both would complement everything and everyone.?" said Marie.

"You are hired is there anything here that would get the interest of the designers for the autos as well as its interior," said Detva.

"See the chair right near you, it is already your top of the car out so put it on its side," said Marie.

"This way.?" said Detva.

"Yes now come over here I want a kiss," said Marie.

"Ok, here it is," said Detva.

"Good, now look while you are kissing me and see the new roof," said Marie.

"Ok, now I see it that was fast," said Detva.

"That is for sure and that short kiss I do not mind now give me the camera and when I say put the chair back the way it was, do so please," said Marie.

"Ok, just few more pictures. Now place the chair back directly in front of me the way it was," said Detva.

"Now get over here and look at your new chair seats. Also place the other chair near it but on its side. Ok, place it now next to the other one for a picture of both, now I have enough pictures," said Marie.

"Finished," said Detva.

"Yes, now see the seat," said Marie.

"The front and back, say the front it looks like a dolphin," said Detva.

"Right and now with the computer see how we take off the round part and its mouth is open and it is a new design and appears helping the person as they sit and rest their neck too," said Detva.

"Now see what I do with its rounder part of the dolphin's head or shoulder I do not know what you would call that part. Not that it is gone just seeing its open mouth with this new logo it is a name.?" said Marie.

"I see it, you are a genius it took up all of the space you clear away from its face and neck and you put in letters filling it up with the name Gale Ets Marie," said Marie.

"Right Gale on the top with ts floating with Marie all in capitols too underneath. Making sure all of the space was filled, you are mine forever," said Detva.

"Not quite I think he has something to say about right now," said Marie.

"He is growing," said Detva.

"Now see the difference of the drawings.?" said Marie.

"Yes, but what about Louie Paul.?" said Detva.

"Here is a picture of Loitering see the door we take it on a clear background and now enlarge the top of it and then place Louie then Paul underneath," said Marie.

"A genius I love you we care going to work here with me all of the time," said Detva.

"See now add the letters in gold and make it very fancy and now it French calligraphy see. ?" said Marie.

"Now there is a logo with the Palace Of Versailles its Fleur de lis so we put it on the doors to the Venice tunnels too for we now see it done with old calligraphy French style," said Marie.

"Their we have it all completed, you have given us the right to run the entire business as the people still run their part of the work like Oseph and the Atlantic tunnels," said Detva.

"There now you do not want any part of the Atlantic project right.?" said Marie.

"No, he has that and there is enough money for them both," said Detva.

"You would take over if something happened to Oseph the reason why is each of the employees have their own journal or files a book to allow all of the other employees," said Marie

"That is perfect we are gaining control," said Detva.

"Right and to see their work now it would look like this a journal with a cover for each file as this is in the computer. I can do that according to positions or titles in order too," said Marie.

"I love you, we are on our way to success in this business and to gain control," said Detva.

"Thank you and I love you too now see here is the cover the logo and then it is Gale or Paul is first and his story then his wife then children and then the business a discription and then its family of employees," said Marie.

"Here is the phone you give this to Paul with his coronations too and of the recent Austrian and Russian mergers of the Euro train and show him in the Hermitage too," said Detva.

"How is it all to you on that computer so far," said Marie.

"I love this and we are next in the line of control and Likus and Oseph are featured just before us so they will not be up set," said Detva.

"Good we will send it off now to Paul," said Marie.

"Wait if you were to say that fast, you would say sent it O Paul right," said Detva.

"Right then we can give him at the end of the book the "Opal he is our Paul and gem too," said Marie.

"See the second page," said Marie.

"Perfect," said Detva.

"Opal is our gem," said Marie.

"We own our castle, when he ask which one would we like.?" said Detva.

"We do enter the business getting all of that money so we will purchase it," said Marie.

"I love you I do," said Detva.

"Here is the result, a positive from Paul, you and I now are in charge of the entire operation includes the Atlantic and the Pacific oceans," said Marie

"Perfect," said Detva.

"True and also while Oseph is using the computer to observe the tunnels being placed in both regions the Atlantic and the Pacific," said Marie.

"That is ok. I can convinced them there should be another set of tunnels," said Detva.

"That is perfect we need the money and they should have another set of tunnels and we can always visit the castle," said Marie.

"Thank you for being on my side," said Detva.

"If you stray I will leave," said Marie.

"I need you, I will not stray we now have to much to loose, look our own accounts," said Detva.

"One trillion between us both here is what I am going to do, see it is now invested and will mature in a 30 days," said Marie.

"Good and the second one stays and that will be mine," said Detva.

"Right but we have to invest again and again," said Marie.

Chapter 22

"There we have all the money we need and now we can enjoy this house we have purchased it and all of the land around us.We are in a good ten blocks from our own closer neighbors," said Detva.

"It is good that we gave a home to each of the staff so the neighbors will not ever object too, to many empty blocks of buildings," said Marie.

"Right the empty ones are right next to us and yet we do use them for many good reasons. Such as our own computer house and electrical also" said Detva.

"It is good for them to have a home each of them having their own space and we will make sure the taxes are very little," said Marie.

"Right and we will pay most of it is a write off anyways," said Detva.

"We will show them how about the taxes and why it goes up without a will and we have to approve of it too," said Marie.

"Good," said Detva.

"Now it has been terrific for the staff when we installed the electrical generator in one of the buildings." Marie.

"Yes, an new electrical system that was so powerful it took care of all of Venice and now we have the city to maintain it," said Detva.

"Right and only our ten blocks do not have a bill," said Marie.

"We were sure the electrical system would make a difference with the castle and yet we could include all of the villages near us," said Detva.

"The small deduction in price for the power did make a difference to all," said Marie.

"We were very fortunate for that to happen again right after Venice, this city has been good for us," said Detva.

"Did you know that Versailles the generator is only to take care of their own and the city was been given over thirty generators over in three years and they are going to add more," said Marie.

"Pay back time is expensive in a city," said Detva.

"Speaking of pay back I know we have four children and thank you for that very large check to be all mine," said Marie.

"Yes, you told me to wait until it was check number ten so I did," said Detva.

"Right and now I can say the second one is for the children. They seem to be happy at the new boarding school and now just one is here at the pre-school little Gale," said Marie.

"You always seem to loose count of your stipends, Gale is five," said Detva.

"I am not loosing count at all I just wonder how it is going to be with these new twins in eight months time," said Marie.

"You are having more I love you so much that I will have to consider them just as number six only," said Detva.

"It does seem as if we are loosing one or two," said Marie.

"No we just did not name them they use their last name as their first with the boy and the girl," said Detva.

"The rich we were given before her father died is a part of this house and will be now that she is adopted," said Marie.

"What I really like the best is when we had one child to many and we decided to change our name and live in France for three months," said Detva.

"That was a good vacation," said Marie.

"The turning point in our lives is when we controlled the world and anyone watched us," said Detva.

"It was nice for you to let them know your name is Ets Marie," said Marie.

"Right and you must give yourself a pat on the back for calling the entire situation to similar to ours eventually," said Detva.

"It is now and a very good reason for it many are now in prision and enjoy themselves for not harming anyone at all, and I love you for that very much," said Marie.

"Thank you dear I needed that," said Detva.

"You had me at and completed too but I needed that too to get wear I am today, with so many children I do know what I need," said Marie.

"Marie Ets Marie there is now way to win it until there is just us together," said Detva.

"So many words do conquer," said Marie.

"Then here is the newest, as a matter of fact here is just what you need right now exactly one hundred of them," said Detva.

"Exactly gift wrapped in a large box," said Marie.

"Yes, and now in a few seconds you will see a large gold box as a jewelry gold box that is real gold and it is materialized too," said Detva.

"You are winning so far," said Marie.

"It has one hundred little sections for all of your tools or rings that are yours before this becomes mine with my rings inside it so I did win again," said Detva.

"I guess so, I guess so, I guess so with all of us answering you and not all at once either," said Marie.

"Thank you, thank you and thank you I won," said Detva.

"Yes you did, yes you did, yes you did and I am out of breath," said Marie.

"Yes, Yes, Yes," said Detva.

"Speechless," said Marie.

"Good," said Detva.

"I need some carrots," said Marie.

"Solid," said Detva.

"Solid and long and with some dip too," said Marie.

"Then I will ring," said Detva.

"So there is no give me a kiss ring.?" said Marie.

"You have them both all ready," said Detva.

"You mean to say there is a hundred rings in this gold box.?" said Marie.

"Solid gold yes, yes, yes," said Detva.

"Ok, truce you won, won, won," said Marie.

"I love you and I did not mean to hurt you at all. Am I forgiven," said Detva.

"Yes you are, it is just uncomfortable with these two," said Marie.

"It will be soon and then we will hear them crying for food and warm and we will get sleep the nannies are very good," said Detva.

"That is the truth we do have excellent staff with us. We will keep warm and enjoy even a cry for hunger now sit here and we can look at some rings," said Marie.

"Alright you will not be disappointed all of them are spectacular," said Detva.

"Please given me a few and open them ok," said Marie.

"Sure here is one wear it and I will open another," said Detva.

"That was interesting a new day and sun shine but what is that," said Marie.

"These rings will tell what is going on if I was not hear you show the police and they will know by the staff and cross bones and skull you are being poison by an employee," said Detva.

"You should be using these rings in Russia not me, or some other place not me," said Marie.

"Here is another a spool of thread, needle and nimble you have to look at it this way," said Detva.

"It is mine but no the other," said Marie.

"Yes it fits you not me and when Ed my Dad died Princess Chardinrey my Mother had to run the business then I took over it for her," said Detva.

"Ok, then show me another if I have to go to Russia," said Detva.

"Thank you my dear because this is business," said Detva.

"I will say it right now if you leave me alone and or die I am not going to like you any more," said Marie.

"You may hate me right now but my Mother was in charge the day Ed died," said Detva.

"What did you do.?" said Marie.

"She worked a little and then I took her place running the business while she had her last child by my father, Her pregnancy was not easy at the end either," said Detva.

"I heard that I think you told me. She did date a boy friend or someone who had left her alone while she was married to Ed, right," said Marie.

"She saw him and they agreed to leave each other after a few visits. Here is a ring that you will enjoy it is a birthday ring for a child just let the staff see it," said Detva.

"Then they will make a cake for all of us. We might go to Russia for a vacation and we can get a lot of good service with these rings," said Marie.

"We should but not all of these rings are for out of the country," said Detva.

"I know but I just want a very long time living with you is that all right with you.?" said Marie.

"It is fine with me," said Detva.

"That is so good to hear. By the way how many rings are for living right here in Venice.?" said Marie.

"There is only fifteen but they are the very expensive ones because this is a gift to you from me," said Detva.

"Ok, I will be brave until I find the brave ring," said Marie.

"It is best to try to be brave and lets think of good things we have and why we enjoy each other," said Detva.

"I know you are right and my babies are talking to one another and I am in the middle too," said Marie.

"Then we must talk about all of the good things we have done and just wear these two rings for now," said Detva.

"My rings, alright," said Marie.

"These look good on you," said Detva.

"They do look nice and I remember having our photos and how the public was amazed with you had the police remove them from Versailles when it was in the small apartment, near the Hall of Mirrors," said Marie.

"I know I got them into Switzerland and it was cut and delivered here all in three days," said Detva.

"Now it is worth a good, nearly a eighty million I am sure I was not going to show my face again and I did," said Marie.

"This is the way we earn our money now and the media does pay when their press announces the wrong thing in public," said Detva.

"You are right even how small it maybe," said Marie.

"We will and we have to even if it means we control all of the media," said Detva.

"That would be hard to do with the harmful information in the press today," said Marie.

"Things will be grand and again thank you for the gifts and I know a gold jewelry in the shape of a tool box is something you do not want to have so I will take it and it will be in my jewelry closet for anyone to see," said Marie.

"Thank you we had a great evening and it lasted until the late night hours and the Doctor is leaving this morning so I will say good bye and I will return," said Detva.

"No, I will go down stairs but we can take the elevator together," said Marie.

"Alright we will," said Detva.

"There that was a good ride and a safe one and very quiet too," said Marie.

"I know I put in a new one for each of the seven we have," said Detva.

"It was very good to live across the canal in the many buildings that we used for it was very quiet for all of the work that was done," said Marie.

"There was very little to due except for the updates and the columns under neither the buildings have extra steel plates to place on the top of the columns," said Detva.

"I know it was quite amazing seeing the workers put them in," said Marie.

"The column is one piece and the top is still permanently there and then an extra section goes in and it is sealed inside," said Detva.

"You did say the first steel forms were removed and one larger one is in its place was more protection if the water leaves us for a while," said Marie.

"Yet it never will that and the steel can never be seen anyways," said Detva.

"It was a good special on the tel too," said Marie.

"It was and it won a lot of awards too," said Detva.

"I need to tel you I just listened to the messages that were approved of so yours is very good one not Paul or Louie Paul or Oseph who won last year but you are going to receive a the Humanitarian Award for help a nations," said Marie.

"Me," said Detva.

"Apparently you get the award for the tunnels to being placed the second time with its affective auto systems too," said Marie.

"I quess that has made my career as an engineer a success," said Detva.

"There is more the University of Versailles and three other major Universities such as Russia, Austria and in England want to give you degrees as Honorary Degrees in Doctor of Science, Engineering and the Protocol Displacement Criterion Degree is for your work in Human Rights," said Marie.

"It is just to unbelievable," said Detva.

"Science is in Austria, Engineering is Moscow and England is Human Rights and last Versailles is for Public Relations," said Marie.

"Do I have to be there.?" said Detva.

"No, the Universities want a speaker, to allow the students to see how important it is not to leave the work place," said Marie.

"Who is going.?" said Detva.

"Detva junior who you approved of and out of all the young adults six are going to help him out and they are going to stay with Urnlee," said Marie.

"Who did all of this planning.?" said Detva.

"Detva junior he wanted to go out of respect and the fact is you and I did not leave until the ten years are up, which is another he wants to be trained so we can visit and finally live in France.?" said Marie.

"Yes, tell him to report tomorrow and I will be there and if a problem when he needs some verification," said Detva.

"That is what he wanted me to say and I let him go there today," said Marie.

"Good so now someone else has a chance to get a slight fortune so we need him to be here for the meetings too," said Detva.

"He is a very husky guy I think he should allow us to have him here with us when he is in the mode and just the three of us per meeting," said Marie.

"Right he can attend when he is on the computer even while working if he wants too," said Detva.

"Then it is a deal.?" said Marie.

"Yes, it is," said Detva.

"Then you made your first error," said Marie.

"Why.?" said Detva.

"Because he is your adopted son, a young adult who is 16 and trying to please you as his father," said Marie.

"Then giving him a position and a check each month and stock I still have to think of him not as a deal is a gift from someone else," said Detva.

"Right and he does not know them and they could not take good care of him," said Marie.

"What about not being in the right place at the right time," said Detva.

"I think as your work is concerned he respects you and wants to do the same thing that you have done," said Marie.

"It is hard work and yet being at the work place I still need to see the computer at all areas of my work it needs to be viewed several times by others and several frames per minute," said Detva.

"This is what he sees and knows and enjoys as a career," said Marie.

"Something as working hard as a meaningful career," said Detva.

"Right, which lead you to me, the replacing of your brother Likus you saw that and now there are four Doctorates too," said Marie.

"I just never did think anyone was paying attention and I was so busy wanting this position and at a good opportunity too I forgot that I am on the tel too," said Detva.

"Everything is perfect with that statement too but the words when are carefully placed they mean just what is declared," said Marie.

"What was needed.?" said Detva.

"Anyone was giving any attention towards me. It is called being human and we do not have anyone invading our privacy, so we should know how to deal with every one or everything," said Marie.

"You are so much better at this," said Detva.

"A lot of this is being very tried and out of practice and it is true woman are now in the media and at first the Europeans did become ruled by men first," said Marie.

"Please explain out of practice.?" said Detva.

"Your penmanship, writing is first then understanding by reading, with writing or just printing a letter again and again of the alphabet and then to corresponded with someone can be done with ease," said Marie.

"Being to tired does make the handwriting unmanageable," said Detva.

"There it is and especially the printing that is needed first," said Marie.

"Thank you, I will give this exercise a try," said Detva.

"Perfect and here is the check from Lalure she has indicated that our weddings and vows here and in the Hermitage," said Marie.

"There is a problem.?" said Detva.

"No, there is a Lloyd's adjustment for her to distribute and she has been given a large amount of money for us and the others," said Marie.

"That is a large check we can actually split it," said Detva.

"Yes split it and invest and then invest again for this money will eventually be the size of our first trillion together," said Marie.

"Wise and beautiful," said Detva.

"That is because of our love and the fact is you are strong and handsome," said Marie.

"This will make money as we have a different accounts but the investment is using all of the money together at once to make a largest sum possible," said Detva.

"Then we invest again and again because once we are in France we might be over looked," said Marie.

"We will invest and invest that is why I did by jewelry for you and always will in case we have to leave immediately we can travel light," said Detva.

"We can give it to our own Exile jewelers to sell," said Marie.

"The most important at that time will be our wedding rings," said Detva.

"Now here is something that you would what to know, there is a new gear for machinery equiptment that has a restoration, if you want to have a better and new one," said Marie.

"It is an automobile of all sizes and it looks as if its design is the way it is put together," said Detva.

"It is like a foreign investment they make only about 2 hundred a year and you are their clients for life," said Marie.

"I know you are thinking the same thing that I am," said Detva.

"Now wait do not tell me now wait ok I give up it is for boys and men using trucks so what is it," said Marie.

"I will give them the rights to use our auntos that are used in the tunnels and they will get three autos and decide what to do for Venice," said Detva.

"I would never want to have to think of that or guess on something that I can not give an answer," said Marie.

"Sorry no more hard questions to answer," said Detva.

"That is why my sentences are long I am thinking for three more. Or maybe four," said Marie.

"I am sorry you know I would not do anything to hurt you," said Detva.

"I know and you may think for me too," said Detva.

"Ok, then I will but right now you are on your and own you are a big boy now," said Marie.

"Where did you hear that.?" said Detva.

"I worked for many lawyers babysitting and I learned and ask questions," said Marie.

"I knew you worked babysitting but I did not know there were lawyers too," said Detva.

"Yes and a few teachers and doctors too," said Marie.

"That was quite an education," said Detva.

"Yes it was and I would only ask a question about the law when something happened," said Marie.

"Excuse me Sir, there is a phone call for the both of you," said the Butler.

"Thank you, here you are dear, please," said Detva.

"Yes, why Paul, I cannot believe you called.? Yes I will tell him and give our best to Duless. Yes ok, good bye," said Marie.

"What did he want.? said Detva.

"Oh, by the way your answer is here they are going to work on the plans for your approval for the new autos to be used with the tunnels," said Marie.

"Good and Paul," said Detva.

"Paul wants us to be in charge for a long time but he can not promise anything so he wants us to invest and there is a new Exile account is for us and here it is," said Marie.

"Let me see, ok," said Detva.

"I can tell you, added to the scource it indicates with apppreciation and taking control of his Venice project," said Marie.

"I am appreciated, we both are," said Detva.

"A new memo, it indicates we are together on this so there is a smaller check for me and a land deed in France and a home in Newport, Rhode Island," said Marie.

"I want to know where Likus Father is I hope he did not move to Europe," said Detva.

"He has moved to Moscow and is in the Hermitage it was his promotion and Likus does not care and I guess this is why they are in Versailles," said Marie.

"Then my brother will not call on Likus in Versailles, I bet Paul has given those two boys their own army as security guards," said Detva.

"They will learn how to controll themselves with anger issues," said Marie.

"That is one good thing they will grow up being men and solders too," said Detva.

"Then if you are worried you must give the boys a vacation time here in their own house and if his father is in France they can live here and stay at the chateau later on when he leaves," said Marie.

"Here is his call from the Hermitage right now. Hey brother congratulations on your promotion," said Detva.

"So that was short, just to say a few words," said Marie.

"Right and I left him know to stay there and do not see Likus at all wait until he is an adult and visit with his children," said Deta.

"Now he will because that is good advice and it seems as if he wants to work I hope if he has listened to you," said Marie.

"I hope so because that is what it will take for them to get back together," said Detva.

"I know. Yet Likus did repel from what I heard," said Marie.

"Yes, he did and his father did let him leave," said Detva.

"Likus will decide," said Marie.

"He will. I just hope everything will be alright," said Detva.

"Now that everything is fine I want to know if you would like too," said Marie.

"Everything is all right," said Detva.

"I know," said Marie.

"We can just rest it should be more calmer for you and you do need to rest do not worry about me," said Detva.

"Ok, then lets just rest or even sleep and day has just started," said Marie.

"It has and we can go outside and take a few minutes of some fresh air," said Detva.

"No, I was just thinking of how Paul waited for Likus and Oseph to be in France and then before they new it, they were both living in Versialles," said Marie.

"He did wait for them both to be on the grounds of Versailles then he gave them the press and the publicity did the rest for they did stay," said Detva.

"That does not happen to us Likus received a very big honor to represent France and Paul's son if anything happended to Paul," said Detva.

"I know even now Duless has a little boy that will look up to Likus some day," said Marie.

"Yes he will and Likus is an appointed protectorate," said Detva.

"That will keep all of us out of there I mean out of Versailles so your Brother is going to stay in Moscow with his wife," said Marie.

"You got that right," said Detva.

"He is not going to France he does not want to loose that position it is all very clear to me now," said Marie.

"Now we have just what we need," said Detva.

"Then when Likus and Prince Oseph with in the Palace of Versailles you know right then you had a new job in Venice. You did right.? " said Marie.

"Yes, I did and I also know that Likus was needed and that all of us were not going to stay after that reception. My Mother left immediately for Austria" said Detva.

"Then there was an award for Paul and she was right there too," said Marie.

"She know she should go to Moscow too and arranged being at the Hermitage for Paul. Not me or Likus just Paul," said Detva.

"That's right, King," said Marie.

"None of us would have what we have now if it was not for Paul," said Detva.

"I really did not know what was happening before I knew it we were living in Venice that evening," said Marie.

"I am very sorry for that but that is working for people who own franchises. When buildings go up to sell a product, people move with these buildings too," said Detva.

"They do.?" said Marie.

"We do and so does the little people who want to get up there and live and make good money," said Detva.

"What is the difference between us and fast foods and autos.?" said Marie.

"A person selling airplanes and catering to his clients can earn a great deal of money as a very important type of automobile he might have a problem," said Detva.

"We know there is a luxury airplane that seats the family and has their dinner the auto is still a fast way of transportation but with the plane there is walking inside," said Marie.

"Still no bathrooms in an automobile just in long distant sleep overs," said Detva.

"Sleep over and we can still use the auto with a second floor," said Marie.

"I do not think those small vans will have that," said Detva.

"I know a big problem in a small auto does provide us with adequate protection just another diversion causing bad driving," said Marie.

"You have heard of objects hitting the driver from the sky maybe going under a bridge and someone throwing an object is a fact and truth," said Detva.

"That is why there are diapers too," said Marie.

"Good to know so we can not have a new auto systems," said Detva.

"No, I quess not so we are up against something that no one else has a severe need to get our own franchise and we have been hit in the face on our first try," said Marie.

"We can but I remember how the others did their work first all of them surprised the public by writing a book," said Detva.

"We can write our own and then share a book.?" said Marie.

"I would like it if you would write the book first," said Detva.

"I will and I will start out mentioning how my ideas and our own franchises were giving me a lot of trouble," said Marie.

"Ok," said Detva.

"But it was easier to have my baby before my ideas got any worse. See I typed just what I said a few seconds ago," said Maric.

"Ok, that is good and creative," said Detva.

"It is a good beginning for a book," said Marie.

"Yes it is," said Detva.

"Now I am on my own and I will just type a few lines until I am done for the day," said Marie.

"Do not get tired," said Detva.

"When I am tried I will quit," said Marie.

"Good and I am looking at the tunnels and how they are getting along placing them into the water," said Detva.

"Alright," said Marie.

"There the last hour is finished and they work together as a team," said Detva.

"Now you are finished," said Marie.

"No, I can help Oseph watch the tunnels on the other side being placed. When he signals then I should help," said Detva.

"Nice overtime.?" said Marie.

"He gives me his stock," said Detva.

"I like that, very nice and perfect of you to buy in too," said Marie.

"It is a good idea and I am very pleased with his choice of payments," said Detva.

"Good and I am sure he is delighted about you working with him, too," said Marie.

"All in the family yet we both qualified for this work," said Detva.

"I know and no one else has ever objected. Not even Likus," said Marie.

"He would not do that," said Detva.

"Of course not he has a good thing now and so do we," said Marie.

"Your right I do and it is you," said Detva.

"You are my one reason why I am here," said Marie.

"Our children are the lucky ones," said Detva.

"I am the lucky one too because you made sure I was right here Detva," said Marie.

"All of you here are grateful to me and I am very grateful to Paul for he is the one who started the business," said Detva.

"He was the one who started the tunnels on Connecticut's Interstates I-95," said Marie.

"He put in sleep on the Interstate at each exit there was is a building. The inside is for the woman and the man are on the outside towards the shore," said Detva.

"Then he wanted Ed to ask his son to put in the tunnels," said Marie.

"Right the sleep was on good faith showing the people Versailles was again there for the citizens of the United States," said Detva.

"Now Canada and Mexico too," said Marie.

"We sound like a comercial," said Detva.

"Let me see if it came out all right and if we are going to use it," said Marie.

"What you had us on film.?" said Detva.

"We always are," said Marie.

"We did nothing wrong right," said Detva.

"It is erased as we speak, that is why we did nothing then I knew we had a chance to have a commercial for France," said Marie.

"Why a commercial.?" said Detva.

"Why not we are honest and we should let the peole know he is responsible," said Marie.

"I did think Paul wanted the press to do the wrong things.?" said Detva.

"He did and he had years of that," said Marie.

"Ok, then label it now with both of us right now we will say." Hello," to Paul," said Detva.

"Hello Paul I know you will be pleased when you see this advertisement for you it is a new approached of having the press on your side," said Detva.

"That is right and justifiable Paul we are for you and we are determined to make sure the world gives you the credit you deserve, so stay in and enjoy yourselves and please double your security. We love you both and say, "Hi." to Duless for us, "Good bye," said Marie.

"There a message is on the tape and here is the second tape made and I will look at it and you send the message ok," said Detva.

"Yes I will and I am going to call Duless just to let her know and to see the tape, there it is sent," said Marie.

"That is finished and I see you have talked just a few words," said Detva.

"We have an agreement when it is work we do not stay on the phone," said Marie.

"It was Likus who could talk to them both," said Detva.

"That is a good observation," said Marie.

"Paul did not make a decision that Likus would be living in Versailles at that time," said Detva.

"He did however wait until he arrived which made anyones life different," said Marie.

"We do not regret it," said Detva.

"You are my hero and genious who did the right thing for everyone do you know that.?" said Marie.

"I do now and I like it," said Detva.

"My hero and I have a very secured feeling, that I have all of the time when I am with you," said Marie.

"It is also called love," said Detva.

"I like to call it being with Detva," said Marie.

Chapter 23

"Good morning it is a good day today," said Detva.

"Here you are, another day another reason to live my search is over I have the love I want," said Marie.

"Me too and I have love for and now I love for me," said Detva.

"We share and we enjoy life," said Marie.

"We do and we will always now with that I have photos and films of the completed house or Chateau in France here is the kitchen," said Detva.

"The living room I like very much, the furniture is beautiful," said Marie.

"Most of the furniture is there and it has been repaired and polished," said Detva.

"The kitchen is absolutely beautiful," said Marie.

"There is a preparation room on the other side," said Detva.

"Still very elegant and so is our bedroom look at those windows," said Marie.

"That is the bedroom of your new wing," said Detva.

"I do want to stay with you," said Marie.

"You will I have a large room myself there is another suite of rooms for us together that is very large for two," said Detva.

"Thank you we will make sure to use our own suites to place our clothes and jewelry," said Marie.

"Our own suites are for storage for your minks, jewelry and shoes," said Detva.

"That is good and the every days thing are with us," said Marie.

"It did take a few weeks with an enormous amount of money did you get it insured for a specific time frame," said Marie.

"Yes, if it was not done in four weeks then we would not have to pay all of the cost," said Detva.

"It was done in five.?" said Marie.

"It took five week and two days," said Detva.

"They did that deliberately.?" said Marie.

"Yes, they did," said Detva.

"Do they do that for all of their clients.?" said Marie.

"No, I was the only one who used Lloyds's for that reason," said Detva.

"Then it was a good deal," said Marie.

"If you wanted the dining room in a very pale aqua marine gold then that would take some time," said Detva.

"Then if I want a bathroom, bedroom or living room done in gold it will take some time," said Marie.

"Yes, it will," said Detva.

"Good then we do have empty of time and I am glad we painted and wallpapered everything anyways," said Marie.

"It at least looks finished so it give a good impression for the next people to work there," said Detva.

"I agree and we need to have this house completed perfectly so we do not get discontented," said Marie.

"I have a call, then and I listened to likus he whas indecatied that he was not intoxicated and remember you are still an inspiration to them as Paul is who did all of their work alone," said Marie.

"That is nice," said Detva.

"No one else was there with you and they both appreciate what you and Paul have done," said Marie.

"This is another reason why Paul did what he did he waited for Likus to show up at Versailles," said Detva.

"He also could not be at the phone to long and he wanted to let you know how much you are to him," said Marie.

"See that is how Paul thinks, he knew I was not getting to many hugs and he does know I did not want any," said Detva.

"You are so bashful and manly you just only show me affection and thank God I do not have to ask you," said Marie.

"I know it is not anything to do with them or any man I just had given hugs and kisses to my cousins when I was younger and all of them were girls," said Detva.

"It is a custom and when anything happens to make a difference then we are unsure and men are always uneasy with anything it is part of the hunt and safety," said Detva.

"Not to get off the track but are we going to give ourselves new names or was that just being in the Hermitage and Versailles," said Marie.

"It will be in those buildings only so you can look forward to being at the Hermitage," said Detva.

"Oh boy, did you hear that kids," said Marie.

"Where," said Detva.

"Over here remember I am only talking to my twins at once," said Marie.

"Right, my brother wants to live here and I can also look forward to never being hugged and only by you., Marie," said Detva.

"Thank you Dear when does he want to move in.?" said Marie.

"Some time I told him I will let him know," said Detva.

"He is Prince regent in Moscow using the Hermitage and he is regent here in Venice when he moves in," said Marie.

"Good way for him to do that here and to keep Likus in Versailles," said Detva.

"Now I do wonder if you have ever talked to Paul alone or on the phone," said Marie.

"No, I told Likus that you and I are taking his and Oseph place in Venice and that Oseph has a job to do there in Versailles using the computer to watch the new Atlantic tunnels being placed," said Detva.

"That is perfect and you never did have to say it was for you or Oseph to do that work.," said Marie.

"You mean I did not want to hurt his feelings that he could not handle this work," said Detva.

"Yes, I hope he never mentioned that.?" said Marie.

"No, because I know he could and yet it would be a hard type of work for him he would get an engineer to act as foreman when he needed to hire someone soon," said Detva.

"Yes, he could do the work," said Marie.

"A price to pay to live in a castle in Venice with the first two floors all in real gold," said Detva.

"Yes, it is," said Marie.

"It really is not a hardship for us to wait for the Hermitage, is it," said Detva.

"No, I do not mind but do you think your brother is going to want to stay," said Marie.

"My good husband, Prince Detva Dovbonovich we are one and with you I am a good wife and your queen at any time and I will say in the Hermitage forever," said Marie.

"My good Queen Marie, who I took you out of the Hermitage and it was only a visit I hope I did not get your hopes up to high. I do know for a fact Princess Ulmake had to go to work in France and eventually in New York if she wanted any money at all," said Detva.

"I know and you saw a way to get Likus in Versailles so that was very good of you and now I can tell you something we all might end up in Versailles because you the children wanting to rule," said Marie.

"So I am ok, as a Prince," said Detva.

"Yes, you are and as a King it would not be that long because I am sure you would want to live in our newly furnished Chateau," said Marie.

"We could in six months rent it out and give them another more than equal too," said Detva.

"What is Lloyd's we have had a return on our money over thirty times and that was invested first," said Marie.

"You are my best investment," said Detva.

"You are mine, I would say that but we do have eight children do to adoptions," said Marie.

"We do have with the fourteen homes across and its staff taking care of the 400 hundred children we will soon yet we do not have to add on to those homes," said Detva.

"That is all we can not duplicate like that again until we are on the main land," said Marie.

"We are going to ask the staff to live in one house and help out so they will take our stock as payment and to be a true owner," said Detva.

"Thank you, I do know for a fact the staff wanted to help out by using those buildings," said Marie.

"I am glad that you agree," said Detva.

"I do agree, now can put a memo up to let them know and the Butler will inform all of them," said Marie.

"He will, I sent a message. He replied, "All will help," said Detva.

"They have been waiting and this was considered their waiting time if there was any negotiating and I guess there was none," said Marie.

"We are in the middle of these twenty blocks or so," said Detva.

"We are a very small island and it is connected in the back to other buildings it is the only irregular water cannal zone and towards the city we are connected and towards to ocean it just looks that way," said Marie.

"You looked at the maps and the overhead photos by the helicopter is quite interesting," said Detva.

"Yes," said Marie.

"I wonder if it is are or is it, is finished," said Detva.

"As you hear it and we are finished islands and not worry for me are talking to our love ones on unfinished islands on borrowed unfinished earths that is different," said Marie.

"Then we can define unfinished earths," said Detva.

"Detva you yourself were apart of it, "Give me your tired humble and weak." When you and Edvard finished the tunnels you were included in his earth while he did it was himself. When the tunnels were finished from Paris to Moscow taking care of all like the States that too is a more finished and is another completed earth," said Marie.

"The controlled wars of European past was the only answer while the new world was ignored," said Detva.

"It is in the Bible the in completed earths having its own grave yard," said Marie.

"True or do we use or is it a fact the gases in the Universe, does it make us sleep while the transfer is going on similar to the gradual difference and slow medieval days to the present," said Detva.

"We are apart of and are being spread to and from by the oceans and then we are in fact part the old and new moons," said Marie.

"We then are in and apart of the new and old earths with it gases that could make all of it less seen and in the distance too," said Detva.

"We did finally control travel and time," said Marie.

"Pluto will cool us off and we will shrink to the earth now as a greater force while we keep what was done and finally the wars did what was suppose be for what we have now," said Detva.

"Buildings up cities making new land for cities and keeping the populations warm is the key," said Marie.

"Man does think better when warm or even hot the work does get done," said Detva.

"The wars did have cold winters too. Yet they were won with hardships too," said Marie.

"Should we say the hardships of just in the way or does the busy city know and the last to get out of and to higher ground does not drown will not celebrate," said Detva.

"The drowning or seeing it is as the last to get into the old earth from the better is the ones who did not help making a large city," said Marie.

"Those who do not help or if they learn then they are involved," said Detva.

"Yes and many will have a life to start and finished they have done within one fourth of ours is an Anorexic, for example," said Marie.

"A boy can loose weight too," said Detva.

"Both are surgical operations and done on the patient without knowing," said Marie.

"I know it is awful and some times it is the only way for them to see that they are beautiful and then the gaining of weight is not done correctly," said Detva.

"An Anorexic or an Asthmatic life time is someone who did have a perfect life for 80 years or more," said Marie.

"25 years for them is 80 years or more for me and we do have a goal," said Detva.

"We are forgiven it is nature it is reality that someone has to get the work out," said Detva.

"Right and many would never think of living here we needed the money and have earned it," said Marie.

"An outsider could have given the photo and computer information center, the referral was not ours," said Detva.

"Do not feel guilty about doing things for others. The referral was ours if someone new gave it to Paul we are the ones who can take it and they could live here under us how long do you think they would like it here," said Marie.

"They would have to earn their way into Versailles even when they still could purchase from us in France and visit the Palace," said Detva.

"We are not in a position to worry any more but what is important is we need to get more ideas before anyone else does," said Marie.

"Like what giving Venice our own picture on a stamp or money," said Detva.

"That is a perfect idea and Likus and Oseph too and then us and your brother and family and then he can move," said Marie.

"Ok, then do we call Paul to notify Venice," said Detva.

"No, I will call now because it is our money anyways then France does owe us and we have done a lot for others again," said Marie.

"Good, thank you," said Detva.

"I will dial now, Hello, may I please be the first to let you know that Detva and I want to be on a stamp and currency for Venice and we will pay for them. Thank you so much, Good Bye" said Marie.

"What did he say.?" said Detva.

"Yes, and send over the photos for us to use," said Marie.

"I love you, I do," said Detva.

"Now I have thought of something, we do not leave for France we go to Sicily and with our money give their new currency a try with our faces on the bills with us being King and Queen before we even leave Venice," said Marie.

"I know this is for the prevention of assignations and there is a King and Queen but are we doing two or three providences.?" said Detva.

"We can do three and place the King and Queen in Rome before we even leave for Sicily," said Marie.

"Good I would like to be a prince regent and stay in Sicily we might not leave and just visit the chateau, is that all right with you.?" said Detva.

"I do not mind and your brother can be told he might leave Russia in five years," said Marie.

"This would be good for both of us and my brother too," said Detva.

"I am sure he will enjoy this building and that Likus will visit them," said Marie.

"It is a safer place for him with canals being seen he will tend to stay where he is," said Detva.

"We can visit the Island and choose a home on the shore towards Italy towards for the main land too," said Marie.

"With the money or currency with our faces on it we do not went to start riots," said Detva.

"No we will not and when the King and Queen are there and the President is still in charge, we are just doing some preparations for the throne," said Marie.

"Perfect," said Detva.

"When we are there and give the throne to the royal family then we may go to France and we will stay at Versailles only for one day," said Marie.

"I hope he does not make us stay there," said Detva.

"No, he will not but you will give him a call before we leave and mention that to him," said Marie.

"Sure I will look forward to it because I just do know what he plans to do," said Detva.

"Maybe by then there is a clearer picture of what he wants," said Marie.

"I do not know unless one of the his older children want to work here," said Detva.

"Could by then. We have an answer for the Sicily currency is has been approved. " said Marie.

"Good, I do know no one is wanting to stay here if we leave, that is 100 %," said Detva.

"There is a lot of things to do for the businesses in France," said Marie.

"True and we can get it will done we have good boys who want to learn," said Detva.

"We should in fact now that it is 100% loyality we should have Paul pick out people from Versailles who are extremely interested in living in Venice to work here until your brother leaves Russia," said Detva.

"He might not and give it a few more years," said Marie.

"He might but I do know he is going to have a new name," said Detva.

"He will but we all do at sometime during this career," said Marie.

"I know he is very strong and yet he was so thrilled to be able to work in Newport, that the one thing he would not want is an assignation attempt," said Detva.

"No one does, that is why we are on the throne of Italy first. Paul could not do that for anyone or we would not be here he took an easy way out of us now we must use this knowledge and because of Lloyd's," said Marie.

"We are now on the run and we must do it very slowly for the others," said Detva.

"Paul made sure Likus was here for a long time for the staff to go with your Mother the Countess," said Marie.

"We are on the run.? " said Detva.

"No, we can visit many times to inform the public we have purchased many homes on the Island," said Marie.

"Maybe just one or two times to see France.?" said Detva.

"That is what Paul wants," said Marie.

"Maybe just twice and are now renting it," said Detva.

"We need to stay in Sicily for the King and Queen and the last President as well, for that is where they confused Napoleon," said Marie.

"Double spies were created out of that and Napoleon did not mention that at all. Until he was very sure they the staff would help he know then they would eventually worked on both sides and they did," said Detva.

"Sounds correct to me," said Marie.

"Of course that is the only think I could think of," said Detva.

"You are right there was an informant who got help," said Marie.

"Now I know my brother wants this place," said Detva.

"Of course and it is a good place to survive an almost divorce," said Marie.

"No one to disturb us," said Detva.

"No one not even a student who are all in security or working else where," said Marie.

"Did you enjoy all of the rings some of them of gold are antiques.?" said Detva.

"Yes, the one that was the most interesting was a small diamond in the middle and very unusual designs around it, I did think it would fit you.?" said Marie.

"I know which one it is and it can see here it is," said Detva.

"Remembering what level it was on you can not unmistaken that is for a man, so it is my gift to you and that was the only masculine ring there was," said Marie.

"Thank you," said Detva.

"It seems as if all is going right and then someone would wear it to allow all that things are coming suddenly to a stop," said Marie.

"Then I will leave it in my pocket and wear it when I require sleep," said Detva.

"Good and we will honor your decision," said Marie.

"Again thanks for this ring, please, do not buy any ok.?" said Detva.

"No, I will not," said Marie.

"By the way do they or we can have a definition of all of this, a logo is done, the ad for the Euro train tunnels is so, what do we say," said Marie.

"Inexpensive yet all of us are insuranced too so go," Go with the Euro train and we will go with the work of technology at its own speed," said Detva.

"Prince Detva Dovbonovich you did it again," said Marie.

"No, you did it, you mentioned about the logo the, Fleur de lis," said Detva.

"Thank you," said Marie.

"We hit a good quote that time so now lets give him the front cover, that Paul is waiting for," said Detva.

"I will call his secretary," Hi, yes could you put a hard card in the fax now and I will send you another copy. Ok it was sent. You have both.? Good thanks. Ok, bye," said Marie.

"What was the ok for.? I think something is going to happen.?" said Detva.

"Just that we are going to have many people here and I was told before Paul will make his call," said Marie.

"Ok, I am whispering, What is it," said Detva.

"Just if a security breach and never any names remember. Please just one more kiss Dear, I love you to love me but I have two others inside," said Marie.

"I forgot, I do not want to make a mistake so please remind me, I do not mind if we do not have any sex," said Detva.

"Just not on the stomach," said Marie.

"Not at all," said Detva.

"Ok, I do not mind you have given me a break at each pregnancy so it is good once and a while to wait," said Marie.

"It is not good for me but I do not think it is good before birth," said Detva.

"It has always been written up instead of having more increased rape charges that is all it ever was," said Marie.

"I know it is strange a world when even visiting or calling it wrong and illegal to do," said Detva.

"Even the abuse a small indication of anger or a tap on the rear and the child knows he has us," said Marie.

"A hit and run if you only a lawyer you might get away with it and it is not against the law to move away or return in a few minutes, when needing the bathroom," said Detva.

"It is when you can afford a chauffeur," said Marie.

"Right so it is a law," said Detva.

"It is," said Marie.

"Laws, what can we do about laws.?" said Detva.

"Stay off the road." A very good quote," said Marie.

"We can start with the island, so why not give them that quote right now," said Detva.

"Conserve on energy stay off the roads," said Marie.

"Very good, I will get it on the bill boards first with my picture," said Detva.

"Good and I will give Paul a plug with his books, all of them," said marie.

"Which ones.?" said Detva.

"All of his books, Grenaire, Versailles, Hermitage, Upstart, Venetian tunnels, Housing, Novitiate, Stipends," said Marie.

"Why we have not finished our own book," said Detva.

"I will give a message now and let him know I will be giving all of names of his books," said Marie.

"Should we have our bill boards together there are usually," said Detva.

"Yes, and have your shirt off," said Marie.

"You are to much you are so funny but I am going to charge the company just a little bit more than I usually do," said Detva.

"To funny, to much and I think you should," said Marie.

"Then you do not mind.?" said Detva.

"There was a calendar if I recall and it will stop the traffic or at least slow it down," said Marie.

"That calendar still gives a lot of money to charities," said Detva.

"Are you.?" said Marie.

"No, it will be a regular guy," said Detva.

"A regular guy what.?" said Marie.

"No, I will be sincere that is what I wanted to say," said Detva.

"Sincere how about Sintoo," said Marie.

"No," said Detva.

"That funny statement just gave a new perfume, Sintoo," said Marie.

"Good," said Detva.

"I do have another fragance I picked out now I will give them a call because I have a name to use," said Marie.

"Good here is our breakfast," said Detva

"Delicious, thank you," said Marie.

"I like the way he nods and is silent," said Detva.

"Yes, he is polite," said Marie.

"Marie, you do not want me to take off my shirt again for charity do you.?" said Detva.

"No, you need to get the idea across to the public," said Marie.

"Ok," said Paul.

"After breakfast if you have the need you can take off your shirt for me," said Marie.

"Instead of being here with you I should go the office for the rest of the day," said Detva.

"What do you mean you should be.?" said Marie.

"You usually have your solitude during the morning," said Detva.

"I need you here and this afternoon you can leave, ok.?" said Marie.

"Sure I do not want to annoy you," said Detva.

"You are not just until this afternoon then I think I will be alright," said Marie.

"Ok, give me a call and I will return, I am not far away," said Detva.

"There is a call Sir," said the Butler.

"It is Paul," said Detva.

"Yes, I will and I understand and thank you Paul, my best to Duless," said Marie.

"What.?" said Detva.

"He could not stay on the phone and there is a check for us, by messenger," said Marie.

"He is very grateful," said Detva.

"He is, in fact so are you and I am very pleased to have this opportunity," said Marie.

"True and we now on our way, I am getting use to the vacation in France," said Detva.

"So am I it is great, huge and wonderful to have the ability to rule an Island in apart of Italy," said Marie.

"We could ask for the Hermitage to help Paul and then we can stay there if you want," said Detva.

"We will know soon first lets see if your brother wants to stay in Venice or does he want to rule in Sicily. What about the people who do not want this" said Marie.

"We have been very generous with our money and we would never raise taxes," said Detva.

"Our brother will open up to a small nation and that is what we do not want to start Sicily does not need independence, and he would never suggest that and will always listen to us," said Marie.

"He would want a good government which is there now. He also is a fisherman he always like the salt water coast line," said Detva.

"I know you told he was thrilled when he could live in Newport by the shore," said Marie.

"There are plenty of large estates by the shore so he will be at home there," said Detva.

"He will and I will keep on reminding him of no independent nation," said Marie.

"Correct or I will let him that he will loose everything and he will be living in Belgium under house arrest," said Detva.

"That is a good scare he should listen to that reason with a lot of concern for loosing ones home," said Marie.

"I could never leave a home and not have another building to go too," said Detva.

"We always knew the ruling is for the better of the people and we have a chance to give them the new tunnels," said Marie.

"We do have that right and now I got a another idea how about the need for a new expansion of Venice, we have the plans for it upstairs," said Detva.

"Could you do it on a scale of six houses and it is in one block six on one side," said Marie.

"For each street having six new buildings and a drive way of water for a large yacht," said Detva.

"That would keep their interest and the six buildings is what is needed per street or canal," said Marie.

"Right canal, it is good talking to you so I am getting prepared to mention this to the committee," said Detva.

"Due to the canals just give them the proposals by fax and emails," said Marie.

"I will, I am sure seeing us before a dedication is not what they want," said Detva.

"We can have them here for an approval picture for the newspaper and films too," said Marie.

"That is right I did not think of it and we can serve refreshments," said Detva.

"It is polite to have the press at one part of the building for photos," said Marie.

"Good and the Butler will handle that," said Detva.

"What if someone is out of line.?" said Marie.

"Anyone that does that should quit and I could decide for them," said Detva.

"No, you act proper because we could still be sued," said Marie.

"Oh, please let me be angry and say a few bad words, ok," said Detva.

"No, the children could hear you so keep quiet," said Detva.

"I got it, we can invite the President and his wife remember he married a model in France about six years ago," said Marie.

"He did and then they can go see Paul and Dulcss," said Detva.

"He once was dated her and they can visit us and we will see their two children," said Marie.

"How about this weekend or the next.?" said Detva.

"Sure and then a convenient visit and time for them to pick also we will have the Pope here too," said Marie.

"Excellent now I am enjoying this place," said Detva.

"They might refuse," said Marie.

"I know or what I think, the President and his wife and two children just might be here unannounced and the public will know when they have left," said Detva.

"That is alright I just think it would be good for them to visit Versailles just one more time or a few more," said Marie.

"Yes, Paul should do this first," said Detva.

"I will mention it to Duless," said Marie.

"They should before the eight years are up," said Detva.

"It could be a few years after they leave. She has decided that she will ask but first they will stop here," said Marie.

"Wonderful," said Detva.

"That was nice of her to do that," said Marie.

"They are going to be here.?" said Detva.

"Yes, in about one year," said Marie.

"Then it is fine with me," said Detva.

"Me too," said Marie.

"Then we can set a date right after they call us," said Detva.

"They will," said Marie.

"Now we can look forward to something incredible," said Detva.

"If all is in our favor," said Marie.

"I know we do not know what is going to happen with our lives never mind about someone else," said Detva.

"We can quess," said Marie.

"What.?" said Marie.

"That you are going to be a proper gentleman," said Marie.

"I will I promise," said Detva.

"Good for me and you," said Marie.

"So lets give ourselves a promising review or give a favorable and positive I think it is easier to just to kiss you and I thank God you are mine," said Detva.

"Sir, here is the mail," said the Butler.

"Thank you, what is it now I hope everything is readable and I could just rip it up in half.?" said Detva.

"Let me take the letters Dear," said Marie.

"Here," said Detva.

"So there are many for the library to read and answer and this last one his a check in it from Paul," said Marie.

"I see it is," said Detva.

"See the amount and it is always to the two of us," said Marie.

"I am ok with that, and he must know that you were the one to invite the newly married couple in the White House not me and they would both go to the Palace of Versailles.?" said Paul.

"I did do that and I did think of it myself," said Marie.

"This is why we both live in a palace," said Detva.

Chapter 24

"A new day and new morning and out in this small walled back yard it is to cold to sit down I just wanted a few minutes in the cold air," said Marie.

"This is a good day, cold, but we do need to go inside," said Detva.

"I do relaize we do not see the children from here from across the canal in front of our house we see a lot of little babies, and their nannies," said Marie.

"We do see a lot the our children during the day and the staff as well," said Detva.

"I just wonder it we are doing the right thing with the pre-school and the enrollment in Venice and the grammar school has taken off and is a success," said Marie.

"We are fine Versailles pre-school is the theme because it was used for the Eurotrain in the States so it is a pre-school grammar and high and a restaurant as a huge success and the runway and studio also," said Detva.

"You are correct and the Hermitage in green and the rooms in blue are starting again and again," said Marie.

"It gives a great feeling of accomplishment and we need all the help we can get," said Detva.

"The Cynthia gold building is coming in second and runway is excellent," said Marie.

"We can thank Paul and Ed and mainly now ourselves for the money is the best and the franchises are selling every day," said Detva.

"We can use this extra publicity for what we have done," said Marie.

"I think the good publicity that got us first, all of us in every large palace or castle adopted many children and people do not forget that. The noise too," said Detva.

"The noise can never be heard now that most of the children are in the middle of the property. Besides you are on my side, I do not want to hear that even in a humorous tone I mean that we need to let nothing stand in the children's' way, not even us," said Marie.

"I am so sorry, I love you so much I would not want to harm you or them at all," said Detva.

"Thank you, and please remember they are young and are babies and they need our laws with them in case something happens to us," said Marie.

"You are a good Mother and no one has ever complained about how many or what we are doing," said Detva.

"Knowing that has made me very delighted and happy to go on especially for the great things that can happen just for them," said Marie.

"Then great things will happen and I sure it is everything will work out, now calm down, it is not good for you or the babies," said Detva.

"Yes, good things," said Marie.

"Sure, all of them are in good wealth it is a law that all children must be in good health when living in a large home in Europe," said Detva.

"We did put 5 children in a group home on the property," said Marie.

"Yes, and because it is Venice their can only be a few in each community and it is not fair as the emergencies can be very harmful while on the canal," said Detva.

"Then in our old age it is good to be on the main land," said Marie.

"I guess so and the ones who could never mind their own business have probably exhausted their desire to communicate," said Detva.

"It has been very functional to be able to have such privacy and work," said Marie.

"Probably it is a very good place to try to get a marriage together, and avoid a divorce. I know I have repeated myself again," said Detva.

"Sure we say these things over and over again but it is the truth these things happen and Venice is the place to work things out," said Marie.

"A place yes, but make sure the couple do not have an bills and it could happen for them especially when he goes to work and gives her space," said Detva.

"Yes, space but he can work in the house like you do on the computer in another part of the building and we do have plenty of buildings to choose from," said Marie.

"I know I even worked in the same house with the babies and of course I did not visit them and I did not have any type of cold, either," said Detva.

"There was no noise either," said Marie.

"How do you know.?" said Detva.

"They were given their bottles, they were having their feeding time and napping too. If you went in at 7:00p.m. then most of them would be awake," said Marie.

"It was very quiet," said Detva.

"It was ok, the babies were being very polite," said Marie.

"They were.?" said Detva.

"No, I do not believe you said that, you are very cute and handsome too," said Marie.

"Thank you and you are very beautiful," said Detva.

"I love you very much but I can not do anything right now is the I doctor still here right now," said Marie.

"I need to say to, I do not want you to ever leave me," said Detva.

"You do all right, it was not your fault about your first divorce," said Marie.

"I know she is in denial and has been in the news twice now," said Detva.

"Before she is in the news again why not ask her if you and I can take care of the children for a little while and then she can get help," said Marie.

"We could it is in the best interest for them at all," said Detva.

"You could give her a call and ask her if you and I can take care of them while she goes in right now.? Let her know that now it is a good time while she is well," said Marie.

"I will go into the next room and let her know I will send her the tickets for the children to be brought here," said Detva.

"Yes, the tickets and with a nanny too. With that I do not think she would object for she could call back in a few hours. There I will find out what is in the tel right now," said Marie.

"Alright," said Detva.

"Now what happened, it was to short.?" said Marie.

"As soon as I mentioned help she interrupted and mentioned to send the money and she will admit herself when they leave," said Detva.

"Did she seem to be intoxicated.?" said Marie.

"A little sad in her voice," said Detva.

"Maybe we have helped her finally.?" said Marie.

"The phone, the Butler mentioned that the nanny has a check and she is on her way to Belgium and she will be dropped her off in her own cab. Good it is still early in the morning time so I think she will be going to the facility too," said Detva.

"I hope the nanny knows how to lure her in the facility and not promise her the extra cash she has," said Marie.

"She knows it is for the children and her," said Detva.

"Did she have uniform on.?" said Marie.

"Yes, but not to convincing," said Detva.

"Did she go with as security guard.?" said Marie.

"He was in a dark blue suit," said Detva.

"Then I guess we can get them out of the country before the media is aware of what is going on," said Marie.

"Of course they want a story and these pictures they would save," said Detva.

"I hope so and not bother them while they are on their way here," said Marie.

"Things will work out remember that we love each other," said Detva.

"She is a mother she knows what to do," said Marie.

"See you are talking to me and I know how she sounds when she is this way and two children are crying in the back ground," said Detva.

"She told them that they are going to see us and now they're getting ready and packing too," said Marie.

"I just found out the Doctor is going and he will help her," said Detva.

"You have been waiting for this for a long time," said Marie.

"I know and it takes the nanny to get them out not me," said Detva.

"This is the chance for you to have them and to take custody, you have found her to be drunk this morning," said Marie.

"I know and the nanny will testify," said Detva.

"I do not think there will be any problems, she will sign them over and you just continue to pay her bills," said Marie.

"I will and she can not visit," said Detva.

"That is impossible even to think of," said Marie.

"When she tries to get out then we have a deal," said Detva.

"You have a deal, when she approved of them being taken away remember that ," said Marie.

"I know I have to remember that this is an agreement with her and I just hope they get them out of there," said Detva.

"You have to remember Detva that if she is was alright and did not drink then she would be going along with her children and even wait next door," said Marie.

"That is very true we have her just where we need her and now those children are mine and I do not have to worry about them. I have been very fortunate that even the tunnels are going well and soon will be finished," said Detva.

"Very nice and I am sure that they will be ok, how about the other the Atlantic tunnels did you appoint someone to watch the computers there too," said Marie.

"No, Oseph did because that person is in Versailles and he liked doing that type of work on the computer," said Detva.

"That is terrific and here is our coffee and dinners we are going to have an early lunch right here," said Marie.

"Besides all of this happening this morning, I am very hungry," said Detva.

"So am I and I could finish this I really could," said Marie.

"You need the food for your strength," said Detva.

"I will have all of this, after all when the chef makes you a homemade lunch like this toast with small bits of oven roast and his own gravy no one ever complains," said Marie.

"It is good and it is keeping my mind off of the children and in fact I know they are now going to be safe," said Detva.

"Yes, they are and I think they are on there way home right now.?" said Marie.

"Here is their location and they are in the the car and the Euro train and are heading this way," said Detva.

"The nanny took the locator with her that was a good idea," said Marie.

"It was only 15 minutes from the airport to the Belgium's airport where the auto was waiting for them," said Detva.

"Yes, that family jet is very helpful," said Marie.

"It is and I do think the staff should be given an award for their perfect timing," said Detva.

"Yes, yes they will for their impeccable timing," said Marie.

"This is worth the salary the staff get they are so good to us Dear," said Detva.

"I know they should all be given cash for this service," said Marie.

"Then the smallest at 5 and the nanny and he security guardsd at 10," said Detva.

"Five thousand for all and the Nanny and the Security guard get ten is fine with me," said Marie.

"Good I have the cash right here," said Detva.

"I will get some small envelopes and place the money in them," said Marie.

"We have to pay them right now so it does not look like a pay off," said Detva.

"Good thinking here is a list of our employees and the Butler will do the honors of giving them the money and having them sign the payroll list we have," said Marie.

"We are the other hand give the Nanny and the Security guard the ten thousand each personally," said Detva.

"Right and we do look fine to welcome the children," said Marie.

"Our children," said Detva.

"Yes thank you. We should give the Nanny and Guard their gift first so the guard may return and sign in again and then the children may enter," said Marie.

"My Lord Detva and Lady Marieca, your Nanny and Security Guard," said the Butler.

"May I congratulate you both on a rather dangerous yet I hope a pleasant drive to the main land. Here are your gifts for services extremely and impeccably done," said Her Ladyship Marieca.

"Yes, congratulations to you both and we want you both to be here with us for now on. The next door for the nanny in the other room later with the children and I would like the guard to be outside of this door when the children enter. Thank you both for a job well done," said Lord Detva.

"Yes thank you both and congratulations," said Lady Marica.

"Thank you Lady Marieca and Lord Detva," said the Security guard.

"Yes thank you Lady Marieca and Lord Detva," said the Nanny.

"Now we have them placed, here are the children," said Detva.

"It is fantastic look at all my lovely little babies or should I say very grown up children. Oh, such hugs and kisses look at all of you, you are so grown up and polite," said her Ladyship.

"Marie look at the little one," said Detva.

"She is so beautiful, Detva she looks you," said Marie.

"Thanks and this one," said Detva.

"So handsome, like their Dad," said Marie.

"Thanks again," said Detva.

"We are all going to sit down at the dining room table and have a dinner right now," said Marie.

"Now this is Christmas and very complete and I am so please and delighted that all of you are here, so we will have a very good evening," said Marie.

"We are pleased and delighted children and we have a few surprises so lets have an early dinner," said Detva.

"Are you hungry, Dear.?" said Marie.

"Yes I am and I enjoy this dinner," said Detva.

"We need help.?" said Marie.

"We need the nannies in here, so here they are," said Detva.

"So how many are there, am I your forth wife," said Marie.

"Dear, I was let go when I was 14 years and very mature," said Detva.

"It was your grandmother who gave you the house," said Marie.

"Yes, it is was my father who introduced them who I live with them for about a couple of years each one," said Detva.

"The South Pacific marriages," said Marie.

"Yes, and you, Marie," said Detva.

"No, but you vaguely smell familiar," said Marie.

"I do like yours," said Detva.

"Thank you and is your food ok," said Marie.

"Yes," said Detva.

"Also thank you for your recent expenses that was very nice indeed," said Marie.

"You are welcome," said Detva.

"Now I did have a big lunch so I will have coffee with the children and you can stay or bring your plate of food with you," said Marie.

"I will and we are going to let them speak I want to hear my children's voices," said Detva.

"I agree but we did know if some of the children were going to cry so now they seem to be calmer and having their dinner quietly," said Marie.

"Wait I will call the AA institute to and find out if my ex-wife is in their or not," said Detva.

"What did they say.?" said Marie.

"I have put an alarm on our own security for she has left and is not home," said Detva.

"Your family knows of this in Belgium right, and now our Butler and staff are aware of this too.?" said Marie.

"All are and she is now in the hospital in Belgium she got a lot of liquor from somewhere because the staff took it with them," said Detva.

"Call the hospital and I will talk to the Doctor," said Marie.

"Here is the doctor I gave him permission of you to speak to him," said Detva.

"He wants to speak to you first," said Marie.

"Yes, I understand and thank you doctor she will be placed in my late parents new castle where the family lives now," said Detva.

"We can not do this to these children they are to young," said Marie.

"I know they are and I will tell them one at a time and it is not going to be easy," said Detva.

"I know what is going on the little ones are crying we left them in the living room to have dinner and the news is on and they know about their Mother," said Marie.

"We will both comfort them and they can not go to see her they will stay here," said Detva.

"Detva they all know now and we are so sorry for you and the children," said the Doctor.

"Thank you and everyone we are going to stay home and we will see Mother's grave in the summer time. Here in Europe we do know death and yet in time of war there are reasons why we stay home," said Detva.

"It is for the best and I know it is too dangerous to go out," said Marie.

"Right now during a sorrow part of out lives we can use the family building in Belgium or the home in Rome can be used for a sorrow get together but Venice is not made for these things in live," said Detva.

"If anyone complains then the homes in Rome or in Belgium will be open by them personally," said Detva.

"Who would want to stop Mommy.? " said the little Boy.

"We can see her in the summy time," said a little Girl.

"You are both correct we will and you are very nice to give all of us permission too. Staimpin. No one is going to stop Mommy from do the right thing she is at Grandmother's house right now ok, Tredsur," said Detva.

"That was very nice indeed," said Marie.

"Now all of us are going to have a fantastic dessert that is why I am here to share that with all of you ok," said Detva.

"That looks so good creamy vanilla ice cream on a chocolate cake it is my favorite," said Marie.

"We have a new cartoon that is out or did everyone see Versailles.?" said Detva.

"Lets see Versailles," said Marie.

"That would be good. Here doctor have some," said Detva.

"It does look good," said the Doctor.

"Here nannies will you bring up these lovely little three babies up stairs and get them ready for the evening. This cake is delicious is there anyone else for Ice cream, here have some more Tredsur," said Marie.

"This is my favorite cake it is the chef who has all of these recipes," said Detva.

"I have the recipes Dear the chef gave me his recipe book last year," said Marie.

"Are you my Mom," said Shouloff.

"Yes I am here sit by me and we are going to watch the cartoon," said Marie.

"I did not see this cartoon," said Shouloff.

"It is just out we got it yesterday," said Marie.

"This is good we can see all of the cartoons," said Shouloff.

"Detva I was wondering if you were to call the landlord to find out if he can deliver," said Marie.

"There all is done he answered just after I message," said Detva.

"Good Dear have some ice cream and cake," said Marie.

"I will thanks," said Detva.

"Sir, there is a Uncle Skillgon here and he is alone too," said the Butler.

"Hello Detva and Marie here is my check I sold all everything just to be or next door I hope you do not mind," said Baron Skillgon.

"No, I do not ind it at all but you might want to uswe the first house next to us and use the crosswalk to that house in the late evening," said the Baron.

"That is right Baron you are going to get any sleep here," said Detva.

"Thank you then late or early in the evening I will withdraw with some of the children as well, so I do not look like an intruder," said the Baron.

"I hope you like roast beef on toast," said Marie.

"Excellent choice and a perfect chef so I was told," said the Baron.

"I am the dark Prince," said Tredsur.

"We can work on that later with William Shakespeare and the novels I will read to all of you in the evening time," said their Uncle.

"Uncle you and I will move this house each night," said Tredsur.

"How is that.?" said the Baron.

"With you reading and my gift of being myself we could be on the stage in this house packed every night," said Tredsur.

"It seems as if I have a contract with Tredsur for tomorrow evening, Detva," said Uncle Skillgon.

"I hope so his face will be on the Versailles and the Hermitage magazines soon," said Detva.

"Suddenly the twins are enjoying the evening," said Marie.

"Like father like son," said Detva.

"Like Mother like daughter I wonder how busy you will be Detva in the evening time, I think the twin are girls," said Marie.

"Dear then you did answer me," said Detva.

"Please excuse me but I think they are liking the male populations around me, we need to get some of their male friends in as soon as they are walking," said Marie.

"We will know very soon, they will grow up and we will let them be in charge," said Detva.

"In charge that is a good idea and they will be paid to help run this house or any other," said Marie.

"Yes all of the houses they can run and stay by paying the bills instead of the rent," said Detva.

"There rent will be $150.00 dollars each and then we will pay the rest for they are taking care of the property," said Marie.

"Then they do not have to pay anything," said Detva.

"No, no one will who take care of and helps with the house yet they can earn very little money and the rest of the cash it can go towards a home a small castle," said Marie.

"Good and it will better than owning stock the ones in charge can do that," said Detva.

"Excuse me sire, here is the phone," said the Butler.

"The police want to speak to the Nanny and the Security guard. I will bring them into the sitting room," said Detva.

"Here we are officer I know we are all aware of my wife dieing when the children and the staff were home with us. So what could be, I am very confused about this visit," said Detva.

"We apologized but we need to know if Lady Brakecaul had told the Nanny or the Security Guard anything.?" said the Detective.

"No, nothing the things were ready and the children got into the car and then her Ladyship saw the security guard and he nodded, and," said the Nanny.

"Very good now I need to know what happened," said the Detective.

"Nothing I nodded to her as she got into her own cab," said the Security guard.

"Now I have apologize again and I am very sorry but as we speak your late wife's husband is going to be arrested for murder," said the Detective.

"Before you continue my wife," said Detva.

"Yes, Sergeant ask Lady Marieca to enter this room," said the Detective.

"Dear I need you to sit down apparently Brakecaul was murdered by her husband," said Detva.

"Yes, that is correct, there were a lot bruises on her body. She was put into the driver's seat after he hit a young boy," said the Detective.

"Those children must of seen or heard them fighting," said her Ladyship.

"Do not worry Dear they are here with us now," said Detva.

"We have sent the smaller ones upstairs to get ready for bed and the nannies have not been down here so I guess there are no bruises or injuries," said her Ladyship.

"We need to get the others ready for bed so we can photo if they are bruised," said the Detective.

"I will go with the nannies," said her Ladyship.

"We need to talk to both of you now," said the Detective.

"Alright Detective it is just the two of us right now," said Detva.

"Your wife was having a child and the baby girl survived, the hospital will deliver her when she is able to travel. While the baby is in the hospital the press will not know it," said the Detective.

"The nanny told me she had a large carrying bag on her shoulders so she did not know she was having a baby, I guess no one knew.?" said Marie.

"There is more, we think he might have embezzled your wife," said Detective.

"The bills are all paid by me she would charge anything," said Detva.

"Do you pay for the other wifes too.?" said the Detective.

"No, their husbands are very good to them and the children," said Detva.

"I am very sorry but there are no other questions may we both stay here until we can learn more about the other children.?" said the Detective.

"Yes, you may and I will send in food and coffee for the both of you," said Marie.

"Thank you and I need to talk to the Nanny again," said the Detective.

"We will like to check with the children right now ok.?" said Detva.

"I will go I want you to talk to the detective and find out everything that had happened," said Marie.

"You are alright I can still bring you upstairs and then return," said Detva.

"Just watch me go to the elevator and listen I will tell you that I am on that floor," said Marie.

"Now we are at a close of this case and if there are any bruises we are going to have ask the children questions," said the Detective.

"I am glad my wife did not hear that and will they be doing this tonight or in the morning. Ok, alright Dear just stay there," said Detva.

"We have not heard if there are any bruises.?" said the Detective.

"Here is the Nanny," said Detva.

"Nanny I need to know what you saw when you met Lady Brakecaul," said the Detective.

"She was sitting down her coat was on and the cab arrived, we all went out and she got into the cab," said the Nanny.

"So she was holding her carring bag over her shoulder," said the Detective.

"She did Detective she did just what you have told me," said the Nanny.

"Doctor thank you for staying and please bring up the nanny to the second room and tell her anything I need to talk to Lord Detva immediately right now so please leave alright and thank you both and Nanny you were very helpful," said the Detective.

"What is it Detective.?" said Detva.

"Did you give your ex-wife any large amounts of money was he hitting the children so you would have to paid him," said the Detective.

"No, I paid all of the bills and I just found out there was boyfriend but he was not living there all of the time," said Detva.

"Alright then we are finished," said the Detective.

"Then I gave them money and he and I caused her death," said Detva.

"No, he helped kill her just like he killed that little boy," said the Detective.

"Detective the doctor wants to see you upstairs right now, please the two of you," said the Nurse.

"Lets go," said the Detective.

"Here is Detva and the detective now," said Nanny.

"Detva look at Tredur and he is starting to shiver too," said Marie.

"I gave him some medicine he should sleep very soon," said the Doctor.

"My little baby boy I am going to," said Detva.

"Detva, please Dear just ask him what happened.?" said Marie.

"What happened Tredur.?" said Detva.

"I will tel you what happened when I am alone with you, just you Dad," said Tredur.

"Now what happened, and I will not tell anyone," said his Dad.

"I was finishing my bath and the bike was in the bathroom and I was still wet and I forgot to put my underpants on and I was wet and I slipped," said Tredur.

"This is how you got those scraps too right here," said his Dad.

"Yes I fill, and I landed on the bike handle which hit my shoulder," said Tredur.

"It is up to you, if I tell that you yourself had an accident in the bathroom and you were alone then you were not hit by anyone," said Detva.

"Ok, that is what happened," said Tredur.

"Then it is alright that I do tell what happened and I was wondering seeing that you are so honest do you want a pony or a jeep in the house to drive.?" said his Father.

"If I lied I only get one and the pony can not be here to get warm for the winter.? Said Tredur.

"That is right," said Detva.

"I did not lie I was on the bike, and I need the pony to get him warm by tonight. Sir," said Tredur.

"You will get him when I know it is safe on the water," said Detva.

"Then by Tuesmorrow.? " said Tredur.

"By the end of the week," said Detva.

"Then I must go to sleep now," said Tredur.

"Why you can watch the tel," said Detva.

"If I fall asleep now my pony will be here by Tuesmorrow," said Tredur.

"Here watch the tel and the nanny will help you get something to see, ok.?" said Detva.

"Ok, but not to far away from Tuesmorrow," said Tredur.

"No, it will be at the end of the week," said his Dad.

"Chitty chitty," said Tredur.

"What.? Ok you can watch that," said his Dad.

"Nanny Chitty chitty," said Tredur.

"Please Chitty chitty," said his Dad.

"Alright here is the movie," said the Nanny.

"Thank you," said Tredur.

"We will talk later ok, Tredur," said his Dad.

"Now dear I want you to talk to him and just let him talk," said Detva.

"Tredsur you are watching, Chitty chitty," said Marie.

"I told Dad I did the mistake, the bike, it should not be in the house," said Marie.

"Mom you Mom," said Tredur.

"I know and who said," It was alright to put the bike in the house," said Marie.

"No me I did See what my bike do," said Tredur.

"Are you alright, does it hurt.?" said Marie.

"No but my bike is hurt and not here," said Tredur.

"Mom can a have a bike too," said his Mom.

"I do want my bike, not someone else's," said Tredsur.

"Your father gave you someone elses bike," said Marie.

"A big boy too," said Tredur.

"Ok, then let me tell you dad ok," said Marie.

"I will put him to bed Lady Marieca," said Tredur.

"Thank you Nanny and try to get some sleep ok Tredur," said his Mom.

"Night Mom," said Tredsur.

"Detva, he mentioned that the bike was to large for him it belonged to a big boy," said Marie.

"Now we can get some answers," said Detva.

"I know but let it go and we can deal with it by ourselves," said Marie.

"I know they are safe now and they are ours," said Detva.

"Right and I am sure he would have mentioned something buy now," said Marie.

"Your right he did want the pony first," said Detva.

"I do not know kids are very clever about those things," said Marie.

"It was not effective," said Detva.

"He has been processed to say No so No will be the answer for even many things to keep control," said Marie.

"Control," said Detva.

"He has the board so all of the evidence is on his side and to work for the answer it must be something clever to say or he still is in charge until then," said Marie.

"We will not give him any more pushing to get an answer. I do not want to loose him by a psychotic injury and he withdraws," said Detva.

"We will not ask him any more questions. He is strong like you" said Marie.

"I was not the one who is injured," said Detva.

"I know but he is home with us and there is a lot for him to do here and they do not have any of their own toys," said Marie.

"We will buy more toys and I will take possession of the property now," said Detva.

"Good, there is still time to call the lawyers in, it is still early," said Marie.

"Alright please sit down with me and I will do the talking. Hello, yes Detva, good and you, positive, fine, I need to put a hold on my wife's property now that she has died," said Detva.

"Away from the care of your fanily in Belgium too, place a guard there," said Marie.

"Now that you did all that for me even took the responsible and to have a guard at the property. Sure, even in spite of the fact that you now have reminded me that you are not the power of attorney and I know there is none, why did you not call.? " said Detva.

"The law," said Marie.

"Now I am understand, Marie just mentioned it," Was the law." Yet you can place a guard there to protect our interest is exactly what was needed," said Detva.

"Does the family know.?" said Marie.

"Yes, they know, Lawrence it is the law, the guard will be there until the trial and sentence and I will have the keys, with your control. Thank you your help again," said Detva.

"The police did it.?" said Marie.

Chapter 25

"Yes they did, it is the law they can protect our properties but with him in prison waiting for the trial of hit and run or hit and murder. The police put up the barricade and then he called them," said Detva.

"I know I interrupted and I did not want too but you have given the hit and murder if he did not put her in front of the wheel there could be another involved," said Marie.

"I am angry and I do not want to say the wrong thing so thank you for helping me," said Detva.

"We can not say or imply anything or anyone we are on their side, the children's side," said Marie.

"Sir, it is Lady Urnlee on the phone," said the Butler.

"Yes, I apologize for all the problems that have occured," said Detva.

"We do not have to talk," said Marie.

"Yes, I will and thank you for calling and give your love to everyone," said Detva.

"There is a good connect with us so I do not think they were with one another to often in fact not at all," said Marie.

"I need to whisper, Urnlee did think there was a lot of drinking but there was so much happening when she got married and Dad died she forgot about it due to the baby being born and remember she was very relax not needing to work anymore," said Detva.

"Then you left her when she was drinking or she kept it very quiet from you," said Marie.

"There was a bottle of vodka quite often but before the divorce she wanted to live in the Chateau before we actually separated even twice we were there to get the marriage back to the way it could be," said Detva.

"Being very occupied with all that has happened to her and for her it was her first marriage so I think she has been more relaxed now and ever before," said Marie.

"That was a lot to face up to," said Detva.

"She endure something that I do not ever want to happen so you better not leave, besides we Sicily," said Marie.

"Plus each other," said Detva.

"We do and still be isolated yet there is no reason why a s a negative, if we pay the help every well and we get the security we need," said Marie.

"All I do not need is my Mother here and when we are in Sicily thank god for the Austria," said Detva.

"Thank God for Belgium and our blessed Lady and Saint Joseph who made a safe but hard journey and we did have to go in that horrible direction and conditions of being poor or with the poor," said Marie.

"I know what you are talking about I kept all of wives out of that environment," said Detva.

"Joseph finally made a comfortable living and I still do not want to go into a poor way of life," said Marie.

"We will not. There are twenty banks accounts in twenty countries " said Detva.

"I know and I have the other twenty in twenty," said Marie.

"We will survive and now lets put the children to bed and they will have lots of toys to be delivered tomorrow ," said Detva.

"We can buy them ten toys small and large and then save the rest for Christmas they believe in Santa so let it be done that way," said Marie.

"You are right again there is nothing better than Santa and it is the right time of the year to give and give greatly," said Detva.

"I did not mind the rings but I do need necklaces and bracelets too but I will buy you a tool box for Christmas," said Marie.

"Also the marching ear rings and rings too," said Detva.

"Sir, the phone," said the Butler.

"Thank the Nanny for me and I know they are tired but I can not do another thing," said her Ladyship.

"Yes my Lady," said the Butler.

"Ok, Mother I will and I will see you sometime soon I hope and enjoy your self," said Detva.

"Your Mother called.?" said Marie.

"She and Auntie are going to the Swiss alps for one month or more," said Detva.

"I hope they have a good time and it is good for their own health too," said Marie.

"They will they are guess of her new boyfriend," said Detva.

"Her second husband Likus father was her husband until he died," said Marie.

"These two were married for a long time," said Detva.

"I know they were quite happy and remained in that old castle for years," said Marie.

"Yes, life was good to all of them he just was very tired of life and had done it all," said Detva.

"We are different we are taking caring of property that is good for the future and a lot better after we are finished," said Marie.

"It will be that way and on the island it will be fun and all ours and the people will love you," said Detva.

"If there is a King and Queen of Sicily as well as Italy and appointed some day we should let it happened.? Just Prince and Princess I think is best," said Marie.

"I know we do have to think of the main land and live in France some day with the children," said Detva.

"You are right they will be working for us but they should be allowed to use Grenaire real estate for a nice castle to own and live there," said Marie.

"Now that everything is mentioned and looks as if is a good plan we are doing the right thing," said Detva.

"Why of course we are and it is for the better of the population," said Marie.

"Then we have done everything right and proper," said Detva.

"Yes or we would have heard from the people sooner if they were upset," said Marie.

"It is a go from here and we are in charge," said Detva.

"Now look at the papers and the news on the tel," said Marie.

"Just Like all of the others and now us look here goes the media and we need to stop them now," said Detva.

"See, "Seven children dead and Detva kills your wife," said Marie.

"I did not," said Detva.

"I know but they do not and you need again to call the lawyers for a retraction," said Marie.

"I will, I will email it" said Detva.

"No settlements go of court," said Marie.

"Then we did ok, I still can not believe them," said Detva.

"They do this for the increase in papers to be sold," said Marie.

"I know it is the circulation, and the amount of clients," said Detva.

"We earn the money so it is ours," said Marie.

"I got it and this will give them something to talk about, we will vacation in Navarre this will make them think we are looking for a place to live and eventually be King and Queen too," said Detva.

"Detva you are a genious I love you so much," said Marie.

"Hold it and hold it you are making me, ok you got it now try to stay away," said Detva.

"Oh, this is wonderful we can look for a house a castle on the computer come on," said Marie.

"Right to me and we can buy it now," said Detva.

"We will, so lets see what there is," said Marie.

"There should be a lot of homes for about 40 million or more," said Detva..

"Then we have made it at last," said Marie.

"It looks that way," said Detva.

"We have," said Marie.

"What is wrong.?" said Detva.

"Wanting Navarre could be considered treason.?" said Marie.

"Then we should tell Paul that he should appoint his son in charge before anyone else does it," said Detva.

"We could mention that it is very vulnerable right now and the appointment is crucial and very necessary for the security of the nation. There it is in, yet no answer," said Marie.

"We will not call that would be wrong," said Detva.

"After this email I would not go into France at all. Paul is not your brother and Likus and Oseph could be dismissed before going to prison. Here is the answer," said Marie.

"Good work you are right on the money you earn. Good keep them coming," said Detva.

"I would not go there any time to soon and now with Likus and Oseph and their child living there we need to watch out for what we are writing and saying to each other in this house," said Marie.

"Ok, we will watch ourselves for now and not be so direct," said Detva.

"I will remind you and that one got away from us both," said Marie.

"It did and it will not happen again, I think we should not mention that to him again," said Detva.

"I have the answer and we should act on it this way we will give him a check for a half a trillion dollars," said Marie.

"That is a lot and say more about why it should be done," said Detva.

"Because if he were King full time and not put the President back or a new one because the he has retired then me could pay the fine and be in prison or exile. Said Marie.

"Not that he is not that angry," said Detva.

"Take your pick I choose exile in the United States with the children," said Marie.

"Then we will give him the money but not half but two halves," said Detva.

"That is just what is needed," said Marie.

"Then here it is, now you are still Lady Marieca," said Detva.

"We will wait, now you are still my Prince Detva Dovebonovich," said Marie.

"This part is still not annoying we did the right thing the better thing is we are not there," said Detva.

"The worst part of it all is what Likus and Oseph were thinking which was yesterday when we just got finished getting the kids to bed and that was an ordeal for them," said Marie.

"Here is the answer, Paul mentioned that we need it more then he does and he and everyone there gives their love to us and let this ride for your sake when the media is on their own side," said Detva.

"Now we know we did the right thing as an answer," said Marie.

"We did and if it was any other year early in the days of the Kings we would be hunted down," said Detva.

"You and I do not want to leave Sicily and we have a house to use in France if we visit," said Marie.

"Now what.?" said Detva.

"We have to wait for the media, remember the Kings of today are educated and yet there needs to be one king then the others are given titles," said Marie.

"True," said Detva.

"Right even Italy where there titles will become lesser than King by the amount of wealth they have," said Marie.

"Wealth works it is tradional," said Detva.

"Your brother will do fine the isolation in Venice is perfect for him, I loved it and so will he," said Marie.

"What part of it.?" said Detva.

"There is no one at the door and they can call first and always make an appointment," said Marie.

"That is why I do enjoy it here but we need a different environment we need to be able to walk outside," said Detva.

"You do understand that I person who calls is doing the proper thing and they can be seen in a few days," said Marie.

"Sure," said Detva.

"To be a weapon as a person is not a social choice among others who are the same, they are replaced person from the prisons," said Marie.

"Now I know I was not," said Detva.

"The best weapon is unaware of who he is," said Marie.

"I know," said Detva.

"You are in the ownership, the receivership position," said Marie.

"He is brainwashed," said Detva.

"He is not you," said Marie.

"Then we need to stay here," said Detva.

"Good," said Marie.

"We are staying here and letting my brother live in the Hermitage when someone else rules there is the best thing I can do for us," said Detva.

"Then you are aware of the position you are in being in charge so give that order and let him know he stays there while someone rules in his place," said Marie.

"Yes, that is right Paul is the only one who rules by using the Euro train to visit," said Detva.

"Do it so he has time to leave and go to Finland if he wants too," said Marie.

"It is done but I did not mention about Finland," said Detva.

"You could Newport in the message," said Marie.

"I just mentioned both," said Detva.

"Here is the answer we need," said Marie.

"I know we are using two different computers but what did he say.?" said Detva.

"Mentioned that it was about time and a very good decision and he would like to live in the middle of the building with his own staff and that just happened," said Marie.

"We are home," said Detva.

"We can still purchase other buildings and repaired them," said Marie.

"We just rent them out.? " said Detva.

"Sure with an obtion to buy," said Marie.

"We need to do another runway in Cynthia again so do not forget it and please put it in the computer," said Detva.

"I just did it," said Marie.

"Thanks, I wanted to tell you something when you were upstairs getting dress for this morning a person was at the door," said Detva.

"Who.? " said Marie.

"Here is his name and he had a little boy with him," said Detva.

"Then he must be given a lure who is you and give a call and if the boy is mentioned then invite him too then find out if he was going to sell him to you, for the hour," said Marie.

"He and the boy were dressed perfectly so I do not think he was going to sell him for the hour. I did think of this joke yesterday and I have a lot of respect for my brother Likus," said Detva.

"What.? " said Marie.

"If Adam and Eve were not so ungrateful being in the garden then do you suppose they were raising a little boy who was given to them by a couple who wanted him to be raised by a Mother. Not a detached female in a dream world," said Detva.

"I do not get it.?" said Marie.

"The purpose is to make you laugh only," said Detva.

"I give up what is the joke, the funny part.?" said Marie.

"The couple who devoted only to themselves," said Detva.

"The couple were two guys," said Detva.

"You are awful this was so bad I had to let it go on and on do not repeat that at all," said Marie.

"Ok, you are right," said Detva.

"Please call him and let him know he can phone from here and you will do the dialing and then he will talk to Likus.!" said Marie.

"Ok here we go, "Hello, I have an answer for you about Likus if you want to you can call from here and I will dial and you do not have to pay and either do we," said Detva.

"What did he say.?" said Maric

"Thank you, I was just taking my nephew out to see Venice he has gone so I do admitt he wanted him to see a beautiful home and a Prince also so I apologize," said Detva.

"So the boy was the reason why he was here so he does not have to call," said Marie.

"Yes, that is what he said and there is more," said Detva.

"What.?" said Marie.

"He used to live across from us and maybe I can call him back if we have some problems with these twenty blocks," said Detva.

"Then call him maybe he would want the work," said Marie.

"Or me," said Detva.

"I do not think so because he probably thought Likus was here.?" said Marie.

"Then I will call him and I hope the nephew does grown up and does not return until is he is a man," said Detva.

"Ok, please call," said Marie.

"Hello, again you are highly recommend for employment I was wondering if you would like to work here doing errands and my wife would like you to baby sit," said Detva.

"Perfect," said Marie.

"Ok, then it is a date for tomorrow for an interview and then have the your last week end off and be ready, what, that is not a problem now I will explain it to you, ok. Bye," said Detva.

"Explain what.?" said Marie.

"That the hourly wage stop interfering while being on Disability checks every one can work 40 or more hours," said Detva.

"Why is that, I am not sure.?" said Marie.

"When Ed started the tunnels the Social Security was saved by all of the people who are disabled and living in those section 8 buildings from Maine to California and in Connecticut it is the Interstate I-95," said Detva..

"I lived here for so long I do not remember any thing about the states. But I want to live here with you for rest of my life," said Marie.

"We are staying my brother did not mind it at all did he," said Detva.

"No, but we will still be a eye on Likus and I think your brother and his wife and children will live in Sicily," said Marie.

"I think so too and now I am going to tell you I am so in love with you," said Detva.

"I love you dear and I need you very much," said Marie.

"I know and I am here," said Detva.

"Thank you," said Marie.

"Now lets have something to eat," said Detva.

"Good idea and I want to have some coffee," said Marie.

"Me too and some of these cakes," said Detva.

"Rich chocolate something that I need and I do crave chocolate," said Marie.

"It is the best," said Detva.

"Do you think your brother will live in Sicily or Russia.?" said Marie.

"I think he will stay there and live in one of the houses in a court yard in the Hermitage that will give him a discipline too," said Detva.

"It would give him a great edge on life and he will have more patience too but he should leave Likus alone," said Marie.

"He will," said Detva.

"It was fun seeing the children but we need to get down to very serious thinking on what to do with the ability to create new cash and it was very good of your brother to recommend the new sitter," said Marie.

"I think so, he is a very pleasant person," said Detva.

"I hope so and I am sure the children will enjoy his company too," said Marie.

"We need more people hired from Venice not the outside it is not good for public relations," said Detva.

"Spoken like a good ambassador you are a good diplomat, Detva," said Marie.

"One thing is good when they are hire then go on, it is time for us to fill their position," said Marie.

"We have always filled in with another and have increased the number of jobs in this building too," said Detva.

"There is a lot of people in maintenance for twenty blocks of buildings," said Marie.

"Next is nannies and nurses it is a good thing to have a doctor with us now I never thought that he would stay and he did," said Detva.

"He has been very busy the first day he started," said Marie.

"Prince Detva the 2:00 p.m. appointment is here a Mr.Theldy or Count Schizotrid," said the Butler.

"Count Schytrid do you think your position here would interfere with your own plans as a title.?" said Lady Marieca.

"No Lady Marieca and Prince Detva thank you both for this position I do need the work my father was quite pleased when I told him you wanted to hire me," said the Count.

"So you lived across the canal," said Detva.

"Yes we moved closer and closer to the city and then to Rome I would like to stay here," said the Count.

"Then you must know several languages and are quite proficient," said her Ladyship.

"Yes I do eleven to be exact," said the Count.

"Would you like to teach instead.?" said her Ladyship.

"This is just what I wanted to know, it is possible so may I start immediately.?" said the Count.

"Yes you start Monday and be with us for this weekend to get to know the children. Call me Detva and my wife Marie," said Detva.

"In front of the children we need to hear our tiles so they will respect us when they are older," said Marie.

"Yes, as you wish and Marie and Detva and if you need a baby sitter my sister would enjoy working here too we have already talked about it.?" said Schizotrid.

"We will have her visit for a interview and the position is then hers," said Detva.

"Thank you and could I call her right now.?" said Schizotrid.

"Yes, please do I need the help today if she does not mind," said Marie.

"Yes she will be right here in a few minutes. It is a lovely home I use to visit when the Prince lived here with his Mother," said Schizotrid.

"Where are they now, I hope you do not mind if I ask you.?" said Marie.

"No, but I did think you would not ask if a sister could babysit.? " said Schizotrid.

"Then what is it.?" said Detva.

"Your neighbors are in Rome, and now my sister and I moved to be near Venice city near land, we moved from here because both of our my parents had died," said Schizotrid.

"Your father," said Marie.

"He is our Uncle and we are all going to Rome and to live in his house and first try to sell our furniture and the two of us never wanted to stay here when they died," said Schizotrid.

"I am so sorry both parents are dead, that is awful you are very lucky to have such a good uncle," said Marie.

"Yes, you are and I am very sorry too, may I ask how they died," said Detva.

"They were in Rome and left my uncle's house and a large truck hit their car. Also thank you and I appreciate the both for understanding," said Schizotrid.

"Then you both can live here and your Uncle would want to go home but the fact is you are to connected to this house so what about that do you think it could work for the both of you.?" said Marie.

"We did not have strong attachments to our parents there was too much of visiting our grandparents because they both wanted to be themselves and we were raised on getting a good education too so we were not at home at all," said Schizotrid.

"Then it is all set and if any of you want to leave we will make sure that you are with your uncle or someplace else," said Marie.

"We could arrangement for you both to live somewhere else," said Detva.

"Your teaching languages is something we might not have again and it will never be seen that I know," said Marie.

"Thank you, the both of you I am sure you will enjoy my teaching my degree is in foreign languages so I am very qualified," said Schizotrid.

"Your sister what degree does she have.?" said Detva.

"Pre-school and graduated from Venice too," said the Count.

"I think everything is in order and you can cross the bridge to your house on our right hand side and it faces the garden." Now here is your sister," said Detva..

"Maybe we should mention first that the both of us are so sorry your parents have died and I hope we can make you both very confortable in our employment," said Marie.

"Thank you and I know by now my brother has told you both everything so if it is final could I start tomorrow. I will bring our things here for us in the morning," said Detva.

"We were thinking we could have you as guests until Monday when you both can start," said Marie.

"It would cause a difference when working with your children to be at the same table with them especially as a home tudor," said Saranee.

"Then we do exspect you both to be at the house celebrating for the holidays.?" said Marie.

"Yes and thank you very much and I do need to get home and we both will see you tomorrow," said Saranee.

"See you both tomorrow," said Detva.

"Yes, good bye," said Marie.

"Now that was a fast but good interview," said Detva.

"Right and if we want to stop this from happening she gave us that right," said Marie.

"I know she is very good about leaving us alone," said Detva.

"Languages are useful and yet fun to learn," said Marie.

"Indeed," said Detva.

"Did not be sarcastic we have interpreters when we need them," said Marie.

"I am a land owner.!!!" said Detva.

"Yes, Detva you are," said Marie.

"We both are," said Detva.

"I am glad I gave them the week end off after tomorrow and I will see them Monday," said Marie.

"When they are here tomorrow I think we should ask them if they want to stay and relax here unitl the weekend. But I am going to ask them on the phone to pack up everything," said Detva.

"Thank you darling," said Marie.

"They need us as much as we need them and we will pay for the cab and let them stay for a long time and you need the help right away," said Detva.

"Thank you dear, please call now," said Marie.

"Hello I was, yes go ahead, your uncle wants to leave tonight and he said,"Before we both change your minds." But he will pack both of you up and say,"Thank you and hello and good bye to all of us. You might arrive late.?" said Detva.

"Wait the security and the maids will help them then their Uncle can leave when they get there," said Marie.

"We are sending over a security guard and three maids to help you pack and we will supply extra cartons," said Detva.

"Ok," said Marie.

"The Uncle is packing right now and he is going to see us here to say thank you while they pack his first and then he going to leave for Rome," said Detva.

"Good meet him outside and pay for the cab right to the station," said Marie.

"Lets pack him some food," said Detva.

"Call the Butler and let him know," said Marie.

"We do need you to pack several dinners for a man and a lot of prepared foods and canned goods in a hurry in a few minutes. The sister and brother are staying with us tonight for good, ok. Thanks," said Detva.

"Thank you dear, now I need you to bring him in yet pay for the cab to stay alright," said Marie.

"That is good food preparation and packing too," said Marie.

"Now the cab is here please pack up the food ok, we will show him out, thank you. All of you it took seconds and yet he has enough food for days," said Detva.

"Hello, I am Uncle Birthfee, Baron Birthfee. Thank you for their employment and this I cannot believe it thank you so much for the food," said the Baron.

"We hope you are pleased you are going home," said Marie.

"I put the house up for sell a few seconds ago it is their house and their money and now they both have enough cash too. Thanks to the both of you," said the Baron.

"We are delighted to help," said Detva.

"Your having twins, my nephew told me how nice an congratulations the both of you and I know I will not be here yet it is joyous event. Said the Baron.

"Thank you and I hope Rome is the same," said Marie.

"We both hope so," said Detva.

"I am sure of it and I should go and see if there is anything else they packed so I will take the food too. I did not do any shopping so there is not much in the house. Thank you both again," said their Uncle.

"Bye now give us a call here is the number can you can leave a message," said Marie.

"Good bye have a good trip and enjoy Rome," said Detva.

"Bye," said their Uncle.

"He was pleasant and very young too," said Marie.

"I guess he was never married," said Detva.

"He did not stay long enough to mention it," said Marie.

"Wait I hear something," said Detva.

"The motors stopped," said Marie.

"I can hear the motors very faintly," said Detva.

"The engines started again," said Marie.

"Here they are, I will help them with there," said Detva.

"We have everything my Lord," said the Security guard.

"Here are the three maids all with luggage thank you staff you are so good us and now I have my new sitter and a teacher as well a God sent, sent from the Gods themselves all of you," said Marie.

"Yes, they are all of them and now you can have a lot of help, Marie," said Detva.

"Good night thank you again," said Marie.

"Yes thanks, so you both met your Uncle outside.?" said Detva.

"Yes and we gave him the extra food so he will not go hungry," said Count Schizotrid.

"He has a car so there will be enough room for anything," said Saranee.

"Let me help you with this Countess I will bring them upstairs for you," said the Guard.

“They do go to the next building with the bridge,” said Marie.

“Here are the rest of the staff and the Butler,” said Detva.

“The maids are in the rooms getting ready to unpack my Lord,” said the Butler.

“Good, thank you so we will have some food in the dining room I could use another dinner,” said Marie.

“Here we go,” said Detva.

“The children are asleep so we can enjoy our dinner. You can both watch so the children do not enter this floor, thank you,” said Marie

“We do feed our staff and extra dinner if they want it or a snack so you can be sure there is enough food during the day and evening too,” said Detva.

“Thank you I could use a dinner right now,” said Schizotrid.

“Now is a good time to let you know when your house is sold we do have a home for you with two apartments. It is the one you are staying in and we will reimburse you when you both choose to leave,” said Detva.

“Yes, we will draw it up and to put in the conrtact the same amount that you both bought it for so here is your money for the month, until you both get a check,” said Marie.

“This is very nice for you,” said Saranee.

“Your welcome, you both have already earn it,” said Detva.

“You do not need to pay us back, this cash is for the both of you and you need to sign an agreement that you will not write a book without us reading it first ok,” said Marie.

“There will be no books written,” said the Countess.

“None our parents ever worked we had our own money from our grandparents,” said the Count.

“Very nice,” said Marie.

“We would never even begin to say you must be employed or work, the average person is to thin and to weak to work It has been established by your Louie Paul the King of France he is know as. He did that when the Euro train was placed in the states with its own tunnels,” said Prince Schizotrid.

“I heard that just recently and I am very pleased to hear of your loyality and devotion,” said Detva.

"So am I are you thinking Detva of what I am thinking of right now the same thing," said Marie.

"A new commercial if you both want it," said Detva.

"Sure, why I think you have said that too in a commercial maybe that is where I heard it," said the Count.

"We do not mind it but what if we are asked to do a film," said Saranee.

"That is also one of our franchises. Versailles and the Hermitage studios," said Marie.

"A toast, we have two new people for the stage with us tonight," said Detva.

"We will take the offer," said the Brother.

"This is two jobs he has given me in one day. As a full day is concerned I am very tired and we will see each other at what time tomorrow.?" said Saranee.

"Why not let all of them sleep late because we have three new children who are very tired from their ordeal so they will need their sleep," said Marie.

"I do agree we will all need our sleep so good night and thank you both again. Also if the children are up early then I will be too," said Saranee.

"Good night the Butler will go upstairs with the both of you and I will give you a call," said Marie.

"Thank you both again and I will be with you early tomorrow too, and again thank you and good night," said the Brother.

"I will let you know in the morning, I will call so good night," said Marie.

"Good night and see you both in the morning," said Detva.

"There this looks promising even in the movies too," said Marie.

"It does do you want another coffee," said Detva.

"I will and we can sleep here and use the bedroom down stairs," said Marie.

"Lets take the food, coffee and desserts to the bedroom," said Detva.

"Alright and here we are before the both of us could finish a sentence," said Marie.

"It did," said Detva.

"This bedroom is the largest on this first floor so will enjoy the fact we have French doors to see the garden in the morning," said Marie.

"It will be the first time we have slept here since we moved in," said Detva.

"We have to be here because I want to be on the first floor for now on," said Marie.

"I am sorry I never thought of that I apologize," said Detva.

"It just started today the moving around is harder so I want to live here on the first floor and relax, the phone I will talk," said Marie.

"I will go up and see if they are all right.?" said Detva.

"Hello, you are in the bedroom and ready for bed I hope, there is food for you both, that is nice the staff is very good that way. Right I will and to make sure you both have a good stay, why not live in those apartments and buy the two homes next to it. Good then we will see you both tomorrow, good night," said Marie.

"All are secured and the guard is posted in the hallway he had a long sleep when he got home and is going to watch for our new employees," said Detva.

"I believe that is part of his job description," said Marie.

"Yes it is and no matter who it is, that is the way he was trained," said Detva.

"Speaking of trained I need you to watch over this house for anyone who might want children for ransom," said Marie.

"I know I am going to call the police and have them put on extra officers for over time and for a long duration too," said Detva.

"You are the only guard that I want watching over me," said Marie.

"Did I tell you that,?" said Detva.

"I will enjoy knowing about that again," said Marie.

"The results of my teaching has been exceptionally," said Detva.

"Lets try it this way, now you can be taught again," said Marie.

"Mentioning ransom here is something that could help out, this is a new company I have started and I have bought out and it is a toll free number systems. All of our friends and family and emergency and police is on this cell phone you just talk to the phone and ask for the police and it will be dialed. No numbers to use just press on the started bottom and you can give the name and phone number of your friend, hang up and then ask for their phone number and immediately it is dialed.," said Detva.

"What a great invention.!" said Lady Marieca.

The End